Tallie lay bac░░░░░░░░░░░░░░░░░░░░░░**e**
protruding abo░░░░░░░░░░░░░░░░░░░░**let**
the ░░░░░░░░░░░░

As Jeb watched her in the spread of silver moon-light on the water's surface, he felt like Odysseus being lured by the sirens. He walked quietly toward the water's edge, not wanting to frighten Tallie. When she became aware of his presence, she sat up.

"The water . . ." She stopped as she watched Jeb remove his trousers.

"Do you mind if I join you?" He stepped out into the current.

He turned to face her, and pulling her to him, he lowered his lips to hers and kissed her deeply as the cool water swirled around their bodies.

Praise for Sara Luck's debut Western romance
SUSANNA'S CHOICE

"It has everything a historical romance reader could want—love, danger, secrets, destiny, fate, seduction, passion, silver mining, and finding true love. . . . An exciting story with strong characters and vivid descriptions of Americana history."
—*My Book Addiction Reviews*

"This one's a keeper! . . . Heartwarming . . . Rab and Susanna have a sweet relationship that slowly evolves into a sensual, loving romance."
—*Night Owl Reviews*
(5 stars, a Night Owl Top Pick)

ALSO BY SARA LUCK

Claiming the Heart

Susanna's Choice

TALLIE'S HERO

SARA LUCK

Pocket Books

New York   London   Toronto   Sydney   New Delhi

Pocket Books
A Division of Simon & Schuster, Inc.
1230 Avenue of the Americas
New York, NY 10020

This book is a work of fiction. Names, characters, places, and incidents either are products of the author's imagination or are used fictitiously. Any resemblance to actual events or locales or persons, living or dead, is entirely coincidental.

First Pocket Books paperback edition September 2012

POCKET and colophon are registered trademarks of Simon & Schuster, Inc.

For information about special discounts for bulk purchases, please contact Simon & Schuster Special Sales at 1-866-506-1949 or business@simonandschuster.com.

The Simon & Schuster Speakers Bureau can bring authors to your live event. For more information or to book an event, contact the Simon & Schuster Speakers Bureau at 1-866-248-3049 or visit our website at www.simonspeakers.com.

Designed by Jacquelynne Hudson

Manufactured in the United States of America

10 9 8 7 6 5 4 3 2 1

ISBN 978-1-4516-7386-9
ISBN 978-1-4516-7391-3 (ebook)

TALLIE'S HERO

ONE

Lord Henry Arthur George Somerset married Tallas Cameron on the Beaufort estate at the Badminton House chapel, a miniature version of St. Martin-in-the-Fields, London, that had been built by the same architect. Following the ceremony, the reception took place in the beautifully decorated twenty-by-forty-four-foot grand hall, the very room where, one rainy afternoon, several of the Duke of Beaufort's friends returning from military service in India had introduced a new sport to the English countryside.

Among the hundreds of people at the wedding were Lord Randolph and Jennie Churchill, along with their three-year-old son, Winston.

"When do we get to play badminton?" Winnie asked the bride as his mother approached her to offer congratulations.

"Oh, honey, I'm afraid you will have to come another day to do that," Tallie answered the lad.

"Did you marry Lord Arthur?"

"Indeed I did. I was going to wait until you were old enough, but I decided you'll probably find someone else by then," Tallie teased.

"I probably will." Winnie looked over toward the fireplace where Arthur was leaning against the mantel, watching the mingling of the guests. "Do you know what my daddy said?"

"What did he say?"

"He told Mama that he was surprised that Arthur got married. Doesn't he like you?"

"Winnie!" Jennie scolded. "Haven't you ever heard that children should be seen, but not heard?"

"I know that. But I think if I have something to say, I should say it."

"You have nothing to say. Now you just skedaddle over to one of the serving people and ask politely for a cookie and a glass of punch. I'm going to summon Mrs. Everest to take you to the nursery."

Winnie looked at Tallie and smiled. "Mama always calls biscuits *cookies*, because she's an American."

"And I'm an American who's going to box your ears right here in public if you don't do as I say," Jennie said.

"Yes, Mama." With a laugh, Winnie walked away.

"He is a delightful and intelligent child," Tallie said.

"Yes, though sometimes his precociousness can be a challenge."

Tallie laughed.

"My dear, I'm so pleased that you married Arthur. You know that the Somerset property he uses when he's in London is right next to my house. That will give us ample opportunity to be friends," Jennie said.

"I'll be looking forward to our visits."

"Lady Somerset, I've not had the opportunity to meet you," a gentleman said as he approached the two women.

"Maybe she doesn't want to meet you," Jennie said, laughing. "Tallie, this is Moreton Frewen. He is one of England's most noted adventurers, and even if I say it begrudgingly, a very good horseman. I'm sure you will see more of him when the Beaufort foxhunting season begins."

"Lady Randolph, you can't fool me. I know you love me."

"That is wishful thinking, my friend, and now if you will excuse me, I must join my husband. Oh, Tallie, I meant what I said. I hope that we can become friends."

"I'm sure that we will."

"You will learn much from Jennie Churchill," Moreton Frewen said. "She has become one of the most influential hostesses in all of London and a principal member of the social set."

"Oh, I'm afraid that I will never be more than an observer of the social set."

"Don't sell yourself short, my dear. You are a beautiful young woman, and I'm told that you have wit and charm. Those are the prime requisites for being influential in London Society."

As Tallie and Moreton conversed, Arthur's father, Lord Henry, the 8th Duke of Beaufort, came over to speak to them.

"Squire Frewen, does my good daughter-in-law need rescuing from your overly abundant charms and exaggerated stories?"

"Your Grace, whatever do you mean? You can't tell me you haven't enjoyed my tales of Africa and India. And now I have just returned from America, with even more stories that I'm sure you will find just as amusing."

"I hope so, Moreton, but if you will excuse us, I would like a word with my daughter-in-law."

When Moreton was out of earshot, the duke spoke quietly to Tallie.

"Your husband isn't by your side. This is a very grave social faux pas, and I shall address him about it."

"Please don't. This day has been stressful for Arthur."

"Has it not been equally stressful for you? Yet you are not avoiding your duties. I would think it would be more difficult for you, because Arthur knows everyone in this room, and you are acquainted with hardly any of the guests."

"Perhaps what you say is true, but Arthur is a sensitive man. Surely, sir, you have seen that about him."

"Humph. Yes. Sensitive. I cannot tell you how appreciative I am of your sacrifice, and if you are in need of anything, please do not hesitate to just ask. Arthur's mother and I will be eternally at your service."

With that comment, the duke turned and quickly walked away, leaving Tallie to wonder what he was trying to tell her. What did he mean by referring to the marriage as her "sacrifice"? She glanced back over toward the fireplace, but her husband was no longer there.

The reception didn't end until well past midnight. Then, when the last guest was gone and the duke and the duchess had withdrawn to their own chambers, only Tallie and Arthur remained in the great Badminton Hall.

"I was beginning to think no one was going to retire until breakfast," Tallie said with a big smile. "I'll just go to our bridal chamber and prepare for you."

Arthur made no reply. Instead, he poured himself a drink, then looked at her over the glass he lifted to his lips.

Hurrying upstairs, Tallie found their rooms among the 116 in the house. Mrs. Ferguson, who had been Tallie's governess and caretaker since the death of her mother, was waiting for her when she entered the bedchamber.

"I'm so glad you're here," Tallie said as she embraced her friend.

"Let's get you out of your wedding dress and into some of these pretty things you've picked out." Mrs. Ferguson chose one of the most alluring nightgowns and held it up for Tallie. "I think Lord Arthur will really like this one."

When Tallie was dressed, she took a deep breath.

"Don't be afraid, little one. This is a rite that all

women dream of, and your husband is a very gentle man. He will love and cherish you as only a husband can love a wife." Mrs. Ferguson moved toward the door to let herself out.

"Mrs. Ferguson, thank you, for taking such good care of me for the last ten years."

"I wouldn't have it any other way. Your parents would be proud of the woman their daughter has become, and I'm proud of you, too. Good night, my dear."

Mrs. Ferguson's words, *your parents would be proud of the woman their daughter has become*, played over in her mind. Would they be proud? she wondered.

Here she was, married to a man that she knew she didn't love. Perhaps that was the legacy she had been left by her parents. George and Millicent Cameron had been married for over thirty years, and not once, in the twelve years of Tallie's life before her mother died, had Tallie ever seen an expression of love between the two of them.

Her father, a sea captain who had gone down with his ship when Tallie was a teen, was stern and stoic, unemotional, even at her mother's funeral, held at the parish church at Downe, Kent. Tallie's neighbors Charles and Emma Darwin had comforted the young girl when she lost her mother, not her father. The one positive thing he had done was hire Mrs. Ferguson.

Mrs. Ferguson and the Darwins had helped to make Tallie the woman she was, not her parents.

Every morning, once her lessons and chores

were done, Mrs. Ferguson and Tallie would cross through the shaw of oak trees that separated the Cameron house from the Darwin house.

She still remembered the day Charles Darwin had given her a precious gift—one that had been her refuge since girlhood. Tallie had entered the drawing room where the renowned author, his flowing beard, gray-white and unkempt, was reclining on the sofa. An inviting platter of current-filled pastries sat on a stool in front of him.

"Ah, Tallie, you are just in time. The plum heavies are hot from the oven, and your aunt Emma is just concluding her Bach fugue."

"My dear, did you practice your piano this morning?" Emma Darwin asked.

"Yes, ma'am." Tallie took a seat on the floor in front of Uncle Charles, as he preferred to be called. "I loved the piece I played. I believe it is the most beautiful song Beethoven ever wrote."

"And what would that be?" Darwin asked.

"'Für Elise.'"

"I know that piece." Darwin began humming the familiar song, so horribly off-key that one could not recognize the tune at all.

Emma shook her head at her tone-deaf husband's efforts, and Tallie hid her smile.

"I think we'd better start our new book."

"What did you choose, Uncle Charles?" Tallie asked as she moved to her favorite horsehair chair in the corner.

"I've chosen one I think you will enjoy. It's one of Jane Austen's books, *Lady Susan*."

When Emma put the book down, it was well past six. Darwin rose from the sofa and, grabbing his cane to assist him, walked into the study.

"This is for you, my dear," he said, returning to the drawing room. He handed a red book to Tallie.

"Thank you." Tallie took the book and opened it, seeing blank pages. She looked back to Darwin with a quizzical look on her face.

"You study your lessons for Mrs. Ferguson, you practice the piano for your aunt Emma, and I want you to do this for me. I want you to write something every day. Someday I want you to write a story. And since you know how much I like happy endings, make sure your story has one."

Since then, Tallie had never been without her red notebook. She had filled many, even writing a book about an orphan girl who had been adopted by a loving family. That story line had closely mirrored her relationship with the Darwins. As she waited for her husband to come to their nuptial bed, she opened a fresh notebook and began to write.

Helen waited expectantly for Lord Londonderry to come to their wedding bed. Lord Londonderry had proven his loyalty to the Queen by his exemplary military service. How lucky she was, a commoner, the daughter of a greengrocer, to have won his love. And now, she was to share his bed, to be deflowered. . . .

Smiling, Tallie lay the book aside. She wouldn't go any further until she had actually experienced her own deflowering. In anticipation, she strategically placed a few drops of perfume on her body, one drop between her breasts, and another drop on her stomach, just below her belly button. She laughed as she thought of Arthur's reaction when he discovered the scent of that drop. Then, she lay back in bed thinking of the great mystery that was about to be revealed to her, wondering what it would be like. She waited for Arthur to come to her.

When more than an hour had passed, she began to worry that something might be wrong, and putting on her dressing gown, Tallie left the room to search for her husband.

She found Arthur in the dressing room that joined the bedchamber to a small sitting room. He was fully clothed, sitting in a chair, staring into the flame of a single candle, a glass in one hand, and a half-empty bottle of whiskey in the other.

"Arthur?" she asked, confused and concerned. "Arthur, is everything all right?"

Arthur looked at her, and never had she seen such an expression of pain on anyone's face. He lifted the glass to his lips and took a swallow before he replied, "No, my dear. Everything is not all right. I have made a huge mistake, and not for myself alone, but for you as well. I have forced you into a position where you must make a choice, and neither choice can be attractive for you."

"What are you talking about? What choice?"

"You must choose between a life of celibacy, or adultery. There is no third option."

"Oh, Arthur, what are you saying?"

"I'm sorry, Tallie." Arthur finished the whiskey in his glass, then, taking the bottle, he rose and stumbled toward the door. "I can't tell you how sorry I am."

Texas Panhandle—late spring 1879

Jeb Tuhill, his brother, Jonas, and three other hands who worked for the Two Hills Ranch were separating out some imported shorthorn bulls that were going to stand as sire at El Camino Largo, a neighboring ranch.

"I don't agree with this," Jonas said. "Why can't Falcon de la Garza buy his own bulls?"

"Pop wants all the herds to be stronger. He thinks these shorthorns have a better chance of beating Texas cattle fever, and the more there are on the range, the better we will all be," Jeb said.

"You could have talked him out of it—that is, if you'd wanted to."

At that moment Travis Wellborn was prodding a bull, trying to force him into the chute, but the bull didn't want to go, and without warning it turned and charged the cowboy's horse. The frightened animal reared up and threw its rider to the ground. As the horse galloped away, the bull turned his attention toward the downed man.

Travis sprinted to reach the fence, but the bull was gaining on him. Seeing what was happening, Jeb urged his horse into a gallop. He grabbed his rope from the saddlebow and began whirling it around his head, making the loop larger and larger, then threw the loop toward the bull.

The loop dropped around the bull's head, and

Jeb wrapped his end of the rope around the saddle horn.

"Dig in, Liberty!" Jeb called to his horse.

The horse, well trained for such things, held its legs out stiff, bracing against the pull of the bull. The bull was jerked up short before he could reach Travis.

By now a couple of other riders were mounted, and they, too, dropped a rope around the bull. Once stopped, he was led into the chute without any further difficulty.

"By golly, Travis! I thought you were a goner there!" Will Tate called.

"I sure would've been iffin' Jeb didn't snare that bull," Travis said.

"My brother, the hero," Jonas teased, and the others laughed, though it was more a laugh of relief than of humor.

Jeb's rescue of Travis was the talk of the evening as the cowboys gathered around the embers of a low-burning fire, the smell of roasted meat permeating the air. The cook had barbequed a goat, and the men were well fed and satisfied.

"Yes, sir, ole Travis's goose would've been cooked if Jeb hadn't roped that bull when he did," Will Tate was telling the others.

"You're a hero," Katarina Falcon de la Garza said as she approached the men. When she reached the fire, its glow reflected off her raven hair and caused her flashing black eyes to sparkle.

"I'm not a hero," Jeb said as he took Katarina's hand and helped her sit beside him. "Anyone else would've done the same. I was just in the right place at the right time."

Katarina, Felipe Falcon de la Garza's daughter, moved closer to Jeb and laid her head on his shoulder as his arm closed around her. He had met her when he'd first wintered a herd in the Palo Duro. The next year, when the Tuhills and Goodnights moved their operations from Colorado to Texas, the two had naturally fallen in together and developed a close friendship.

"That's my big brother," Jonas said rather sarcastically, as he poured a drink from a jug of liquor that Senor Falcon de la Garza had brought for the cowboys. Jonas took a swig of the tequila. "To the hero." Jonas raised his cup, then threw its contents on the ground. "How is it that he's always in the right place at the right time? Can you answer that, Katarina? What makes him so special?"

"Jonas, you ought to go easy on that stuff." Jeb chuckled to ease the comment.

"You might get away with telling everybody else around here what to do, but you don't tell me. I'm my own man. I don't need you for anything, and don't you forget it."

Just then one of the cowboys jumped up. "Dancers, form your squares!" he shouted.

"Come, Katarina." Jeb pulled her to her feet as he stood.

Katarina looked back at Jonas, who was once again filling his cup. "Jonas, are you all right?" she asked, concerned.

"I'm fine. Just fine. Go on. Dance with the *hero*. You don't need me."

"I don't understand him sometimes," Jeb said, watching Jonas head toward the bunkhouse. "It seems like no matter what I do, it gets under his skin."

"Jonas is jealous of you," Katarina said.

"Jealous of me? What have I done to make him jealous?"

"You really don't know, do you? Everything you do makes him jealous. You're the only educated man in the canyon, and besides that, you still do all the cowboy things better than almost anybody else. Every cowhand who is anywhere near the Palo Duro Canyon looks up to you. When there's a problem, who do they come to? It's not Jonas."

"That's because I'm older than he is."

"That's not a good enough reason. Your father is older than you, and yet you have the final say about everything. Papa knows that the bulls that are being put on El Camino Largo would not be coming if Jeb Tuhill didn't think it was the right thing to do."

Just then the skirling sound of a fiddle started, and the caller began to call a dance. He was clapping his hands and dancing on the wood floor that had been put down on the ground as if he were part of a square himself.

"Let's dance," Jeb said, glad for the diversion, because the direction of the conversation was making him uncomfortable.

Only two women were on the Two Hills Ranch besides Jeb's mother—Edna, the cook, and Tess, the foreman's wife. Edna and Tess joined Katarina and an alternating cowboy to stand for the fourth woman to complete one square for a dance.

Jeb and Katarina danced the first set. After that, he enjoyed watching her, her eyes flashing, her long hair swinging, and her colorful skirt swirling about her. She had to be exhausted, having ridden with her father and the men from El Camino Largo all day, but she danced with every cowboy who asked her. It seemed that she could make each man feel as if he were the most important person in her life. Jeb admired that trait in her.

"Jeb," one of the men in the band called. "Why don't you come up here and play so Miss Katarina can dance for us?"

"Yeah, do it!" one of the cowboys called out, and the others mimicked the call.

"All right," Jeb said. "I'll have to go get my guitar."

"No, you won't," Edna said. "I knew they'd ask you to play, so I brought it out for you."

Jeb looked over at Katarina. "It's up to you. Do you want to do this?"

"I love to dance." She raised her hands over her head and struck a sultry pose.

Jeb removed his guitar from its red-felt-lined case, handling it with care. After a bit of tuning he looked at Katarina, who took her position. He lifted his leg to put it on an overturned bucket, and resting his guitar against his knee, he began to play. His fingers were flying over the strings, the melody rising and falling as he thumped on the body of the guitar to keep the rhythm.

Katarina whirled and dipped as her boots made a staccato beat on the wooden floor. The strenuous performance of song and dance continued for more than three minutes, then ended with a grand crescendo.

Their performance was met with loud cheers and applause. Just then, Jonas stumbled out of the bunkhouse, obviously inebriated.

"You missed it, Jonas," Pete Nabro said.

"The hero again?" Jonas slurred his words. "Nah, I didn't miss a damn thing."

Jonas went directly to Katarina and pushed aside the cowboys who were standing around. He pulled Katarina to him, and in front of everyone, he kissed her deeply, forcing her body back in a deep bend. Instinctively, she placed her arms around his neck.

Jonas pulled her up into an intimate embrace.

"You like that, don't you, Katarina?" He gave her another crushing kiss.

Jeb stepped up to his brother and put his hand on his arm. "Back off, Jonas."

"Says who? Looks to me like the lady is liking my attention. She's been waitin' aroun' for you to make a move, and where's it gotten her?" Jonas said indistinctly. Once more he tried to kiss Katarina. This time she turned her head to one side, but her arms were still wound around his neck, and Jeb noticed she was smiling.

"Come on, Katarina, I think it's time to call it a night," Jeb said, taking her by the hand and leading her away from Jonas.

"The boss man is telling us what to do, is he? Well, not this time, big brother, you're feedin' off your range. She's mine." With that, Jonas started swinging wildly.

Jeb ducked under the swings, then picked Jonas up bodily and carried him, still flailing ineffectively, to the bunkhouse.

The next morning Jeb headed toward the house for breakfast. He and Jonas had both slept in the bunkhouse, allowing Katarina and her father to use their rooms. When Jeb went in, his father and Senor Falcon de la Garza were sitting at the table, where James Tuhill was reading over some papers that Felipe had brought.

"Good morning, Jeb, where's your brother?" Elizabeth Tuhill asked when he entered the kitchen. She was standing over the cookstove watching bacon twitching in the pan.

"I expect he'll be along shortly."

"I understand things got a little rowdy last night," James said.

"It wasn't bad."

"Humph. That isn't what Edna said when she came in. She said Jonas got a bit out of hand."

"Really, it was nothing. He was just letting off a little steam. No harm was done."

Just then Jonas came into the kitchen and went straight to the coffeepot. "I don't need you to speak for me," he said as he poured himself a cup of coffee with trembling hands.

"Sit down, Jonas, and get that chip off your shoulder," James said.

"Where's Katarina?" Jonas asked, then took a drink of his coffee.

"She's still in bed," Falcon de la Garza replied. "She was tired from the ride over and then the dance last night. I'm glad she'll have a few days to rest before we go home."

"Oh, then we're not driving the bulls out today?" Jeb asked.

"No, take a look at this." James handed the paper he had been reading to Jeb, as Elizabeth set bacon, fried eggs, and hot biscuits in front of the men. Then, after filling their coffee cups, she joined them at the table.

The paper was an invitation to visit Charles Goodnight's ranch. With more capital from John Adair, the JA had grown to about one hundred thousand acres, making it the largest spread in the Palo Duro Canyon. Adair had tried to talk the Tuhills into expanding as rapidly as Charles had, but Jeb had thought it would be better to pay off their original note and own their land outright. The JA and Two Hills were now the most efficient and prosperous ranches in the Texas Panhandle.

"Are we going?" Jeb asked.

"Of course we're going," Elizabeth answered. "How long has it been since I've seen Molly?"

Jeb chuckled at his mother's comment. "I guess that settles it. We're off to see the Goodnights."

"It's not just the Goodnights," James said. "If you read on, John Adair will be there as well, and he's brought several of his English countrymen with him. I'd bet that they know the kind of return John is making on his money, and they want to get in on this American cattle bonanza, too."

"It could be that, or maybe they're coming to us for investment capital," Jeb suggested.

"That's a possibility."

"When do we leave?"

"Will's loading the wagon now. Your mother wanted to ride, but Pattie's got a lame foot, so I think we'll leave her horse behind. You boys and Felipe will ride along beside us."

"Is Katarina going?" Jonas asked.

"No, I want her to stay here and rest. Anyway, she won't be up before noon, and when she does wake up, Edna can take care of her," Felipe said.

"I'll need to go over a couple of things with Travis, and then I'll be ready to leave when you are," Jeb said, then finished his cup of coffee.

"I'm not going," Jonas said.

"The invitation was for all of us," James said. "I think you'd better come along."

"Pop, you know, and I know, that nobody will even know I'm there. Jeb's the only one Mr. Goodnight will listen to. He thinks Jeb knows everything there is to know about cows, and if he's trying to get money from some of these English dandies, you know how the conversation will go. 'Jeb, why don't you tell us a little bit about the profit-and-loss statements, if you don't mind,' and then my big brother will stand up and rattle off all the numbers. No. I'm not gonna go listen to all that bull. I'm stayin' right here."

"Who put the burr under your saddle?" Jeb asked.

"You did!" Jonas shouted. "Do you think I don't get sick and tired of it? 'Boy, ole Jeb sure got all the brains in that family. If you want somethin' done, and done right, don't bother goin' to Jonas. Jeb's the one you need to see.' Well, I've had enough. I don't plan to go over to the Goodnights just to sit there and twiddle my thumbs while you play the big expert. And it's not just outsiders. Even you, Pop. You think I can't tell that Jeb's your favorite?"

"That's enough, Jonas!" James said sharply. "You're wrong. You're both our sons."

"I'm not going." Jonas folded his arms over his chest and slumped back in his chair.

"Well then, suit yourself. It'll be your loss," James said as he rose from the table.

TWO

Jeb was thoroughly enjoying the ride through the Palo Duro Canyon to the JA Ranch. It had been some time now since he'd first come to the area. He loved the rugged gorge that slashed the surface of the plain, running for more than 120 miles. With walls in some places over a thousand feet high, and often twenty miles wide, the canyon was a natural corral. It had plenty of grass for the cattle, with an abundance of runoff from the escarpment as well as water from the many springs that formed high in the red sandstone.

The only complaint Jeb had was its isolation.

He thought of Katarina. Her family had been on the land since before there was a Texas, and she was happy here. She would make the ideal rancher's wife, and he knew she cared for him. Jeb believed it was time for him to take a wife, and when he returned to Two Hills following this visit with Charles Goodnight, he would ask Katarina to marry him.

∽∞∾

After a little more than two hours' ride, the main house of the JA Ranch came into view. The official greeters were always the chickens that had free range around the place. They were so used to the comings and goings of horses that they fell in behind them like soldiers and followed them to the hitching rail.

Just then, Molly Goodnight came running out of the house.

"Elizabeth! I didn't know for sure if you would come with James. It's so good to see you." She hugged her friend, and the two women walked arm in arm toward the house, both talking at the same time.

"I guess we can assume she's happy to see us, too." James said.

Jeb chuckled as he shook his head. "We won't get Mom away from here for a week."

"Don't be so hard on her, Son. You know how few women there are out here. They enjoy it when they can get together."

"It's too bad Elaina didn't come. I think she would have enjoyed the visit as well," Felipe said.

"I suppose we need to get in there and give Charles a little relief from his highfalutin guests," Jeb replied.

Charles Goodnight was standing at the door waiting to meet the men. When he saw them, he raised his eyebrows and rolled his eyes, then a small smile crept across his face.

"How are things going?" Felipe asked.

"They're here, and they're ready to spend their money."

Jeb chuckled. "That's better than asking us for it."

"Don't kid yourself. There's one of 'em doing that, too."

Inside, John Adair took control of the introductions. "Gentlemen, I present to you the very brightest and best investing minds that Great Britain has to offer. Mr. Robert Fleming, the man who has single-handedly started the investment-trust movement in Scotland. Mr. Archibald Coats, a simple thread merchant from Dundee who has made a fortune. Thomas Nelson, a publisher from Edinburgh. And Lord Henry Somerset, the eighth Duke of Beaufort. All of these gentlemen know how to make money, and they plan to start a company that they will be calling the Scottish American Investment Company, Limited."

"What, exactly, will you be investing in?" Jeb asked.

"I'm hoping they'll consider me," a tall, thin man in buckskins answered.

"And who are you?" Jeb asked, turning to the man.

"I'm Moreton Frewen, at your service, and if I do say so myself, I'm the best investment in all of America."

Lord Somerset chuckled. "Leave it to Moreton to toot his own horn. But I will concede he is most successful in convincing people to part with their money. He already has some of mine."

"I'm not asking you to invest in me, exactly. My brother and I have started an operation on the Powder River in the Big Horn Mountains of Wyoming, and we are negotiating for the 76 brand. Now we want to build that brand to be the biggest and best known in the whole Territory. We'll get money from England, Scotland, Texas, or even Timbuktu, if that's what it takes."

"Why would a Texas cattleman want to invest in a Wyoming ranch?" Jeb asked.

"Let me ask you this," Moreton replied. "Do you own the rangeland whereon you run your cattle?"

"We do."

"Unfortunately for me," John Adair said. "I planned on drawing interest on my money for a good long time from what I invested in Two Hills, but Jeb, here, was hell-bent on getting clear title to the land as soon as possible."

"He did push us unmercifully," James said, "but I'm glad he did. It's a good feeling to own our land."

"Well, in Texas that may be, but things are done a little differently in Wyoming. Where I am, the Powder River is wide-open range, and no one has to spend precious capital on acquiring land. All I'll have to do is run my cattle, let the herd multiply, and then take my profit when we ship the cows to market in Chicago."

"How much money are you trying to raise?" James asked.

"Ha! I like a man who gets to the point. I need to raise three hundred thousand pounds."

"How much is that in dollars?" Jeb asked.

"It's about one and a half million."

"Whew," James whistled. "That's a lot of money."

"Yes, it is. But if I can entice a minimum of twenty

investors, that's only an average of seventy-five thousand dollars apiece. I'm still trying to convince all of these gentlemen to join me, and I'm open to any and all who would be interested."

"I can tell you right now, Moreton, I'm putting my money in Texas," John Adair said.

"You're making a big mistake."

"Well, you've made your case with me," the Duke of Beaufort said. "And besides the money to be made, of course, what sold me was your tales of the game in the Big Horns. I plan to take you up on your offer to join you for a hunt."

"I welcome you." Moreton extended his hand to Lord Beaufort.

"How many cattle are you running up there?" Jeb asked.

Moreton chuckled. "Well, none, at the moment."

"Wait a minute. You have a cattle ranch, but you have no cattle?"

"That is a condition that I'm about to change. I'm here to cajole Mr. Goodnight out of at least a thousand head of what John says are the best-bred cows in Texas. We have just about sealed the bargain if I can get him to throw in some men to trail them to Wyoming. And then I'm trying to get Mr. Farrington to act as trail boss on the drive, but Goodnight won't budge."

"You're damn right, Farrington stays in Texas. I've trained him to do things my way, and there's too much for him to do here to let him go," Goodnight said.

"I haven't given up yet," Moreton said. "Every man has a price."

Just then Molly entered the parlor and called the men to dinner.

During the meal, Moreton Frewen regaled the group with preposterous tales of adventure, from riding a steeplechase in England, to big-game hunting in Africa and mountain climbing in Switzerland, to the wonders of the Wyoming Territory.

All these stories were told with humor and self-deprecation, and Jeb found himself truly enjoying the evening. This man was only a year younger than he was, and yet the life Moreton had lived, if his tales were to be believed, made Jeb question, for the first time, if he really wanted the hard life of a cattle rancher. There was a lot of the world that he had never seen.

Then he thought of Katarina. With her by his side, he was sure that the Palo Duro would be as satisfying as any place on earth.

THREE

The next morning Jeb got up early. When he went into the kitchen, he saw his father and Charles Goodnight sitting at the table, a coal-oil lamp pushing away the predawn darkness.

"Did you two get up this early, or did you not go to bed?" Jeb asked.

"A lot to talk about, Son, a lot to talk about."

"I didn't get a chance to ask you, Jeb, what do you think about Frewen's idea?" Goodnight asked.

"It's probably not a bad investment," Jeb said. "I mean, look how much money we've had to put into buying our land. If his only expenses are the operating expenses, and if the business is handled smartly, I don't see how you couldn't get a quick return on your money. But I don't know; there's something about that man that just doesn't ring true. If I made an investment in his operation, I think I'd want to be right there seeing how my money was being used."

"Sounds reasonable," James said.

"I know one thing, he'll have a good start for his herd," Goodnight said. "He just bought a thousand cows from me."

"Tell me, Jeb, what are you doing up before sunup? I thought you'd stay in bed a bit after you and Moreton had a few toddies last night," James said.

"I did enjoy the conversation, but I need to get home. Will you say my good-byes to Molly and the others?"

"You're not fooling me. It's that little black-eyed girl you want to get home to," James said with a chuckle.

"Oh, that's right. She is there. I forgot."

"Yeah, I'm sure you forgot," James teased. "Get out of here. I don't know when your mother and I will come home. She and Molly have a lot of catching up to do."

Jeb made good time going back to Two Hills, getting there just at cock's crow. He unsaddled Liberty and rubbed the horse down before he went to the bunkhouse to deposit his gear. When he stepped into the room, Pete Nabro and Josh Kendrick were the only two cowboys around.

"What are you doin' here?" Pete asked.

"What do you mean, what am I doing here? I live here, remember? Where's Jonas?"

"Uh, I don't know where he is right now. Have you seen him, Josh?"

"No, can't say as I have." Josh hurried out of the bunkhouse.

From the way the two men were acting, Jeb

sensed that something was wrong. He didn't know what it was, but he would bet it concerned Jonas. Whatever it was, it would fall upon him to straighten it out, but right now he was hungry. Maybe Edna would have a pot of coffee and some oatmeal on the stove at the main house.

When he stepped in the door, Edna was surprised. "You're not supposed to be here. Not yet."

"And why not? What smells so good?"

"I, uh, made some muffins and I put a little cinnamon and sugar on them."

Just then Jeb heard laughter. Jonas and Katarina came down the stairs; Katarina was in a dressing gown and Jonas was shirtless. Their arms were wound around each other.

"Oh, Jeb, I—I . . . ," Katarina gasped, unable to say any more.

Jonas and Jeb locked stares, but neither said a word. Jeb's jaw twitched as he clenched his teeth in rage. He left, going straight to the bunkhouse. There he gathered up his clothes and tack, then saddled Liberty and rode away.

As Jeb rode through the canyon, a coyote loped across the trail in front of him, turning to give him a stare, but he didn't take notice. He had something to figure out.

What had just happened? His brother, his little brother, had taken the woman Jeb wanted to marry away from him. They couldn't love one another—not after just one night. Jonas had obviously slept with Katarina just to get even with him. And everyone else at the ranch—Edna making muffins for the lovebirds as they descended the stairs arm in arm—wasn't that sweet? And then Pete and Josh acting so strange. It was as if everybody knew what was going on except him. Well, they could get along without him. If Frewen would take him, he was going to Wyoming. To hell with the whole bunch.

Just then, a wild turkey hiding in the sagebrush took wing while a hawk circled in the sky. He pulled Liberty up and got off, leading his horse over to a bubbling spring that was flowing down from the escarpment. As his horse drank in the cool water, Jeb looked around at the red clay stone, the white gypsum, and the yellow mudstone that made up the walls of the canyon. Could he really leave the Palo Duro?

Yes, if only for a little while. In his heart, he was a Texan now, and he would be back.

When Jeb reached the JA, he saw his father and Charles leaning on the corral fence, watching the cowboys cutting out some bulls.

"That was a quick trip. Did you forget something?" James asked.

"Did you mean it when you said you thought Frewen's operation would be a good investment?"

"Yeah, we did," Charles said, "but you didn't seem too keen on the idea when you rode out of here."

"Well, I am now."

"What changed your mind, Son?"

"I need to leave the Palo Duro for a while. I'm going to invest in Frewen's ranch, and I'm going to take his cows up to Wyoming."

James and Jeb exchanged a long, hard stare, neither saying anything.

Finally James broke the silence. "Your mother won't like it, but maybe it's best."

"A hundred and fifty thousand?" Moreton asked. "You know I'm only soliciting seventy-five thousand dollars to be a partner."

"As I see it, a hundred fifty thousand will give me a ten percent stake in your company. Who, besides you, would have a larger stake?"

"Well, my brother has a share, but other than Richard, there'd be nobody with that big of a stake."

"If I do invest money, there's one contingency that I'll have to insist on."

"And what would that be?"

"I'm to take an active part in the management of your operation."

Moreton smiled and stuck out his hand. "From what Charley Goodnight and John Adair have said about you, I'd be a fool to turn that offer down."

A herd of a thousand cows, a string of twenty-four horses, a chuck wagon, a hoodlum wagon, eight men, a bull named Homer, and Jeb Tuhill left in the early dawn of a mid-June day.

Homer was trained as a lead bull, and taking his position in front of the herd, his long strides caused the brass bell around his neck to ring in a steady rhythm. The cows fell in behind him as he headed out of the Palo Duro Canyon, across the Staked Plains. The bull was uncanny. He seemed to know where he was going, leading the way toward New Mexico following the trail of countless thousands of cattle that he had led before. He moved with a purpose, as if he could smell the black grama grass of the high plateau, or the spring at Trinchera Pass in the Raton Range.

Somerset town house in London— late summer 1879

Marrying Arthur had given Tallie entrée into London's highest society. Known as the Marlborough Set by those who were a part of it, it was dominated by Prince Albert Edward, monarch in waiting to Queen Victoria. In the convoluted rules of the social set that swirled around the Prince of Wales, extramarital affairs were not only tolerated, but expected.

But the game had rules: first and foremost, under no circumstances was a scandal to reach the newspapers and thus become common knowledge to the lower classes; and second, only married women were to be dallied with, but not until they had produced an heir for their husband. If, after the first few children were born, a child was born who looked out of place, no questions were asked and these children were accepted as full-fledged members of the family.

Tallie knew these rules, not as a participant, but as an observer, and she was calling upon that knowledge to write her second book. Returning late from one such social event, Arthur went to his bedroom, and Tallie to hers, as was their custom. She changed into a dressing robe, sat down on the chaise, and, picking up her notebook, returned to her work in progress she was calling *The Prince's Folly*, by Nora Ingram.

The Prince's Folly

by
Nora Ingram

To sleep discreetly with Prince X was an impossibility. One had only to drive by a residence to see Prince X's carriage waiting outside the front door. The man who would be king was afforded opportunities for dalliances that were not available for the other men of the Marlborough Set. There was no need for His Royal Highness to, as did the other men, adhere to the tea hour. For the Prince, only, it was permissible to arrange a grouse shooting for the lady's husband, then while his lordship was absent, take lunch with her at midday or entertain her at a secluded midnight supper. The Prince made no effort to keep his affairs secret, and he was neither ashamed nor boastful of his conquests.

The Prince bestowed no gifts of rings, pendants, or bracelets, nor did the women of his sexual entourage expect such things. The Prince considered sharing his bed reward enough. . . .

After a few hours of work, Tallie closed her red notebook and stared out at the blooming flow-

ers in the carefully tended beds that were behind
the house. She rose from the chaise and went to the
window. The sun was just beginning to brighten
the sky over the rooftops of London.

The cattle drive—summer 1879

Jeb had to admit the country was beautiful, with
unbroken grassland leading to the valley of the
Arkansas, the mountain ranges making up the
Rockies to the left, the Spanish Peaks, the Green-
horns, Pikes Peak, and other ranges, as the herd
continued to trek north. They crossed the Platte at
the mouth of Crow Creek and followed the creek on
to Cheyenne.

Goodnight had allowed them to use his guide
bull, Homer, with the strict requirement that Homer
be returned as soon as possible. Homer made the
drive unbelievably easy. When cows strayed, his
bawl and his bell brought them back. At night the
cowboys muffled the bell and tethered the bull with
the horses, feeding him corn from a skillet. The next
morning, no matter what time they started, when
the cows heard the bell, they fell in behind their
leader.

On the seventy-fourth day of the drive the herd
reached the Powder River Basin, and Jeb was struck
by the majesty of what he saw. Rising dramatically
to the west were the Big Horn Mountains, but to
the east was a limitless prairie. There was buffalo
grass, bluestem, slough grass, bunch grass—miles
and miles of it—and in some places it was as high
as Liberty's knees. He now understood Frewen's
unbridled enthusiasm for Wyoming. With the river

providing ample water and the grasslands undulating in gentle folds toward the Black Hills, this river basin was better than a gold mine for making money.

Moreton was right. In this country, all you had to do was brand the cows, turn them loose, then sort them out at a roundup and put them on the train for the Chicago stockyards.

Yes, Jeb was beginning to think he'd made a wise investment.

About midmorning, Jeb looked up to see several men riding hard toward him.

"Will," he called to one of his trail hands, "I don't know who these men are, but tell the boys to be ready for them."

"You think maybe they're rustlers?" Will asked.

Jeb pulled his pistol and checked the chambers to see that it was loaded. "I don't know. But I've come this far, and I'm not taking any chances."

Because of the clear air, distances were foreshortened, and it was several minutes before the men were close enough to make them out individually. The man in the middle leading the others sat tall in his saddle. He was dressed in buckskin, and Jeb smiled when he recognized him.

"It's all right, boys," he called to the others. "That's Moreton Frewen."

Jeb urged his horse into a ground-eating lope, closing the distance between them. Moreton, seeing Jeb coming toward him, galloped ahead of the others. Jeb and Moreton met in the middle of the two groups.

"By Jove, you're here! When my man told me he saw a herd moving this way, I knew it had to be you," Moreton said, holding out his hand to clasp Jeb's. "Welcome to the 76 Ranch. Any trouble on the drive?"

"No. Homer did his job. It's been tiring for the men and the livestock, but we didn't have any real trouble."

"How many head do you think we lost?"

"Last count, as near as we can tell we have nine hundred fifty-seven cows."

"So we only lost forty-three! That's excellent. The cattlemen at the Cheyenne Club told me to expect at least a ten percent loss."

Jeb didn't reply. Ten percent would be one hundred cows, and no way was he going to lose a hundred cows. As it was, he was a little upset with himself for losing forty-three cows, but the losses couldn't be helped. Broken legs accounted for most of the losses. The rest, for one reason or another, just couldn't keep up and fell off as stragglers, so far behind the main herd that it wasn't feasible to go back for them.

"My men will help drive them the rest of the way," Moreton said.

"How much farther is it?"

"You're almost there. Only a few more miles." Moreton pointed to a hill just behind him. "Once you crest that rise, you'll be able to see Frewen's Castle."

"Castle?"

Moreton laughed. "That's what the settlers call it. I guess it's a form of American humor, but I don't mind it. In fact, I rather like the appellation."

A few minutes later the two men were at the crest of the hill Moreton had pointed out, and some few miles in the distance Jeb saw a ranch compound on a curve of the Powder River. A house was located several yards from the river on a flat plateau. Behind the house lay several outbuildings.

But the house caught his attention. The big, two-story, pitched-roof house was made of squared pine logs. It had imported slate shingles and an impressive plastered and beamed gable over the entrance, giving the place what Moreton referred to as an Elizabethan look. It was much larger than the house at Two Hills, or even at the JA Ranch, and Jeb could see why it had been dubbed Frewen's Castle.

Later that same day as Moreton was entertaining Jeb, a redheaded man, a foot shorter than Frewen, entered the room carrying a tray with a crystal decanter containing brandy and two snifters. He set the tray on a small table between two tufted, brown leather chairs. They sat in front of one of the stone fireplaces that flanked each end of the great baronial hall.

"Mack, I want you to meet someone. Next to Richard and me, Mr. Tuhill is now the senior partner of the 76 Ranch," Moreton said. "Jeb Tuhill, meet William MacVittie. Mack is the best damn manservant a man could ever find."

Jeb stood to meet him.

"My pleasure, sir, but I prefer the title *valet*."

Moreton laughed. "I hired Mack to groom horses, but I soon found out he was better at grooming me, so I keep him around. He's a good man."

"Shall I pour, sir?"

"Please do. Will you join me?" Moreton asked, picking up a snifter and offering it to Jeb.

"Thanks." Jeb looked up at the majestic head of an elk that hung above the mantel. "An impressive rack." He took a sip of his brandy and settled back into the chair.

"I bagged that animal within a mile of where we are sitting right now. No question, this is a hunter's paradise. Do you enjoy the sport?"

"It's been a long time since I thought of hunting as a sport. Where I come from, game is used for food."

"But of course, and that's equally true here. But I do have friends, friends with money, who ofttimes visit the wilds of Wyoming for the express purpose of taking down an animal or two."

"John Adair," Jeb said. "That's how I first met him. When we all lived in Colorado, he hired Charles Goodnight to take him and Cornelia out on a buffalo hunt." A smile crept over Jeb's face.

"You smile. Were you a part of the hunt?"

"Oh, yes, I was there."

"Well, what happened? Did he shoot a buffalo?"

"No. He shot a horse."

"He couldn't tell the difference between a horse and a buffalo?"

"He could. But while he was sighting on a big bull, he swung his rifle around, and when he fired, he shot his own horse in the head. The fall came close to being the end of Mr. Adair."

Moreton laughed. "I've never heard John tell that story, but then I suspect it isn't a story he would willingly share."

"No, I don't suppose it is." Jeb took in the opulent architectural details of the great room. From his vantage point, he saw a hand-carved, massive staircase that, from the wood used, Jeb knew had to have been imported from someplace. This stairway stopped at a mezzanine gallery that displayed oversize paintings of the mountains and all kinds of animals that one might find in Wyoming. In addition, the two stone fireplaces were each large enough to allow a man to stand upright. Off to the side of this forty-foot-square room, Jeb caught a glimpse of a library that was lined with shelves of books, stretching from floor to ceiling. No, this was in no way an ordinary ranch house.

Wyoming Territory—fall 1880

When Jeb had first arrived at the 76 Ranch, he had stayed in one of the extra bedrooms in the main house, but he wanted a place of his own, so he and some of the cowhands built a small cabin for his use, set apart from the ranch proper.

Jeb had been here for an entire year now, including what Moreton called the hunting season. Last fall, several wealthy Englishmen, including the Duke of Beaufort, whom Jeb had met in Texas, came to enjoy the house, which was in many respects like the royal hunting lodges of Europe. On the first hunt, Jeb saw firsthand the skill with which Moreton Frewen could handle a rifle. A mountain lion had crept to the edge of a rock and was about to leap down upon an unsuspecting Lord Billingsworth. Frewen, who was riding behind Billingsworth, saw the animal poised to jump, and he aimed. But the animal jumped before Moreton could pull the trigger. Undaunted, Moreton shot the animal in midair, and the cat fell lifeless to the ground right beside Billingsworth's horse.

Now, standing at the window of his cabin, Jeb looked toward the Big Horn Mountains. They were at least fifteen miles distant, but in the cold, clear air they looked as if they were no more than a half hour's walk.

On one side of the room a potbellied stove pumped out enough heat to take the morning chill out of the air. A bluesteel, enameled pot sat on the stove, filling the room with the aroma of coffee made from freshly ground beans. Jeb walked over to the pot and, using a cloth to pad against the heat, poured himself a cup. He picked up a hand-numbered calendar and made a mark through Friday, September 24.

Finishing his coffee, Jeb emptied the dregs onto the fire in his stove. Then he walked from his cabin to the main house and went inside without knocking. Moreton's brother, Richard, was sitting near the fireplace, staring at the dancing flames.

Richard had been absent for most of the time Jeb had been at the ranch, only arriving a month ago.

"Good morning, Richard," Jeb greeted him.

"Quite," Richard replied shortly, then got up and left the room. Jeb watched him leave, curious as to his strange behavior.

"What's wrong with Richard?" Jeb asked when Moreton came into the great room.

"We've been having a family discussion. Tell me, Jeb, have you ever been to sea?"

Jeb chuckled. "I've never even seen the ocean, let alone been to sea. Why do you ask?"

"Because there's no other way we can get to England. I have to meet with some investors, and I'd like to take you with me. That is, if you'd be interested in going."

"Why, yes." A big smile spread across Jeb's face. "I'd love to go to England."

Two weeks later, Richard Frewen stood on the platform of the Rock Creek depot as Jeb, Moreton, and Mack prepared to board the eastbound train.

"I don't know why you're taking Jeb with you. I can understand Mack having to go, but Jeb should stay here with me," Richard complained.

"I ask you, do we need money or not? Jeb is a good spokesman for this organization, and all our friends will be delighted to see a real cowboy. Everybody thinks you and I are just playing at this, but anyone who sees Jeb will know he's genuine. He goes," Moreton said.

"But what about the fall roundup? He should be supervising that."

"You've got a new foreman," Mack said.

"And you've got Will Tate to help you," Jeb added. "He was one of the best hands the Palo Duro ever had. The roundup will be just fine without me."

Richard lowered his head. "It's not the cows I'm worried about. Who's going to take care of Lord Desborough and Lord Tankerville when they come for their hunt?"

"That's been taken care of, too. The last performance of *Scouts of the Plains* is in Denver this year, and when it's over, I've arranged for Bill Cody to act as a hunting guide. He'll so bedazzle your guests that they'll probably forget about the hunt just to listen to him," Moreton said.

"Wait a minute. You didn't tell me Buffalo Bill was coming. If I'd known that, I wouldn't be going to England with you," Jeb said.

Just then the train whistle blew, announcing the train's approach.

"Too late to change your mind now," Moreton said.

Jeb picked up his valise, while Mack handled Moreton's bags. The relationship between these two men constantly amazed Jeb. He knew they were friends, and they had respect for one another, but there was never a question as to who would do anything that required physical effort. Jeb would never understand how the aristocracy lived.

When the train reached New York, Jeb was disappointed that they had no time to explore the city, although if Moreton's idea of sightseeing in New York was similar to what he had shown Jeb in Chicago, he was more than happy to forgo the experience. Moreton had insisted that they go to the Chicago stockyards, and the stench they had encountered could still be smelled on the clothing Jeb had worn.

Alongside a dock in the New York harbor lay the SS *Adriatic*, a four-masted, square-rigged vessel, augmented by a steam engine and twin screws. Jeb was impressed when he was told that the ship had once set a speed record of seven days and nineteen hours for a crossing between Liverpool and New York. Once aboard, they were shown to their staterooms on the first-class promenade.

When the ship got under way, Jeb stood at the

rail watching as the buildings of the city got smaller and smaller until he could no longer see them. He had heard many times that the Llano Estacado, the Staked Plains, of West Texas were said to be as level as a sea. As he stared at the calm water of the Atlantic, for the first time since he had left the Palo Duro, he felt a twinge of homesickness.

The crossing took eight days, and when the ship docked at Liverpool, Moreton, Jeb, and Mack were met by the afternoon coach. It was dark blue with red wheels and was drawn by four matched bays. In fancy lettering across the back was the word QUICKSILVER.

"Where to, gents?" the driver asked as Moreton opened the door to the coach.

"Badminton," Mack said as he swung the valises into the boot of the coach.

"Ah, the Beaufort Hunt. They come from far and wide, and where be ye from?"

"Texas," Jeb said.

"I'm just waiting for the day you say you're from Wyoming. Then I'll know I've got you snared," Moreton said as he climbed into the coach.

The carriageway leading to the entrance of Badminton was at least three miles long, flanked by what Moreton said were lime trees. They passed through a clock arch, and the house in all its magnificence came into view. Jeb thought the house was the largest he had ever seen. The overwhelming structure had three stories and looked more like a Palladian pavilion than a residence.

"Is this one family's home?" Jeb asked.

"That's right, but the duke doesn't live here alone. I believe all five of his children are here at one time or another. You remember Beaufort. He came to hunt last fall."

"I do remember him, but I had no idea this was where he lived, or rather, how he lived."

"I will agree, it is impressive," Moreton said as the coach rolled to a stop.

The men stepped out, once more leaving Mack to handle the valises.

"I believe we're expected." Moreton pulled a long cord hanging by the door, and from somewhere in this cavernous house they could hear a bell.

When they were admitted to the entrance hall, the footman told them he had been given instructions to inform the duchess immediately. The room was huge with many large paintings, mainly of men on horses surrounded by dogs, but Jeb's attention was drawn to a troughlike item that he guessed to be about three feet wide, over seven feet long, and about three feet tall. Its most noticeable features were the relief carvings of a couple dozen nude males in various poses.

"Do you have any idea what that is?" Moreton asked.

Jeb chuckled. "No, but I'm pretty sure it isn't a horse trough."

"It's a Roman sarcophagus. The Duke of Beaufort is very proud of his art collection."

Jeb nodded his head without saying anything. Then he smothered a laugh. He could see this in a brothel if it had nude women, but where would you put nude men?

"Squire Frewen! I have missed you terribly," a

matronly woman said as she hurried across the hall toward the two men. "The Beaufort Hunt has not been the same since you left Melton Mowbray. Are you here to stay?"

"Your Grace, I fear it will be only a short stay at Badminton, although you know I would rather be here than anyplace in England." Moreton took the woman's hand in his.

"And who do you have with you, my dear boy?"

"Please forgive me. Duchess Georgiana, may I present my friend and American cohort Mr. Jebediah Tuhill."

"I'm pleased to welcome you to Badminton, Mr. Tuhill."

Not knowing the proper way to respond, Jeb bowed his head slightly. "Thank you, ma'am."

"I know you'll need to refresh yourselves, so Simon will show you to your rooms now, but I can't wait for the dinner hour. You always provide such lively conversation at the table, Moreton. Please don't disappoint me."

Jeb and Moreton followed the footman up the stairs, where they were assigned bedrooms at opposite ends of a long hall. When Jeb stepped into the room, his valise had already been unpacked, and a formal black wool suit with a tailcoat was hanging on a gentleman's clothes valet. There was a white waistcoat with a pleated shirt and a white bow tie, but the black patent-leather pumps with the bows on them made Jeb laugh out loud.

"Mack, are you in here?"

"I am." Mack stepped out of a small room off the bedroom.

"When did you have time to get this garb for me?"

"If you recall, I didn't visit the stockyards, and I knew you would need the proper attire."

"Moreton is right, you're a good man to have around."

"Are you ready?" Moreton called as he tapped on Jeb's door at precisely 7:00 p.m. "I should have come for you earlier because we need to get to the drawing room, where the duchess will give us our assignments."

"Our assignments?"

"Yes, the duchess will hand you a card with the name of a woman that will be your responsibility for the entire evening. You'll escort her to the table, and you'll engage her in conversation."

"But I thought I heard Lady Beaufort say you were to entertain us tonight."

"It's not like it is in America. I'm sure I'll be assigned to Lady Georgiana herself, and I'll entertain her. Let's hope the lady you get can hear. It's most dreadful when you're forced to shout to make yourself heard."

"This evening sounds like it's going to be a lot of fun." Jeb rolled his eyes.

"Don't give up yet. It could be."

The drawing room was large, but quite comfortably furnished with overstuffed chairs and sofas. About fifteen or twenty people were in the room conversing. The duchess approached when she saw them enter, then she introduced Jeb to all the guests, Moreton not being a stranger to anyone.

"Squire Frewen, it is my honor to have you as my personal escort tonight. Mr. Tuhill, I've assigned my daughter-in-law to you, but as of the moment, she's tardy. However, I'm sure she'll be along shortly."

Moreton quickly melded into the conversation, but Jeb was left to his own devices. He wandered over toward a recess that housed a cabinet that was perhaps the most beautiful piece of furniture he had ever seen. The ebony wood piece stood fourteen feet high and seven feet long and was embedded with hard and semiprecious stones. A clock was surrounded by gilding, and Jeb saw that it was now almost eight o'clock.

"Mr. Tuhill?" The voice was feminine and well modulated.

When Jeb turned to see who had addressed him, his breath caught in his throat. Based on most of the women he had seen here, he was expecting a plain or only moderately attractive woman. The creature standing before him was beautiful. She was dressed in a long, flowing gown that followed the curves of her body. The emerald coloring seemed to bring out her blue eyes and the red highlights in her brown hair, which was pulled tightly away from her face. Her shoulders were bare, and just above the décolletage a diamond pendant glistened, hanging from a thin silver chain.

"Mr. Tuhill?" she repeated, this time with just the hint of laughter in her voice.

Not until then did Jeb realize he had been staring. "Oh, uh, yes. I'm Jeb Tuhill."

"I'm Tallas Somerset, and I'm to be your companion at dinner."

"I'm glad to meet you, Miss Somerset. Or, is it Lady Somerset? I'm not really up on titles and protocol."

Tallie laughed out loud, and Jeb thought he had never heard anything like it. Neither abrasive, shrill, nor intrusive, it had an enchanting lilt.

"I'm only a lady by marriage."

"No, ma'am. From my perspective, you're a lady through and through."

"What a delightful dinner companion you'll be." Tallie offered Jeb her arm. "Won't you escort me to the dining room?"

FOUR

Dinner was served in several courses by a dozen footmen, all of whom were wearing waistcoats in the colors of Badminton House, tan with horizontal stripes of blue. Their brass buttons bore the Beaufort family crest, a lion rampant in the shield, the shield topped by a plumed helmet.

"I'm told that you are a real American cowboy," Tallie said to Jeb. "Is that true?"

"In a manner of speaking, I suppose it's true. Though I prefer to think of myself as a cattleman, rather than a cowboy."

"Oh, I'm sorry. I didn't mean to be diminutive."

"It's not that. There's nothing demeaning or diminutive about being a cowboy. The only difference is that a cowboy generally works for wages and found, where a cattleman provides those wages and found." Jeb chuckled.

"And where do you ply this cattleman's trade?"

"Right now, I'm one of the many partners in Moreton Frewen's Wyoming ranch."

"Wyoming? That's in the American West?"

"Yes."

"What's the American West like? Here in England, one reads so many tales about it that it's hard to sort truth from fiction."

"If your only source of the West is what you read in the dime novels, then you can consider very little of it to be true."

"Do you mean to tell me that every word that Buffalo Bill has written in his books is not the absolute truth?"

"Lady Somerset, don't tell me you're a fan of Buffalo Bill's books?"

"I'm not, but my father-in-law is. He was very disappointed that he didn't get a buffalo when he went to America."

"In my opinion, the buffalo is probably our most majestic creature, but unfortunately, its numbers are dwindling."

"You can't mean they're disappearing? Buffalo Bill says there are hundreds of thousands of them."

Jeb smiled. "Are you sure you haven't read some of Bill's books?"

Tallie lowered her head as her face flushed. "Well, I have to admit, I have looked through a few of them, but it was only for research purposes, you understand."

"Lady Somerset, I think you may be a cowgirl at heart."

There was that laugh again. "Are there wild Indians? I have read of your gallant General Custer and how every soldier in his command was killed and scalped."

"There are some who suggest that Custer wasn't all that gallant. But that was four years ago. There is very little trouble with Indians now."

"But you have highwaymen and outlaws, do you not?"

"And schools, churches, trains, telephones, and newspapers. We don't do things any differently from anyone else—we just have a lot more room to do it in."

"I should like to come visit your American West someday."

"I'm sure Moreton would make you and your husband feel quite welcome."

Again Tallie laughed. "Oh, dear, I can hardly imagine Arthur in your West."

"Arthur is your husband?"

"Yes."

Jeb looked around the table at the other guests. "Which one is Arthur?"

Tallie dropped her eyes, and for the first time in their conversation her response was not animated. "Arthur chose not to attend the dinner."

After saying good-night to Lady Somerset, Jeb returned to his room, humming a tune that he didn't recognize. He felt good, almost giddy, as he opened his door. He didn't know what it was about this woman, but he couldn't seem to get her off his mind. She was pretty, but he couldn't say that she was more beautiful than Katarina. But nobody, not even Katarina, or perhaps he should say, especially not Katarina, had ever affected him the way Lady Somerset had. The conversation he'd had with her was engaging, amusing, and entertaining, yet he couldn't remember anything significant that they had said to one another. He did remember that she'd said she would like to visit the American West. Perhaps he would suggest to Moreton that he extend an official invitation for her to come to Wyoming.

But why should he want to do that? The lady was married.

The next morning, Jeb woke before sunrise. He didn't share Moreton's excitement for the foxhunt that was to be because he couldn't see how a group of men riding behind a pack of dogs, chasing after a fox, could be anywhere near as exciting as taking a bear or stalking an elk in the Big Horns. But he was here, and the Beaufort Hunt had been all the talk last evening. Even his dinner companion had spoken of it enthusiastically, and if for no other reason, he would enjoy it for her sake.

Jeb was still thinking about last evening's dinner. He wished the English custom of conversing with only your assigned partner could be adopted in the States, and he smiled when he thought of the boisterous dinner conversations that were sometimes held at Two Hills.

"I can just hear the catcalls I'd be getting from the boys back home if they could see me now," Jeb said aloud as he pulled on the tight moleskin riding breeches and tucked in a silk shirt. The ever-efficient Mack had chosen what he called a sober black jacket with a velvet collar, telling him that as an outsider, it would be an unpardonable sin to wear the honored Beaufort colors of blue and buff.

A white stock-tie, tall black dress boots, and a black velvet hunt cap completed the outfit.

When Moreton came for Jeb, the Englishman was dressed in the Beaufort colors, the buff-colored pants being paired with a blue jacket with canary-colored facings.

Moreton looked carefully at Jeb's attire. "You'll pass, but I have one suggestion. Take the coins out of your pocket."

"What do you mean?"

"It's not considered proper when I can count your change."

"What's with this getup anyway?" Jeb pulled the coins out of his pocket.

"Tradition, my man, tradition. Now let's go choose our mounts."

The duke had nearly a hundred horses in his stable, and when Jeb and Moreton arrived, the grooms and the servants were busy getting tack and saddles assembled. Nearby, the master and the huntsman were supervising the loading of the hounds into the enclosed wagons called hound vans. Jeb asked a groom how many dogs would be used, and he was told at least fifty couples.

More people began coming into the stable, and Jeb was surprised to see so many women drawing horses. "I thought this was a gentleman's sport."

"Not by a long shot. The Austrian empress Elisabeth came here to hunt a few years back, and now all the women think they can ride as well as any man. According to Lady Georgiana, the empress is in England right now, and there was talk that she may come today." Moreton stepped toward a stall. He read the name above the door. "Toreador. Let me look you over. Are you going to be the horse that carries me after the hounds?"

Jeb, too, began looking over the horses. He stepped up to one named Hoarfrost. Then he saw Dunster Boy, Mackintosh, and Duebar, and he wondered where these people came up with these names. Where were such names as Duke or Bandit or Red Devil—names that told you something about the horse's personality? And where was a Liberty?

He stepped up to Hoarfrost, a bay with enormous quarters. "You look strong enough." Jeb patted the horse on its neck.

"Oh, sir, he is quite strong," a groom replied.

"Is he fast?"

"Fast enough for any hounds, sir. And no horse in the stable can beat him when he wants to jump."

"When he *wants* to jump?"

"More than likely he'll jump all right for you," the groom said.

Jeb took little comfort from the "more than likely," but this was the horse he had chosen, so this was the horse he would ride.

"A good choice," Moreton said as he led Toreador up beside Jeb.

"There's something about this that makes me a little uneasy."

"That's poppycock. I've seen you ride. You can cut any cow out of a herd, rope it, and tie it down with one hand tied behind your back if that's what it takes."

"Are we going to rope the fox?"

Moreton laughed. "I don't know, I don't think I've ever seen a fox-roping."

Once they were saddled and mounted, Jeb and Moreton joined in a slow parade of horsemen as they rode the three miles to Worcester Lodge. The four-story stone structure served as a combination banqueting pavilion and entrance gate to Badminton Park.

The assembly of the lawn meet was to begin with breakfast in the dining room, located above the groin-vaulted archway of the lodge. Like everything else about this place, Jeb was awed with the details: the stairs that were partitioned so that each had a different height for each foot, the plastered ceiling depicting the flowers and fruits of the four seasons, and the convex mirror overhead that had a radiating sunburst pattern.

"It's beautiful, isn't it?"

Lowering his gaze, Jeb saw Lady Somerset standing in front of him. He had admired her beauty at the dinner, but he was not prepared for what he saw today. She was dressed in a light blue jacket similar to the one Moreton was wearing, but he had never seen a lady wear pants, at least not the body-molding livery of a riding habit.

Although it seemed strange to Jeb—no, more than strange, it seemed almost scandalous—nobody else seemed to even take notice. Apparently the body-molding pants the women were wearing was an ordinary thing. He tried not to stare, but it was difficult.

"I believe some introductions are in order," Lady Somerset said. "Lady John Beresford, my sister-in-law, I would like you to meet Mr. Jebediah Tuhill, from Wyoming."

Jeb acknowledged the introduction, noticing that Lady Beresford, too, was wearing the snug pants. However, her body was a bit more ample than Lady Somerset's, and she did not present quite the same alluring picture.

"When I'm introduced as Jebediah, I hardly recognize my name. I'm called Jeb."

"That's good to know, and I'm called Tallie. It would be my honor if you would call me by my given name."

"It's not an honor to be called Lady Arthur Somerset?" a rather short man asked as he joined the group.

"Lord Henry Arthur George Somerset, may I present Jeb Tuhill?"

Jeb nodded.

"My brother Arthur, always the smart-alecky arse," Lady Beresford said. "Why didn't you just stay in bed?"

"Because I want to wish my wife well as she prepares for the hunt. And I want to grant my best wishes to"—Arthur paused in midsentence and took in Jeb with an appraising gaze—"her handsome paramour."

"Arthur! I believe you owe Mr. Tuhill and me an apology. Your mother assigned Mr. Tuhill—Jeb—to be my escort last evening. I would hardly say he is my paramour."

"Ah, my dear, I love it when you become inflamed with passion, no matter what causes it. I am sorry. Will you both accept my apology?"

Tallie took Arthur's hand in hers and turned to Jeb. "Will you join us for breakfast? I believe the pheasant will be quite good."

After breakfast, as they gathered for the hunt, Tallie looked around for her husband. Arthur wasn't there, but she wasn't surprised. Arthur was sensitive and artistic, but not particularly athletic. This was in stark contrast to his father, the Duke of Beaufort, who was the most consummate sportsman in the entire county, even for a time acting as his own huntsman while riding to hounds.

Tallie and Arthur's father had got along quite well over the past two years. The duke found Tallie delightful and refined her riding techniques, first on a more sedate hunter, then on one of the most powerful mounts in his whole stable. Tallie loved the challenge.

As the riders gathered in the morning mist, she saw that Jeb Tuhill was close by, whether by accident or by design she didn't know. But she was pleased by it, even though she did feel a little guilty over her unexpected reaction to him. She mentally took notes on his appearance: a shock of wheat-blond hair that tumbled onto his sun-bronzed forehead, blue eyes—so blue that she would describe them as cobalt—deep set with small creases around them, broad shoulders, a trim waist, and legs with powerful muscles displayed by the tight breeches he was wearing.

She imagined him as the hero in a novel and even mentally wrote a few lines: *Sweeping her into his powerful arms, he spoke in a commanding manner. "My struggle to repress my feelings for you has*

*been futile. My love for you cannot be contained
and will not be denied. Do you know how passion-
ately I admire and love you?"*

"If it gets any foggier, we won't even be able to
see the fox," Jeb said.

Hearing his voice in a timbre that was as deep
and resonant as the imagined voice of her hero
startled her, as if one of her characters had stepped
from the pages of the novel. "Oh, uh . . . " Tallie
struggled to shake herself out of her fantasy.

A lopsided grin formed on Jeb's face, as if he
were privy to her private thoughts. "I guess that's
what the dogs are for," he said, the grin still in place
as his eyes twinkled with amusement. He kneed his
horse and rode over toward Moreton Frewen.

The hounds were released and they began running, the men and women on horseback starting
after them. Tallie loved the hunt, loved the feel of
a powerful horse under her. She was quite skilled
and rode comfortably in the saddle as the horses
thundered out across the wide, green meadow. She
glanced over at Jeb Tuhill, surprised at how easily
and confidently he was riding.

But then, why shouldn't he be easy and confident in a saddle? After all, he was a cowboy. No, she
edited her thought. He was a cattleman.

The hunt continued for most of the morning, the
hounds entering covert after covert only to draw a
blank. As the fog thickened, Tallie was afraid the
huntsman would call in the dogs, but the whips
were doing a good job keeping the hounds together.
By one o'clock they had not found a single fox, and
the duke called for a break.

Tallie searched out Moreton and Jeb. "Did you bring your lunch?" she asked.

"I forgot," Moreton said. "Mack usually takes care of things for me, and he's not here today. We'll just have to wait till we get back, unless you, Lady Somerset, have something to share?"

Tallie laughed openly. "Lady Georgiana takes care of you, Moreton. Guess who's here?"

Just then an old man carrying a knapsack approached the threesome, with a broad grin on his face.

"Lum, my old friend," Moreton said as he shook the man's hand wildly. "Jeb, this is my groom from Melton Mowbray, where I grew up."

"It's good to lay eyes on you, my boy. We miss your antics around here," Lum said.

"Did you bring what Lady Georgiana asked for?" Tallie questioned.

"I did." He handed the knapsack to Tallie, and she withdrew a pastry.

"Will you have a pork pie, Mr. Tuhill?"

"Not any pork pie—a Melton Mowbray pork pie," Moreton said, snatching the first one away from Jeb. "Come, catch me up on what's going on at home."

"I'll bet that's the end of the hunt for Moreton," Tallie said as she slid off her horse. "Would you like to stretch your legs a bit?"

Jeb followed and they led their horses to a low stone wall.

"Now no one will take your pork pie." She retrieved another pastry and handed it to Jeb.

"Whoever thought of this couldn't have come up with a better food for a foxhunt," Jeb said. "The next time I see my mom, I'll have to tell her about this, because it would be great for men on a cattle drive."

"Does your mom live in Wyoming?"

"No. She lives in Texas."

"Aren't Texas and Wyoming far apart? How did you get to Wyoming?"

"It's a long story." Jeb took another bite of the pastry.

Tallie hesitated before she asked her next question, but she had to know the answer. "Does it involve a woman?"

Jeb looked directly at Tallie, his eyebrows rising and his forehead furrowing. He opened his mouth as if to speak, then he looked away.

Just then the tone and pitch of one of the baying hounds changed, one of them in particular sounding a new note. The huntsman blew his horn and all the horses were off.

"Let's go! That's a find!" Tallie shouted as she swung up on her horse, riding astride just as a man would do. Her horse quickly broke into a gallop, and Jeb had to ride hard to catch up to her. Just then, a horseman riding faster than anyone else broke off from the pack, and Tallie followed his lead.

Damn, that woman can ride, Jeb thought as he urged his own horse faster. Then, ahead, as patches of fog were clearing, he saw the fence. The fence itself wasn't imposing, but on the other side of the fence was a ditch and a great bank constructed of clay.

The horseman ahead of them cleared the fence and the ditch. His horse balanced itself for an instant on the bank, then with a second leap made it into the field beyond.

Jeb had jumped many an arroyo in his day, to say nothing of banks of rock and sage. His horse was moving rapidly, its head stretched out, gathering itself for the leap ahead. But a little twitch in his mount's ears gave Jeb some concern, and he recalled the groom's words: *More than likely he'll jump all right for you.* That *more than likely* had Jeb a little concerned. Would his horse take the jump?

The horse was still in full gallop, and Jeb rode him to the very edge of the jump, then the horse suddenly stopped, planting his forefeet and lowering his head. The horse stopped, but Jeb didn't, and his momentum threw him from the saddle, over the horse's neck, headfirst into the ditch.

Tallie stopped her horse and dismounted. She climbed the fence and scurried down the embankment.

"Jeb!" she yelled as she knelt beside him. "Can you hear me? Are you all right?" Tallie lowered her ear to his chest to see if his heart was still beating, placing her hand on his forehead.

Jeb had managed to turn his body in such a way that he didn't break his neck, but he was shaken and covered with dirt. He lay on the ground, aware of what had just happened. He should say something to let Tallie know he was all right, but in a perverse sort of way he was enjoying her ministrations.

When Tallie was convinced that he was still alive, she looked up, and when she did, his eyes were open and he was grinning.

"You! Why didn't you say something? You scared

me half to death." She started to get up, but Jeb pulled her to him.

"Aren't you supposed to check to see if I have a broken neck before you leave me here?"

"I guess I can do that, but, Mr. Tuhill, I think there's not a thing wrong with you."

"It's Jeb."

"Yes," she said in a bare whisper as she removed her riding gloves and began to examine his neck. "Seriously, you seem to be all right. It's a good thing this berm is new because it's softer. Let me help you get up."

"That does a lot for my pride," Jeb said, but he was glad to have her assistance. When he was upright, he realized his body was aching and he tried to stretch, but when he did so, he felt a sharp pain in his side. "Ohhhh," he groaned.

"You *are* hurt, aren't you? And it looks like your horse has decided to go home without you."

"He's probably going home in embarrassment. Where did everybody else go?"

"Who knows? Wherever the scent took the hounds, but we're in luck. When we stopped for lunch, we were in Bodkin Wood, so I think if we angle northeast, we'll find Swangrove, even if the fog gets thicker."

"And what is Swangrove?"

"It's a hunting lodge. Do you think you can get on my horse?"

Jeb winced with pain, but he did manage to get on the horse, and Tallie got on behind him.

"Who gets the reins?" Jeb asked as he looked over his shoulder at her.

Tallie reached around him to grasp the reins. As the horse broke into a trot, she could feel him wince, though he made no sound. "Are you all right?"

"I think so."

"It's not much farther."

"Good."

Tallie thought she could hear his discomfort in his voice.

The ride took no more than five minutes, though it seemed much longer to Tallie, who was so empathetic that she could almost feel Jeb's pain. Then, finally the lodge appeared out of the fog, a huge stone building two stories high with castellated walls around the two wings.

"There it is."

"That's the hunting lodge? I was expecting a little log cabin. That thing is as big as a hotel."

Tallie rode up to the front of the impressive building, then called out, "Mr. Greenlee? Mr. Greenlee, are you in there?"

A middle-aged man with a bald head and muttonchop whiskers came outside at the call. "Lady Arthur?"

"My friend has been injured. Can you help me get him down from the horse?"

"Yes, yes, of course. Crashed over some timber, did ye?"

"I'm afraid he tried to go over a fence and didn't make it."

"On the contrary, madam, I did make it over the fence," Jeb said. "It was my horse that didn't make it."

Despite the situation, Tallie chuckled, as she and

Greenlee helped Jeb dismount, and though he tried not to, he called out in pain.

With Tallie on one side and Greenlee on the other, they walked him into the building, then led him over to a large sofa, where he sat down.

"Help me get him out of his clothes," Tallie said, "and then let's get him to lie down."

"Is this a proposition, Lady Somerset?"

"I hardly think so."

Greenlee and Tallie got Jeb's jacket off, then removed his shirt.

"I think I would feel better if I continued to sit up."

"No, I want you to lie down. More than likely you have a cracked rib, but I'll need to check and see."

Jeb lowered himself to the sofa, and Tallie watched as he winced in pain. When he was reclining, she watched his chest as he breathed, and she was glad to see he was inhaling normally. She placed her hand on his chest and ran her fingers through the curly hair that covered it, her actual observation proving what she had imagined earlier. Then she traced the well-defined muscles of his broad shoulders, powerful arms, and flat stomach. She was acutely aware of his masculinity then, in a way that she had never been aware before.

"Unless I am a much different animal, I would think you would be checking my sides, if you suspect I have a broken rib," Jeb teased.

"I was checking for a broken collarbone." She moved her hands to his rib cage, and when she applied the slightest pressure on his right side, once again he called out.

"That seems to be the place. Mr. Greenlee, will

you hitch up a team to a wagon so we can get him back to Badminton?"

"I'm afraid my wagon was pressed into service this morning. When the fog was so bad, several of the ladies gave up the hunt and went home early, but I can ride over to the stable and get it."

"Good. I'll stay with Mr. Tuhill and make him comfortable."

Tallie took Jeb's shirt and made a tight roll out of it. She placed it next to his injured rib, then, taking her own stock-tie, she fashioned a sling that drew his arm close to his side.

"That feels better, but how did you know what to do?"

"The duke taught me. There's always some sort of accident happening during a foxhunt—cracked ribs, broken bones, broken necks . . . That's why Lord Beaufort insists that any Badminton woman wears breeches instead of a skirt."

"What's the connection?"

"His niece fell from her horse and her skirt caught on the pommel. When she died, the duke decided that none of the women he cared about would ever be subjected to that again."

"The duke seems like a very caring man."

"He is."

"What about your Arthur? Is he a caring man?"

Tallie hesitated before answering, raising her eyes to Jeb's. "Yes, in his own way."

"But he's not a loving man."

"Why would you say that?"

"Because a loving man would never have suggested that I was his wife's paramour."

"You're not familiar with English Society, are you, Mr. Tuhill?"

When Tallie went to bed that night, she couldn't get the image of Jeb Tuhill off her mind. She saw him lying on the sofa undressed, allowing her hands to move over his body, feeling—no, caressing—every part of him. She pictured how he would look totally naked. She had never seen a live nude male body, but her curiosity was more than aroused when she studied Lord Beaufort's sarcophagus in the front hallway. And Jeb's riding breeches left little to the imagination.

She and Arthur had been married for a little more than two years now. In all that time, she had never seen as much of his body as she had seen of Jeb's today. Somewhere in the sixty-five bedrooms of Badminton House, Arthur was sleeping. And this night, in one of those rooms, Jeb Tuhill was sleeping.

When on their wedding night Arthur had informed her that there would be no consummation of their marriage, Tallie had accepted it. He had told her that she must choose celibacy or adultery, and until this very night she had never even considered adultery, though there had been ample opportunities.

Tallie rose from her bed and slipped on her dressing gown. She moved to the door and quietly opened it, then stepped out into the hallway. Which room was Jeb in? Could she find him?

How stupid! Of course she couldn't find him. The house was full of guests, and she couldn't knock on each door trying to find the one person she wanted to see. She returned to her bed and lay for a long time, thinking of the lot she had drawn in life. It could be worse.

She was sure that Arthur cared for her, in his own way. He was certainly providing well for her. And, unexpectedly, his father, the duke, had been exceptionally nice to her. Through his contacts Tallie had been able to get her first book published, using the pseudonym Nora Ingram.

So, why was she thinking of Jeb Tuhill? Why did she have this feeling of expectation? Of unfulfilled desire? He was the first man she had been seriously attracted to, and tomorrow he would be gone, never to be a part of her life again.

The first time she had met Arthur, Tallie, along with the Darwins, had spent the summer on the Isle of Wight, and during that idyllic summer she had met Alfred Lord Tennyson, Henry Wadsworth Longfellow, and Mary Anne Evans, who wrote as George Eliot, one of the most popular writers in all England.

Miss Evans had told her, "Experiences are a writer's stock-in-trade. Embrace them, store them away like commodities on a shelf."

Thinking back on Miss Evans's words, Tallie took notice of this strange and disquieting sense of awakening that Jeb Tuhill had aroused in her, and she knew that she had just added an experience that she would store on her shelf.

FIVE

Following the foxhunt, Jeb—his chest tightly bound—and Moreton left for Dundee, Scotland, where they met with Robert Fleming and anyone else they could convince to listen to them talk about investing in American cattle.

"Gentlemen, I thank you for coming," Moreton said when all were gathered at Fleming's trust company. "I think you will find this meeting has the potential to be one of the most profitable you have ever attended. But don't take my word for it. I am no different from any of you—a subject of the Crown with an interest in making money, and a willingness to invest in an exciting venture.

"Rather, I would have you listen to a presentation given by one of the newest investors in the Great Western Cattle Company. Mr. Jeb Tuhill is a lifelong cattleman, not only born to the profession, but educated in it as well, having studied ranching at a Western university that specializes in such subjects.

"Ah, but, gentlemen, disabuse yourselves of any idea that Mr. Tuhill is all academia. He can ride, rope, and shoot as well as any cowboy I've ever seen. This man standing before you is the consummate cattleman, and now, I leave it to him to explain the machinations of earning more money than you ever thought possible just by investing in American cattle in general, and the 76 Ranch in particular. Mr. Tuhill."

Moreton held his hand out toward Jeb, who stood to the polite applause of those gathered.

"Thank you, Moreton. Gentlemen, the steak you have just enjoyed is the end product of the most lucrative branch in all agriculture, the raising of beef cattle.

"And in Wyoming, we have a unique situation that is made to order for prudent investors. As of today, about ninety-five percent of the Territory of Wyoming is public land, and on that land grows the most cattle-nourishing grass in the world. Understand this—the grass is there for our use. We don't have to put our money in land or feed. All we have to do is buy our initial herd of cows and turn them loose; they will feed themselves, and the herd can be expected to double every three years.

"Now, if a rancher chooses to sell off a third of his herd each year, conservatively he will have an immediate return of at least ten percent on his investment, even as that investment grows. What this means is, should you choose to invest in the Great Western Cattle Company, with proper management, you can expect to double your capital every three years."

"Mr. Tuhill, to a Scotsman like myself it sounds

like you have invented a money machine," Archibald Coats said. "It makes my lowly thread business seem like a pauper's mite."

"I hardly think you can say that, Archie, but the American cattle business does seem like a bonanza," Robert Fleming said.

"Oh, it is," Moreton chimed in. "You can't lose."

"Yes, I believe you told us as much when we visited you in Texas," Fleming said. "You were quite as exuberant then as you are now."

"Moreton is filled with exuberance," Jeb said, "and by and large he is correct. But as in every investment there is some risk, though in this case it is minimal."

"What sort of risk could you foresee, Mr. Tuhill?"

"Weather. We can't control a prolonged drought in the summer, or a severe blizzard in the winter. However, the Powder River valley has been blessed so far, and I have no reason to believe that things will be any different in the foreseeable future."

"We appreciate your honesty, Tuhill. Let us consider our options and get back to you," Fleming said.

The trip to the United Kingdom proved to be one of the most lucrative calls for investment that Moreton had ever conducted and on the return trip to New York on board the SS *Germanic*, Moreton was in rare form as he extolled the virtues of cattle ranching to any passenger who would listen. Jeb and the ever-present Mack occupied their time playing the French card game *écarté*, which seemed to have been the latest craze in London.

Tonight, having grown weary of listening to Moreton regale the other passengers with his stories, Jeb went outside to take a stroll on the promenade deck. He took in deep breaths of the salt air, appreciating that he was finally able to inhale with minimal discomfort. It had been more than two weeks since his injury, and he felt his side, noticing that the pain was beginning to subside.

Even though he probably didn't still need it, he continued to wrap Tallie's silk stock-tie around his trunk. In the past two weeks, he'd come to find it soothing, both physically and mentally.

He was in the middle of the ocean, but found something comforting in looking up and seeing the same stars and constellations he could see on the range in Wyoming, or down in Texas. He knew, also, that if Tallie Somerset was looking up at the sky at this very moment, she would be looking at the same stars. Walking up to the taffrail, he rested his arms on it, his hands clasped before him, and looked down at the sea. He could see, in the dark and almost black water, the white foam kicked up by the twin screws and the passage of the hull. The ship's wake appeared luminescent in the bright moonlight, and he followed it with his eyes as far back on the water as he could see.

Lives also left wakes, and he wondered how it would be if, in some way, he could follow his own wake back far enough, and fast enough, to relive some of his own life. He did not regret his decision to go to Wyoming, but he did regret the circumstances under which he'd left Texas.

His action had been motivated by anger. But since then he had had a lot of time to think. If he was hon-

est with himself, he couldn't decide just why he had
been so angry. At first, he thought it was because
he had lost Katarina. He had thought he wanted to
marry her, but was that really true? Had he wanted
to marry her only because she was there, because
she was handy, and because she would fit into his
life?

The more he thought about it, the more he realized that his brother had done him a favor. A man
didn't marry a woman just because she was there.
There had to be a better reason than that. He
couldn't put his finger on it, but he believed there
must be something to what the poets called love.

He just hadn't found it yet.

Then, in a totally unbidden thought, the face of
Tallie Somerset popped into his mind.

"Well, she's married, so you can just get her out
of your mind right now," he said aloud, angry with
himself for letting that thought surface.

Jeb turned from the railing and started toward the
first-class lounge, but he stopped and went back to
the railing. Unbuttoning his shirt, he withdrew Tallie's stock-tie and threw it over the rail. He watched
the white cloth flutter down to the water, and when it
disappeared into the black, he went into the lounge.

Mack was sitting in a chair against the wall, separated from the others, but watching everything.

"Do you mind if I join you?" Jeb asked, taking a
chair from an empty table and carrying it over to
put it alongside the Irishman.

"Your company would be a pleasure, sir."

"You're missing out on all the stories," Jeb said
as he sat down.

"They're not new stories."

Jeb chuckled. "I guess you've heard them all before."

"I haven't only heard them, I've lived most of them."

When they docked in New York, much to the surprise of everyone they were met by Richard.

"What in heaven's name are you doing here?" Moreton asked. "Why aren't you in Wyoming?"

"Because I've booked passage on the return trip of the SS *Germanic*. It's your turn to mollycoddle the ranch, where it's too damn cold to function as a civilized human being. I'm going back to England, where I intend to have a life."

"But you can't give up now, Richard. Jeb and I have raised a tremendous amount of money. Will you just turn your back on that?"

"I suppose not, but I'm not staying this winter."

"And I'm not going back either. I have things to do in New York," Moreton said, turning toward Jeb. "Will you take over for us?"

What kind of businessmen were these two? Jeb thought about selling his shares of the Great Western Cattle Company right there on the spot and going back to Texas, where he belonged. But he had more integrity than that. He had just spent two weeks convincing honest men to part with their money, and he knew what he had told them was true. Raising cattle could be a profitable business, but someone had to assume some responsibility, and these two clearly weren't inclined to do that.

"I'll be on the train west as soon as my valise is off the boat."

76 Ranch, Wyoming Territory—December 1880

It was a lazy Sunday afternoon and Jeb Tuhill and Buffalo Bill Cody were sitting on the floor in front of the fireplace, cleaning Moreton's hunting guns. Moreton had a veritable armory, with eight rifles of various calibers and actions, and six double-barrel shotguns. A fire popped and cracked in the fireplace, the flames warming the two men, as well as painting their faces golden in the glow.

Cody finished the rifle he had been working on and leaned it up against a wall before starting on another.

"Was it a good hunting season?" Jeb asked.

"It would have been better if . . . "

"If what?"

"If I didn't have to wet nurse a bunch of dandified cullies."

Jeb laughed. "But you have to know that's the whole purpose of this place. The blue bloods come, they hunt, and they lay down their money. And do they ever have it! The folks around here call this Frewen's Castle, but let me tell you, the place I stayed when I 'rode to hounds' had one hundred sixteen rooms, including sixty-five bedrooms. Now that really is a castle."

Cody chuckled. "So you went on a foxhunt. Tell me, did you wear some of those tight little breeches like all these dudes wear when they're here?"

"I did."

"I'll bet you were quite a sight to behold."

"Well, I wouldn't have wanted any of the men to see me dressed like that."

"Ha, I don't doubt that. Now, tell me, what is it you say when you see a fox?" Buffalo Bill stood and, with the rifle on his shoulder, yelled, "There goes the little son of a bitch!" He lowered the rifle and smiled at Jeb.

Jeb laughed. "Something like that."

"Really, was there anything to it? The foxhunt, I mean."

Jeb's hand went to his rib and Tallie's face came to his mind. "There were some interesting moments, and if I had the chance, I'd do it again. Especially if the circumstance was right."

"Hand me the oil, will you?" Cody picked up a flask of whiskey and took a long drink.

Jeb handed Cody the oil. "Here I am, sittin' on the floor cleanin' guns with Buffalo Bill Cody, the great Western hero. Who would've ever thought it?"

"Cut that out, now." Cody took another swig of whiskey.

"Oh? What about this?" Rising, Jeb walked over to the mantel and picked up a dime novel.

"What have you got there?"

Smiling, Jeb held up his finger. Clearing his throat, he began to read in a stentorian voice.

Hearing that the desperadoes had said they would kill him on sight, Buffalo Bill boldly rode into the town where they had their haunts, and clutching the reins of his horse between his teeth, he drew both his pistols and called out to them. "It is I, Buffalo Bill. I have heard that you would do me harm, so I am here. Will you face me like men? Or will you hide like cowards?"

Four came to face him, and at the first shot Bill was wounded in the right arm, which destroyed his aim, and a second shot caused his horse to fall dead beneath him, pinning him to the ground.

Instantly his foes rushed upon him to complete their work, when, rising on his wounded arm, Buffalo Bill leveled his revolver with his left hand and, with but four twitches of his trigger finger, dispatched the evil brigands as they were almost upon him.

Jeb closed the book and, smiling, looked at Cody. "Is just one word of that true?"

"Well, there—might be—a little exaggeration here and there," Cody said as he wiped down the barrel of a shotgun.

"I'd say. Tell me, Bill, if you had the reins clutched in your teeth, how could you possibly yell out at them?"

Cody laughed out loud, laughing so long and so hard that Will Tate came into the room. "What's the joke?"

"Will, I don't think our friend Jeb believes everything he reads about me."

Somerset town house, London—February 1881

Tallie was at her desk, writing, when she heard a light knock on her bedroom door. Thinking it was Mrs. Ferguson, she called out, "Come in." The door opened, but Tallie didn't look around. "It's a little early for tea, isn't it, Mrs. Ferguson?"

The reply was a discreet cough, a male cough. Curious, Tallie looked around and saw her father-in-law, the Duke of Beaufort, standing there.

"Your Grace," she said, surprised to see him. She stood quickly. Never, in the over two years that she had been married, had the duke ever been on her private floor, let alone stepped into her bedroom.

"Tallie, I'm so sorry," the duke said ominously.

"Sorry?" She gasped. "It's Arthur, isn't it? Has there been an accident?"

"No."

Tallie put her hand to her chest. "Oh, thank God. You had me frightened."

"Arthur's, uh, *inclinations* cannot be a secret to you. And I am afraid his proclivities have gotten him into a great deal of trouble. Some young men have been arrested for, uh, certain indelicate acts. They were in a gentlemen's club of sorts on Cleveland Street. It seems that Arthur has been named in the investigation."

"Oh, poor Arthur."

"I appreciate that you are thinking first of my son and not of yourself. But I'm afraid that isn't the worst of it. It would appear that Eddy—that is, Prince Albert Victor—is involved. And the Queen is blaming Arthur for having a corrupting influence on her grandson. The specific details concerning both Arthur and Eddy will be kept secret, so nobody is to know. Nevertheless, the Queen has given orders that Arthur be exiled to the Continent. If he ever returns to England, he will be sentenced to hard labor."

"Oh!" Tallie gasped, raising her hand to her mouth.

"So I have come to make you this proposition. I want you to divorce Arthur. If you will do that, I will deed this house to you, and I will add a generous remittance."

"You want me to divorce Arthur?"

"Yes. The details surrounding this scandal must forever remain secret. But once you institute a divorce, Arthur will be seen as the aggrieved party, and you will be reviled by society. You will be scandalized. That, I'm afraid, cannot be helped."

The duke's words were overwhelming. Tallie couldn't bring herself to speak.

"I realize that I am asking a tremendous sacrifice from you, my dear. But under the circumstances, I think this will be best all around. If you agree to it, I will have my solicitor make all the arrangements. That way it will not be necessary for you or Arthur to appear in court."

With tears gathering in her eyes, Tallie looked directly at the duke. "I have no choice, do I?"

"Yes, you do have a choice. But with the involvement of the royals, it could mean the revocation of the Beaufort title. Our fate is in your hands."

Tallie turned away from the duke and walked to the window, looking out at the winter garden. A few birds were darting in and out of the holly trees. They would grab a berry, then quickly fly away to eat in private.

Tallie lifted her chin and turned to face her father-in-law. "Send your solicitor."

"Thank you." Then Beaufort did something

that Tallie could never have predicted. He came to her and embraced her as a father would hold his daughter. "You are a wonderful woman, Tallie. Such is the shame that Arthur could never see that."

"Are you sure you won't be ostracized for being my friend?" Tallie asked.

"No, it will be for entertaining you in my home," Jennie Churchill replied.

"What? Oh, Jennie, yes, of course, I never thought!"

Jennie laughed. "Tallie, you have become a very dear friend. Nobody is going to tell me who I can have as a friend or, for that matter, who I can entertain in my own home."

"I—I should have listened to you. I was prepared for the criticism that would come from the divorce, but I never once thought the book would get such a reaction. *The Prince's Folly* is a novel. Don't people realize that a novel is fiction?"

"Is it really, now? Who in their right mind doesn't recognize the Prince of Wales and the Duchess of Manchester?" Jennie picked up a copy of the book, finding a random line to read. "'The Duchess's husband conveniently rode to hounds and broke bones frequently enough to provide his wife, the most beautiful woman in England, opportunity for dalliances with the Prince.' Let me think. Who could that be?"

"That's not Prince Albert and Louise at all," Tallie insisted. "I was very careful to call my characters Prince X and the Duchess of W."

Jennie laughed. "What a crafty ruse you devised! I'm quite sure nobody would ever recognize either of your protagonists."

"Do you think I was a bit too blatant?"

"Perhaps a bit, but I love it. You do realize, though, that you will be persona non grata for the foreseeable future, and you definitely will be out of favor for this season. No matter what the prince may think, Queen Victoria will see to that."

"Oh, Jennie, what have I done? I've upset just about everyone with this book, haven't I? That is, everyone except my publisher. Did you know George Smith told me that the book is in its third printing at Smith, Elder already? He says everyone is buying it."

"Yes, and it's not just the commoners. The dirty little secret, my dear, is that all of Society is reading *The Prince's Folly*. They talk so contemptuously about it in public, while in the privacy of their own chambers they enjoy every juicy tidbit. I think they're even titillated if they recognize themselves."

"I shouldn't have written the book. You tried to tell me, but I didn't listen. And now, without Arthur, I really don't know what I'm going to do."

"Well, I can tell you. First, you don't need Arthur. I never thought he was right for you anyway. And secondly, you should stop accepting the blame for ending the marriage. You have no idea how many remittance men are going to come out of the bushes when they realize how much money you will make from your book. Why, every third or fourth son who's not a priest will be begging to court you. You'll have your pick of men."

"I don't want another husband," Tallie said emphatically.

"You can't really mean that. We both know Arthur was not the right mate for you, but that doesn't mean there isn't someone out there who could make you very happy. I know this is a delicate subject for you, but rumors are beginning to circulate about Arthur. . . . "

"No, Jennie. I don't want to talk about it, even to you."

"Then we will never mention it again. But let me ask you one more thing. Would you consider taking a lover?"

Tallie let out a long sigh. "I don't want a husband. I don't want a lover, and that's that."

A broad smile crossed Jennie's face. "That's exactly what I want to hear, because I have just fallen in love with the most wonderful man. Count Carl Kinsky zu Wehinitz u Tettau. Don't you think even his name sounds gorgeous?"

"It sounds totally unpronounceable. Does Randolph know?"

"Yes, of course he knows, and he's quite all right with it, as it leaves him free for his own dalliances. But I have a problem, and you, my dear friend, can help me immensely while at the same time you will be helping yourself."

"Pray tell this does not involve your count."

"Oh, but it does. For propriety's sake, and because Randolph thinks that Winnie is at an impressionable age, my husband insists that Carl not call at our home. And he may be right. Anyway, we've been having our trysts at Bay Middleton's hunting lodge, and that dreadful man has been filling Carl's head with tales of a possible hunting excursion to a place somewhere in Wyoming."

"Wyoming? Where in Wyoming?" Tallie asked, immediately recalling that Jeb Tuhill, the subject of many of her latest fantasies, had said he was from Wyoming. How many times had she relived the scene at Swangrove when Jeb was injured? In her mind she was feeling the hard muscles of his broad shoulders, running her hands through the mat of hair on his chest, inhaling the scent of him. Then in an unbidden moment that caused her face to flush, she remembered his tight riding breeches, and what she had seen. If Jennie only knew what the word *Wyoming* conjured up for her.

"It's on a cattle ranch, but the worst news is, one of the men who is a partner in this place is a miserable cad, and now he's engaged to marry my sister."

"What's—what's his name?" Tallie asked with trepidation. For some unknown reason, she feared that Jennie would say the name Jeb Tuhill. Nothing had happened between the two, but when she imagined a man who could be a heroic character in a novel, Jeb's features formed in her mind.

"I'm sure you probably don't remember him—the egotistical bastard—but I do recall he was at your wedding. Now, I think Squire Frewen only wants to marry my sister so he can get some of my father's money."

"Squire Frewen? Would that be Moreton Frewen?"

"Yes, that's him. Don't tell me he made such an impression on you that you remember him?"

Tallie didn't say that it was Moreton's partner

that she vividly remembered. "I just recall the name. He's marrying your sister?"

"Clara, yes. And in my opinion Moreton Frewen is an utterly abhorrent man. Why, he even calls our dearest mama Sitting Bull behind her back. Anyway, Bay Middleton has convinced Carl that there is the most wonderful opportunity for adventure at this man's ranch, and Carl is determined to go, so he's going with Bay to my sister's wedding in New York City, and then out to this Wyoming ranch."

"That sounds like a perfectly reasonable thing to do for a sportsman."

"Well, it's what could happen before he gets to the ranch that I am concerned about. I just know there will be some New York socialite who will see Carl and hear his title, and she will try her hardest to snare him for a trophy. That's why I need you, Tallie. Will you go to Clara's wedding and keep an eye on Carl?"

"This is a man you say you have fallen in love with, and yet you're concerned that he'll take up with someone else?"

"Oh, Tallie, you just don't understand the hunt—the excitement that only a virile man can bring out in a woman. You need to become more adventurous, get out in the world."

"But aren't you going to your sister's wedding?"

"No, I can't. Randolph has started a war with the prime minister, and now Gladstone's determined to get rid of him. My husband would never admit to this, but I'm writing some of his speeches, so he has begged me to help him while his position in the

House of Commons could be in the ascendancy. I owe him that, so I've agreed to stay behind.

"But I can't stop Carl from going. And I've been thinking, if you would take this trip to the States, it would be good for both of us. You would get away from the gossip that you are currently fueling with *The Prince's Folly*, and I would know you were standing guard over my count. If you stay by his side, no other woman would dare try to put her talons in him."

"If I say yes to this trip, would I go with your sister all the way to Wyoming?"

"Why in heaven's name would you want to do that? New York is exciting, but I can't think of anything more dreadful than being on a cattle ranch in Wyoming."

"You just said I need to become more adventuresome. Who says a trip to Wyoming couldn't be the place to start?"

SIX

New York—April 1881

allie, Count Carl Kinsky, and Bay Middleton made the trip to New York on board the SS *Adriatic*. A North Atlantic storm came up, causing the seas to swell and the ship to be tossed about. In spite of her father's profession, this was the first time Tallie had ever been on board a ship, and in the beginning she was a little apprehensive, knowing that her father had been lost at sea. But the two men had been gracious traveling companions, entertaining her with stories from each of their exploits.

Tallie soon understood why Jennie was infatuated with the Austrian count, who was both handsome and extremely wealthy. She thought that both of these gentlemen would make good studies for characters for a new novel, and she began to look forward to spending time with each of them on the ranch in Wyoming.

When the ship docked, a week later than scheduled because of the storm, Tallie was certain that they had missed the wedding. Bay arranged for a carriage to take the three of them to the home of

Mr. and Mrs. Leonard Jerome, Jennie's parents. The Jerome home, a six-story mansion, was at the corner of Madison Square and Twenty-sixth Street. When the three were admitted into the opulent home, they presented their cards and were ushered into a drawing room.

Within minutes Clara Jerome came hurrying into the room. "Tallie, how happy I am to meet you at last. Jennie speaks so well of you. Count Kinsky, Captain Middleton, welcome to America."

"Do we have the honor of addressing you as Mrs. Frewen?" Bay asked as he took her hand in his and lifted it to her lips.

"Not yet. The wedding was scheduled for last week, but for one reason or another, Moreton telegraphed to tell me to postpone it. I have now set the date for June second, and that is ever so much better, because now you will be able to be a part of it."

"I hope that there wasn't some unforeseen accident," Tallie said.

"I'm sure it's nothing like that, although Moreton didn't give a reason. Oh, the unexpected—that's the caprice I love about my future husband!"

"Are you sure you and Lady Randolph are sisters?" Kinsky asked with a broad grin. "I have a hard time believing that Jennie would consider the delay of a wedding to be a caprice."

"Neither did Mama. In fact she was furious with Moreton when we had to reschedule everything. But the wonderful thing is, now all of you will get to enjoy springtime in New York."

"I'm sure we will," Tallie said.

"Tallie, Mama said that she wants you to stay in Jennie's room, but she thinks it would be better if you gentlemen stay as our guests at the Fifth Avenue Hotel."

"That's very gracious of you," Tallie said. "But won't that be an inconvenience for you? Perhaps I should stay at the hotel, too." She was thinking of her promise to Jennie to watch Kinsky. How would she do that if she stayed at the Jerome household and he stayed at the hotel?

"Nonsense. You'll be in Jennie's room, and if you choose, we'll hardly know you're here."

"Well, if you'll excuse us, Miss Jerome, we'll be taking our leave," Kinsky said. To Tallie he added, "I've arranged a livery to deliver your baggage, Lady Somerset."

"Thank you," Tallie said as the men were escorted out of the drawing room.

"Isn't he the most unbelievably handsome man you've ever met?" Clara asked, once the men were out of earshot.

"Which one?"

"Why, Kinsky of course. I can see why Jennie is head over heels in love with him, and I daresay if I weren't already engaged, I do believe I'd set my own cap for him."

"I think one could say you're a little beyond just being engaged," Tallie said, feigning a laugh.

"I suppose that's true, but it never hurts to know what's on the market. Come, let me show you to your room."

The 76 Ranch—May 15, 1881

Moreton and Richard were sitting on the front porch. Jeb and some of the cowboys were playing a game of baseball in a field on the plateau. Jeb was at bat, and there was a loud crack as he hit the ball. The ball flew deep into the outfield, and Jeb began running toward first base as his teammates cheered him on.

"What a silly game that is," Richard said.

"You can't mean that. If you took the time to look into the game, you would find that it tests the athletic skills of all who play it."

Richard chuckled derisively. "You're becoming too Americanized, Moreton. We're here to make our fortunes, not to be assimilated into this uncultured wasteland."

"It's my thinking that our venture will be more successful because we are investing our time as well as our money. Most capitalists are only interested in their return, but I think understanding the culture of the American West is every bit as important to making money as is buying the right breed of cattle."

"Yes, well, you can be the one who studies this culture all you want. But for me, I recognize this for what it is—a business, and that's all. And you may have noticed, whenever any of our countrymen come here, they enjoy their time spent, but they are only too pleased to return to civilization."

"You can't deny, Richard, that this is some of the most glorious scenery you've ever seen. It is a virtual paradise."

"I signed on to your scheme because you told me we would make a fortune. So far that fortune seems to have eluded us."

"We're making an adequate return. Anyway, there's more to life than money," Moreton said.

"Tell that to your gaudy nouveau riche American friends. They think money can buy them social acceptance, and it's pathetic. Just look at your future father-in-law. He's one of the worst offenders."

"And what are you trying to do, Richard? Are you not trying to make enough money to buy yourself a place in their company?"

"I know the difference between money and social position. But I do admit I'm a hedonist, and I'll have to confess that I enjoy the gauche playthings the American rich invent. Take the champagne fountain in your father-in-law's ballroom. Who wouldn't want to drink a toast to your new bride from that?"

"I thought you said you didn't want to go to the wedding," Moreton said.

"I don't. The last place I want to be is surrounded by loudmouthed, know-it-all Americans who think they're rich."

"It might help if you tried to change your attitude. We do live here, at least part of the time, and we make our money here. We both should try to get along with the Americans. It would do you good to come to the wedding."

"Well, I'm not going."

"Very well, have it your own way, but I do plan to ask Jeb to come to New York with me. Mr. Jerome has some powerful friends, and I think no stone should be left unturned where there's any chance of money coming our way. Leonard's sent word that the tobacconist Pierre Lorillard is interested in coming to the 76, and so is August Belmont, so I want Jeb there to help me talk up the place."

Jeb had always been intrigued by the telephone at the 76 Ranch. The telephone line was stretched over twenty-five miles connecting the Castle with Frewen's Trading Post in Trabing. After some shouting and repeating of questions and verifying of answers, Moreton learned that the river was crossable, so the next morning Jeb, Moreton, and Mack started on the long journey to the wedding. Reuben Marshall would drive the coach that the Frewen ranch kept at Trabing, the little settlement at the fork of Crazy Woman Creek and the Powder River.

Because the river was at flood stage, the trip to Rock Creek took longer than usual, but once they boarded the train, it was only a three-hour trip to Cheyenne.

"Mack, I want you to outfit Jeb and then meet me at the Cheyenne Club," Moreton said.

"What do you mean?" Jeb asked.

"For the big shindig tonight. You have to be dressed properly," Mack said.

"Shindig? I do believe the cowboys are making their mark on you, Mack. But what kind of getup do I have to have for Cheyenne? This is a cowmen's town."

"You've not been to the Cheyenne Club," Mack said. "It's a little different."

"That's right. I'm throwing a stag party tonight

in honor of my forthcoming marriage, and I'll be inviting any fellow stock-grower who's in town," Moreton said.

"You mean there are other cattlemen here? I can understand why you're not at the spring roundup, but why wouldn't your 'fellow stock-growers' be there? The roundup is the most important part of ranching, and besides, even though it's hard work, it's a lot of fun. I'm sorry I'm going to miss it."

"My friend, many of the men you'll meet tonight barely know the difference between a bull and a heifer. All they know is that the steer they buy in Texas costs five dollars, and four years later at a Chicago market, that same steer is worth around forty-five dollars. That's their only interest in the cattle business. But Mack is right about your clothes. Tonight everyone will be wearing white tie and tails."

Jeb looked around at the other people he saw going about their business in Cheyenne. Most everyone was dressed just as he was—working pants and shirt, maybe a vest, cowboy boots, a wide-brimmed hat, and a gun in a holster.

"Moreton, I think I'll go down to the saloon and see if I can find Reuben. I know he hasn't started back for Trabing yet, and I just think I'll join him. You can get married without me."

"But I want you to come to my wedding."

"Then stop treating me like your pet sheepdog."

"I'm sorry, Jeb. I don't mean to be an ass. In my own clumsy way, I'm just trying to be helpful."

"Try being helpful without being so damn patronizing, will you?"

"You'll come to New York, then?"

Jeb smiled. "Yeah. You stop being an ass, I'll come." He looked over at Mack. "Come on, let's go get me properly attired for this . . . shindig."

"Very good, sir," Mack replied with a wide smile.

SEVEN

25 May 1881
New York, NY, USA

My dearest Aunt Emma,

Please forgive me for being so remiss in writing to you, but I have been so busy during my visit that I am neglecting all the social graces. It is a poor excuse to say that social graces are easily overlooked here, for Americans seem totally unaware of such things; a cabdriver will speak to a banker with no sense of awareness of differing stations, while at the same time one or two people can dictate who can and who cannot attend society's coveted events.

I miss you and Uncle Charles and all my Darwin "brothers and sisters." I had to laugh at your last post when you wrote of Bernard's interruption of one of the worm experiments. He is so fortunate to have you both as grandparents. The love that all of you show for each other, and for me, has not been duplicated in any other setting I have ever experienced. I know that I can never fully express my enduring gratitude.

I apologize profusely for not coming by to bid you adieu before leaving for America. It was just that the trip arose rather quickly, and my time was consumed in making all preparations for the voyage. For the first time, I can appreciate how Uncle Charles feels when the negative letters arrive expressing disdain for his work. While The Prince's Folly can never be compared with the significance of The Origin of Species, nonetheless, the feelings of rejection are universal.

On a lighter note, New York is a wonderfully exciting place. There are so many marvelous things to see and do here, and Mr. and Mrs. Jerome (you know they are the parents of my neighbor Jennie Churchill) have been wonderful. I must describe the house. It is of the French Second Empire style of architecture, having a slate-shingled, mansard roof. Then there are two stories of redbrick and stone, and two stories of rusticated limestone. The service floor is all belowground. (I can't imagine that Mrs. Ferguson, or Eliza and Parslow, would appreciate being separated from our families like that!)

But that is the outside. I shall try to share some thoughts about the inside. The breakfast room can seat seventy people, which when compared to Badminton doesn't seem like much, but this house is located on a plot of land *that could barely accommodate Uncle Charles's greenhouse. Can you imagine what the tourists who come to Downe wanting to meet the famous Charles Darwin would say if they were invited in for a scone in that kind of setting? But let me tell you about the ballroom—it has two fountains, one that spouts champagne and the other French perfume. Personally, I am aghast at some of the tacky attempts to convey wealth that are displayed in this home. I should correct that and say* house, *for I cannot see that this structure could ever be a home. Even now, I can recall the times when we sat on the floor while you read to all of us, or I can see you and Uncle Charles playing backgammon. I cannot find a place in this house where those small pleasures might occur. I miss you all very much, and I love you.*

   As ever,
   Tallie

P.S. Miss Jerome's wedding to Mr. Moreton Frewen will be June 2nd, and then I am off with the newlyweds to Mr. Frewen's ranch in Wyoming. I am looking forward to visiting America's "wild" West.

Tallie was staying in Jennie's old room, and she thought of her friend as she looked around, trying to imagine her here. Her time in New York had been exciting, but Clara had monopolized most of her time, leaving little chance for Tallie to "chaperone" Carl Kinsky. At times, she felt she was remiss in honoring her friend's direct request, but circumstances prevented her from being in his presence. If he had done anything untoward, Tallie could honestly report she hadn't seen it.

Clara had been a most accommodating guide. She took Tallie to all the well-known sites and introduced her to all the right people, but never once did Clara even hint that Tallie was the well-received English novelist Nora Ingram. A part of Tallie was glad no one knew who she was, but when she heard people discussing her work, she had wished that Clara might drop some hint that Tallie was the author.

A few days later, Tallie and Clara were perusing the paintings of Albert Bierstadt in the Metropolitan Museum of Art, exclaiming appreciatively about those with Rocky Mountain subjects.

"Do you think the mountains in Wyoming will look like these?" Tallie asked as they stood in front of one particular painting.

"I do hope so. Moreton says it is some of the most beautiful scenery he has ever seen. And I'm so pleased that you're going to share a part of it with me, even if it's only for a month or two."

"You have to be so excited about the wedding, but aren't you even more excited to know you will start your married life together in such rugged country?"

"I would never admit this to anyone, especially not to Mama, but I will tell you, I am a little afraid of what's to come. I love Moreton and I trust him, but when I think how far away it is, it scares me." Clara took Tallie's hand and squeezed it as tears began to cloud her eyes.

"Oh, Clara, is something wrong?"

"It's just that—I just wish . . . "

"You wish what?"

"I wish Mama was a bit more receptive to Moreton. She just preaches to me all the time, telling me what a mistake I'm making. And Jennie doesn't help matters at all. She positively abhors him. She could have come, but—"

"What about your father?" Tallie interrupted.

Clara's face brightened. "Papa's the one bright spot in this whole thing. He says he doesn't wonder why I'm in love with Moreton, because he's enamored with him, too. But you've met him. He's wonderful, and I know I'm going to be happy."

Tallie looked at Clara. She wished she could reassure her that she and Moreton would live happily ever after, but in Tallie's experience—her own marriage, Jennie and Randolph's, all the different prototypes she had parodied in *The Prince's Folly*, even her own parents'—no one had a happy marriage. That wasn't quite true. There were the Darwins. If it could ever be said that a man and woman truly loved one another, it would be Charles and Emma.

"When do you expect Moreton to get to New York?"

Clara looked at the big clock on the wall of the gallery. "Oh, dear, we must leave right now. He could be arriving even as we speak, and I can't let Mama be the first to greet him!"

A dozen trains were backed in under the glassed-roof train shed of the Grand Central Depot, and they echoed back the sounds of chugging engines, clanging bells, and wheels rolling along steel rails. Coal smoke hung in a cloud just under the roof, and wisps of steam drifted through the shed like fog rising from wet ground on a warm day. Jeb noticed a chalkboard listing the schedules for trains, and he calculated that no fewer than eighty trains would arrive and depart every day.

Adding to the sounds made by the locomotives and train cars were the sounds of scores of conversations, some of them in languages Jeb couldn't understand. He stood on a long strip of cement pavement between the train he had just left and the one on the track next to it. In the window of the car of the next train he saw a young boy staring at him. Jeb smiled and waved, but the boy ducked his head in embarrassment.

Jeb was wearing one of the outfits that Mack had helped him select while they were in Cheyenne—a brown tweed frock coat with striped trousers, a dark green vest, and a white silk shirt. While these clothes were not his usual attire, they were acceptable, but the two things that Mack had insisted upon his buying—a silk puff tie and leather brogans—he could have done without. Jeb didn't like the hat either. He thought it looked like a gambler's hat, but at least it was better than the derby Mack had tried to convince him to buy.

"I must say, Jeb, don't you look like the bon vivant," Mack said as they stepped into the cavernous waiting room that resonated with the echoes of a thousand travelers.

"I'm sure I do, whatever that is," Jeb said.

"Ah, to be back in the city," Moreton said, raising his arms in exclamation. "Isn't it wonderful?"

"I really don't understand why so many people

want to live in a place like this. It's crowded, smoky, dirty, stinky."

"I'm going to change your mind about New York, you just wait. It's probably the most vibrant city in the world," Moreton said. "I think we're staying at the Fifth Avenue Hotel. Mack, you take care of things here while Jeb and I go on."

"Yes, sir," Mack said, remaining behind.

Jeb always felt a little self-conscious when Mack was left to discharge the menial tasks because, in truth, Mack was probably a better friend to Jeb than Moreton was. But Moreton just expected it, and the few times Jeb had protested, Mack seemed offended.

Jeb and Moreton walked through the terminal with its frescoes and varnished woods lining the immense public concourses where labyrinthine arcades of shops handled multitudes of passengers, coming and going.

Once outside the huge redbrick terminal, Jeb saw portals that had ironwork arches painted to resemble marble. On these arches were labels reading NEW YORK & NEW HAVEN RAILROAD, NEW YORK CENTRAL & HUDSON RIVER, and NEW YORK & HARLEM. Jeb wondered how anyone would know which of these trains to board. Wyoming was much simpler. At Rock Creek, you could get on, and if the train was headed west, you would reach Rawlins; if it was going east, you would go to Cheyenne.

Outside, Forty-second Street ran in front of this temple to commerce. It was just as busy as the depot had been, with people moving quickly and purposefully from one place to another. Just across from the terminal was the Grand Union Hotel, which advertised rooms for a dollar a day and had a dining room that would accommodate six hundred guests. Where did all these people come from?

Moreton hired a hansom cab that was standing by the curb. Once he and Jeb were sitting behind the front gate and Moreton had given their destination, the driver snapped his whip, and the horse took off in a trot.

The drive took them down broad esplanades bordered by luxury hotels and beautiful buildings called apartment houses. Everywhere Jeb looked, he saw people, especially women, who were wearing walking dresses that dragged along collecting dust from the walkways as they went from shop to shop. Parked along the curb were victorias, landaus, broughams, and coupés—all sorts of carriages waiting for their ladies to return.

The street was filled with cabs, such as the one he was in, omnibuses, and trolleys that ran on tracks but were pulled by a team of horses. The occasional horseman looked out of place among the many wheeled vehicles.

The way the people seemed to be moving around, in and out of buildings, passing each other apparently without seeing each other, reminded Jeb of an anthill. How could anyone live in such a place?

Jeb's room was on the fourth floor of the Fifth Avenue Hotel, and he was standing at the window looking out over the city when there was a rather loud knock on his door. Opening the door, he saw Moreton and two other men standing in the hall.

"Jeb, my good fellow, I want you to meet a couple of friends of mine. This is my countryman Bay Middleton, who is undoubtedly the best foxhunter in Melton Mowbray, and this handsome fellow is Count Carl Kinsky."

"Count?"

"Don't let the title intimidate you, he's just like us. Or, as like us as an Austrian can be."

The three men laughed.

Us, Jeb thought. No, he was not a part of the "us" because he didn't think any of the three men were like him.

The four of them "did the town," in cowboy terminology, going from saloon to saloon—though Jeb quickly learned that they were referred to as *clubs* rather than saloons. He was surprised that Moreton didn't want to see his future bride immediately, but he seemed in no hurry to do so.

The second night in New York was a repeat of the first, but this time they were joined by Moreton's future father-in-law, Leonard Jerome; his good friend Pierre Lorillard; and William Bagot, who was to be Moreton's best man.

They were dining at the Union Club, when an excited telegrapher approached their table. "Mr. Lorillard, is Iroquois one of your horses?"

"Indeed, he is. Is there any news of the derby?"

"The ticker tape just came through and it says that Iroquois won."

The table erupted in cheers and shouts at the news.

"That's the first time an American horse has ever won the English Derby," Moreton said. "Bring on the champagne. We have to celebrate."

And celebrate they did. They went from club to club, starting in the fashionable places and eventually moving to establishments with names such as the Star and Garter, the Bohemia, Buckingham Palace, the Alhambra, and the Tivoli.

Jeb noticed that each of these had a ladies' entrance to the side, and he was told that these establishments were known as houses of assignation. As they drifted farther west from Broadway, he saw pickpockets and con artists working the crowd. Mack had been right in insisting that Jeb not wear his Western clothing because he would have been an easy mark for these masters of deceit.

At around 3:00 a.m. the revelers finally reached the tenderloin, the city's sleaziest party area. Women, whom Leonard Jerome dubbed hell's belles, approached all of the men, not hesitating to solicit each of them for paid sex.

How different it was in the West. Yes, there were brothels out West, but the women, called soiled doves by the cowboys, were not as brazen with their solicitation. Most had been forced onto "the line" due to circumstances beyond their control. That didn't seem to be how it was here. In a city this large, and with so many ways a woman could earn a living, Jeb believed that these women had entered the avocation by choice.

Working their way through a crowd of people,

even at this early-morning hour, the group finally got into the Haymarket. This was a combination saloon, restaurant, and dance hall, and the noise was so great, it was hard to hear anyone speak. Nonetheless, a woman approached them.

"I heard you gentlemen talking, and it sounds like one of you is about to get married."

"He is," Kinsky said, pointing to Moreton. "This is his last night of freedom."

"That doesn't have to be, does it, honey?" The woman walked over to Leonard Jerome and put her arm around his neck as he smiled up at her.

"Don't come to me tonight, Mamie. I'm on my best behavior."

"Well, if I can't have the best, who wants a taste of honey?"

"What do you say, Moreton? Are you going to take this last chance?" Middleton asked.

"Never. I'm happy with the woman I have."

"Would you say that if Mr. Jerome wasn't here?" Kinsky asked.

"Absolutely."

"And I believe you, my boy," Jerome said, lifting his glass of champagne toward Moreton.

"But that's the point, Moreton," Kinsky said. "You don't have her yet."

Jeb had not joined in the teasing, but he was glad to hear Moreton's response.

"You seem to have a lot to say," the woman said to Kinsky as she moved closer to him. "Maybe you can get a little sugar, then come back and tell your friend what he's missing?"

"Ha!" Middleton said. "The shoe is on your foot

now, Carl. You aren't married, and you aren't about to get married. Are you going to take her up on her offer?"

"No offense to you, love," Kinsky said to the woman, "but I don't need to go looking for it. I brought my own woman to the States with me, and I'll be escorting her to this gentleman's wedding tomorrow."

"Bah!" the woman said, pouting as she stood up and backed away from the table. "There's not a man among you."

"There you go, Moreton. That was your last chance," Middleton teased.

At about four in the morning, Jerome and Lorillard parted company with them, while the others returned to the hotel. Jeb, who was not used to drinking so heavily, excused himself and went to his room, but the others continued their conversation in the lobby of the hotel.

When Jeb came down for a bite to eat the next day, the morning was long gone, but Moreton and Bay Middleton were still in the same chairs where he had last left them, and they were drinking more champagne.

"Jeb," Moreton said, raising a glass in a salute. "You gave up much too early last night. Bay and I have solved all the problems of the world."

"I'm impressed with your stamina, Moreton. There's no way I could be as chipper as you are," Jeb said.

"Years of practice, my friend. Both Bay and I were asked to leave Cambridge for this very thing, you know."

"Are you sure you want to get married today?"

"I am absolutely positive." Moreton took another drink of champagne.

Jeb was glad Mack had laid out his clothes for him one more time. Even though the wedding was to be at 3:00 p.m., he was told he would be wearing a morning coat. He thought all the rules that society imposed upon people were ridiculous, and he could hardly wait to be back where it didn't matter what you wore—it only mattered what you could accomplish.

But what was he accomplishing by being at the 76 Ranch?

Jeb thought he liked Moreton, but this trip to New York had been a revelation into a world that Jeb didn't think he cared for. He didn't consider drinking all night long on the eve of your marriage right.

It was as if all of these people weren't real. He had heard the comments of neighboring ranchers back in Wyoming. They all called the Frewen brothers and their many titled guests "upper-class" playboys.

By association, was Jeb falling into that same category? Why hadn't he insisted on staying behind and working the roundup? That was what he loved to do.

But, no, here he was dressed up like some dandy expected to attend a wedding that no one, not even the bridegroom, seemed anxious to have happen. If Moreton loved this woman so much, why had he not even taken Jeb to meet her?

Jeb picked up the top hat, put on the silly gloves, and walked out of the hotel.

The doorman stepped toward Jeb, holding his whistle. "Would you want me to summon a cab for you, sir?"

"No, thank you." The church where the wedding was to be held was several blocks away, but Jeb needed to walk. He had much to think about.

The city seemed to echo with bells, not the peal of bells like in a church or a school, but rather a jangle from some device that made a higher-pitched, rapid staccato of rings. All of the vehicles seemed to be equipped with the devices, and the more impatient of the drivers used them incessantly as a warning to others, so that the sound was always there. In addition, he heard hoofbeats and the scrape of iron-rimmed wheels, much louder on the paved streets than on the dirt roads Jeb was used to.

When Jeb reached Grace Church, he was met by an usher.

"Are you a friend of the bride or the groom, sir?"

Jeb stared at the usher, fighting to keep from saying neither, but he saw Count Kinsky sitting next to the aisle near the back of the church, and because, at the moment, Kinsky was the only person he recognized in the entire church, he pointed to him. "If I may, I would like to sit with that gentleman."

"Very good, sir." The usher escorted Jeb down the aisle until they drew even with the pew Jeb had indicated. Kinsky smiled when he saw Jeb, stood up, stepped out into the aisle, and extended his hand.

"Glad to see you made it." Kinsky made a motion with his hand, inviting Jeb into the pew.

Jeb started in, then stopped in surprise when he recognized Tallie Somerset, the woman he had met at Badminton. "You! What are you doing here?"

Tallie smiled at him. "I must say I could say the same of you. Seeing you is a pleasant surprise."

"I wasn't aware you two knew each other, Jeb. I guess introductions won't be necessary," Kinsky said.

"Are you with . . . ?" Jeb didn't finish the sentence because he wasn't quite sure what to call her.

"I have the privilege of being m'lady's escort, yes," Kinsky said.

Jeb failed to see that the prayer kneeler was down, and in his attempt to pass by Tallie, he tripped. Instinctively, Tallie reached out to him.

"I'm sorry," Jeb said when he was seated. "That was very clumsy of me."

"It happens to all of us at one time or another," Tallie said, smiling. She scooted closer to Kinsky to make room for Jeb.

Jeb felt a little self-conscious sitting beside Lady Somerset. As he looked at her white-gloved hands folded demurely in her lap, he couldn't help but remember how those same hands, then gloveless, had trailed across his bare skin as she inspected his injury.

He was having a hard time reconciling that Tallie Somerset with the one sitting beside him now, so prim and proper. But then, how proper could she be? She was married, Jeb had met her husband, and yet here she was in Kinsky's company. Wait. What was it Kinsky said last night? *But I don't need to go looking for it. I brought my own woman to the*

States with me, and I'll be escorting her to this gentleman's wedding tomorrow.

Had he been talking about Tallie? He had to be, he was sitting here with her, wasn't he?

Tomorrow Jeb would be on the train headed west, and it couldn't come soon enough. Though a small part of him thought it might be nice to stay a day longer if he had any further opportunity to visit with Miss Somerset.

No, it's Mrs. Somerset. Lady Arthur Somerset of Badminton House. Apparently, that she was married didn't matter to Mrs. Somerset, so why should it matter to him?

EIGHT

Tallie was sitting between two handsome men. Count Carl Kinsky was the quintessential gentleman, so sophisticated and polished, his hair always oiled, his mustache carefully trimmed, his clothing perfectly tailored. He seemed to anticipate every move she made, and his solicitude was to be admired, but something about him bothered her. He was what Uncle Charles would call *slick*.

That word could never be used to describe Jeb Tuhill. It wasn't that Jeb was unsophisticated; he had seemed reasonably comfortable during his visit to Badminton House last fall.

But she was equally sure he would be more at home out on the range among cows and bears and Indians. Though she didn't really know anything about the range and cows, or bears and Indians for that matter. She knew only what she had read in the novels of the West, and what she could imagine.

She tried not to look at Jeb, but in her peripheral gaze, she couldn't help it. He was a good-looking man, yes, though he wasn't as handsome as Carl Kinsky, or even Moreton Frewen. Yet, he had a strength about him, a powerful and disquieting attraction.

Tallie had said she was surprised to see Jeb, but was she? She knew that Jeb worked with Moreton Frewen, and she couldn't deny she had entertained the hope that she would see him when she came to America. Though she hadn't said anything to Jennie about it, the idea that she might see Jeb again was one of the reasons she had agreed to Jennie's proposal.

Tallie had thought about him on the ship on the way over, revisiting in her mind the tactile sensations of running her hands over the bare skin of his muscular chest. The thought then, and, indeed, the thought at this very moment, caused her to feel a tingling warmth, and using the closeness of the pew as an excuse, she repositioned herself slightly, so that her hip touched his. She wondered if he felt the same sensation through that contact. Was she imagining it? Or did he just move a bit closer to her?

Had she moved closer to him on purpose? Or was it merely the conditions by which they were sitting? Jeb decided to test it, and he pressed a bit closer to increase the pressure at the point of contact. She made no effort to move away.

Tallie tried to shift her attention away from the man. She began to focus on the beautiful architectural details of the church—anything to lessen her awareness of him. She was concentrating on the beautiful stained-glass Te Deum window that was above the reredos, and listening to the organ music, when the priest, Moreton, and his best man, who had been standing up front, left the chancel.

Kinsky checked the watch that was hanging from a fob on his waistcoat. "Was the wedding not to have started at three o'clock?"

Seeing that the time was half past three, Tallie asked, "Yes, but where are they?"

"Maybe Sitting Bull has put her foot down."

"You don't think Mrs. Jerome has called off the wedding, do you?"

"If she has, Moreton will be devastated. I've never seen him this animated about anything, except maybe when he gave Redskin to Lily Langtry."

"I find that most disgraceful," Tallie said as she playfully struck Kinsky's arm with her fan. "You can't compare the possible loss of a wife to giving away a horse."

"Lady Somerset, I just did," Kinsky said, a broad smile crossing his face.

Jeb was listening and watching the interplay between his pewmates when he heard a commotion in the narthex. Looking toward the rear of the church, he saw Bay Middleton. Middleton disappeared back into the narthex, then reappeared a few seconds later, escorting an angry-looking older woman down the aisle. If this was Clara's mother, he could see why Moreton called her Sitting Bull. Then, even as Mrs. Jerome was seated, Moreton and his best man reappeared from the transept. Jeb figured the wedding was on, and to Wagner's "Bridal Chorus," Leonard Jerome escorted his daughter down the aisle, where he gave her away, then slipped back to sit beside the bride's mother as the wedding continued.

When the wedding was over and the four white, prancing horses pulled the carriage carrying Mr. and Mrs. Moreton Frewen away, Jeb stood for a moment alone, in front of the church. He put the top hat on his head and turned to walk back to the hotel.

"Oh, Jeb?"

Turning, Jeb saw Tallie. He smiled at seeing her.

"Carl and I would be honored to have you join us for the rest of the afternoon. The reception doesn't start until seven, and the count and I plan to have one last tour around the city."

Then she *is* with him, Jeb thought. What kind of woman is this? She is married, but she has come to America with Kinsky, if Kinsky is to be believed. And nothing Jeb had seen this afternoon suggested that Kinsky hadn't been telling the truth when he said he had brought his own woman to the States with him.

"Thank you, but I don't think I'll be at the reception. I need to get ready to leave tomorrow," Jeb said.

"Oh, but you can't miss the reception. Unless you are the bride or groom, that's the most important part of any wedding. And won't you please come with us now?" Tallie asked.

"We can't convince him, Tallie. His mind is made up. Anyway, I think Clara's sister and Bay are going to join us. I know it would just be a bore for Mr.

Tuhill to have to listen to all the latest gossip from London," Kinsky said.

"All right, so you won't come with us now. But please promise me you'll come to the reception," Tallie said.

Jeb nodded, and as he did so, his top hat fell to the sidewalk. At the same moment, both Tallie and Jeb knelt to retrieve it.

"Your hat, sir," Tallie said, putting it in his hand, their bodies now just inches apart. "Please come tonight, Jeb. I'll save a dance for you." Her voice was almost a whisper, as if she did not want the count to hear her.

Jeb stood quickly and offered her his hand to help her rise. "I'll be there."

Jeb watched as Tallie and Kinsky joined the people who were now entering carriages to be taken from the church. He wondered why Tallie had invited him to join them when it was obvious Kinsky did not want that at all. Jeb decided he didn't understand women well enough to even guess at her reason. He turned to walk back to the hotel.

The reception was held in the grand ballroom of the Jerome Mansion. If any ballroom ever deserved to be called grand, it was this. Rainbows of crystal light played across the ceiling from the huge chandeliers that hung above the room, while bronze statues supporting gas jets were set in any unused space. But the focal points of the ballroom were the two fountains, one spewing champagne, the other eau de cologne. For the reception, banks of roses, gardenias, and orange blossoms surrounded the splashing fountains. On a table beside one fountain stood a twelve-tiered wedding cake, which Moreton and Clara were attempting to cut.

Tallie was standing with Leonie, the youngest Jerome sister, who had only arrived from London three days ago.

"I'm so glad you got here in time for the wedding. I'm just sorry Jennie couldn't join you," Tallie said.

"Oh, she could have. It's just that she detests Moreton almost as much as Mama does, but I find him delightful."

"But Clara loves him, and that's the most important thing."

"Tallie, do you really believe that? Don't you think position and money are more important than love?"

Tallie looked directly at Leonie, and thinking of her relationship with Arthur, she answered with one word: "No."

"Well then, Lady Somerset, let's just look around this room and pick out someone that you can 'love,' as you call it. Count Kinsky would be my first choice for you. He's rich and handsome, and I could tell this afternoon, he is interested in you."

"Ha! Never in a thousand years."

Count Kinsky would never be the man for Tallie. She had heard the rumors connecting him with the Austrian empress Elisabeth, and she knew first-hand that he was romantically involved with Jennie. Affairs were entirely permissible, if not encouraged, in London Society, but Tallie knew she wanted more than stolen trysts hidden from the husband and the help. In her mind, she thought of the last line of a letter from the Darwins. Uncle Charles had added a postscript: *Now the tally with your aunt Emma in backgammon stands thus: she, poor creature, has won only 2,490 games, whilst I have won, hurrah, hurrah, 2,795 games!*

This was the standard against which she would judge all relationships. A man and a woman who found absolute contentment solely in one another's presence—she knew such companionship, such love, was rare, but that was what she knew she wanted.

"I've found him," Leonie teased. "Look, over against the wall. That exquisite gentleman looks like he was made just for you." She began tugging at Tallie, trying to pull her toward the man.

The man Leonie had pointed to was Jeb Tuhill. Tallie smiled when she looked toward Jeb. "He does look good, doesn't he?"

"Well, let's go meet him." Leonie took Tallie's arm and began to walk in Jeb's direction.

Just then Bay Middleton approached the two women and asked if Leonie would join him in a set forming for a quadrille. Count Kinsky was right behind Bay and took Tallie's hand as the music began, and they moved onto the dance floor.

Jeb moved to what appeared to be one of several opera boxes on an upper level of the grand hall. Here he had an unobstructed view of the main floor without being observed. He found himself watching Tallie Somerset. She danced most often with Count Kinsky. And why wouldn't he dance with her? In Jeb's eyes she was clearly the most attractive of all the women present.

She was wearing a pale yellow dress that was cut low to accentuate a well-endowed chest and cream-colored skin, but unlike many of the other women present, she wore no jewelry. Her hair was arranged in a pompadour decorated with short ostrich feathers. Jeb watched with fascination from his elevated view as the feathers moved with her swaying body as she danced so effortlessly.

Jeb had come to this reception because this woman had specifically asked him. *I'll save a dance for you,* she had whispered when she had handed him his hat, and he had come for that favor, but watching her swirl around this room, he knew that was not to be. This was not any kind of dancing he had ever before seen.

"Jeb, would you like me to take your hat?" Mack asked as he approached Jeb.

"What? No, thanks." Jeb had been holding the hat by its brim, as again and again he turned it in a circle. He looked down at it. "It's sure not much of a hat, is it?"

"Why, what are you talking about? It's an elegant hat worn by a most aristocratic gentleman. And if I do say so myself, you look exceptionally well turned out this evening."

Jeb chuckled. "Mack, can you see me wearing this hat against the sun? Or using it as a pillow? Or scooping up a drink of water for my horse?"

"Well, when you put it like that, I have to agree with you. But, Jeb, I haven't seen you dance one dance, yet I've watched any number of young ladies cast their glances in your direction. When are you going to ask one of them?"

"I'll ask someone when they call out, 'Form your squares.' But that's not likely to happen, is it?"

"No, sir, I don't suppose it is."

"I'm not one of these people. Tonight, I feel like a mule in horse harness."

Mack laughed.

Glancing back toward the ballroom floor, Jeb found that he had lost sight of Tallie. He looked at all the dancing couples and saw neither Tallie nor Kinsky. Had they left the reception together? He found the idea disconcerting, though he certainly had no right to be upset by it. Tallie was nothing to him. And she was married. If anyone should be upset, it should be her husband.

"Look, Mack, I think I'm going back to the hotel because I want to make sure I'm ready to leave in the morning. I doubt that Moreton will miss me, but if he should, will you tell him I've gone?"

"I will, and, Jeb, if I could, I would come along with you."

Jeb came down from the opera box, then left the ballroom, walking down a wide, curving stairway to the gaslit courtyard below. At the bottom of the stairs, he heard something that sounded like the whicker of a horse. Curious, he turned back to the marble-and-brick building, the second floor of which housed the ballroom. He tried one of the doors under the stairway and, finding it unlocked, stepped inside.

What he saw nearly took his breath away. It was a stable, but unlike any he had ever before seen, and that included the huge stables he had seen while he was in England. This stable had a crimson carpet on the floor and highly polished walnut-paneled walls. Each of the stalls had its own window, with the gaslights diffusing through brilliant colors of stained glass. At least a dozen horses were in the stalls, all of them now looking out over their gates to see who had entered their domain.

"Well, I'll be damned," Jeb said under his breath. "I guess it *was* a barn dance after all."

He walked down the line of stalls, seeing the four beautiful white horses that had pulled the carriage away from the church following the wedding. Stepping toward one of them, he began to stroke the horse's face.

"You've had a big day, boy," he said as the horse began to toss his head asking for more. "If I'd have known you were here, I would've spent my time with you instead of—"

Just then, Jeb heard the door opening, and he instinctively moved quickly into the shadows.

Tallie stepped into the stable, her face and skin taking on a rosy glow from the reflected light. She moved along the horses quickly, stopping in front of one horse not more than fifteen feet in front of Jeb. The horse whickered softly when she approached.

"I couldn't leave tomorrow without saying good-bye to you." She took off her long, white glove and held out her hand. The horse immediately began nuzzling her hand. "Go easy, girl," she said softly.

She withdrew some sugar cubes from a small reticule and put them in her hand. As the horse ate, Tallie laid her head against the mare's neck.

"Thank you, Sugar, for being my friend while I've been in this place. I'm going to miss you." She continued rubbing the horse and feeding her more sugar cubes.

After a few minutes, Tallie turned to go. Something caught her eye and she looked toward the back of the stable, where she made out what she took to be the white of a man's shirt.

"Is someone here?" Tallie asked tentatively, uncertain.

"Yes." Jeb stepped out of the shadows.

"You." Tallie dropped her purse, sugar cubes falling onto the carpet. "Why didn't you make yourself known?"

"First of all, I didn't want to frighten you, and then I didn't want the horse to miss out on her sugar." Jeb stooped to pick up the little white cubes that lay on the carpet and began feeding them to the horse. "Is she a good horse?"

"The best in the stable. I saw you upstairs. Why didn't you ask me to dance?"

"It looked to me like you were busy."

"Things aren't always what they seem, Mr. Tuhill. I would very much have enjoyed a dance with you. But now it's too late. I'll be leaving tomorrow."

"As will I."

As they stood there looking at each other, Jeb took in every detail of this woman: her hair, her face, her eyes, her lips. He raised his hand to touch the feathers that were pinned to her hair. When he did, it broke the spell.

"You came on the ship with Kinsky?"

"Yes."

"What does your husband think about you being with him?"

"As I said, things aren't always how they seem."

As Tallie spoke, she tilted her head up toward his, and the breath of her words blew softly against his cheek, as sweet as mint.

If Tallie had been writing this scene in a novel, the hero would kiss the heroine right now. But how could Tallie make that happen in real life? She thought she wanted to be kissed by this man, but did he want to kiss her?

Brow furrowed, she watched as if she were an observer while Jeb slowly lowered his face to hers. She had always wondered what one did during a kiss. Were your lips closed or were they open? Now for the first time in her life she was going to find out. But she was frightened. Not by the kiss. She was frightened that Jeb would learn that she had absolutely no idea what to do.

When he brought his lips down to hers, she was surprised by the gentleness of the kiss, and she closed her eyes trying to lock this kiss in her memory. She had been married for more than two years, and in this one kiss, she realized what a sacrifice she had made when she married Arthur. This was what real men and real women did.

She wanted this kiss to go on. She pressed her lips closer to Jeb's, and when she did, she felt a tingling that spread throughout her body and warmed her blood. She felt that her legs were about to buckle under her as this feeling grew more intense.

After a long moment, Jeb pulled away from her,

looking into her eyes with a tenderness that was almost palpable. Reaching up, Tallie touched her lips and held her fingers there for a long moment as she stared up at him.

"I—I'm sorry," he said. "I had no right."

"Will you escort me to the main house?" she asked, her voice little more than a whisper.

Jeb gave Sugar a final pat on her nose, and taking Tallie by the arm, they left the stable.

As they were walking through the courtyard, Tallie turned to Jeb. "Tell me, do you play backgammon?"

"I'm afraid not, but I've just learned *écarté*. Does that count?"

"It doesn't matter. Good night, Mr. Tuhill."

"Lady Somerset," Jeb said with a slight bow, as she turned and entered the mansion.

As Tallie lay in her bed that night, the tactile memory of Jeb Tuhill's kiss lingered, and she reached up to touch her lips with the tips of her fingers, as if in that way she could duplicate the sensation she had felt.

Is this what a kiss felt like between a man and a woman who were in love? Of course, she wasn't in love with Jeb Tuhill. My goodness, she scarcely knew the man. But she could not deny that she'd had an unexpected reaction to the kiss.

She wished that she could discuss this with Jennie. Or even Aunt Emma. She had so many questions, questions to which a woman of her age should already know the answers. And the first question she would ask, if she could, would be, why, when nothing but their lips touched, did her entire body react in such a pleasurable way?

She had to put these unsettling thoughts out of her mind, so she began thinking of her trip to Wyoming. She'd believed that two months away from London would cause the gossip surrounding *The Prince's Folly* to die down, but Leonie told her it was even more intense. So Wyoming seemed to be her best course of action for now.

She was committed to going with Clara to her new home, and she had to admit, she was a little anxious about what she would find. The stories Mrs. Jerome had told when she was trying to discourage Clara from marrying Moreton were not a source of comfort. Were there wild Indians who would carry her off into the wilderness? Were the cowboys uncouth louts? Were wolves and bears always on the prowl?

Tallie tried to imagine what the West would look like and be like. But the last image in her head before she fell asleep that night was of Jeb Tuhill. How surprised he would be to see her there.

NINE

Before her marriage to Moreton Frewen, Clara had lived with her mother and sisters, much of the time in England and in France. In Paris, Marie Garneau had become her personal attendant. Marie tended to share Mrs. Jerome's mistrust of Moreton Frewen, and she, too, thought Clara had made a terrible mistake when she married him. Despite that, when Clara said she would be living in Wyoming, Marie's loyalty was such that, with some reluctance, she agreed to accompany her employer.

"Il est insensé d'aller à un endroit où nous pouvons tous être tués par les Indiens sauvages," Marie said.

"Don't be foolish, Marie. Do you think Mr. Frewen would take his new bride to a place where she could be killed by savage Indians?" Tallie asked.

"But I am afraid," Marie said.

"Don't be so timid," Tallie teased. "I'm looking at this as a bold adventure, and so should you."

The ladies were just about to board the barouche,

one of four vehicles that would be transporting the Frewens and their considerable luggage to Grand Central Depot. One vehicle was dedicated entirely to the large, square trunks that Marie had carefully filled with the latest Parisian fashions for Clara, as well as new Imari china, glassware, and linens for Frewen's Castle.

When they reached the depot, Mack was standing out front, waiting for them. Ever the efficient valet, Mack had gone ahead to engage several freight handlers to unload the trunks and transport them to the train.

"Are the cars in place?" Moreton asked, as he helped Clara down from the carriage.

"Yes, sir. There's a beauty of a private car for you and Mrs. Frewen, and a very comfortable car for the rest of us. I must say, we will all be traveling in style."

"Yes, well, we have the Commodore's son Billy to thank for that. It was one of the Vanderbilts' wedding presents to us," Clara said. "All my father's friends have been just wonderful, and they all promise to come visit us."

"The cars are sitting on a spur track, but all the arrangements have been made," Mack said. "The Chicago Limited will connect to the cars at ten thirty."

"That gives us just over an hour," Moreton replied. "That should be plenty of time to get loaded and settled in."

Mack led the little group, which included Carl Kinsky and Bay Middleton, through the crowded depot. When they reached a door that read TO TRAINS, they entered the shed and encountered quite the commotion. Tallie counted six trains discharging or receiving passengers, while two more seemed to be standing by. Two were moving—one backing in, and another pulling out. At the far end of the train shed, set away from the activity, were two detached cars parked on a separate track.

As they approached the two cars, Tallie saw Jeb jump down from one, and she felt a flare of excitement. She had secretly hoped that he would be traveling with them, and seeing him here, she presumed that would be true.

Jeb looked up, and seeing the group advancing toward the cars, he waved and started toward them.

He stopped dead in his tracks when he saw Tallie. For a moment, surprise was on his face. "I wasn't expecting such a delightful send-off party, but I'm especially pleased to see Lady Somerset one more time. I'm afraid I didn't get a chance to say my proper good-byes."

Moreton chuckled. "She isn't here to see us off, old boy, she's coming with us."

"Coming with us?"

"I am," Tallie said. "I hope that doesn't inconvenience you?"

Jeb nodded approvingly, a smile curving his lips, and then he saw Carl Kinsky and Bay Middleton coming up behind them. "Oh, yes, the hunters have arrived," Jeb said, acknowledging the two men as they joined the group.

Kinsky shook his head. "As much as I'd planned on this trip, I'm afraid it's impossible this time. My two delightful months in this country"—he bowed slightly toward Tallie—"must come to an end.

Apparently the embassy can't function for long without their Austrian connection."

"The embassy?"

"Yes, I am an attaché to the Austrian ambassador to the Court of St. James, and it seems our young empress is in need of my services."

"That sounds very important," Jeb said.

"Don't let the title fool you. The empress probably wants someone to supervise the movement of her beloved horses from one stable to another, or something just as silly. Believe me when I tell you my position is in name only, because it was inherited by birth. I would like to say I earned it because of some particular skill or talent I may possess, but I can't."

"I think that everyone is quite aware of your particular talent, Count Kinsky," Clara said with a knowing smile.

As Clara spoke the words, Jeb noticed Tallie's fair skin take on some color, and she turned away in what Jeb took as embarrassment.

"Why, Mrs. Frewen, whatever do you mean? I'm sure you mean my prowess as a horseman, and nothing more?" Count Kinsky bantered.

"Of course. Absolutely nothing more," Clara said, continuing the repartee.

The luggage cart arrived, and as Mack saw to the trunks being put aboard, Kinsky and Middleton began to say their good-byes to the group. A railroad official approached them.

"Mr. Frewen?"

"I'm Frewen."

"The Chicago Limited has left its track, and it will

be connecting to your cars in a few minutes. I suggest, sir, that you and your party board your cars."

"Thank you," Moreton said. "All right, everyone, let's start this glorious adventure."

"Moreton, my heartiest congratulations," Kinsky said. "And I'm holding you to your invitation for me to come to the ranch for a hunt."

"You will always be welcome," Clara said as Kinsky stepped back.

He reached out to take Jeb's hand in his. "And, Jeb, it was my pleasure in meeting you. All I ask is that you take care of my girl here. Don't let some wild Indian take her scalp because she's much too beautiful for that."

Kinsky casually brushed a curl aside that had escaped from Tallie's topknot as he pulled her to him in a close and lengthy embrace, but Jeb noticed he did not try to kiss her.

"Middleton, we'd better get out of here before I do something careless, like jump on this train and head west," Kinsky said.

"Thank you for an enjoyable two months," Tallie said as she backed away from the embrace. "I wish you were coming along, but please remember me to Jennie, when next you see her."

"Consider it done." With a salute Kinsky turned and walked away with Middleton.

Moreton and Clara boarded Mr. Vanderbilt's private car, marked the *Wayfarer*, while Jeb, Mack, Marie, and Tallie boarded the Wagner Palace car.

One half of the Palace car had roomettes for each of the passengers, while the other half was fitted with comfortable reclining chairs. With a slight bump the cars were connected to the train, then they slowly started to move out of the station.

The seats were built to swivel, and when the train cleared the train shed, Tallie stared out a window. "It's a beautiful city," she said to no one in particular.

Jeb rose from his seat on the other side of the car and came to squat down right beside her.

All thoughts of scenery were gone as Tallie was overwhelmed by Jeb's nearness. In her mind she felt his muscles beneath her hands from when she had examined him after his fall, and she longed to touch him now, to run her fingers through his hair, to inhale the scent of soap that clung to his face. Forgoing her temptation to reach out for him, she constructed a descriptive passage to remember and transcribe into her notebook.

> His chest was broad and his shoulders wide upon his powerful-looking frame. His face was bronzed by wind and sun, and the shadow of a beard on his chin and square jaw gave him a manly aura that transcended the fine clothes he was wearing. His hair, the color of ripened wheat, contrasted with his deep tan.
>
> He had a distinctive and pleasant aroma, a hint of soap, old leather, and an essence that could only be described as masculine.

She thought of the kiss they had shared the previous night, and she balled her hands in tight fists, trying to put some governor on her feelings. This trip was just starting out. She would have to control her thoughts.

Jeb had said something to her, but she stared at him without responding.

"I said I don't know how so many people can live so close together," he repeated.

"Being close together. That's not a problem," she said in a rush, and then she thought about what she had said. "I mean in a city, that is."

Jeb sensed that he was too close to Tallie and moved to the seat next to hers. "Do you mind if I sit on your side of the car? That way we can share the same scenes."

"I'd like that very much. Clara said she thinks this trip may take a week or more. Is that true?"

"I'm afraid it is. You'll be stuck with us for a long time. I'm sorry your count couldn't make it this time."

"Oh, Mr. Tuhill, I didn't mean to imply anything like that at all."

"I thought we had it established that you were to call me Jeb. If it goes back to Mr. Tuhill and Lady Somerset, this will be a long trip, indeed."

"All right, Jeb. But let's establish something else. Count Kinsky is not *my* count. He is a friend of a friend of mine, a very good friend, I might add, and until this trip to America, I only knew him in strictly social settings."

"Is he a friend of your husband?"

Tallie lowered her head. If she was going to spend the next several months with this man, she should tell him right now that she was no longer married. But something inside her kept her from doing so. Part of the reason for coming on this trip was to find out who she really was. Lady Somerset was a persona, no more her true identity than Nora Ingram was. Yet Tallie was as much both of those identities as she was Tallie. She knew that, right now, she was vulnerable. And that vulnerability had to be protected.

"No, he is not a friend of Arthur's."

At the mention of her husband, Jeb noticed a perceptible change in Tallie's demeanor. Undoubtedly something was going on between them, and he had no right to pry. His thoughts went back to his own departure from Texas, and how he refused to tell anyone why he was in Wyoming. He would give this woman her privacy and enjoy her company for what it was if that was how she wanted it.

For the next several minutes they did nothing but stare through the windows as the train passed through the city, first on the ground, even with the carriage and wagon traffic, then on an elevated track, moving quickly, almost as if flying over the city, then on a ferry across the Hudson until finally they were in open country and the train was going much faster.

"Oh!" Marie said. "We are going so fast! I wonder how fast we are going."

"Just a moment and I'll tell you," Mack said. Pulling his watch from his waistcoat pocket, he opened the cover so he could see the face of it.

Marie laughed. "You cannot tell how fast we are going by looking at your watch."

Mack didn't answer, but he held his finger up as

if calling for quiet. For a long moment he stared at his watch, then he brought his finger down and smiled. "We are doing twenty-eight miles to the hour."

"I don't believe you!" Marie said.

"Mack, what sort of tall tale are you telling the young lady?" Jeb asked, teasing his friend.

"Oh, I assure you, it's no tall tale. We're doing exactly twenty-eight miles to the hour."

"How do you know that?" Tallie asked.

"It's a trick I learned from a railroad conductor. It's how they determine how fast the train is going. You count the number of clicks you hear when the wheels cross a rail joint. The number of clicks you hear in twenty seconds is how fast you're going."

"What a handy tidbit of information," Tallie said. "I know I'm going to learn much on this expedition. Thank you, Mack, for sharing that with us."

Just then the door to the parlor car opened, and Moreton and Clara entered. Clara had changed to a colorful summer dress, and she was clinging to Moreton's arm in a proprietary way. Moreton had doffed his jacket and was now dressed in a silk shirt and trousers.

"I don't know which of you to ask," Clara said, addressing both Marie and Mack, "but will one of you fetch some lunch for Moreton and me? We're both famished."

"Allow me to *fetch* it for you," Jeb said, coming down hard on the word *fetch*.

Tallie sensed that Jeb was reacting to Clara's request. Did he resent that either Mack or Marie was always at the beck and call of the Frewens? It seemed to her that he was uncomfortable having his friend ordered around, and she respected that.

"We'll both do it," Tallie said as she rose from her seat.

"Just tap on the door when you return," Clara said as she began pulling Moreton back in the direction of their car.

Jeb and Tallie made their way to the dining car, which was usually the last car on the train, but because of the two special cars was now adjacent to their car.

"I wish Clara would have given us a suggestion of what she wants for lunch," Tallie said as she glanced over a printed menu that the waiter had handed her. They were seated at a small table covered with a crisp, white tablecloth, and although it was past noon, the dining car was full of other passengers.

"I know what I'm going to order for Moreton. He will need a good piece of steak," Jeb said.

"Why do you say . . . " Tallie pursed her lips and put her fingers to her mouth as her eyes grew wide.

"That was a very indecent thought on your part, Lady Somerset," Jeb said with a charming smile and a little wink.

"No lady would have those thoughts, I fear." Tallie blushed.

"You are every bit a lady to me, both by title and by grace."

"Jeb, let's agree to put the title part away. From now on, I want you to think of me—to call me—just plain Tallie. That's how I grew up, and while I'm on this trip, that's who I want to be."

"All right," Jeb said, but he thought it a strange request. Who else would this woman be?

When they returned to their car after taking Moreton a steak and mashed-potato plate and Clara lettuce cups with pounded cold fish, Jeb reclined his seat and, with his hat pulled down over his eyes, took a nap, or so it appeared. Mack and Marie were conversing on the opposite side of the car, their voices low and indistinct. Tallie sat in her seat watching the countryside roll past for a while, then she lifted the table from the side of the car and locked it into place. She had an overwhelming urge to write, so she took a notebook and pencil from a case and quickly put her thoughts on paper.

The Lady and the Cowboy

by
Nora Ingram

He was a man of great strength, not the strength of muscle and tissue, though no doubt that, too, could be attributed to him. Rather, his strength came from some inner source, a degree of contentment with himself, a sense of extreme confidence that no man, regardless of wealth or station, was his superior. He was an American Westerner, called a cowboy and proud of that moniker.

He was also a ruggedly handsome man, square jawed, with a strong chin, piercing blue eyes, and blond hair. Not the effete, slicked-back blond hair of drawing-room dandies this, but rather the lusty blond of sun-ripened wheat. No woman could look at him and not feel . . .

What was she doing? Had she not learned a lesson after she wrote *The Prince's Folly*? She had told herself that her writing career was over, but here she was starting another book that was potentially as consequential to her own emotions as her first book had been. *The Orphan* closely mirrored her own experiences, while *The Prince's Folly* had been written as a lark. She had watched the superficial people who hovered around the Prince of Wales and, based on her own observations and Jennie's revelations, wrote the roman à clef that had caused her so much trouble. What kind of book would this new one be?

She looked toward Jeb Tuhill, who sat across from her as he feigned sleep. A smile curled her lips as she thought about this book. A diary—that was what she hoped it would become. *The Lady and the Cowboy*, or would a better title be *The Lady and Her Cowboy*? She put her pencil down and closed her notebook.

Jeb wasn't asleep. He was merely pretending to be asleep so he wouldn't disturb Tallie. He had to admit that he was most intrigued with her. She was an exceptionally pretty woman, yes, but more than her looks intrigued him. He liked to hear her talk, liked the way the words rolled off her tongue, not slow and drawn out the way most people that he knew talked. Rather each word was said with its own unique pronunciation. "Count Kinsky makes me laugh," she had said. Only she didn't say *laugh*, she said *loff*. "Count Kinsky makes me loff."

By now Jeb was used to the British accent because that was the way that both Moreton and his brother, Richard, talked, and it was the dialect of many of the visitors to the ranch. And, of course, he had visited England last year.

But when Tallie spoke, it was different. The British accent made her words sound almost like music, and it made some part of Jeb—which part, he couldn't figure—come alive.

He tipped his hat back and looked over at her. He wanted to find another reason to talk to her, but she was busy writing, so he let her be.

Tallie retired to her roomette in the early evening. She was physically tired, but she was mentally exhausted. She had written more pages than she had written at any time since she'd finished *The Prince's Folly*, and the words just seemed to flow from her. It had been her intention to write a novel about her experience at Badminton House, but she couldn't exclude her relationship with Arthur from that manuscript. She hadn't wanted to describe the failure of her marriage because, no matter what the cause of a divorce, the woman always became the suspect when blame was assigned. And was she to blame?

She thought back to the summer when she first met Arthur. He had come to the Isle of Wight with the Darwins' youngest son, where they had joined the Darwins and Tallie for a family vacation. It had been a carefree summer filled with happy memories, and Arthur had been especially caring toward Tallie as the rambunctious Darwin boys teased her unmercifully.

When Tallie's father died, and for some years after that, Arthur had visited her on occasion, always treating her with respect and dignity, despite the lack of parity in their social positions. It had been on one such visit that Arthur had approached Tallie with a proposition.

"I have considered this very carefully and I find you a fit companion. I have watched you interact with the Darwin family, and I think you would be a welcomed addition to the Somerset household. You are now without a family; I would like to ask you to become a part of mine."

"Arthur," Tallie said with a laugh, "do you have any idea what you just said? It sounds like you're asking me to marry you."

"I think I am doing just that."

Tallie had indeed accepted his proposal. She knew she didn't love Arthur, but at the time she didn't think that was as important as security. She assumed that love would grow with the marriage. But it didn't happen. Nothing happened. She always asked herself if she was at fault. If she had loved Arthur, would things have been different?

She lay back on the small bed feeling the gentle, rocking rhythm of the car, and listening to the click of the wheels as they passed over the rail joints. She smiled as she thought of the trick Mack had taught them about counting the clicks to gauge the speed of the train.

But it wasn't MacVittie who was occupying her thoughts. It was Jeb Tuhill. What was it about him that created such a dominant character for her? What so held her interest? Even as she asked herself the question, she knew the answer. She had known the answer from the moment he had kissed her. This sensation was something new to her.

You must choose between a life of celibacy, or adultery. There is no third option, Arthur had told her.

She had remained celibate throughout her marriage, and since that time. She had hidden behind her marriage vows, subverting any kind of desire she might have felt, and it had worked well. Though the handsome, wealthy, and titled men of England, up to and including the crown prince, had made advances toward her, her resolve of celibacy had never seriously been threatened.

The Prince's Folly. She could just as easily have named that book *The Lady's Folly*, because that was what it had become. Her folly. She had thought by using a pseudonym she could remain anonymous, but that was not to be. The publisher had intentionally released her real identity as soon as the book began to make so much money because, by title, she clearly was a part of the Marlborough Set. But by actions, she was far from it. With Nora Ingram exposed, it had been Tallie's intention to never pick up her pen again, but on this trip she had an unquenchable desire to write. She was attracted to Jeb Tuhill, but just as she and Arthur had nothing to build a bond between them, except for physical attraction there was probably nothing that could build a bond between her and Jeb. The lady and the cowboy. That said it all. The reality was they came from two different worlds. But with writing, she could create her own piece of fiction, fiction that came straight from her heart, and that could satisfy every desire Tallie might feel toward Jeb. And in this country, no one would know the true identity of Nora Ingram. Her anonymity was safe.

TEN

The train reached Chicago at midmorning of the third day. Here the two cars were shunted aside, where they would remain until they were attached to the Chicago, Burlington and Quincy train for the final leg of their journey to Wyoming. The CB&Q wasn't scheduled to leave until six o'clock the following evening, so that gave them a day and a half to spend in Chicago.

"We may as well see some of Chicago," Moreton said as he helped Clara down the steps of the car. "Once we leave here, you ladies will think you've left civilization behind you."

"Or you could think you're seeing God's country for the first time," Jeb said.

"You can't really think the plains are beautiful?" Mack said.

Just then a porter approached them. "Are you the passengers just arriving from New York traveling on Mr. Vanderbilt's private cars?"

"We are," Mack answered.

The man held a yellow envelope. "I have a telegram for a Mr. Frewen."

"I'm Moreton Frewen."

The messenger handed his delivery to Moreton, who tipped him generously, then opened the envelope to read the message.

"What is it, darling? Has something happened?" Clara asked.

"No, it's something quite special. A friend of mine is in the city and he wants to meet you, my dear. It is true serendipity that we have this layover. So, Tallie, I would like to invite you to join us. Jeb, would you like to join us, too?"

"I'll stay with Mack," Jeb said.

"All right, but you're going to miss a good dinner at the Palmer House."

"That does it, Jeb," Clara said. "You can't miss the Palmer House. It may be the finest hotel in the country." She took Tallie's arm and began hurrying down the walkway.

Moreton laughed. "Rule number one in married life seems to be, sometimes you can be overruled, and this may be one of those times. We'd best step lively if we are to keep up with the ladies."

"Moreton, in all honesty, I'd rather stay with Mack."

"My wife has spoken and you can't disappoint her. And besides, aren't you getting just a little tired of the food we're getting on the train? I'm ready for some real beef, and since we're in Chicago, there's as good a chance as any that it's Wyoming beef. "

"If it's good, we can pretend it's from the 76, and

if it's tough, we'll say it came from the LX Bar," Jeb teased, and Moreton chuckled.

The two men hurried to catch up with the women, who were already in front of the depot.

"Are we really going to the Palmer House?" Tallie asked.

"That's where the telegram says my friend is staying. Why do you ask?" Moreton asked.

"Because look over there. I see a carriage with the name of the hotel written across its side. Do you suppose they have their very own carriage that waits at the train station just for their guests?"

"We'll only know if we ask," Jeb said.

The four entered what they were told was a courtesy carriage, which took them to the Palmer House. The hotel was on Monroe Street, an imposing building, six stories high and occupying the entire block.

When they stepped into the marble foyer, Moreton walked up to the concierge.

"My dear sir, I am here to call upon John Campbell, the governor-general of Canada, and his wife. Would you be so kind as to tell me what suite they are occupying?"

Upon hearing the name of the friend Moreton was meeting, Tallie gulped.

"They are in suite 612. If you would like to call them, you can use the lobby phone, and our operator will connect you directly to their attendant."

"Thank you," Moreton said.

As they started toward the phone, Tallie stuck her hand out to touch Moreton on the arm. "Moreton, if you don't mind, I think I'll explore the lobby of the hotel while you're visiting with the duke and the princess."

"Why, Tallie, surely you will want to visit with Princess Louise—oh, wait," Clara said. "Yes, I understand. It's probably best that you not join us."

"Come, Jeb. Let's find something to do," Tallie said, pulling Jeb's arm as she hurriedly walked away.

"What was that all about?" Jeb asked when they were away from the Frewens. "I'm very happy not to meet some duke or princess, or whatever titles these people have, but I got the distinct impression that you didn't want to be with them either."

"I didn't."

"But why?"

"It's really quite complicated. First of all, Princess Louise is Queen Victoria's daughter."

"Are you telling me you know the Queen's daughter?"

"No, I don't know Princess Louise, but I do know her brother, the Prince of Wales, and right now, he's not very happy with me. Let's just enjoy the afternoon."

Jeb stared at Tallie. Who was this woman? If he understood her, she had just told him she was friends with the future king of England, or, if not a friend, at least acquainted enough with him that, somehow, she had incurred his displeasure.

"All right," he said. "Let's enjoy the afternoon. What do you have in mind?"

"I think a bite to eat is the first order. I saw a sign saying the restaurant is on the office floor. We can take the lift up there."

"The lift?"

Tallie chuckled. "I'm sorry, I think you Americans call them elevators. Have you ever been in one?"

"Yes, there was one at our hotel in New York, but they aren't something I've used a lot."

Tallie led Jeb to one of the two elevators. A uniformed elevator operator was standing just inside.

"We'd like to be taken to the restaurant, please," Tallie said as she and Jeb stepped in.

"Excellent, madam, you won't be disappointed," the operator said as he closed the door with a click. He moved a lever, and the elevator started to rise.

"This makes me think of a jail," Jeb teased. "A jail that moves."

Tallie chuckled. "Have you had a lot of experience in jail?"

"Just one night."

Tallie laughed. "I didn't expect that answer from you. There's a lot I have to learn about the Wild West."

"It's not called wild for no reason. You'll see what it's like soon enough."

"Is this your first time in the Palmer House?" the operator asked.

"Yes," Jeb replied. "It is. Do you have any suggestions for something we can do to kill a few hours before we rejoin our friends?"

"I've just the place for you, especially if you're headed to the 'Wild West' as you called it. And it's right here in the hotel. It's called the Garden of Eden."

"What?" Jeb choked out, thinking of the assignation houses he had seen in New York on the night before the wedding.

"Oh, no, sir, it's not what you think. A gentleman named Eden runs it, and the *Garden of Eden* is a play on his name."

"What exactly is this place?" Tallie asked.

"It's, well, it's a barbershop, but it's a whole lot more. You'll have to see it to believe it."

"Look, mister, you'd better not be pulling my leg. I may be a country boy, but my lady friend was to the manner born," Jeb said, pulling out a line that he remembered from having read *Hamlet*, "and if you're sending us to a place where she wouldn't be comfortable, I'll come back and see to it that you don't lead any other lady astray."

"Sir, you are in the Palmer House, the finest hotel in America. Our owner, Mr. Potter Palmer, has searched the world to bring our guests the most elegant of furnishings and amenities. You will find the Garden of Eden unlike any experience you have ever had in any hotel in the world."

"You still haven't answered the lady's question. I find it hard to believe it's just a barbershop if Mr. Potter Palmer, as you call him, allows you to direct people to this place."

"Well, sir, it is also a bathing room."

"A bathing room? You can't be serious?"

"Oh, but I am. You will want to experience it for yourself." Just then the elevator stopped and the two got out.

"I'm sorry, Tallie. We'll have to find something on our own."

"Why? The bathing room sounds tempting."

"We'll talk about it later," Jeb said as he placed his hand upon her back, directing her toward the restaurant.

The restaurant was a large, circular room, completely surrounded by mirrors, and illuminated by Edison's incandescent lightbulbs. It had a large dome supported by marble columns, and the wainscoting and the floor were of the same material.

When the menu was put before them, Jeb studied it for a moment. "Humph, not much of a menu."

"Why, whatever do you mean? It is a very complete menu," Tallie replied.

"Really? I see no buffalo, elk, or bear."

"No doubt you would also want fox, I suppose?" Tallie teased.

"Why not? What's the sense of hunting something if you don't eat it?"

Tallie laughed. "You are impossible. I think I'll have broiled lamb chops with green beans, scalloped potatoes, and carrot puree."

"I'll have the same thing, without the carrots. But, whatever you do, when we get to Wyoming, please don't tell anyone I ate lamb."

"What? Why not, for heaven's sake?"

"Cattlemen and sheep ranchers don't get along."

"I see that I shall have much to learn about your American West."

On the dining table was a pamphlet advertising the Garden of Eden. "Oh, look, this is what the lift operator was talking about."

Tallie picked it up, and after glancing at it for

a moment, she looked across the table at Jeb and smiled. "Listen to this." She began to read:

"'The Bathing Department is a marvel. Every known bath can be had. Marble floors, marble baths, and marble scrubbing beds are everywhere. In the "Macerecure" room twenty different kinds of baths are furnished. In one room is a diving tank, 15 by 50, with a depth of five and a half feet. The 'needle' shower bath, with its million sprays, cost $1,000. The Russian and Turkish bath rooms are fitted up in the highest style of perfection, and throughout the whole department nothing is wanting to make it the most consummate triumph of modern art and taste.'"

"It sounds like they are pretty proud of their bathing rooms," Jeb said.

"No, you remember what the lift operator said. They aren't just bathing rooms. It is the 'Garden of Eden.'"

"Are we to wear nothing but leaves? And are you planning to tempt me with an apple?"

"If I wore nothing but leaves, I would hope that I wouldn't need an apple to tempt you."

Jeb looked up in surprise.

Tallie put her hand to her mouth. "Oh, my, what did I just say?" Tallie's cheeks flamed as she blushed. "That was most indecorous of me."

"It was also quite accurate." Jeb smiled devilishly. "You really wouldn't need an apple."

"Please, Mr. Tuhill, forget that I said that."

"Mr. Tuhill, is it? I'll tell you what. You go back to calling me Jeb, and I will forget all about it."

"Thank you—Jeb."

"Would you be up to trying this marvelous bath?"

"Yes," Tallie said with a smile. "I think I would."

After lunch they went to the Garden of Eden, which, though attached to the hotel, was in a separate building. It actually was a barbershop, and Jeb decided to get a haircut and a shave before heading west. Sitting in one of the chairs in the huge room, he watched through the surrounding mirrors as Tallie took her place on one of the plush velvet sofas to wait for him. Tilted back in the chair to allow the barber to lather his face for his shave, he could watch her unobserved through the overhead mirror. As she sat, he noticed she took out a small, red notebook and began to write. He would love to read what she was writing, see what made her bite her lip in such a fashion, as though she were laughing to herself. The haircut and shave took about half an hour, and Tallie wrote for most of that time. Finally the barber concluded his services by spinning Jeb around so he could examine himself in the mirror.

"There you are, sir. What do you think?"

Jeb stroked his cheek, feeling the absence of stubble. "It's fine, thank you."

"You look like a man of the city," Tallie said when Jeb stepped away from the chair. She leaned into him, smelling the fresh scent of the shaving cream. "I think you should have a splash of cologne."

"Cologne? I think not."

"That's because you've never tried it." Tallie stepped to the barber and picked up a bottle of men's cologne that the barber told her was a leather fragrance with a touch of wood and balsam. "Let me pat some of this on your cheeks."

Jeb allowed her to pat his face with the cologne, as her face was but inches from his. He watched her expression of satisfaction as she finished.

"Now, doesn't that smell good?"

"Whatever you are wearing smells better," Jeb said as he drew her to him, pulling her against his now smooth face. The mirrors in the barbershop captured the scene of the two young people in what appeared to be an embrace.

"Did you say something about a bath?" Jeb asked.

"A bath? Yes, I did say that, didn't I?"

"Maybe I should make it a cold bath." Jeb moved away from Tallie and headed toward the Bathing Department.

Paying the fee, they received keys to their exclusive bathing chambers, as well as to the needle-shower bath. Their private rooms were on either side of the one that contained the shower.

Tallie and Jeb went into their individual cubicles, but before Tallie drew the bath in her tub, she changed her mind and decided she would rather use the shower first.

Stepping into the shower room, Tallie undressed, then folded her clothes and put them carefully on the marble table to one side. Completely nude, she stepped into the shower and turned the knob, which sent a thousand needle streams of water against her body.

This was the first time Tallie had ever experienced such a shower, and it felt wonderful. At first, she was aware only of the delightful massage of the high-pressure streams of water as they relieved the stress and tightness from her muscles. But then, as the little needles of pulsating water covered her body, she began to feel sensations of pleasure unlike anything she had ever before felt.

She imagined Jeb just on the other side of the wall, as naked as she was right now. Her thoughts of his being so close to her, combined with the sensual effect of the cascading water, made her body tingle from the top of her head to the tips of her toes.

Just next door, the object of Tallie's fantasies turned the knob that promised hot water, but none appeared. Then, when he checked the water heater that serviced the room, he saw that the gas fire was out. Jeb lit the flame, but knew that it would probably take a few minutes for the water to be heated.

Deciding to try the shower while the water heated, he stepped outside and realized that he had given the key to the shower to Tallie. He didn't have the key, but the door to his bath hadn't been locked, so he figured this one might not be as well. He wasn't worried about Tallie. If the door was locked, that would mean she was inside; if it wasn't locked, it would be free to use.

Tallie stepped out of the shower, her skin pink, not only from the pulsing of the spray, but also flushed with the eroticism of her thoughts. She was dripping wet but still feeling the wonderful tingling sensation of the many streams of water. She was just reaching for the Turkish towel when the door was opened and Jeb stepped in.

Was he really here? Or was this a part of her fantasy?

When he stepped inside, Jeb was shocked to see Tallie standing there, and not just standing there, but standing there nude. Droplets of water clung to her naked skin, one of which hung from a very erect nipple. No painter's brush or sculptor's chisel had ever created a work of art as beautiful as that which stood before him.

Tallie remained in place for a long moment, unmoving and too stunned to make any effort to cover her nudity. Jeb was so captivated by this unexpected vision of loveliness that he, too, remained riveted to the spot.

Together they created a tableau vivant that was broken only when Tallie said without hysteria or even alarm, "As you can see, Jeb, this room is occupied."

"Yes, I, uh—I'm sorry."

Despite Tallie's declaration and Jeb's apologies, the scene didn't change. Tallie made no effort to cover herself, and Jeb continued to stare.

"You were right, by the way."

"I was right?" she said, confused, but still she made no effort to cover herself.

"An apple would be unnecessary."

Jeb left the shower room, restoring Tallie's modesty. But even as he closed the door, he saw in Tallie's face not anger or embarrassment, but a mystic smile.

Tallie and Jeb returned to the lobby of the Palmer House, where they were to rejoin the Frewens. As they sat in comfortable chairs, they spoke of inconsequential things. Though neither mentioned the incident in the shower, neither of them could ignore its presence. Tallie's hair was pulled into a chignon, though an errant curl fell by her ear. Her reddish brown hair shone in the artificial light, its dampness a vivid reminder of what had happened earlier. The tension continued to grow until they saw Moreton and Clara leave the elevator and walk toward them.

"Well, there you are," Moreton said. "Have you enjoyed your day? I understand you partook of the most consummate triumph of art and taste that Chicago has to offer, the renowned Palmer House shower."

Jeb and Tallie glanced at each other quickly, but before they could speak, Moreton explained, "The concierge told me that you had taken keys to the baths and shower. How was it?"

"It was exhilarating," Tallie said.

"Good, I'm glad you enjoyed it. We are spending the night here in the hotel, and I've secured rooms for the two of you and arranged for some of your things to be sent over."

"Moreton, I don't think that's wise," Jeb said.

Moreton laughed. "I said *rooms*, Jeb. I have one for each of you. This is the finest hotel in America, and if I may say so myself, having sampled first-class hotels in Europe, Asia, and Africa, it may well be the finest in the world."

"It's a foolish waste of money," Jeb said. "We've perfectly fine beds in the parlor car."

"Which is currently parked in a depot car shed. There will be trains coming and going all night, and all you will hear will be bells, whistles, trackmen shouting, and cars banging together. Believe me, Jeb, if you want any sleep at all, you'll appreciate the Palmer House."

"What about Mack and Marie? If they can sleep there, I can sleep there, too."

Moreton chuckled. "Mack can sleep through gun-fire. Absolutely nothing bothers him, and I suspect Marie isn't that far behind. Besides, if you don't stay, you will be denying Tallie the opportunity to stay. She needs an escort, and you are the most likely candidate to do that for her."

"All right, for that reason I'll stay, but that's the only reason."

The room was unlike any hotel room Jeb had ever before seen. Most of the hotels where Jeb had stayed were rather dark and uninviting, with somewhat nondescript furniture, but this room was cheery and bright and clearly filled with quality pieces. Virtu were scattered about, and several fine paintings were displayed on the walls. That, in itself, would have set this room apart from any place he had ever before stayed, but what really gave him pause was the oversize bed with a canopy.

Beside the huge bed was a table with an engraved card. Jeb picked it up and read:

ALL BILLS PAYABLE WEEKLY.
AN EXTRA CHARGE WILL BE MADE FOR BURNING GAS AFTER 12 O'CLOCK.
OCCUPANTS OF ROOMS MUST LOCK THEIR DOORS ON RETIRING FOR THE NIGHT; ALSO DURING THE DAY, KEYS MUST BE LEFT AT THE OFFICE.
CARRIAGES CAN BE HAD BY MAKING APPLICATION AT THE OFFICE.
THE PROPRIETORS WILL NOT BE RESPONSIBLE FOR BOOTS OR SHOES LEFT OUTSIDE THE DOOR.

Just as Jeb was reading over the card, the telephone rang in his room. When he answered it, he heard a tinny voice.

"Jeb, it's Tallie. Since you are to be my escort, would you like to escort me to dinner?"

"I'd love to."

"Delightful. I shall meet you in the restaurant at nine."

Tallie reached the restaurant a few minutes before nine and, when greeted by the maître d', explained that she would be meeting a gentleman friend.

"Would you be comfortable waiting at a table in the dining room, ma'am, or would you prefer to wait in the ladies' lounge?"

"The dining room will be fine."

Tallie was seated in a secluded area near the back of the restaurant, the light of a single candle creating an intimate setting. A setting made for lovers.

Was her placement at this table intentional? Was this the table for those who were meeting secretively? Perhaps for an extramarital tryst?

Were these the thoughts of Tallie Somerset or the imaginings of Nora Ingram? She didn't know. Which persona had stood in the bath this afternoon without shame or humiliation when Jeb stepped in? Was she subconsciously inviting him to join her, and what would she have done if he had? Looking up, she saw Jeb arrive at precisely nine o'clock, and Tallie smiled because she knew he would be exactly on time. He said something to the maître d', then she watched as he was directed to her table. He crossed the room toward her, carrying himself not with arrogance but extreme self-confidence. When he arrived at the table, he took her hand in his and lifted it to his mouth for a gentle kiss, his eyes reflecting the candlelight, causing them to twinkle.

"Have you been waiting long?" He took the seat across from her.

"Yes," she said, giving voice to an unbidden thought that caused her pulse to quicken and her body to tingle. She had waited for this feeling for a long time. "No, no, I mean no. I . . . I just got here."

She had written about midnight suppers in her novel, and now she was tongue-tied because such events were often the opening act for an indiscreet rendezvous. So much so that, in her world, having a midnight supper with someone other than your spouse had practically become synonymous with adultery. But what was it called when neither party was married?

A date. She took a deep breath. She would make this a perfectly enjoyable evening.

"I have to say I'm enjoying Chicago more this time than I did when we came through on our way to New York," Jeb said.

"What happened then?"

"Moreton insisted that we visit the stockyard and the meat-processing plant. I don't know what he expected, but that little visit almost changed his mind about being a rancher."

"Why?"

Jeb shook his head. "It wasn't a very pleasant experience."

"Have you always lived on a ranch?"

"I guess I have. I was born on a cattle ranch in Colorado, and then my family moved their operation to Texas. Except for going to Kansas for college, I've always been on a ranch. And now I'm in Wyoming.

"Is ranching the same everywhere?"

"In some ways it is. Everybody raises cows and sells them for beef, but Moreton's ranch is a little different from any I've known."

"How is that?"

"Most ranchers take an interest in their livestock, but I think Moreton would go for years without ever seeing a cow if he could."

"Would the cows survive?"

"The best ones would."

Tallie smiled. "Sounds like the theory of natural selection to me."

"I had to read a book about that in college. I believe that theory is called evolution."

"Yes, *The Origin of Species*, written by my next-door neighbor."

"You know Charles Darwin?"

"I not only know him, I love him."

Jeb's eyes opened wide at Tallie's statement.

"Oh, no, silly, not like that. Uncle Charles and Aunt Emma practically raised me after my parents died."

"I'll bet that was fun—did he use you in any of his crazy experiments?"

"He observed all the time—earthworms, plants, birds, dogs, his wife, and his children, and I'm happy to say he included me as one of them. All the time he was keeping careful notes about everything."

"Did he write in a red notebook?" A grin crossed Jeb's face.

"Yes. How did you know that?"

"Because this person I met recently always has a red notebook on her lap, and I'm just curious what she writes."

"Now that's something I'm sure that person will never share."

"I'll bet you show me that notebook before you leave Wyoming."

"That will never happen. A lady has to keep some secrets." Tallie rewarded Jeb with a captivating smile.

For the rest of the evening, the conversation flowed as if Jeb and Tallie had known one another for a long time. Never once did Jeb even by innuendo hint at the Garden of Eden episode. A part of Tallie was disappointed that he did not.

❧

After dinner, Jeb escorted Tallie to her room, and as they stood outside the door, she wished that this evening didn't have to end. Jeb Tuhill was not at all like any other man she had ever known. He was knowledgeable without being overbearing, he was witty without being ridiculous, and he was confident without being arrogant. He was, in a word, charming.

And now more than anything, Tallie wanted Jeb to kiss her.

She thought back to the kiss they had shared in Leonard Jerome's stable, and recalling it, she could feel a tingling in her lips. Surely he could see them quivering, surely he knew that she wanted a kiss. She told him as much with the expression in her eyes, the gentle parting of her lips, the rose in her cheeks, the shortness of her breath.

Jeb stared at those sweet lips, gently parted, and knew that he wanted to kiss her, and not just a gentle brushing of her lips as he had done in the barn. He wanted this to be a crushing kiss, one that would pull her body against his, against the thrusting demand that was now manifesting itself.

If he did kiss her, even if she allowed it, and he believed that she would, what could come of it? He not only wanted her, he wanted all of her. But he didn't see how that could ever be. And if he couldn't have all of her, then why torment himself with a few teasing kisses? After all, he was but a cowboy, and she was a titled lady with a husband.

"Good night, Tallie," Jeb said with a slight nod. "I'll see you tomorrow."

"Good night, Jeb," Tallie replied, trying not to let her disappointment color her response.

Please, God, **she** prayed that night after she went to bed. *Don't let Jeb be like Arthur.*

Even as she was silently mouthing the prayer, she knew it wasn't something she had to worry about. She had seen an obvious display of his masculinity when he stepped into the shower and caught her naked.

She smiled now as she thought of that moment. Had her failure to lock the door been an honest mistake? Or was it an open invitation for him to come in? She knew that she would have given herself to him, right then and right there, on the marble table.

At that very moment, Jeb was standing at the open window of his room, looking out over the city of Chicago. Even though it was after midnight, many windows of the buildings he could see were still gleaming, the brightness decreasing according to whether they were illuminated by Edison's incandescent lights, gaslights, kerosene lamps, or, the dimmest of all, candles.

The supper conversation had been most unusual. By word, gesture, and touch, Tallie seemed to be telling him that she was receptive to him. But was she really? Or was this merely some sort of game she was playing with him? They were from two different worlds in just about every way such a thing could be measured. She socialized with royalty; he worked with cows. She was a polished diamond; he was a piece of rawhide cord.

Jeb tried to assess the situation with a clear mind, but a clear-minded assessment was almost impossible. When he was around this woman, he wanted her with every fiber in his being. But he saw danger at every turn. *Married, Jeb,* he told himself. *Married to an English lord.* He shook his head and stepped away from the window.

ELEVEN

The next morning the travelers boarded their private cars to continue their journey to Wyoming. Clara had insisted upon a last-minute shopping trip for the women before leaving the exciting city. Tallie returned to the Garden of Eden, where she purchased a bottle of the leather-scented fragrance she had splashed on Jeb following his shave. She didn't know if she would have the opportunity to use it again, but she bought it anyway, tucking the bottle among her belongings in her valise.

Jeb had brought a newspaper on board and was hidden behind it at the moment, so Tallie took out some paper—it had a drawing of the Palmer House—and a pencil, and began to write:

Dear Aunt Emma,

So much has happened since my last letter that I scarcely know where to start. The Frewen wedding was beautiful and I'm so glad I came. Clara has invited me to spend some time with her in Wyoming, so on the next day after the wedding, we boarded a train for the West, or rather I should say we boarded two special cars, furnished for the journey by William Vanderbilt.

Unlike the trains in England, where one can normally reach one's destination in hours, in this vast land of America one can be on the train for many days. We were in transit for three days and two nights from New York to Chicago. The railroad refers to our two cars in a most unique way, as on the schedule board of the Union Station in Chicago we were listed as "Special Varnish, on track number 10." There our cars were connected to the train that will take us to Wyoming. It will take us as long to get to Wyoming from New York as it took me to cross the Atlantic Ocean. When one realizes that we are traveling at better than twenty miles to the hour, every hour of the day and night, one can get an idea of just how big this country is.

On either side of the train are the prairies, where I can see nothing but wildness, and even desolation. Then I look back inside the car and there is a sharp contrast. Outside, there is the glow of nature, inside the epitome of civilization.

Clara and Moreton Frewen are luxuriously ensconced in the Wayfarer, *their own special car, separated from us by a vestibule that invites them to visit us in our car, but acts as a barrier between our car and theirs, thus ensuring their privacy.*

Mr. Frewen has brought his valet, William MacVittie, whom everyone calls Mack. Clara has her personal maid, Marie Garneau. There is one other traveler with us, that being Jebediah Tuhill. Mr. Tuhill is one of Moreton's business partners, but he is much more than that. He is a genuine man of the American West, and one who would be well worthy of a study by Uncle Charles.

Jeb, for that is how he likes to be called, is certainly a handsome specimen, a little over six feet tall and with all the proper body conformity. He is the kind of man one senses would make a powerful ally, or a dangerous enemy, though his nature is of such equanimity that I would be hard-pressed to know whom he might regard as an enemy. I am glad he is traveling with us because one hears such stories about the West that I feel safer in his presence than I would without him.

Aunt Emma, I can share with you, as I can share with no other, these disquieting feelings I have about him. He thinks I am married, and I have not disabused him of that idea, and that has put me quite on the horns of a dilemma. I so desperately want him to know that I am not married. But in order to let him know that, I would have to tell him I am divorced and possibly risk his condemnation.

I know I have no right to think such a thing, but I can't but wonder if there could be some sort of . . .

Tallie put her pencil down and folded the paper and put it away. What was she doing?

She was fantasizing about this man who was sitting across the train car from her, but what right had she to do that?

He had kissed her in the stable, yes, but that could have been a spur-of-the-moment inclination, and he had seen her naked in the bath, but that, too, had been just one incident. Had he truly wanted to pursue her, would he not have kissed her after their midnight supper at the hotel, like a proper suitor?

She was so confused. She was a grown woman, yet she had no clue how to let a man know she wanted more than a mere friendship with him. For the rest of this trip, she would have to stay busy. She would write.

They were three days out of Chicago, and Mack and Jeb were conversing while Marie was napping. Tallie turned her chair so she could look outside. The train began to slow, and she saw the beginnings of a town. The first house, small and painted white, was surrounded by canes of pink and white rambler roses. A woman was standing beside the house, hanging clothes on a clothesline. Two children were playing nearby.

Tallie couldn't help but project herself into the scene. How different that woman's life was from her own. Tallie had social position, money, and success as a writer. But something in her wanted, desperately, to trade places with that woman, to be the one hanging up her husband's clothes and keeping watch over her children as a train swept by. She wondered if the woman ever thought about any of the people on the trains that passed daily, on their way to distant places.

Tallie was still contemplating the clothes-hanging woman when the train stopped at the depot. The small, red-painted building sported a sign, black letters on a white board, reading LODGEPOLE, NEBRASKA.

Tallie watched the happy embrace and kiss of a man and a woman who had been reunited by the train, and the sorrowful embrace and kiss of a man and a woman about to part. As the train left the station, the woman who had said good-bye was still standing on the platform, wiping away her tears. Tallie felt a lump in her own throat as she empathized with the woman.

"Tallie, would you like to go to the dining car and get a bite of lunch?" Jeb asked, interrupting her thought.

"But . . . " Tallie stopped midcomment. She was about to say that so far the group had generally dined together on the train. Then as she considered dining alone with Jeb, she found the idea quite pleasant. "Of course."

As they were on the vestibule between their car and the diner, the train hit a rough spot on the track and jerked, throwing Tallie against Jeb. He caught her, pulling her to him for support. He held her.

And he held her.

Tallie could feel his breath against her cheek as he held her close to him, his powerful arms wrapped around her, her soft curves pressed against his hard body. The connection between them sent a shiver through her. She wanted to stay just like this, wrapped in his arms, but she knew she should not and could not.

When Jeb made no move to let her go, she knew she would have to take the initiative. "I'm, quite all right now," she finally said.

"Oh, yes, of course." Jeb held her for just a moment longer, then let her go.

In the diner, they sat across from each other at a small table. A flower in a vase separated them, and Jeb moved it, putting it against the window. A white-jacketed porter placed a menu in front of them, and after a moment's perusal, they both ordered a bowl of oyster stew, and for dessert a deep-fried sweet cake known as a cruller.

The meal was delivered rather quickly. "How long will you be staying at the ranch?" Jeb asked as they began to eat.

"Clara has invited me to stay for the rest of the year, but I don't know yet."

Jeb smiled. "That would be great if you could stay that long. There aren't many women around the 76."

"What about you, Jeb? Have you been with More-ton for very long?"

"For about a year and a half. I drove a herd up from Texas."

"Drove a herd? How does one drive a herd?"

"You get a group of drovers—uh, men on horse-back—and you ride alongside a herd of cattle, keeping them all moving in the same direction at the same time until, eventually, you get to where you're going."

"That sounds quite—exhausting."

Jeb laughed. "It will put a tired on you."

Now Tallie laughed. "'Put a tired on you'? That's a rather quaint expression. American, I suppose."

"I'd say it's more James Tuhill than American. It's an expression I picked up from my father."

"Besides driving herds, what else do you do at Moreton's ranch?"

"I'm sort of a liaison between the ranch owners and the cowboys. I go to the roundups and I sometimes go on cattle drives with them. I try to be involved in all aspects of actually running the ranch because I guess I'm the only partner with any real ranching experience."

"That sounds terribly involved."

"Well, it's not all work. Some of it is quite enjoyable, the hunting for example. Most of Moreton's guests that come from England like to hunt, so I get to act as a guide."

Just then Moreton, Clara, Mack, and Marie came into the dining car.

"Well now, did you two slip off to be by yourselves?" Moreton teased.

"No, I—" Jeb smiled sheepishly. "I guess we did at that."

"I don't blame you. I don't blame you at all."

"Here, you can have our table. We were just finishing." Jeb stood and then helped Tallie from her seat.

Tallie and Jeb made their way back to the parlor car. "I have something for you," she said. "Now would probably be as good a time as any to give it to you."

Tallie headed for her roomette and stepped

inside. "It's really nothing." She withdrew a small package, handing it to Jeb. "I got it just before we left Chicago."

Jeb opened the package. "From the Garden of Eden?"

"Do you remember how it smelled? The barber said it smelled like leather, and I think that is the perfect scent for a cattleman." She held the bottle up for Jeb to sniff.

"I think it smelled better when it was on my face."

"Let me take care of that." She poured a small amount on her hands, then began to pat his cheeks. Immediately she knew she had made a mistake and quickly withdrew. "You'd better do this."

"I think not." Jeb drew her to him and placed his cheek against her hand.

Now she felt the texture of his skin. The aroma of the cologne assailed her nostrils, and more than anything in the world she wanted to kiss and be kissed by this man.

"You are beautiful," Jeb said as he pulled her to him, wrapping his arms around her. Unlike the time in the stable, nothing about this kiss was innocent or hesitant. It was urgent and demanding, and Tallie wound her arms around his neck, feeling the texture of his hair as she ran her fingers through it. Jeb held the kiss for a long moment, as if testing how far he should go, how far he *could* go. Tallie made no effort to end it, nor to make things progress. It was as if she had made herself completely pliant to his will, subservient to his desire.

The caress of his lips on her mouth set her aflame, and then she returned his kiss with a hunger that she couldn't control. It stretched out, seemingly into an eternity, but was over much too quickly.

When at last their lips parted, Tallie kept her eyes closed, the better to control her emotions. The kiss had made no declarations, it had implied nothing. It was what it was, a kiss, no more and no less. After all, didn't she know about such things? Hadn't she written about them? Weren't such kisses mere play among her friends of the Marlborough Set? Didn't they exchange kisses, flirtations, tender caresses, and more? Yet, though she had observed and written about such behavior, this was a new emotion for her and she found it disturbing.

No, not disturbing—*disturbing* was totally inadequate to describe what she was feeling. She felt a sense of disconnection from reality, as if she were in a small boat on a storm-tossed sea. When he had kissed her in the stable, it had been her first real kiss with a man. At least, she had thought so then. But this kiss went so far beyond that, this kiss so filled her senses, that she felt for a moment as if she might swoon.

Tallie's reaction to the kiss had both pleased and surprised Jeb. She had been a willing participant so he didn't feel that he had forced himself on her, yet a vulnerability about her made him instantly protective.

Jeb had kissed girls and women before, including, of course, Katarina, but never before had he experienced a reaction like this. He felt both protective and invasive.

◈

Opening her eyes, Tallie saw Jeb looking at her with a bemused smile.

"Maybe we should go back out into the car," Jeb suggested.

"Why?"

Jeb chuckled. "I'm not sure how it would look if we are still in your bedroom when the others come back."

"Oh! Oh, yes, you're right. We should go back."

Returning to her seat, she quickly let the table down while Jeb stepped out on the vestibule that separated the Frewens' car from the parlor car.

When the others returned, Tallie was reading over her work, as if nothing had happened.

> He is a man of the American West, a man without property or station, yet that does not seem to bother him. He is supremely confident and self-assured. It is not known if this is a trait that elevates him, or a flaw that finds him wanting.

Putting down her pencil, she looked out the window at the rapidly passing countryside. The last phrase of her writing was running through her head. *A flaw that finds him wanting.* That phrase she found hard to justify. Nothing about this man found him wanting.

Jeb stood on the vestibule letting the wind blow against his face, totally disgusted with himself. Whom was he kidding? He could never have a relationship with this woman, she was married, and what he had done to her by kissing her was every bit as bad as what Jonas and Katarina had done to Jeb before he left Texas. He was attracted to Tallie and he thought she was attracted to him. Why had he kissed her like that? Hadn't he already told himself that any real relationship with her was impossible? A better question would be, why did she react to the kiss as she did? Was she the kind of woman who could enjoy a man without the commitment of a real relationship?

She must be. She was married, yet she was clearly reacting to him in a way that suggested she was not only willing to respond to him, but would go further. How much further?

Jeb believed she would go as far as he wanted to go. She had certainly made no effort to limit any advance of his. And he had seen her as a willing companion to Kinsky. Was this the way women in high society acted? Did they care nothing about commitments? Evidently, Tallie didn't, or she wouldn't be acting in such a way. What kind of marriage did she have that she could leave her husband for so long? It couldn't be a happy marriage.

It wouldn't be like that if Tallie were his wife. If he could make her love him, he would do everything he could to make her happy. He would . . . what in the world was he thinking? Tallie love him?

What was it about this woman that had so quickly captivated him? She was pretty, yes, but Jeb had been around many beautiful women, not the least of whom was Katarina. Tallie had a sense of humor and he enjoyed her easy laugh, genuine and delightful—never loud and forced like the laughs of the saloon girls, who often used laughter as a mask. She was as good a rider as he had ever met, and he found that particularly appealing.

But she was also married, and something about that troubled him. Was he attracted to her because she was married? Was there some appeal in forbidden fruit?

As Jeb stood against the railing on the small vestibule, he pinched the bridge of his nose to drive that far-fetched thought from his mind. But he could no more do that than he could stop breathing.

Tallie returned to her roomette and sat on the side of the bed, reliving the kiss that Jeb and she had shared. She thought of the last glance she had of Jeb. He had returned the glance, and something in the way he'd looked at her had both thrilled and frightened her. She wasn't frightened of him; she knew instinctively that he would never do anything to hurt her. She was frightened of herself. She was still a virgin, a secret that she had kept even from her closest friends. She was ashamed, embarrassed at being a virgin even after she had been married for over two years. What sort of woman wasn't wanted enough by her husband for him to even consummate their marriage?

What had she missed by being in a marriage without any physical contact between husband and wife? Until now, she had never really been able to imagine, but this trip had changed all that. First there was the intimacy of the moment when he saw her naked. Then there were the kisses they had shared. The one in the stable, while arousing, was, nevertheless, innocent. But the kiss this afternoon was not innocent. She had pressed her body against his, mashing her breasts against his chest, and feeling, for the first time in her life, albeit through two layers of clothes, the hardness of a man's desire.

Even though Jeb was still wearing the clothes of a gentleman, something about him belied the suit and vest, something gave her a sense of leather and steel.

As she lay in the dark of her room, feeling the rhythm of the car's movement and listening to the click of the wheels passing over the rail joints, she realized that just her thoughts of Jeb had, once more, caused a warm tingling all through her body. Only this time, something new was added. The sensations that were pulsating between her legs were maddening.

TWELVE

The train rolled into Rock Creek just before breakfast the next morning. Tallie would have slept through it if Jeb hadn't knocked on her door about half an hour earlier. As it was, she was in her seat looking through the window at just one more of the scores of small towns they had passed through since leaving New York. What made this town different from all the others was that this was where they would leave the train.

"Oh, Lady Somerset, please tell me that this is not where we are to be," Marie said.

"We won't be staying here," Tallie said. "It is my understanding that we will just be getting off the train."

The train stopped, then backed up for some distance. At first Tallie was confused, then she realized this was done so the two cars could be disconnected from the rest of the train.

By the time they stepped down from the cars,

the train had already left the station. Suddenly, and frighteningly, five desperate-looking men came running across the track toward them with shouts and cheers. A couple of the men began firing their pistols into the air.

Tallie reacted, and Jeb reached out to put his hand on her shoulder. "Don't be frightened. It's only Rudy Brock and some of the cowboys from the 76 Ranch, come to welcome us."

"That's their idea of welcome?" Tallie asked.

"Hurrah for Mr. Frewen and his new wife!" Rudy Brock shouted, and hurrahs were given.

"His new wife? What happened to his old one?" another cowboy asked, and everyone laughed.

"Gentlemen!" Moreton said, holding his hands up to get their attention. Then moving his arms toward Clara in a grand, sweeping motion, he announced, "May I present the joy of my life? This is my bride, Mrs. Moreton Frewen, who, from henceforth, will be the chatelaine of the 76 Ranch."

"Ha, and more 'n likely she'll wind up boss of the whole spread, I'll bet," Rudy said, and again there was laughter.

"My dear," Moreton said to Clara, "this rather vociferous fellow is Rudy Brock, one of my cowboys. And these gentlemen"—Moreton turned to the gathered men—"and I trust that you *will* be gentlemen, are some of the other cowboys of the 76."

"I'm glad to meet all of you," Clara said.

"Hurrah!" one of the men shouted, and all threw their hats high into the air.

Rudy came up to Clara and, with his hat in his

hand, said, "Mrs. Frewen, if the boss don't treat you right, why, you just let me know."

"Why, thank you, Mr. Brock." Clara smiled. "But I'm quite sure he will treat me—right."

"All right, boys, let's get their gear loaded."

The cowboys began loading the luggage onto the stagecoach that would be used for the long trip north.

"Jeb, we brung Liberty to you," Rudy said. "We figured you'd more 'n likely rather ride a horse back than be closed up in the stagecoach. We brung you your gun, too." Rudy handed the belt, holster, and pistol to Jeb. "We would'a brought you some clothes to wear if we'd know'd you was goin' to be all decked out in them dude clothes."

"Thanks," Jeb said, strapping on the gun belt. "I'll be fine."

Rudy looked over at Tallie. "Course, none of us know'd you'd be bringin' your own woman with you. Maybe you'd rather ride in the coach?"

"Oh, she's—"

"Just a friend. I'm Tallie Somerset."

"Pleased to meet you, Miz Somerset," Rudy said. "You talk like Mr. Frewen. I reckon you must be from England, too?"

"I reckon." Tallie smiled broadly.

"Mack, you came back? I thought for sure Mr. Frewen would push you off the train somewhere along the way," one of the cowboys said.

"Now why would he do that when he needs me to keep the likes of you straight?" Mack bantered back.

Despite the obvious good cheer of everyone present, Marie was obviously uncomfortable.

"C'est un endroit horrible. Comment peut-on vivre ici?"

"What do you mean this is a horrible place?" Clara asked. "Why, it's wonderful, and we can live here quite happily. Think how much fun it will be."

Mack climbed up to sit beside the driver of the coach, and with shouts and whistles the coach got under way, preceded, flanked, and followed by men on horseback.

The coach was pulled by a team of four horses, and because the body of the coach was slung on leather straps, it dipped and swayed so that it reminded Tallie of her time on board ship, and though she wasn't disturbed to the point of seasickness, she could see how such a malady could occur.

"Monsieur Frewen, will we encounter wild Indians on our way?" Marie asked apprehensively.

Moreton smiled at her. "There are no wild Indians between here and the 76. And even if there were, look out the window. There are six armed men accompanying us. That is enough protection for any contingency."

Tallie looked through the window and saw that Jeb was riding close to the coach. She saw, too, the pistol at his side, and somehow that made her feel secure.

They rode across the plains for three hours without stopping, then Tallie was startled to hear the sound of a trumpet.

"What is that?" Clara asked, giving voice to Tallie's question.

"That, my dear, is our driver giving word to the way station that we are arriving.

At least another five minutes passed before Tallie heard the driver calling to his team. The coach rolled to a stop, but was, for a moment, engulfed in the dust cloud that while they were under way had trailed behind them.

"Cooper's way station!" the driver called down.

"How long will we be here?" Clara asked.

"Long enough for the driver to change teams, and for the rest of us to get something to eat."

"Good, I'm starving," Clara said.

Even before anyone from inside had moved, the door to the coach was opened, and a smiling Jeb Tuhill was standing there to help everyone down. Tallie was the last to disembark, and it seemed to her that he held her hand just a bit longer than necessary. But rather than be annoyed by it, she found it quite pleasurable.

Stepping away from the coach, she studied the little building. Constructed of rip-sawed boards, unpainted and drying in the sun, it had two windows in the front, one on either side of the door. A crudely lettered sign was just over the door.

COOPER'S WAY STATION
EATS DRINKS BEDS

"Surely, we aren't to eat in such a place," Marie said.

"Marie, where is your sense of adventure?" Tallie asked with a bright smile.

Once inside, though, even Tallie began to have second thoughts about having chosen to come on this trip.

Crowded close together in the small room were eight tables. Their tablecloths bore the stains of many meals between launderings. Only one table was empty, and a man, whom Tallie thought must be Cooper, seated them with great fanfare.

"This is the best table in the house. It's a special table, for someone like Mr. Frewen and his guests."

"Mr. Cooper, are you sure you aren't Irish? You've a gift of blarney that would put the best Irishman to shame," Mack teased.

The table could accommodate six, so Jeb and Mack joined Tallie, Marie, Moreton, and Clara at the table, with Jeb sitting directly across from Tallie.

Rudy Brock and the 76 cowboys found places at the bar. The other tables in the way station were filled with men, all of whom, Tallie noticed, were wearing belts with holstered revolvers. The oppressive smell of sweat mingled with the odor of frying bacon and roasting venison being prepared in the kitchen corner of the building. The men, with little regard for the presence of the three women, carried on raucous conversations, often interspersed with loud laughter and crude expletives.

When the food was delivered, the men at the table ate heartily, and Clara bravely joined in. It was too much for Marie, who, looking pallid, mumbled, *"Excusez-moi, s'il vous plaît,"* and got up from the table. She walked rather quickly through the room and out the front door.

"Oh, dear, I'd better go check on her." Clara started to get up.

"No, you stay here with your husband. I'll go," Tallie volunteered.

"Thank you, Tallie, that's very sweet of you," Clara replied.

When Tallie stepped outside, she saw Marie standing next to the coach, leaning toward it, supporting herself with one outstretched hand.

"Marie, are you all right?" Tallie asked, walking up to her.

"I am so sorry if I embarrassed Madame Frewen. But that room, the smell, the food, it is so awful."

Tallie smiled. "I will admit that it isn't like dining at Delmonico's."

"No, it is not."

"Are you going to be ill?"

"I—I don't know."

"Perhaps if you walked a bit."

"*Oui*. I think that would help."

"I'll walk with you."

A short distance from the coach was a tree, which was quite an anomaly in what was a mostly barren landscape. The two women walked over to the tree and stepped under the shade. Just on the other side of the tree was a swiftly flowing stream, and as they were standing there, a fish leaped from the water, then went back in with a splash.

"Oh! How marvelous!" Marie said, and Tallie smiled, because it was the first time Marie had said anything during the entire trip that wasn't negative.

"See, if you'll just let yourself, you can find many things to appreciate out here, I'm sure of it."

"Well, now, Roscoe, lookie here. What do you think about this?" A man's voice, it was gruff and frightening.

Turning toward the sound, they saw two men. Neither of the women had seen or heard them approach, and now the men were no more than a few feet from them. One was a big man with a bushy, unkempt beard and long, matted hair. The other was thin, with a prominent Adam's apple, a hawklike nose, and snakelike, obsidian eyes. Like nearly all the other men here, they were wearing pistols.

"I tell you what I think," the snake-eyed man replied. "I think these two women could be a couple of soiled doves."

"I think you're right. That's what you are, ain't it, ladies? A couple of soiled doves?"

"Soiled doves?" Tallie was not certain of the term.

"Well, we was just tryin' to be polite, callin' you that instead of what you be. Whores. Now, girlie, does that suit you better? But whatever you call yourselves is fine with me. Don't you think, Leroy?"

"Yeah, they can call themselves anything they want. But, I tell you what, ladies, afore you go to set up your trade, how 'bout you givin' me an' Roscoe here a free sample?" the big man asked. He grabbed himself pointedly and smiled, showing a mouth of crooked, stained, and broken teeth.

"Tallie, mon Dieu, nous sommes à être tué!"

"No, Marie, I don't think these gentlemen mean to kill us. I think they have mistaken us for *prostituées.*"

"Des prostituées? Mais non, dites-leur qu'ils ont tort."

"Gentlemen, you have made a mistake," Tallie

said as she placed her hand on Marie's arm, trying to reassure her. "We are not what you think we are."

"I say you're whores, all right. Iffen you wasn't, why would two pretty young things be out here all alone?"

"They aren't alone." The voice was clear and resolute, and when Tallie looked around, she saw Jeb coming toward them. She had never been more relieved to see anyone in her life.

"Mister, go get your own whores. These here are our'n," Leroy said.

"They aren't whores, and they aren't yours."

"Mister, maybe you'd better just go mind your own business."

"This is my business." He held his hand out toward Tallie and Marie. "Lady Somerset, Mademoiselle Garneau, come, I'll walk you back to the coach."

"You don't hear all that good, do you, mister?" Leroy said. He and Roscoe both went for their guns, but Jeb drew first, his hand a blur as he jerked his gun from his holster and pointed it at the two men. He pulled the hammer back, and as he did so, the sound of the sear engaging the cylinder made an ominous click.

"No, wait!" Leroy shouted, and he and Roscoe both jerked their hands away from their pistols and put their arms in the air.

"Pull your pistols out slowly and hand them to me, butt first," Jeb ordered.

Tallie had never heard that tone in Jeb's voice before. She had never heard that tone in any man's voice before, and it both frightened and thrilled her.

"Here they are, don't shoot," Leroy said as he and Roscoe handed their guns to Jeb.

"They'll be with Cooper," Jeb said, returning his gun to his holster.

Jeb turned and started back toward the way station with Tallie and Marie hurrying alongside him.

"Thank you, Jeb. I was certainly glad to see you come along when you did," Tallie said.

"I shouldn't have let you go out alone."

"Would you really have shot them?"

"Yes," Jeb answered immediately, without equivocation.

"Oh!"

"Tallie, while you're here, there's something you should know. Never, ever, point a gun at anyone unless you're one hundred percent committed to shooting them if you have to. Do you understand that?"

"Oh, dear. Then I shall certainly endeavor to never point a gun at anyone."

"If that's the case, you need to be more careful about getting yourself into another situation like the one you were just in."

"You say that as if it were my fault."

"No, it wasn't your fault, it was my fault. I had no business letting the two of you go out by yourselves in a place like this."

"Jeb, please tell me that it isn't like this all over the West?"

"There are men who would do others harm

everywhere. That is true of Washington, New York, or even London," Jeb said, his voice softer now. "Most of the West is just like it is anywhere else— men and women living together peacefully, trying to make homes for themselves and for their children."

"You're right," Tallie said. "Forgive me for trying to judge the entire West by what happened here."

By the time they returned to the way station building, a new team had been connected to the coach and the others were just coming out.

"Is everything all right?" Clara asked.

"Yes," Tallie said. She was about to add, *Thanks to Jeb,* but she thought it best to say nothing.

"Where'd you pick up those guns?" Moreton asked, seeing the two pistols Jeb was carrying.

"I got them down by the creek," Jeb replied without further elaboration. "I'm going to leave them with Cooper."

Before he went inside, he emptied the two pistols of all their cartridges. Tallie watched the confident way he handled the guns, then followed him with her eyes as he took the weapons inside.

"Tallie, aren't you coming?" Clara called.

Looking around, Tallie saw that she was the only one not back in the coach, and with a sheepish grin, she hurried back. "I'm sorry, I'll be right there."

"Heeyah!" the driver shouted as soon as Tallie was inside, and he popped the whip, the sound as loud as a gunshot.

"Oh!" Marie said with a little jump.

"It's just the popping of the driver's whip," Tallie said as she put her arm around the frightened woman. "There's nothing to worry about."

"Did something happen back at the way station? Just how did Jeb find those two guns down by the creek?" Moreton asked.

"Monsieur Tuhill is a hero. He rescued Madame Somerset and me from *deux meurtriers*."

"They weren't murderers," Tallie said. "They were just a couple of very unpleasant men."

"What did they do? Did they try to accost you?" Clara asked.

"Two men mistook us for prostitutes and wouldn't accept our denial."

Moreton smiled. "Let me guess. Jeb convinced them that they were in error?"

"I believe you could say that. Yes."

"What did he do? Did he fight with them?" Clara asked.

"He didn't, but he was quite—persuasive."

"He drew on them, didn't he?"

"Yes, he did, and I must say, he did it very quickly," Tallie replied. "He probably drew faster than even Buffalo Bill could draw."

"You, Lady Somerset, are a fan of Buffalo Bill?" Moreton asked.

"I wouldn't say I am a fan, but the Duke of Beaufort introduced me to several of his books, and I learned that withdrawing a pistol rapidly is a skill that a cowboy would want to have."

"You may have the opportunity to meet Buffalo Bill because he is often a guest at the ranch. Perhaps you can convince Jeb and Bill to have a fast-draw contest."

"Would Jeb win?"

"Hard to say. Both men are fast draws."

As the coach rolled on, Tallie reached into her reticule and removed a small mirror. Holding it up as if looking at her reflection, she turned it slightly so she could see Jeb, who had now caught up with them and was riding right beside and slightly behind the coach. She held the mirror for a long moment, then when she saw Clara looking at her quizzically, Tallie smiled and put the mirror away.

Would Jeb have actually shot those two men?

Never, ever, point a gun at anyone unless you are one hundred percent committed to shooting them if you have to, Jeb had told her.

Tallie wondered if Jeb had ever actually shot a man. The thought was abhorrent to her, yet she knew that his willingness to do so had saved Marie and her from . . . from what?

She didn't know, and she didn't want to know. She was just thankful that Jeb had come when he did.

Three hours after they left the way stop, Tallie heard the driver calling out to the team. The coach came to a stop, and looking through the window, Tallie saw Jeb ride up close by.

"Jeb, what is it?" she asked. "Why are we stopping?"

"It appears that we're being met by a welcoming committee from the fort."

"The fort?"

"Fort Fetterman." Jeb dismounted and opened the door to the coach. "This would be a good time to stretch your legs, if you would like."

Tallie and the other three occupants of the coach stepped down, just as a troop of soldiers arrived.

The officer in charge, a young lieutenant, called his troop to a halt, then dismounted. Handing the reins of his horse to one of the soldiers, the lieutenant came toward them and saluted. "Would you be Mr. Frewen, sir?"

"I am."

"I am Second Lieutenant Kirby, sir. Colonel Gentry's regards, and he has sent me to escort you the rest of the way to the fort."

"Thank you, Lieutenant. That is most gracious of the colonel."

"Driver, are you ready to get under way?" the lieutenant called up.

"Anytime you are, Lieutenant."

Moreton and the others returned to the coach, and with a jerk they got under way once more.

"It's nice to have a military escort," Moreton said.

"Oh, Moreton, is such a thing really necessary?" Clara asked. "What I mean is—are we likely to be attacked by Indians, or road agents?"

Moreton chuckled and took Clara's hand in his. "Not at all, my dear. Look at this as purely an honor guard, accorded to yours truly."

When the coach rolled through the gate at Fort Fetterman half an hour later, the guards at the gate rendered a salute as the band played "The Girl I Left Behind Me." Stepping out of the coach, the travelers were greeted by Colonel Gentry, the post commander.

"Mr. Frewen," Colonel Gentry said. "How good of you and your bride to pay us a visit."

"How good of you to offer us your hospitality," Moreton replied.

Moreton made introductions all around, and the cowboys were told they were welcome to mess with the enlisted men and sleep in the barracks for the night, while Jeb and Mack could stay in the officers' quarters. Tallie and Marie would be guests of Major Powell, while Moreton and Clara would stay with Colonel Gentry.

"We don't often get to entertain anyone outside the army," Major Powell said. "So if you would take dinner with us, we would be honored. You folks will be a most welcome diversion."

Major Powell's wife, Laura, and his eighteen-year-old daughter, Marjane, prepared a wonderful dinner of roast venison, noodles, fresh peas from the post garden, and apple pie.

"The food is delicious," Tallie said as she took a second helping of the fresh peas.

"I take it you tried to eat at the way station," Mrs. Powell said with a laugh. "That place is a disgrace."

"Shall we say, it was an interesting introduction to the Territory for Lady Somerset," Jeb said.

"*Lady* Somerset?" Laura said.

"That is true, but, please, I am much more comfortable being called Tallie."

"Oh, but I am most intrigued by lords and ladies and such. I've recently read a wonderful book that is all about such people. My sister sent it to me. Perhaps you know of it."

"Perhaps. What's the title?"

"*The Prince's Folly.*"

Tallie was, at that moment, lifting a forkful of the green peas to her mouth, but upon hearing the title, she dropped the fork, the peas scattering on the table.

Tallie glanced toward Clara, who was covering a smile with her napkin. While Tallie was picking up the peas, she pleaded with her eyes that Clara, who well knew that Tallie was the author of the book, say nothing.

"Are you all right, dear?" Laura asked.

"Yes, I'm so sorry. That was very clumsy of me."

"Think nothing of it," Laura said. "About *The Prince's Folly*. Have you read it?"

Tallie debated with herself for a moment before answering, "Yes, I know that book."

"I must say I found the book enjoyable, but is that really the way the upper crust live? If that's the way it really is, those people have no morals at all."

"Oh, I must read it," Marjane said.

"You will not, young lady."

"But why not, Mama? You said it was a good book."

"It's not the sort of book a young, unmarried girl should read, that's all I am saying."

"Mrs. Powell, you do realize that it's a novel," Tallie said. "Not everyone behaves as do the characters in *The Prince's Folly*. I'm sure that Miss Ingram was exaggerating the situation in order to make a story."

"That may well be, but my sister said that book has caused quite a stir. She read all about it in a gossip sheet some friend of hers got from England.

It's called *Truth*, so you know that story can't be all made-up lies."

"I've heard of Mr. Labouchere's publication," Tallie said, growing more uncomfortable with the conversation, but not knowing how to get out of it.

"Whether it's true or not, I think the book is very entertaining. Besides, sometimes it's good for highbrow people to get their noses tweaked," Mrs. Powell said, "that is, present company excepted."

Tallie looked around the room, seeking a possible way to end this conversation, and her eyes hit on the very thing to do just that. "Oh, I see that you have a piano. Do you play?"

"As a matter of fact I do, and Sergeant Wooley just this week tuned it for us," Mrs. Powell said. "Marjane loves to sing. Let me play a piece for you."

Mrs. Powell sat down at the piano and began playing so poorly that soon Clara, who was an accomplished pianist, claiming exhaustion, asked to be excused.

Jeb, Tallie, and Moreton dutifully listened as Marjane, who had a surprisingly good voice, sang several songs accompanied by her mother, who misplayed about every third note. Mrs. Powell then searched through her music for another song for Marjane to sing.

"You play, don't you, Tallie?" Moreton asked.

"I do."

"Good, good, perhaps you would play something for us," Colonel Gentry said.

"I would be delighted."

Tallie played a couple of pieces for them, including "Für Elise," smiling as she recalled how badly Charles Darwin butchered the song when he tried to hum it so many years ago.

"That was beautiful," Jeb said as he moved to the piano bench and sat beside her. He began to pick out a few notes, making a simple melody.

"Do you play?" Tallie asked.

"Not the piano, but I do pluck around on the guitar."

"Marjane, go get Lieutenant Padgett's guitar. We'll have a regular concert tonight," Major Powell said.

When Marjane returned with the guitar, Jeb took it in his hands and began to tune it carefully.

"Shall we play a duet?" Jeb suggested.

"I don't know. I probably don't know . . . "

"How about Bach's 'Air from Overture Number Three'?"

Tallie's eyes opened wide in surprise. "All right, I know that." She turned to the piano.

"Can you transpose it from D to C?"

Tallie began to play the first bars of the song, then changed the key. "I think I can do it, but I must say, Mr. Tuhill, you have kept your talents very well hidden."

Jeb laughed. "Don't say that yet. You've not even heard me play."

Jeb sat on a chair, pulled the guitar up, looked at her, then with a nod started. With the piano providing the accompaniment, Jeb picked out the single-string melody that wove its way through the music like a golden thread through a beautiful tapestry.

When they were finished, the applause was genuine and enthusiastic.

"My word, Jeb," Moreton said. "I knew that you could play the guitar, in fact I've heard you play it, but generally it is some ditty or other. I've never heard you play like this."

"This isn't exactly the kind of music a bunkhouse full of cowboys would normally appreciate," Jeb said.

"Where did you learn to play classical guitar?" Tallie asked.

"I've picked at the guitar for about as long as I can remember. But I never really played until a very talented gentleman named Felipe Falcon de la Garza taught me."

"Ah, yes, Senor Falcon de la Garza. From one of the original Spanish land-grant families, right?" Moreton asked.

"Yes. You met him at the Goodnight ranch, the same night you met me."

"A very fortuitous meeting, I must say."

"Oh, Jeb, do play something else for us," Tallie said.

Jeb played "Sheep May Safely Graze," the plaintive piece bringing a lump to Tallie's throat. There was much to know about this man.

When the last note died away, Jeb stood. "It has been a most enjoyable evening, Mrs. Powell, Major, but tomorrow will be a hard run to the 76, and I, for one, need to call this a night." He stood and left the room without saying good-night to Tallie, and she felt a loss.

After Tallie was shown to her room, she took out her notebook.

> Lady Anne found her cowboy, for that was how she was now thinking of John Tuttle, as her cowboy, to be a man of such contrasting personalities as to be one of the most fascinating people she had ever met. She had been a witness when, with a gun in his hand, he had confronted two brigands. He had been both heroic and terribly frightening. Then, later, that same hand that had so quickly brought a gun to bear caressed the strings of a guitar in a way that exposed the beauty of his very soul. How complex was this man—how fascinating—and how attractive. She had never known anyone like him. Certainly not among the dandies who were members of the social set to which she belonged back in England.
>
> Lady Anne couldn't help but wonder, what would those hands do to a woman? Closing her eyes, she imagined those hands in her hair, on her cheeks, caressing her shoulders, and cupping her breasts. She was sure her cowboy could entice her into a journey of pleasurable discovery by . . .

Tallie flushed and put her pencil down. What was she doing? Was she writing, or fantasizing? She walked over to the open window where a light breeze was blowing in, cooling the summer night. The flagpole stood in the middle of the quadrangle, devoid of its banner, and the barrel of a nearby cannon shimmered silver under the nearly full moon.

She thought about the lines she had just written. Was this book a novel or a diary?

Not everyone behaves as do the characters in The Prince's Folly. *I'm sure that Miss Ingram was exaggerating the situation in order to make a story.*

Those were the words Tallie had so confidently told Mrs. Powell when she was defending *The Prince's Folly*, but could she with conviction say those same words about *The Lady and the Cowboy*?

She was just injecting her personal feelings into her writing. That was all.

Alfred Lord Tennyson himself had told her that a writer's soul should be exposed by the words on the page. That was what she was doing. Exposing her soul. Or was she exposing her heart?

Tallie's mind was too active for her to go to bed right now, so silently she slipped out of the quarters to feel the cool air of the night. As she looked up at the cloudless sky, the moon was shining so brightly she could see the empty flagpole, the gleaming cannon, and even the shape of each pebble on the paths that led to the surrounding buildings.

Jeb was in one of those buildings. She wondered which one.

Jeb should never have played the guitar the way he did. He had not heard the haunting strains of the classical guitar since he'd left Texas, and now as he walked along the bank of the North Platte, in his mind he was walking beside the Red River, which flowed through the Palo Duro. He missed Texas. It had been two years since he'd left. He had received letters from his mother, but she was careful never to mention Jonas or Katarina, and he never asked about either of them in his replies. That was silly. The next post he exchanged with his mother he would find out what had happened. Jonas was his brother, and he loved him, and Katarina—well, she was the girl next door. He knew he did not love her now, and that he had never loved her.

He left the riverbank, climbing up the bluff, walking between the barracks, entering the quadrangle. And then, he saw her in the moonlight, sitting on the barrel of the cannon under the flagpole.

His first reaction was anger. What was this woman trying to do? Hadn't he rescued her once already today? What was to keep some sex-starved soldier from seeing her sitting so beautifully in the center of the parade ground and taking her off to the hayfield?

He quickened his pace as he headed toward her. To do what? To yell at her? To gently take her back to her quarters? To take her to the hayfield?

Whom was he kidding? It wasn't a sex-starved soldier he was protecting her from, it was from himself.

"What are you doing out here?" Jeb asked when he got to Tallie. He took her by the arm, jerked her off the cannon, and began pulling her toward the major's quarters.

"Jeb, I didn't do anything. I just came out to get some fresh air," Tallie said, almost running to keep up with him.

"You're on an army base."

"I know that. How much safer can I be?"

"An army base full of men. Full of men who probably haven't seen a woman, at least a beautiful woman, in months. What do you think a man wants to do to you?"

Jeb glared at her in the moonlight and saw her lip begin to quiver. "Oh, Tallie, I'm sorry." He folded her into his arms. "I didn't mean . . . Come on, let me walk you back to the major's quarters."

He took her hand in his and began walking toward the house. "You have to understand. Men out here are different from the men you have known before. They take whatever they want."

Tallie smiled weakly as she looked up at Jeb, her eyes glistening. "I should have listened to what you were saying when we were at the way station. I just didn't think."

They stepped up onto the stoop of the major's quarters.

"It's all right. Nothing happened. Now go to bed."

But Tallie didn't move.

"It's time for us both to go to bed."

But still, Tallie didn't move.

Jeb took her in his arms and she wound her arms around his neck as her body began to shudder.

"It's going to be a long summer," Jeb muttered as he found her lips and began a kiss that started innocently enough, soft and tentative, but then deepened.

She felt his tongue trace the soft fullness of her lips, and the kiss sent the pit of her stomach into a wild swirl. His mouth covered hers hungrily, then something happened that she had never before experienced—his tongue slipped through her lips to explore the recesses of her mouth.

At first she was startled, but then she felt as if her mouth were burning with fire. What was he doing? When his tongue withdrew from her mouth, she followed it with her own tongue, moving it into his mouth, returning the kiss with reckless abandon.

He pulled her to him with an agonized moan. She felt a hardness prodding into her stomach as he lowered his hands to cup her buttocks and force her against his bulging member.

Jeb realized that this was wrong, she was married after all, but feeling this soft, beautiful woman pressed against him, he was powerless to resist despite his sense of propriety. When her lips parted under his and her tongue darted into his mouth, his blood turned to molten steel and he wondered if he would have the strength to turn back.

Her arms were wound around Jeb, and she was kissing him wildly, sending her tongue in repeated deep probes into his mouth. Jeb moved his hands to the front of her dress and began to undo the buttons. He thought she would stop him, perhaps he even hoped she would stop him, but to his surprise she seemed more than eager to go on.

Tallie had lost all control over her actions. Whatever happened now was completely up to Jeb. She felt the front of her dress part, then, when he pulled her camisole down, she felt the unusual sensation of cool night air caressing her naked breasts.

He pulled his lips away from hers, and she wanted to cry out in protest, to tell him no, she wasn't ready to stop, but then he moved his lips to her neck and kissed the hollow at the base of her throat. After that, his lips seared a path down her throat, then moved unerringly to one of her breasts. She gasped as he pulled a bare nipple into his mouth and began running his tongue around it.

She felt his hands return to her buttocks, but this time they began bunching up her dress, inching the skirt up a bit at a time, exposing her bare legs to the same cool night air that was caressing her naked breasts. She felt as tightly wound as a coiled spring; never before in her life had she experienced a sensation quite like this.

An unexpected and loud burst of laughter came from one of the barracks and rolled out across the moonlit quadrangle. Both of them froze at the sound; it was as if, until that moment, they were totally unaware that they were standing in the middle of an army fort.

That realization brought them both to an immediate halt; then Jeb stared at her with a look of torture on his face that she could not understand.

"You must go inside, Tallie," Jeb said, his voice ragged and raspy. "Good night." He kissed her one more time, this time as lightly as a butterfly might land on a flower. Then he turned and walked back toward the bachelor officers' quarters.

Tallie was shaking when she reached the door to her room. She entered and, closing the door, leaned against it, taking several deep breaths. She had never before had such feelings. From the first time she had met this man at Badminton, she had been attracted to him. But what did he do to her that made her behave like a helpless ninny?

She had heard him say this was going to be a long summer. Right now in this room, she made a vow that she would make this man care for her. Dare she even hope that some way she could make this man love her? But first she had to find the right way to tell him about Arthur, and to tell him that she wasn't married.

THIRTEEN

When the coach and outriders reached the 76 Ranch at nearly eight o'clock in the evening, the passengers disembarked and cautiously began stretching their legs after the long ride from the fort.

"Well, Clara, what do you think of your new home?" Moreton asked, taking everything in with a sweep of his arm. The sun was just dipping low toward the Big Horn Mountains, painting the sky red, while purple haze was gathering in the small fissures, chimneys, and narrow canyons.

"Oh, my, Moreton, it is absolutely beautiful!"

Moreton smiled broadly. "I knew you would like it. I just knew you would."

"Oh," Marie said, "it is so . . . empty!"

"Yes," Moreton said. "Isn't that wonderful?"

To be sure, the house was more than adequate, especially when compared to others Tallie had seen on this trip, but she felt that Clara was trying a little too hard to see the grandeur of the house as Moreton had portrayed it. The one thing he had not exaggerated was the scenery, and Tallie looked toward the mountains with awe.

Then Jeb, still mounted, rode up. "What do you think?"

"I think it's magnificent," she said with genuine enthusiasm. "But I thought this was a cattle ranch, and I haven't seen any cows."

"They're here, but they pretty much take care of themselves."

"If they take care of themselves, who needs a cowboy?"

Jeb smiled, but didn't answer. Instead, he tipped his hat and, grabbing his bag from one of the men, rode away, following the path that wound through the copse to his cabin.

Once inside, Jeb stripped out of the Eastern duds he had been wearing for nearly a month and got into his old jeans and chambray shirt. He had just lain down on the bed when there was a knock at his door.

Without waiting for Jeb to rise, Richard threw open the door and said by way of a greeting, "We've got some trouble brewing."

"Yeah, I had a good time. But, I'm glad to be back."

"Oh? Oh, yes, how was the trip?"

"What's the trouble?"

"It's John R. Jones. He's diverting water from Crazy Woman into an irrigation ditch, and besides that, he's fenced in some of the range."

"And you don't think he has a right to do that?"

"Well, of course he doesn't have the right. It's

been preempted by the doctrine of prior appropriation."

"Prior appropriation. Now that's one I've not heard of." Jeb swung his legs over the bed and sat.

"It is a doctrine that the first ranchers into the Territory have adopted. It states that the rangeland is closed to any further settling."

"Richard, have you thought about what you just said? A group of cattlemen can't just declare a thing so and have it take on the authority of law. This prior appropriation doctrine would have to be enacted by the government. And since Wyoming isn't yet a state, I don't even think the territorial government could make such a thing law. Besides, in my opinion, it's just plain wrong."

"What John R. Jones is doing is stealing our grass and our water."

"Correct me if I'm wrong, but doesn't *free range* mean 'free range for everybody'? It seems like I remember Moreton's biggest selling point for investors, and that includes me, was that you didn't have to spend capital on the land."

"That's the point. It's our land because we were here first, and Jones can't have it. If you want your investment to make big returns, you'd better come around to the Powder River cattlemen's way of thinking."

"Good night, Richard. I'm tired." Jeb walked to the door and opened it.

The next morning, Tallie was awakened by what she thought was the booming of a cannon. For a moment she was at a loss to remember where she was, but looking around, she remembered that finally the coach had come to Moreton's ranch. The previous evening, everyone had gone directly to bed, following a light meal of cheese, fruit, and a hard cracker, reminiscent of those her father had brought from his ship.

Just then Marie Garneau came bursting into Tallie's room, yelling, *"Monsieur Frewen va me tuer! Monsieur Frewen va me tuer!"*

"Don't be silly, Marie. Mr. Frewen isn't trying to kill you. What are you talking about? What has happened?" Tallie jumped out of bed, going to comfort the frightened woman.

Both Clara and Moreton immediately came into the room, and Tallie found herself, still in her nightgown, playing host to all three of them.

"Marie, for heaven's sake, calm down," Clara said. "You aren't hurt."

"He was trying to shoot me!"

Moreton shook his head. "Not unless you were standing in the garden, I wasn't."

"I heard the gunshot. What was it?" Tallie asked.

Moreton chuckled. "I killed a deer in the bedroom."

"You killed a deer in your bedroom?"

"No, I mean I killed a deer from the bedroom window. It was in the garden, eating our cabbages."

"Marie had the misfortune of coming into our room just as Moreton shot the creature," Clara said. "But, Marie, I assure you, you weren't in any danger. Think about it, I was there, too, and I wouldn't let anything happen to you."

"I want to go home," Marie wailed.

"Go home to where? Back to France?"

"To Paris, or London, or New York. Anywhere but here. Please, let us go home."

"Marie, this *is* my home now," Clara said. "If you feel you must leave, I'll see to it that you get back to the train at Rock Creek."

"No, I . . . I cannot leave you, and besides, I could never go by myself."

"Please, Marie." Clara turned her attention to the maid, who was now cowering in a corner. "We've only just arrived, and I'm sure we're all going to have a marvelous time here. Promise me you'll give it a chance."

"And I promise I won't shoot another animal from the house," Moreton said with a chuckle. "That is, if you're anywhere around, Marie."

"Mon Dieu, qu'ai-je me suis mis dans?"

"You've gotten yourself into a family that loves you, and you know we'll not let anything happen to you." Clara hugged the frightened Marie to comfort her.

For the first evening's meal with Clara Frewen as the new mistress of the Castle, she invited as many cowboys as would fit around the huge wooden table in what she was now calling the banqueting hall. She had carefully put out place cards indicating where each of the men should sit, and she had instituted the feudal system of having newer cowboys sit below the salt, although few recognized the significance of their seating arrangement.

One of Marie's first tasks had been to find flowers for the table, which was covered with a white cloth. Tallie smiled when she saw that the center of the table was lined with the yellow blossoms of the prickly pear cactus.

In deference to Jeb's position, he sat to Clara's left, while Tallie sat to the right of Moreton.

"Gentlemen and Lady Somerset," Clara said as she rose from her seat. "I welcome you to our home, and I anticipate many hours of, shall we say, togetherness. In that respect, I ask for one thing. I expect conversation at this table to be civil and mindful of the presence of ladies."

Tallie lowered her head as she watched cowboys sit up a little straighter and remove any hands or arms that had been placed on the table. If anyone could attempt to "civilize" this ranch, it would be Clara. But because of Clara's statement, there was little conversation during this first social evening in the Frewen household.

Jeb was sitting directly across the table from Tallie, and when he had come in, she had taken a sharp breath of quiet approval for the way he was dressed. He was wearing denim trousers and a khaki shirt that appeared to have been boiled, making it as crisp as any starched shirt she had ever seen. It contrasted sharply with Moreton's fringed buckskin. It was the first time she had seen Jeb in what she would call cowboy clothes, and she liked how he looked. His sleeves were turned back, allowing her to see the corded muscles in his forearms, the same arms that had pulled her off the cannon at the fort and then held her in an embrace. The tight shirt accentuated his chest muscles, where she had placed her head following a kiss that had challenged her senses. This man exuded an earthy manliness that made it difficult for her to take her eyes off him.

She was relieved when Moreton broke the silence, telling with great glee the story of his shooting the deer in the garden and scaring Marie, who was conspicuously absent. Jeb laughed, and the silent cowboys, following his lead, joined him. When the meal was served, it was a hearty venison stew, taken from that very deer.

"Moreton, shame on you. You nearly scared the poor girl to death," Clara scolded, but it was hard for even her to keep from laughing.

"Speaking of shooting, I heard from Bill Cody in your absence," Richard said. "He wanted to know if he would be welcome at the ranch this fall."

"Buffalo Bill? Will he be coming here?" Tallie asked.

"Yes, of course," Moreton said. "Mr. Cody is such a colorful figure all of our guests take great delight when he serves as a guide on our hunts, but I'm curious, Tallie, why are you so interested?"

"My former father . . . " Tallie caught herself midsentence. "I've read some of his books. That's all."

"I think Tallie fancies herself a cowgirl," Jeb said.

"That's very true, and I intend to take full advantage of my time here."

"I'm sure you will." Jeb took a bite of his stew.

Following the meal, the cowboys filed out in what seemed to be relief that their first evening in the banqueting hall was over. Jeb was following them out when Moreton suggested he stay for a while.

The two women and Richard joined Jeb and Moreton in seats in front of a painted fireplace screen. It depicted a herd of buffalo, the animal now almost extinct from the Powder River valley.

"Would you care for some brandy?" Moreton asked as he went to the hunt table and poured himself a glass. Offering wine to the ladies, he poured a drink for Jeb and Richard.

"To the end of John R. Jones," Moreton said as he lifted his glass.

"The end of John R. Jones? Isn't that a bit ominous?" Jeb asked.

"Well, I didn't mean it literally, but he and his ilk have to be shown that they can't come into this valley and take what we've worked so hard to build up."

"I don't understand you, Moreton. You've come into this valley, and, yes, you built this house and this home ranch, but on a much smaller scale John R. Jones has done exactly the same thing. He's running maybe fifty to a hundred head of cattle, where we're running close to thirty thousand. How can he possibly be a problem?"

"You're thinking like a commoner. It starts with something little and then the whole thing is ruined. Tallie can tell you. The timber you flew over headfirst when you nearly broke your neck. That was put there because some farmer didn't want the foxhunt on his precious land. And now, what do you think this little rancher will do to the rest of us? He and others like him will fence us all out, and where will we be then?"

"We'll be just like the 'commoners' in Texas. Everyone will buy their own land," Jeb said.

"And just you watch. Our profit levels will fall drastically."

"All this because one man is diverting water from Crazy Woman Creek," Jeb said.

"It's just the beginning. We let John R. Jones and the others who follow him take our grass and water today, and tomorrow it's our cattle."

"Oh, my dear, don't you think that's enough of this needless chatter? Tallie and I aren't interested in some little spat with your neighbors. We want to know how soon we can go for a ride," Clara said, taking Moreton's arm in hers.

"You're right, and I'm so sorry you had to hear this nonsense. You ladies may go for a ride tomorrow if you wish. Jeb can pick out a gentle lady mule that will be just right for you, dear, and we'll find something for Tallie as well."

"Oh, Moreton, I do hope you have something a bit more spirited than a gentle lady mule," Tallie said.

Jeb laughed. "I don't think he meant that, Tallie. We've both seen you ride, and I would trust you on the most spirited horse on the ranch."

"I'll take that as a compliment, coming from you."

"That was my intention."

The conversation continued until Tallie could no longer suppress her yawns and she excused herself, but before she retired, she stepped out onto the porch to take one last look at the bright moon and clear stars.

While she was standing in the pool of light that came from a suspended lantern, Jeb came through the door. Seeing her, he came to stand beside her.

"Isn't it beautiful?" she asked as she continued to look up.

"It is, and at this altitude, the stars seem so much closer, but obviously they aren't."

"I know I'm going to enjoy it here. Will you be going with us on our ride tomorrow?"

Jeb shook his head. "I'm afraid not. I've been away for too long now and I have quite a bit of work waiting for me."

"But you owe me."

"I owe you?"

"A guided tour around the place. You do remember that I provided one for you at Badminton." She turned to him and placed her hands on his chest, looking up at him with a most seductive smile.

At the mention of Badminton, reality set in, and the smile left Jeb's face. "Badminton, yes, I remember."

Tallie noticed the immediate change of expression. "Jeb, what's wrong?" She dropped her hands from his chest.

"What makes you think something is wrong?"

Tallie thought of Uncle Charles's book *The Expression of the Emotions in Man and Animals* and wished she had studied it more carefully. "Your expression changed, and I thought I may have said something that upset you."

Jeb shook his head. "Nothing is wrong. I just need to remember who I am, that's all."

"What an odd thing to say. And just who are you?"

"I'm a cowboy." Jeb forced a grin, then pulled his hat down over his forehead. "A cowboy who knows horses, so tomorrow, I'll pick out a good one for you."

"I'll appreciate that."

"Good night, Tallie." Jeb squared his hat and walked off in the darkness.

Sleep was elusive for Jeb, and he lay in bed far into the night, his hands laced behind his head as he stared up into the darkness. He was attracted to Tallie, perhaps more than to any other woman he had ever known, but no matter how much she might flirt with him, he would not take the bait. Tonight, her hands on his chest, the smell of her hair, her skin—all of that was there in the moonlight, just asking for another kiss, but he must keep up his guard.

And he must keep reminding himself that this was a friendship that would only last a little while, and then she would return—return first to a world he could never be a part of, and second to the arms of a man who had married her. He couldn't bring himself to say to a man whom she loved, because for the brief time he had spent in the presence of Tallie and Arthur Somerset, he didn't feel any love between them. And that made him suspicious. Why was she here in the first place?

The next morning Clara and Tallie showed up at the corral. Both were wearing trousers for the ride, although Jeb was glad to see they were not the tight breeches Tallie had worn to the foxhunt. As did many Englishmen, Moreton didn't believe in women riding sidesaddle.

"It is dangerous," Moreton had expounded. "A woman riding sidesaddle has less control of the animal than someone who is riding astride. While sidesaddle, you have only the reins by which to impart directions, whereas riding astride you guide the horse by the touch of your knees."

Jeb picked out a horse for Tallie and a mule for Clara.

"His name is Gallant, and a gallant steed he is," Jeb said as he passed the reins to Tallie. "I think you and Gallant will get along just fine."

Tallie stood waiting for Jeb to assist her in getting on the horse, but Jeb made no such offer. He had seen this woman easily mount a horse, and he felt it was best to keep his hands off her.

"Thank you, Jeb."

As he knew she would, she swung easily into the saddle and headed the horse out of the corral in an easy lope.

Jeb did offer his help to Clara as she got on her mule. "Don't go where you can't see the house," he cautioned.

Just then, Mack rode up. "Don't worry about the ladies, Jeb. The boss gave me the day off so I'm going with them. I've even got a knapsack here with a tasty lunch."

"Good, take good care of 'em." Jeb glanced toward Tallie, who was now cantering her horse toward the rise of the plateau.

Tallie, Clara, and Mack rode that day, and every day for the next several days, until Mack was sure the ladies recognized the terrain enough that they wouldn't get lost. Then one day Clara chose to ride with Moreton down to Trabing to the general store. Tallie rode out alone this time, wandering quite some distance from the house. She enjoyed riding with Clara but enjoyed it more when she could ride by herself and not be restricted by Clara and her plodding mule.

Today, as she was riding alone along the slope, her gaze took in the sweep and color of the mountains and rangeland. Since her arrival at the 76 Ranch, Tallie had learned just how unique and diverse this country was. She stopped to watch a troop of antelope come down to the river to drink, and so enthralled was she by the scene that she didn't see another rider coming toward her. He was almost on top of her before she noticed.

"You should be more observant when you're out here by yourself. I rode up on you without you even being aware I was here," Jeb said, reining up alongside her.

"I was just watching the antelope. They're so graceful." She shifted in her saddle and looked again toward the snowcapped Big Horn Mountains. "Everything out here is so rugged, and yet so beautiful."

"Yes, it is. I'm glad you have an appreciation for it."

"Did you think I wouldn't?"

"It's not the same as the woodlands around Badminton. And it's a far cry from London or New York."

"All the more reason for liking it here. Clara and I have ridden every day since we arrived, and everything seems so peaceful. In the city, one has to watch every corner to make sure a pickpocket or, even worse, a gunman isn't lying in wait for some unsuspecting target, but here everyone seems so trusting."

"Don't let the tranquillity fool you. There are those who are resentful, and there are those who are downright mean. Don't ride this far from the house without an escort, even when you and Clara are together."

"You've not been to dinner for a while," Tallie said, changing the subject.

"I've been working. A few of the cowboys and I were out locating different parts of the herd, and we tried to drift them back closer to the home ranch."

"I'd like to see some cattle. My friends wouldn't believe I've been on a cattle ranch for weeks and the only cow I've seen is the cook's milk cow."

"Moreton will have to take you out to the herd someday."

Tallie started to say she would rather have him take her, but she didn't. "Oh, look at those beautiful flowers! What are they?" Tallie dismounted and walked over for a closer look.

"The cowboys call them weeds. Moreton calls them longleaf phlox." Jeb dismounted as well.

"And I call it decoration." Tallie picked a small, pink blossom off a stalk and playfully stuck it through a buttonhole on Jeb's shirt. She stepped back and looked at it, then laughed.

"What's so funny?"

"I was just thinking what the cowboys would say if they could see a weed decorating your shirt."

"No doubt they'd be envious."

"It's crooked." Stepping back up to him, she made a slight adjustment to the flower, which brought her close to Jeb.

He put his hands on her shoulders. "Tallie?" His voice had a strange, almost plaintive sound.

Tallie stared deep into his eyes, which were smoky, confused, hungry. More than anything she wanted him to kiss her, and she turned her face up to him, parting her lips slightly in invitation. Jeb put his arms around her and drew her close to him, burying his face on her shoulder. She took the initiative and turned her face as she brought her lips close to his, hovering for an instant before she kissed him. She allowed her lips to part only slightly, just enough for her to taste him as her body began to warm. She knew the instant Jeb took control of the kiss because his lips hardened against hers, and he drew her closer to his body, molding her shape to his. Ending the kiss, he dropped to the ground, urging her to join him, and when she did, he lay down, pulling her beside him. He wrapped his arm around her, finding her lips again. His hand began to stroke her back, working down to her bottom, where he began to knead the curvature of her buttocks. Instinctively, she threw her leg over his body, trying to get closer to him, and he pulled her on top of him. She could feel the hard bulge, and she lowered herself for another kiss. He met her lips, but then withdrew his face and held her body tightly against him as he struggled to pull himself to a sitting position.

"No, no, no," Jeb said in a racked voice. "We can't do this."

He pulled away from her, then he jumped to his feet and walked toward his horse, leaving Tallie sitting among the flowers. "You've got to go back to the house. Go now."

"Jeb, there's something I need to tell you."

"No. Not now." He turned his horse and galloped off.

Jeb could still taste her lips and knew he had to do something to get his mind away from what had just happened, and what more he had wanted to have happen. He was riding with no destination in mind when he arrived at Crazy Woman Creek, and he knew then what he was going to do.

He followed the Crazy Woman until he found the irrigation canal that Richard had mentioned. The canal looked to be about three feet wide and about that deep. Dismounting, Jeb walked alongside the waterway, following the slope down from the creek.

He saw a small cluster of buildings that he knew made up the John R. Jones Ranch. John was busy hoeing around some plants while his wife was picking green beans and putting them in a woven basket. Two children were scattering dried grass between some of the carefully tended rows.

Jones looked up and, seeing a man approach, walked over to the fence and picked up a rifle. He held it as Jeb walked up to him, but made no threat with it.

"Good morning," Jeb said when he reached the fenced-in garden.

"Mornin'."

"You've got a fine-looking garden here."

Jones nodded. "Me and my wife here, we work at it."

"I suppose the water helps," Jeb said, noticing the pipes that ran from the irrigation canal.

"You're that Texas fella that works for Frewen, aren't you?"

Jeb didn't consider himself to be someone who worked for Frewen, but he didn't correct Jones. "I am. Jeb Tuhill's the name." Jeb extended his hand.

Jones made no move forward to take it and lifting the rifle, answered, "John R. Jones. What do you want, Tuhill?"

"I don't want anything in particular. I didn't mean to bother you, but I was over this way and I just thought I'd stop in to say hello." Jeb got back on his horse and turned to leave.

"Uh-huh," Jones grunted, never taking his eyes off Jeb.

As Jeb rode away, Jones put his rifle down, then walked back over to pick up the hoe he had been using.

"What was that all about?" Jones's wife asked.

"Don't know, but you know good and well he didn't just wander off up here. Those damn foreigners are up to something. You just mark my words."

"He didn't sound like a foreigner."

"Don't matter none. He works for 'em, that's the same thing."

FOURTEEN

When Clara and Moreton came back from Trabing, the wagon was filled with supplies, including several cases of champagne in stone bottles. Clara jumped off the wagon and came running over to Tallie.

"Guess what? Jennie is coming! Can you believe it? Jennie is coming to Wyoming." Clara was so excited she grabbed Tallie and danced around her, much as a child would. "Isn't it wonderful?"

"Yes, it is. It will be good to see her."

"Oh, I almost forgot. She has a post for you, too." Clara handed an envelope to Tallie.

Eagerly, Tallie took the letter, but she didn't open it immediately. She walked down to the river and sat on a bench under a cottonwood. There she opened it and began to read.

> *My dear Tallie,*
>   *The season has been such a bore without you. And, as about every word that anyone*

can say about The Prince's Folly *has been spoken, it no longer seems to be causing the uproar it once did. There are many who were once so vehemently against you who now speak in your defense. Some have even gone so far as to express the opinion that your book has done London Society a great service by suggesting that not even a crown prince should be above the standards of civil society.*

And, speaking of members of the royal family, rumors about Eddy abound. I must tell you in all candor, the rumors link Arthur's name to a brewing scandal. Your circumspection regarding the dissolution of your marriage has been most admirable; however, as your dear friend, I have been one to speculate as to the cause of your separation. Knowing you as I do, I know that you were and are honor bound to never divulge the true reason for your divorce, and because you haven't, there were those who held you wholly responsible. But as these rumors continue to circulate, many are reassessing their attitudes, albeit no one but you and Arthur know the absolute truth. But do know, my dear, as one who knows you and loves you, I can warmly report that your social standing is once more in the ascendency.

I hope you are thrilled by the news I have conveyed to my sister. I will be in Wyoming before the end of July, and I am asking that you serve as an arbitrator between me and my "dear" brother-in-law. I have begged

*Mama to accompany me, but she will have
nothing to do with the lout.*

*I trust that you are keeping the wild Indi-
ans at bay. Or would it be the cowboys who
should concern me?*

Yr. loving friend,
Jennie

Tallie folded the letter and put it back in the envelope. Little did Jennie know how much one particular cowboy should concern her. Tallie sat on the
bench a long time, listening to the running water,
watching the fish jump. Did she even want to go
back to London Society? The rumors that constantly
swirled around people—who was sleeping with
whom, whose party was the grandest of the season,
whose foxhunt drew the biggest crowd—all of that
seemed so superficial.

But was this the real world?

Jeb Tuhill was part of the real world, but was she?
She was trying in every way she could to tell him that
she wanted to deepen their friendship, but he had
ridden away to leave her sitting among the flowers.
Intuitively she knew why. His standards were too high
to dally with a married woman. With Jennie coming,
it would be the perfect opportunity to tell him she was
divorced, and she would. But was divorce as big an
issue in America as it was in England? If it was, she
would run the risk of losing him, but until the air was
cleared, she could never have him.

When Tallie returned to the house, Clara was in a
rush of exuberance as she ordered cowboys around.

They were carrying crate after crate into the house and then moving furniture.

"You'll never guess what is coming to the Castle. Moreton has bought a piano and it will be here before nightfall. Have you ever known a more generous and loving man? He bought it as a surprise for me."

"That's wonderful," Tallie said, thinking of the night at Fort Fetterman when she and Jeb had played a duet. "With Jennie coming, there will be much music around here."

"We're going to try it out for the Fourth of July. Moreton is sending for all the cowboys to come in for the day, and I believe he is sending for some women from Miles City. Don't you just love this country?" Clara went on excitedly.

Tallie shook her head as she watched Clara go from one thing to another. She was directing the hanging of bunting from the mezzanine. "Do you think we can put the piano up here? Don't you think the music would sound the best floating out over the great room?"

"You are probably right, but think about the poor men who will have to get it up there. I think a place here in the great room will do quite nicely."

"Oh, pooh, Tallie, you are too practical."

Tallie left before she was asked any more opinions. She went out to the corral, and Gallant came hurrying over to her when he saw her. She gave him part of an apple, leading him to the stable, where she saddled him herself and went for a long ride, being mindful to stay within sight of the ranch. She was on the bluff when she saw a lumbering wagon approaching the house. The piano had arrived.

The Fourth of July turned out to be a big event. A cow was slaughtered, and Hank, the cook, supervised the barbeque. The aroma of the roasting beef could be smelled from a long way, and every cowboy rode in, anxious for the festivities.

But the food wasn't the only draw. Three wagonloads of women had been imported from Miles City, and they were freely conversing with the cowboys.

Tallie was sitting off by herself on a blanket when Jeb approached her. "Is this your first celebration for the Fourth of July?"

"As a matter of fact, it is. We have picnics, but not like this. I don't think I've ever seen a whole cow roasted. Will all of this meat be eaten?"

"Maybe not. If there is some left over, do you think you could make a beef Mowbray pie?"

"You remembered," she said with a smile.

"That's not all I remember." He rubbed his ribs thinking of the time she had taken him to Swangrove.

"The women. Why have none of them visited here before?"

Jeb looked directly at her. "Because they are paid to be here."

"Paid? What do you mean *paid*? Where do you come from?"

"Right now, these live in Montana. They tend to congregate around railheads during cattle drives, but when the season is over, they'll go back to Chicago or St. Louis or whatever city they live in during the winter."

Tallie laughed. "There's a season in America, too?"

"Yeah. The cattle season. Very soon, cows will be sent to market, and Miles City will be full of cowboys. These women will make a lot of money, and then they will go home until next year."

"Don't any of them want to stay? Don't they want to get married and live happily ever after?"

"Every single woman you see out there wants that, but sometimes there are circumstances that prevent happy endings."

Just then someone yelled that a baseball game was forming and anyone who wanted to play should join in.

"That's me." He stood.

"Well, hit a home run for me."

"Hit a home run?" Jeb smiled broadly. "Why, Tallie, I'm impressed. We're going to make an American out of you yet." He ran toward the other men.

The festivities went on well into the evening. There were roping contests, shooting competitions, and a square dance, but the final extravaganza from Moreton was a huge display of Chinese fireworks. Tallie observed that the ladies from Miles City were pairing off with various cowboys, but Jeb stood off by himself. She was disappointed that he had not come to join Clara and her as they sat on their blanket, but she thought perhaps he was watching to see that none of the cowboys got out of hand.

Just then a rider came in, waving a newspaper in his hand and yelling. Jeb hurried over to him.

"The president's been shot! It's President Garfield! He's about to die."

Jeb took the newspaper and began to read aloud from the *Helena Independent*:

PRESIDENT GARFIELD SHOT
HE IS SINKING RAPIDLY
IS NOT EXPECTED TO
SURVIVE TWELVE HOURS
NO POSSIBLE HOPE OF RECOVERY

Washington, July 2, 9:50 a.m.—President Garfield was shot before leaving on the limited express this morning. Private advices say the President's condition is more serious than any of the dispatches intimate. According to this, which is reliable news, he is almost necessarily fatally hurt. An effort was just made to probe for the ball but was ineffectual.

The evening's bulletin says that the President was not dead as reported, but a dispatch from private sources says that he is growing weaker.

"Who would do a thing like that?" one of the cowboys yelled.

"The article says his name is Guiteau," Jeb said.

"I knew it! A damn foreigner," the cowboy said as he stomped off.

The news put a definite pall on the festivities, as everyone began to drift off or else sit quietly staring into the fire.

Jeb came to sit beside Tallie, as Clara had left to be with Moreton.

"I am so sorry about your president," Tallie said.

"The article goes on to say that it doesn't appear that any internal organs were hit, and the external bleeding seems to be minimal. Let's pray that the president survives."

Tallie sat for a moment without speaking. Then she turned to Jeb. "I heard that cowboy say he knew it was a foreigner. He even used an expletive. Do they not like foreigners?"

Jeb took Tallie's hand in his. "A lot is going on in this valley. The Frewen brothers aren't the only Europeans in this cattle game. There's Sir Horace Plunkett who owns the EK outfit and the Swans down Chugwater way are Brits. They're everywhere, even down in Texas where I come from."

"Is that bad?"

"No, it's not bad, but it does lead to some resentment. What do all these Englishmen have in common?"

"My guess would be money."

"Yes, and lots of it. Just look at this celebration tonight. Think of how many dollars were just blown up in fireworks. Do you think the little guys who are just barely scraping out a living would ever do that?"

"There's a lot that I just don't understand," Tallie said.

"There are crazies everywhere, and I'm sure that they'll find this Guiteau had some personal gripe against the president. It probably didn't amount to anything, but those people are everywhere, even out here, so be careful when you're out riding. Will you promise me that?" Jeb stood, pulling her to her feet. "You're one foreigner I sort of like having around."

Tallie smiled. "Well, that's comforting, to know that you—*sort of*—like having me around."

Jeb returned her smile. "All right. You're one foreigner I *very much* like having around."

After the Fourth of July celebration, the ranch got back to normal, but Clara did not. She sent several couriers back and forth to Denver in anticipation of Jennie's visit. New Belgium carpets, new chintz-covered chairs, new canopied beds and special linens—anything she could think of, she bought.

And the food she ordered was unbelievable. There were imported cheeses, dainty cakes and sweetmeats, fresh vegetables and fruits as well as tinned meats and seafood. But the most extravagant thing were the wagonloads of fresh flowers, all to be purchased again when the anticipated guest did not arrive on the scheduled coach run.

At last the telegram arrived from Fort Fetterman via a messenger who delivered it to the general store at Trabing.

Clara was standing by anxiously when Moreton took the telephone call from the store.

"Mr. Frewen, there is a telegram here for Mrs. Frewen. Would you like me to read it to you? Or shall I bring it tomorrow?"

"No, please, read it now."

The store clerk cleared his voice, then began to read, shouting because he still did not fully trust the telephone.

"Will reach Rock Creek on Thursday stop Will take coach to Trabing stop Love Jennie stop."

"Is that it?"

"Yes, sir, Mr. Frewen. That's all it says."

"All right, Ed, call as soon as Lady Churchill gets to the store."

"I'll expect her about Sunday, don't you think?"

"If nothing slows her down. Thanks, Ed."

Clara could scarcely contain herself until Sunday afternoon when the coach rolled up at Frewen Castle. As soon as Jennie disembarked, Clara rushed to her, hugging her sister in a loving embrace.

"I can't believe it! You're here, you're really here. I've missed everyone so terribly." Tears of joy ran down Clara's cheeks.

"It was quite a journey, I can say, but I'm glad to finally be off that rocking coach. You live so far away from—from everything."

Tallie waited politely until the sisters had greeted each other, then she, too, embraced Jennie.

"I've missed you, too, Tallie, but you look wonderful. You've not been wearing a hat, though. Look at your coloring." Jennie patted Tallie's cheek.

"It's from happiness. I love it here."

"I don't think your glow is from the location. Where is this cowboy you've written about? I'm dying to meet him."

"Jennie!" Tallie exclaimed as she looked around to see who might have heard her friend. Then she saw Carl Kinsky emerging from the coach. Her mouth fell open as her eyebrows lifted in total surprise.

"Hello, Tallie. Have you missed me?" Kinsky took her in his arms in an embrace.

"Not for a minute, but I must say your visit is a surprise to me."

"To all of us," Clara added, "but welcome to our castle."

Tallie saw Jeb standing at the head of the team that had brought in the coach. He had been observing the greeting of the newcomers.

"Jeb," Tallie called. "There you are. I'd like you to meet my friend Jennie, and of course you already know Count Kinsky."

Jeb walked over to the group, an unreadable look on his face. "Count," he said as he nodded an acknowledgment, then he turned to Jennie.

"This is my friend Jennie Churchill."

"Lady Churchill," Jeb said, again not adding anything.

"Oh, yes. You have to be Jebediah Tuhill. I'd know you anywhere," Jennie said. "May I call you Jeb?"

"That's what everyone else calls me." Jeb smiled, wondering how in the world this woman could possibly have known his name.

"Well, I'm Jennie." She embraced Jeb.

"It looks like you've found your long-lost friend," Kinsky said as he casually draped his arm around Tallie. "Well, now that we are here, shall we step inside? I'm anxious to get a look at this abode Moreton is so proud of."

Everyone moved into the house, where Clara chatted incessantly. Before Jennie had settled comfortably, Clara insisted that she and her sister sit down at the new piano and play a duet.

"She's excited to see her sister, I would say," Jeb said, "and I suppose you are just as excited to see your count."

"I'm excited to see Jennie."

"Of course. How could I get that wrong? I'd best leave now." Jeb turned toward the door.

Just as he was leaving, Clara hurried to the door. "Don't get so busy that you miss dinner tonight. Come at nine."

"Thanks, Clara. But I do have a lot to do."

"I absolutely insist that you be here tonight. It's going to be so special."

When Jeb had gone, Jennie came over to sit beside Tallie.

"I believe your writing talent is slipping."

"And why do you say that?" Tallie asked.

"You did not describe that man with nearly enough superlatives. He is gorgeous!"

Tallie laughed. "Don't let him or any other cowboy hear you describe him with that word. He would prefer *rugged*, or *individualistic*, or *confident*."

"What about *loving*?"

"I'm not at liberty to say." Tallie's cheeks colored.

"Aha! Just as I've thought. You've found yourself a man that you can fall head over heels in love with. It's about time, Tallie."

"Not quite."

"What do you mean? That luscious man is made for you."

"He doesn't know."

"What doesn't he know?"

"That Arthur and I are divorced."

"What? Why, that's the dumbest thing I've ever heard. If you can't tell him, I'll tell him myself."

"No! I'll tell him, but the time has to be right."

Jennie gave Tallie a hard stare. "You're only hurting yourself, you know. Love is wonderful. Just ask me about that. Carl is the greatest lover I've ever had, and you know very well I've had some good ones."

"I know, but I don't think it's the same in America."

"Great lovers are great lovers no matter where they are, and I can tell you right now, your cowboy will be a fantastic lover. Would you like me to find out?"

"Jennie! You embarrass me so much."

"And that's why you love me. Come on, let's go see what my sister is up to."

Jeb entered his little cabin and slammed the door behind him. Seeing Kinsky here was a surprise. An unpleasant surprise, he told himself, though in truth Tallie had done nothing to lead him to believe that she was interested in Kinsky. It did make Jeb wonder, though, just where he fit into this picture.

The answer was simple. He didn't fit into the picture at all. He was a cattleman. No, on this ranch he was a cowboy, and he wasn't about to forget it. Moreton had a herd of about three thousand steers ready to go to the railhead in Miles City, bound for the Canadian market. And even though Fred, Will, and Rudy could easily handle the drive, which in itself would hardly take fifteen days, Jeb decided he would join them. He had no intention of staying here to watch Lady Somerset put on her tight breeches and ride "to hounds" with the count.

Defiantly, he chose to skip the special dinner that Clara had arranged. He saddled Liberty and rode up among the pine trees in the mountains. Finding a soft pile of pine needles, he bedded down and spent the night.

FIFTEEN

The next morning when Jeb rode in, Moreton was standing near the corral with a smile on his face. "You ran out on me last night. I guess you couldn't take it."

"That's close to being right," Jeb said, not offering any explanation of where he had been.

"Well, last night was just a precursor. My wife has planned the shindig of all shindigs for Friday night. She's sending word for everybody who's anybody in three counties to come meet her sister. She's even engaged an orchestra ensemble to come up from Cheyenne."

"Moreton, I'm going with the boys to Miles City."

"That's ridiculous. Fred Hesse can run a trail drive just about as well as anybody I know. Why would you want to be miserable for weeks, eating camp food, sleeping on the ground, following dusty cows? You know how much fun we're going to be having right here. Clara wants Carl to teach the hands cricket. She thinks they'll excel at the game, and since you're so good at baseball . . . "

"You've just given me a good reason to go to Miles City."

"But Carl wants to take back a sheep head, or at least a wapiti rack. I told him you would be his hunting guide."

"Find somebody else. I'm going on the trail drive tomorrow."

"All right, you can go, but I say the trail drive doesn't start until after Clara's party, and you will promise me you will come. And maybe you could play your guitar."

"I'll come, but I'll not play."

"But you're so good. I heard you."

"Music has to come from the heart, and right now mine isn't in it."

For the rest of the week, Jeb coordinated with Fred on necessary provisions for the cattle drive. Even though it was to be only three hundred miles, the same equipment as for a long drive had to be made ready. Because Jeb kept busy, he did not see Tallie and the visitors except from afar. The three women did seem to be enjoying their visit, often taking a picnic basket down by the river, or going out riding horses, or just sitting on the porch.

He also noticed that Kinsky spent most of his time with Moreton and Richard. They raced horses, putting up temporary barriers to substitute for steeplechase fences, and they played cards and drank champagne. They reminded Jeb of college boys. Or playboys, as he had heard the local people call them.

Jeb had never seen anyone operate a ranch quite

the way Frewen ran the 76. The closest thing Jeb could compare it to was the Cheyenne Club, and Frewen's Castle was, indeed, a social club.

"You have to understand, Jeb, that this kind of activity is necessary to bring in the investments we need. For most of the people who invest with us, it isn't at all about business. For them, investing in an American cattle ranch is about adventure, or social station. They love to be leaning against a fireplace mantel in some English manor, discussing their American property." Moreton affected a stilted, upper-class accent. "Yes, yes, dear boy, well, I do have holdings in the American West, don't you know."

Jeb had chuckled at Moreton's mimicry, in part because it seemed to Jeb that Moreton was doing no more than parodying himself.

And now Jeb was being forced to be a part of this charade.

On the day of the event, the guests began arriving by midafternoon. They came from neighboring ranches, from Cheyenne, some even from as far as northeast Colorado. By early evening more than a dozen coaches and carriages were drawn up outside the main house. A stagecoach, three days out of Cheyenne, arrived and five men got out, slapping their hands against their clothes and raising a cloud of dust. They looked around at the house and the other coaches and carriages.

The driver climbed down from the box of the coach and walked around to the boot. Opening it, he began setting cases on the ground.

"Look here, driver, you be careful now with those instruments," one of the men said. "They are quite fragile."

"Hell, mister, you think I haven't hauled a fiddle before?"

"It isn't a fiddle. It is a violin."

Clara and Marie came out of the house to meet the musicians of the Cheyenne Chamber Orchestra.

"Welcome, gentlemen, to the 76 Ranch," Clara said. "We're so excited to have you. If you'll come with me, I'll show you where you will set up for your performance."

"We'll need to freshen up a bit," one of the musicians said.

"Of course, I'll show you to your dressing room."

"Ma'am, I got a box of these here flower corsages that stays with you," the driver said. "They was sent from the mayor's office."

"How thoughtful. Does that mean Mayor Carey and his wife won't be here tonight?"

"All's I know is what I been told, ma'am."

"Very well, then. Marie, please see to it that each of our women guests gets a corsage."

"Yes, ma'am," Marie said as the driver placed the box of corsages in her outstretched arms.

Jeb had been told that this dinner would be in formal attire, including white tie and gloves. As Jeb was standing in front of a mirror tying the bow tie at the winged collar at his neck, Will Tate and Rudy Brock appeared at the open door to Jeb's cabin.

"Whooee, I tell you the truth, Jeb. In that outfit I

can't tell the difference between you and all them English dandies," Will teased. "Next thing you know, you'll be drinkin' tea and holdin' your little finger out."

Will mimicked holding a cup with his little finger extended, and he made a show of raising it to his lips. Rudy and Jeb both laughed at his antics.

"Damn if you don't do that just perfect," Rudy said. "You got an extra one of them suits, Jeb? Ol' Will here might just fit right in."

"He can take my place anytime," Jeb said.

"No, thanks." Will held his hands out in front of him as if pushing Jeb away. "There ain't no way you can ever get me into one of them fancy getups."

"Are you sure, Will? There's always a lot to eat at one of Moreton's affairs," Rudy said.

"It could be all apple pie and ice cream and you still couldn't get me to go."

Jeb chuckled. "The truth is, my friend, I don't much blame you. I wouldn't go either if this wasn't a commanded appearance."

When Jeb stepped into the Castle a few minutes later, the musicians were on the mezzanine and their music was filling the hall. Jeb recognized Frank Bosler, John Coble, Francis Warren, and Harry Oelrichs, all from the Cheyenne Club. He also saw Sir Horace Plunkett, who was the nearest neighbor to the 76. Each of them was accompanied by a well-dressed woman, none of whom Jeb had ever seen before.

Just then Moreton stepped out onto the first landing of the staircase and called upon the band to play a fanfare so he could get everyone's attention.

"Ladies and gentlemen, I want to welcome you one and all to my home for this gathering of friends and neighbors from the great Territory of Wyoming, as well as old friends from England."

There was polite applause.

"To my English friends, I invite you to meet and get to know my American neighbors. When you do, you will see why I love this wonderful country and these magnificent people so.

"And to my American friends, I want to introduce my beautiful bride, who, by agreeing to marry me and come to Wyoming, has made me the happiest man in the world. Clara, step out here and let everyone see how beautiful you really are."

With the ease of a performer, Clara stepped out far enough to be easily seen. She made a small curtsy to the polite applause of the guests.

"Next is my wife's equally beautiful sister, the Lady Randolph Churchill. Her absent husband, a renowned member of our Parliament, could not accompany her on this trip, but Jennie has been handsomely"—Moreton paused for effect—"escorted by Count Carl Kinsky zu Wehinitz u Tettau from Austria. Now, if you think I am pretentious, wait until you talk to him."

This time there was loud applause and uproarious laughter at Moreton's self-deprecating humor.

"And finally, I would like to introduce you to a lovely young lady who has been a houseguest here at the ranch for more than a month now. She came here, from England, to help my bride settle in. Lady Tallas Somerset." He motioned toward Tallie, and as had Clara and Jennie, Tallie made a slight curtsy. Again, there was a polite round of applause.

"And now as a sop to my heritage, my bride has decided that this dinner party will be handled according to the rules of English etiquette. Each gentleman will be handed a card containing the name of the lady he will entertain this evening. It is the hope that no one will be paired with the woman he brought. Now isn't that a shame for some of you?" Moreton laughed, but his guests did not. "Mack, will you distribute the cards?"

When Mack handed the card to Jeb, he took it out of the envelope, hoping that his friend had paired him with Tallie, but when he read the card, it said Jennie Churchill. Jeb thought it could be worse, and seeing Jennie across the room, he started toward her.

When he reached her, she grabbed the card out of his hand. "I believe there has been a mistake. Let me look at your card."

When Jeb got a card back, Tallie's name was on it. "Thank you, Lady Churchill," Jeb said with a slight nod. "Evidently I did make an error."

Jennie smiled, obviously pleased with her shenanigan. "I must find my partner."

Jeb quickly found Tallie and escorted her to their places at the long table.

"I thought Moreton said it was his hope that everyone has a partner they don't know," Tallie said.

"Don't you want to know me better?"

"You know what I meant," Tallie said as Jeb withdrew the chair for her to sit.

"It looks like Marie has been busy." Jeb picked up a small, hand-lettered menu from the table in front of him. "I'm glad you're my dinner partner because I daresay most of the women here won't be reading French."

"All right. I'll translate. *Consommé de boeuf clair*, that will be a clear soup. *Whitefish à l'Orlay*, that's fish with a tomato sauce, and *ris de veau aux choux-fleurs*, that's sweetbreads and cauliflower with a cream dressing over both."

"Cauliflower? I can't stand that."

"Then I'm not going to translate anything else for you. You'd never have guessed this dish was cauliflower if I hadn't told you," Tallie said with a giggle.

The meal continued for more than three hours as course after course appeared. At first the conversation among the matched guests was lively, but once the initial background talk was exhausted, each couple had little to discuss, therefore many ate in silence as the music played through the hours.

The dinner had one definite faux pas as the diners discovered what *agneau rôti aux épinards* meant.

"This is sheep meat!" Harry Oelrichs bellowed when he tasted the roasted lamb. "You can cover it up with all the fancy sauces you want, but I'm not going to eat it. Now, get this out of my sight."

Clara was flustered as she frantically rang her bell calling Mack and Marie to the dining room.

"Remove this dish immediately and have Hank prepare the *selle de venaison à la purée de pommes de terre*."

"Our meal will only be delayed for a moment, ladies and gentlemen, and I'm sure we can agree that if we don't eat lamb, we can all eat venison," Moreton said. "My wife has a few things to learn about this country."

From that moment the conversation became much livelier as all the men began to talk at once.

"Mark my words, gentlemen, right now we're all into cattle, but who's to say our cows won't get Texas fever and nobody will take our beef. Sheep may be something some of us would want to look into," Francis Warren said.

"Aw, Francis, don't tell us that. Are you on the side of the sheepmen taking our grass and water, too? We've got enough trouble with all these squatters coming in. Our very livelihoods are being threatened," Moreton said.

"That's why we've formed the Powder River Cattlemen's Association," John Coble said. "We're going to fight for our rights."

"I hope you mean to fight in a court of law, and not to fight literally," Jeb said, entering the conversation for the first time.

"Look, Tuhill, you're a Texan. Wyoming does things differently," Coble continued.

Just then Tallie reached over and took Jeb's hand. She squeezed it gently. He didn't know if she was supporting his statement or insinuating that he should stop talking.

It was nearly midnight before the dinner ended.

Clara was organizing a dance, but Jeb stepped out. He was sure the dance would be some cotillion or quadrille or some other dance that proper society enjoyed, but it was not for him. He left without saying good-night to anyone, even Tallie, walking back to his cabin, just glad to be out of the hub-bub. He had to get out of these clothes and con-centrate on the trail drive that would be heading out tomorrow.

Once inside his cabin, he lit a kerosene lamp, then began undressing, carelessly throwing his jacket on the floor. Next he removed the bow tie and the studs from his shirt, letting them fall. Removing his shirt and pants, he was wearing only his draw-ers when he looked up and saw her standing in his doorway.

"Tallie," he said, not bothering to put on his pants. "Why aren't you at the dance?"

"Because my partner left me," she said, her voice soft and silky. She had never looked more beautiful to him than she did right then. Her hair was down around her shoulders, and the copper highlights were gleaming, as her eyes seemed to shimmer. "Go back, Tallie. Go back and dance with anyone but me. Kinsky, Coble, Warren, anyone . . . " He stopped himself in midsentence. "Please go back."

Tallie watched Jeb expose his raw emotions. Everything about her told her to follow his admoni-tion and turn around and leave him, but she stepped into the cabin and closed the door. Their eyes locked as she moved slowly, cautiously toward him. Instinc-tively she knew that she wanted this man and there was no turning back. She stood in front of him, her chest heaving as her heart beat rapidly. In her mind she had written this scene many times:

> Awestruck by her beauty, he took her into his arms, showering her with kisses whilst his hands loosened ties and undid fastenings, divesting her of clothing and making her a willing slave to his manly urges. "Yes, my darling, yes," Lady Anne said. "I am yours."

Never once had she contemplated what her heroine would do if the hero rejected her.

She stood just inches from Jeb, her eyes taking in his features, the shock of hair falling onto his forehead, the crinkles around his piercing blue eyes, the hint of stubble that was appearing on his firm jaw. Then her gaze moved to his chest, where the muscles were clearly defined, the mat of light-colored hair on his chest. His stomach was taut and she noticed that he, too, was breathing raggedly. But never once did she make a move to touch him. She watched with wonder as he moved toward her, in what seemed like slow motion. Then she closed her eyes as his mouth met hers and she felt an exquisite jolt of pleasure.

"Come." He took her hand and led her to the bed. He turned her around and with trembling hands began to fumble with the many buttons that closed her gown. When her dress was free and he was standing behind her, he lowered it to the floor, letting it drop in a puddle around her feet. Turning her around, he took each of her breasts into his hands, and through the covering of her chemise, he began to massage each one, causing her nipples to strain against the light cloth. Seeing them become erect, he lowered his mouth and, untying the strings with his teeth, moved the cloth away, taking one breast into his mouth, causing ripples of exquisite pleasure. This one action, so new to her, caused a gentle throbbing to begin in her most private part. Grabbing his head, she pulled it away, not daring to let him take her to some place she had never been, yet wanting him with all her heart to continue. She wanted him to show her what it was that real men and real women did together.

Then she had a moment of doubt. *You must choose abstinence or adultery.* Arthur's searing words came into her mind. Why had she never wanted a man before this one?

Jeb worked her petticoat off her hips until she, too, was standing in her drawers, her opened camisole still covering her chest.

"This is it, Tallie. Tell me to stop, or tell me to go on, because after this, there'll be no turning back."

Smiling at him, Tallie removed her camisole and dropped it onto the floor to join her petticoat and dress. Then she sat on Jeb's bed, the feather mattress cushioning her bottom as she lay back. Jeb knelt in front of her as one hand began to unfasten the waist while the other found the slit in her drawers.

When he touched her, Tallie had an instant jolt of reality. Was this actually happening? Yes, it was. A man—a man who was not her husband—was touching her in an intimate place, a place that had never before been touched. Would he want her? Was she desirable?

She soon had her answer as Jeb began to stroke her in a way that she had never experienced. Her drawers were still on her body, affording her some modesty, but she struggled to lift her hips and Jeb slipped them off. He lifted her nude body, placing her in the middle of the bed as he climbed in beside her, kissing her on the lips, and then trailing kisses down her chest, all the while his hand stroking her. She could feel moisture between her legs as his finger moved back and forth, going first to the heart of her womanhood, then trailing to a definite point that seemed to be getting more and more sensitive each time he touched it. She knew there was something more, something wonderful and mysterious just ahead of her and she—

"Jeb! Jeb! Are you in there?" a man yelled as he banged on the door.

Jeb didn't answer, but rested his head on Tallie's chest.

"Jeb, it's me, Rudy. Come quick. We've got a big problem."

"Just a minute," Jeb said raggedly.

"Come to the stable."

"I'll be there in a minute." He kissed Tallie gently. "Stay here, I'll be right back."

Tallie felt a ragged disengagement, and she watched as Jeb dressed quickly, then left.

Stay here, Jeb had said.

But Tallie knew she wouldn't stay. After Jeb left, she dressed and let herself out of the cabin and hurried back to the main house. The dance was still in progress, but she went immediately to her room and closed the door. What had just happened?

The next morning Jeb got the trail drive started early. He was thoroughly disgusted with Tim Middleton, the cook who was supposed to be going on this trip. Some of the cowboys had got into a horrendous fight with some of the men who had come with the other ranchers to Moreton's party. More and more Jeb appreciated the wisdom that his father and Charles Goodnight had shown when they disallowed any alcoholic beverages among the cowboys, except when they were in town. It always led to trouble.

Tim was so thoroughly beaten he couldn't move, let alone start out on a trail drive. Now the cowboys who were sober were grumbling because Jeb had insisted they start on time, adding plenty of beef jerky and pilot bread to the supplies in the hoodlum wagon.

"Who's going to cook?" Rudy asked Jeb.

"Nobody. It's only a fifteen-day trip to Miles City, and if we're hungry, maybe we'll drive harder. Besides, if Tim sobers up and he finds out he can walk, he'll catch up with us in a few days."

"I don't know," Rudy said, "you might be making a mistake, boss. You know a cowboy works best on a full stomach."

"Well, what's your suggestion? Hold up the whole herd?"

"No, sir. Let's roll 'em out." Rudy spurred his horse to get away from Jeb.

"Damn." Jeb knew Rudy was right. This was going to be a hard drive, and the main reason was because of Jeb. Yes, he was aggravated at Tim, but he was really aggravated at himself. At what he had done, or at least wanted to do, with Tallie last night. With him out of the way for weeks, maybe she would renew her friendship, or whatever it was, with that slick bastard Kinsky. He hated that man, with his slicked-down hair and his fancy clothes. What could any woman see in a cully such as him?

The cattle that were to be driven had been gathered into a cohesive herd, and men in the saddle were calling to each other, and whistling to keep the cows in check. Trail drives were nothing new to Jeb; he had been taking part in them from the time he was a boy. He sat on his horse with one leg hooked around the saddle horn as he looked at the scene laid out before him.

He saw one hoodlum wagon, twelve cowboys—fourteen counting Rudy and himself—forty-eight horses, and three thousand head of cattle.

Rudy rode up to Jeb. "Jeb, I've got the boys all divided up. Will's goin' to be ridin' point, Johnny's on drag, I've got four men ridin' on either side, and I'll be sort of ridin' all over the place keepin' watch. That is, unless you have a different idea."

"No, that'll be fine."

By midmorning, Jeb had regained control over his temper as the pace of the lumbering cows slowed everything down. The cacophony of bawls and snorts started a song that every cattleman longed for, and he was no exception.

Jeb liked trailing cattle; he liked the sounds of

the shuffling hooves and clacking horns, and the whistling cowboys as they kept the herd moving. He liked the sight of a sea of brown and white moving slowly but steadily across the plains, with mountains beside and behind them. And he even liked the smell, pungent to an outsider, but familiar and comforting to him. It didn't take long to settle into the rhythm of the drive.

Back at the Castle, Clara and Moreton were presiding over a combination breakfast and lunch, most of the guests having slept late after the night's activities.

"Did you hear about the brawl last night?" Harry Oelrichs asked.

"It must have been something," Francis Warren said. "My man said if Tuhill hadn't got in the middle of 'em, somebody would have likely been killed."

"Really," Moreton said. "I wondered why Jeb was so anxious to get out of here at daybreak. Mack tells me he loaded down the hoodlum wagon with jerky and left the chuck wagon behind. Don't you think that's rather odd?"

"It's crazy," Oelrichs said. "If his cowboys don't have anything to eat but jerky, he'll have a mutiny on his hands before he gets those cows to Montana."

"His cook is the one who got the worst of the fight last night," Mack said as he poured fresh coffee for those who needed it. "I'd be surprised if he'll be able to walk for a while."

"What do you have to cook on a cattle drive?" Tallie asked.

"Beans and bacon, honey. And maybe throw in

an apple pie now and then, and those cowboys will be as happy as a pig in— Let's just say they'll be pleased," John Coble said.

"Moreton, could I do it?" Tallie asked.

"Of course not," Clara said. "But my question is, why would you want to?"

"I think I know," Jennie said with a smile. "Miss Ingram needs some material. Is that the right answer?"

Tallie blushed a bright crimson before she recovered. "Yes. Isn't a cattle drive as true a depiction of the American West as anything?"

"I would say so, yes," said Oelrichs.

"But a woman?" Louisa Warren said. "I think not."

"I have a woman cook," Sir Horace Plunkett said. "And she does a real fine job, too."

"Then that settles it, Moreton. May I have the job as cook?" Tallie asked.

Moreton thought about her request for a moment. "The herd can't be too far away." He looked toward Jennie, who was nodding her head. "I'll let you go, but only if I can send one of my most experienced hands to watch out for you."

"Thank you, Moreton. I'll be the best cook you've ever had." Tallie jumped up from her chair.

"Mack, get with Hank, and the two of you get the chuck wagon ready. And I think I'll ask Ken Corliss to go with her," Moreton said.

Jeb felt guilty about feeding the cowboys jerky and hardtack, so he rode up to Will and suggested that they find a good place to water the herd and bed them down early.

"There's no sense in pushing them so hard the first day," Jeb said, "and see if you can get a fire started. We did bring the grates, didn't we?"

"We did," Will said with a slow smile. "Jerky not enough for you?"

"I'll see if I can get us an antelope that we can cut up into steaks. The men will like that."

"Good idea. And maybe it'll give Tim time to catch up with us. That is, if he's coming."

"Just get the coals ready for the meat." Jeb slapped his legs against Liberty's sides.

Jeb had to ride farther than he had wanted to, but he finally saw a small herd of antelope. Taking off his bandanna, he began to slowly wave the red cloth, hoping that the curious animals would see it and allow him to get close enough to get a good shot. When he was within range, he fired, and a small animal fell.

Just then Jeb saw a boy run out to the fallen animal.

"Hey," Jeb yelled as he approached the boy. "What are you doing out here?"

"I could ask you the same thing, mister. This animal belongs to me. It's on my land."

Jeb looked around, locating where he was. "Would your name happen to be Jones?"

"Yes, sir, it is. Sammy Jones."

"Well, Sammy Jones, would you like to share this animal with me? I'll skin it and cut it right down the middle. You can even have the skin for your mama. Will you do that?"

The boy smiled. "Yes, Mom'll like that."

Jeb worked quickly, admiring the spunk of this young boy. He had no means to kill an animal, yet he claimed it as his. Sammy reminded him of himself when he was that age.

When Jeb returned to the camp, he saw the chuck wagon was pulled up beside the hoodlum wagon. Tim must have joined them. That was good. Tomorrow would have to be a better day.

SIXTEEN

Ken Corliss stepped out from behind the chuck wagon carrying a big iron skillet.

"Did you get us some meat?" he asked when he saw Jeb riding up. "I think the coals are just right to fry some steaks up fast, and the missus sent some of the taters that was left over from last night's bash. Fanciest camp food these cowboys'll ever eat."

"What are you doing here? Where's Tim?"

"He's pretty sick. Got a lump on his head the size of a baseball. Somebody got him good last night."

"You can't cook, can you?"

"I can sure serve up taters." Corliss guffawed.

"That's today. What about tomorrow?"

"Then I'll be cooking."

Recognizing Tallie's voice, Jeb turned toward her in surprise. "You? Are you out of your mind? This is a working cattle drive, not a fancy foxhunt," Jeb bellowed.

"Now, Jeb, just take it easy," Rudy said. "It might

be nice to have Miss Tallie along with us. She might keep you from chewin' us out all the time."

"You're going back if I have to take you there myself. Get your stuff and let's go. Now."

"No! I'm staying." Tallie put her hands on her hips and glared at Jeb. "Moreton said I could come if I brought Ken to look after me, and there he is, so I'm staying." She turned to the wagon and took out the long-handled cooking utensils. "I believe your job was to procure meat for this bunch of men who've had nothing to eat but jerky all day. Did you get it?"

Jeb tried to keep a straight face, but seeing Tallie's defiant stance, he smiled as he tossed the side of antelope on the back of the chuck wagon. "Fresh from the corner market," he said, then turned his horse and rode off to check on the herd.

That night around the fire, the men were in an unbelievably good mood, considering the inauspicious start they'd had that morning. The meat was good, but it was cut into pieces unlike any cut of meat Jeb had ever seen. Undoubtedly Tallie had done it herself. If she was really going to do this fool thing, he would have to make certain Ken did things like that for her. He would not be responsible for her cutting off a finger.

Jeb took the first shift riding herd on the cattle. He didn't want to find himself having to talk to Tallie, and he thought she was probably tired enough that she would be long asleep when the shift changed.

For the next three days, Jeb avoided Tallie, talking to her only when it was necessary. Surprisingly, she had no difficulty getting the meals ready, and with Ken's help they selected good spots for the nightly forage.

Jeb had mixed emotions about having her along on the trail drive. On the one hand, he was sure that she was looking at it as a lark, something that she might find entertaining, a good story she could tell when she returned to England. But being the cook on a trail drive was a serious job, and so far she was taking the job seriously. The cowboys were genuinely enjoying her company, always displaying their best manners, never cursing and roughhousing around the way it would be on a normal cattle drive.

On the other hand, taking her along with him meant that he would be in contact with her for at least twenty days, twenty days that she would not see Kinsky. Though she would be with the chuck wagon and he would be riding with the herd, he would see her at least twice every day, at breakfast and again at supper after they made camp for the night. He found that a pleasant prospect, even though he had carefully avoided any private conversation with her.

As he rode, he thought about the night before the drive started. What he had done, or was about to do, to another man's wife had been unconscionable. But looking back on it, she certainly wasn't putting up much resistance. What kind of marriage did she have? If she were Jeb's wife, he would see to it that he slept beside her every night. Hell, maybe having her on this cattle drive was good. She could get used to being a cattleman's wife.

Jeb shook his head, trying to physically force such thoughts from his mind.

He remembered meeting Lord Henry Arthur George Somerset, the third son of the 8th Duke of Beaufort. His title made him sound important, but Arthur was a most unimpressive man. And apparently he was indifferent to Tallie. What was it Arthur had said about Tallie? Oh, yes, Jeb remembered it now. *I want to grant my best wishes to her handsome paramour.*

Tallie deserved more than that. She deserved someone who could love her and be true to her. If only he had met her before she was married.

Then he remembered something that, at the time, he didn't think was significant. The night of the party, Moreton introduced Clara, then Lady Randolph Churchill, but when he introduced Tallie, he called her Lady *Tallas* Somerset. Why wasn't her title Lady *Arthur* Somerset? That was how she had been introduced to him when he had first met her in England. Did Moreton know something he didn't know?

One evening Jeb was standing off to one side, drinking coffee and watching as the men were going through the chow line. Tallie was dishing up the food to them, smiling and speaking to every one, and the men were reacting well to her presence.

Corliss came over to speak to Jeb. "You know, don't you, Mr. Tuhill, that I'm the most experienced cowboy you've got on this drive? I was trailin' cattle afore most of these boys was even born."

"I know, and the other hands speak well of you."

"Yes, sir, well, what I'm tryin' to do is make a point here."

"All right. What's your point?"

"Somebody with my experience has no business bein' a cook's helper."

"Well, Mr. Corliss, I didn't—"

"Hold on now, hear me out," Corliss said, holding up his hand. "Like I say, somebody with my experience has no business bein' a cook's helper. But this is different. Mr. Frewen his ownself asked me to come along and keep a lookout for Miss Tallie. And that's just what I'm adoin'. And look at the men. You ever seen a better-natured bunch of men in your life? It ain't only the food, it's somethin' else. It's, well, sir, I don't rightly know how to explain it, but it's just havin' someone like Miss Tallie around. And it ain't just 'cause she's a pretty woman, though she is. I can't hardly explain it."

"You don't have to explain it, Mr. Corliss. I know exactly what you're talking about. And I want you to know how much I appreciate what you're doing. She's sort of . . . special."

"Yes, sir, she is."

"No, I mean she's special to me."

Corliss smiled. "Yes, sir, I kinda thought that. I mean, seein' as how she's always alookin' at you."

Tallie was well at home around horses, and though she would rather be riding a horse than driving a wagon, she wasn't intimidated by the task. After breakfast, she hitched up her own team every morning, then started out. It was not a quiet move because hanging pots and pans tended to bang and clang as the wagon was under way.

Jeb watched the two wagons drive off. He was

glad Ken Corliss had agreed to take over as driver of the hoodlum wagon. He knew Corliss would look out for her.

Their route would take them north alongside the Powder River, which was said to be a mile wide and an inch deep, until they found the best place to ford. The river wasn't a mile wide except when in freshet, but fording the river was dangerous in some areas. The river was spotted with quicksand, and it was deceptive, but Corliss got the two wagons safely across.

After crossing the Powder they would move overland to the Tongue River, whose water was less alkaline. When they reached the Tongue, they would turn north, keeping the Tongue to their left, following it all the way to Miles City, Montana.

That evening, before the herd was even in sight, Corliss helped Tallie select a good camping spot and get her wagon set up and her fire going.

"Moreton said you are very experienced. I suppose you've been a cook's helper many times before?"

"No, ma'am, I ain't never been a cook's helper before," Corliss said. "That's a job you give somebody who's maybe on his first drive."

"Then, I don't understand. Why are you doing it now?"

"Because Mr. Frewen asked me to. And because Jeb sets a big store by you."

"A big store? I don't think I know what that means."

"Why, it means he likes you, ma'am. He likes you a heap, he told me so his ownself."

His words thrilled her, but Tallie didn't know exactly how to respond. "Well, I appreciate that, Mr. Corliss. And should anyone inquire, I will say that you have done a marvelous job of looking out for me."

"Thank you, ma'am. I intend to do my best."

The first pink fingers of dawn stretched out over the range, and the light was soft and the air was cool. The herd had been on the trail now for well over a week, and to Jeb's amazement, and he had to admit his admiration, Tallie had worked out fine. She had got every breakfast out on time, then had moved the chuck wagon ahead to find a place for supper and the night's encampment. So far there had been no problems on the trail, so the drive had been easy.

The last morning star made a bright pinpoint of light over the purple mountains that lay in a ragged line to the west. The coals from the campfire of the night before were still glowing, and Jeb threw a few chunks of wood onto them, then stirred the fire into crackling flames.

A rustle of wind through feathers caused him to look up just in time to see a golden eagle diving on its prey. The eagle swooped back into the air carrying a tiny field mouse, which kicked fearfully in the eagle's claws. A rabbit bounded quickly into its hole, frightened by the sudden appearance of the eagle.

Jeb walked over to the chuck wagon, where Tallie, wearing men's trousers and a shirt, was scrambling eggs. This would be her eighth breakfast, and she had tried to vary the things she served. Ken had done a good job bartering for eggs along the way, trading with the few settlers who were homesteading along the Tongue. They seemed to be happy with the pilot bread Jeb had loaded up on when he thought there would be no cook.

Two coffeepots sat on a grate over a fire, and Jeb started to reach for one.

"Just a moment there, sir," Tallie called out. "I don't believe I heard you ask for a cup of coffee. And according to Mr. Corliss, nobody can come up and just poor himself a cup without first securing permission from the cook, not even the trail boss."

Jeb chuckled. "You're taking this cooking job pretty seriously, aren't you?"

"Would you want me to take it any other way?"

"No, you've got me there."

"I know you've had your spies out watching me. I'd like to know. What's the general consensus?"

"You're doing all right."

"All right? Just all right?"

"Just all right. The men say they'd sure like it if you made biscuits, but they won't ask you."

"Biscuits? These men want sweets out here? I'm not sure how I would bake them. . . . " She began rummaging through her utensils, looking for a suitable pan. "Wait a minute, we're not talking about the same thing, are we? You're not talking about cookies, are you?"

"No, I'm talking about biscuits. Little rolls of dough that you put in a Dutch oven and bury in the coals of a fire until they cook. It takes about fifteen minutes."

"I don't think I can make biscuits. That's not

something Mrs. Ferguson ever made, so I don't know how to do it."

"I'll show you how."

"You can cook?"

"You'd be surprised what I can do." Jeb raised his eyebrows.

Tallie was thinking of a witty retort, but because this was the first conversation they had had since the night of the party, she kept her tongue.

"I'm talking about what I can cook," he said. "It's too late for breakfast, but I'll help you make some for supper."

"All right. And for being so nice to me, you may have a cup of coffee."

"Well, I thank you." Jeb smiled and poured himself a cup and sat down to enjoy it. It was black and steaming, and he had to blow on it before he could suck it through his lips. He watched the sun come full disk above the horizon, then stream brightly down onto the open rangeland.

Will Tate had taken a ride around the herd, and Jeb heard his horse coming back in.

"I'll tell you, that coffee smells awful good," Will said, swinging down from his saddle and walking toward the fire, rubbing his hands together in eager anticipation.

"You'd better ask the cook if you can have a cup," Jeb said. "She's pretty mean with it."

"Of course you may have a cup, Mr. Tate. Unlike someone I know"—she glanced over at Jeb—"you didn't sleep in this morning. Some of us have been up and working."

"Speaking of up and working, it's time to get the

others up." Jeb looked out at the dozen lumps that were actually bedrolls occupied by sleeping men.

"No, let me do it," Will said.

"Go ahead. Just remember, keep it clean. We've got a lady in our midst," Jeb said, shaking his head.

Will crept over quietly until he was exactly in the middle of the sleeping men. He stood there for a moment, listening to their soft snoring as he smiled in anticipation. Then he yelled, at the top of his voice, "All right, you men, off your tails and on your feet! Out of those sacks and into the heat! Up and at 'em, boys, we're burnin' sunlight!"

Will's shout woke the men up, some of them jerking up quickly in their bedrolls, others grumbling and complaining.

One of the men groaned, "Damn, you, Will, from the way you were carrying on, I thought the cattle were stampeding."

"No, no, nothing like that, boys. But our cook's been up for a long time making breakfast, and she deserves to serve it hot."

Jeb leaned back against the hoodlum wagon watching as the men passed through the line to get their breakfast. Tallie dished up their tin plates with a smile and cheery conversation, and he knew she was doing more than just cooking for the men. Her very presence seemed to lift everyone's spirits.

"Hello, Tommy," she said to one of the younger cowboys. "I hear you lost your good-luck piece."

"Yes, ma'am, I did. And I've looked all over for it."

"I know a place you haven't looked."

"Where's that?"

"Here." Tallie reached back into the wagon to produce a rabbit's foot.

"Yes! That's it!" Tommy said excitedly. "Where'd you find it?"

"You must have laid it down on the back of the chuck box. Mr. Corliss found it when he was cleaning up last night, and I knew it was yours."

"Thank you, Miss Tallie. Thanks a lot." Tommy beamed happily as he stuffed the rabbit's foot into his pants pocket. "You may not know it, but this lucky rabbit's foot's got me through some terrible scrapes, and I sure hated to lose it."

Jeb couldn't help but pause as he walked away. How different was his perception of Tallie now, out on the open range with a dozen cowboys and three thousand head of cattle, than it had been when he had first met her, or even at Moreton's wedding reception. There, she had interacted with the highest society, matching the best of them in grace and decorum. Yet here, now, she was equally at home with the most common of the cowboys. It was enough to make a man scratch his head in puzzlement.

Moreton was sitting at his desk in his office when Carl Kinsky came in. "I say, Moreton, five very disreputable-looking men have ridden up, asking for you."

"Oh? Did they state their business?"

"No, they just asked for you."

"Well, I'd better see what they want."

Moreton walked out onto the stoop, and as Kinsky had reported, there were five men on horseback. They were rough-looking with dirty clothes and unshaven faces. All were wearing pistols, and the saddle sheaths of each sprouted a rifle.

"Moreton Frewen?" one of the men asked, spitting chewing tobacco in a long stream.

"I am."

"Jake Slater." The man held out a hand that looked as if it had not seen soap in a week. "At your service."

Moreton did not take the man's hand and even took a step back. "Sir, at my service? I think not."

"Are you a part of the Powder River outfit?"

"The 76 outfit? Yes, I would say I'm a part of the Powder River."

"That's not what I mean, Frewen. The Cattlemen's Association. Me 'n' the boys here are your new employees."

"What are you supposed to do? I have all the hands I need right now."

"That's not what some of the other cattlemen are sayin'. They's athinkin' they've got a problem that we can sorta take care of."

"You're talking about the squatters."

"And the rustlers."

"What directions have some of the other cattlemen given you men?"

"Directions? They don't tell us what to do. We just—what's the fancy word one of 'em used?— *eradicate*, that's it. We're supposed to eradicate the problem."

"And just how do you plan to do that?" Moreton said.

"Maybe we'll just have some sucker climb a ladder with a rope round his neck, and we can't help it none iffen the ladder falls over and the rope don't break, now can we?"

Moreton blanched. "Oh, gracious no! I'm sure that's not what the Association had in mind."

"Well, you rest easy. Remember the name. Slater. Ol' Jake'll do you right."

Slater touched the brim of his hat, then turned his horse as he and the others rode away.

"For heaven's sake, Moreton, what are you getting yourself into?" Kinsky asked once he was sure the riders were out of earshot.

"I don't know. But I suppose if the action of these men was approved by the Cattlemen's Association, it will all be aboveboard."

"You are a very trusting man, Moreton."

After breakfast and cleanup, Tallie drove the wagon to the place where the herd would spend the night. She couldn't recall when she had been so tired, a bone-aching, backbreaking tired. Yet transcending the tiredness was an exhilaration that came from the excitement of the drive and from meeting the challenge. She knew that Jeb had not believed she could do this, and she was enjoying his reaction to her success.

The yellow glare of the sun-filled sky mellowed into the steel blue of late afternoon by the time Tallie reached the place where the herd would be halted for the night. To the west, the sun dropped all the way to the foothills. Behind the setting sun, great bands of color spread out along the horizon. Those few clouds that dared to intrude on this perfect day were underlit by the sun and glowed orange in the darkening sky.

She had just got the chuck wagon set up and her cooking fire going when she heard someone approaching. Corliss was out hunting and that left her alone, so she was a bit apprehensive about who it might be. Jeb had put a shotgun in the wagon, telling her that if she ever actually needed a weapon, the shotgun would be best.

"You don't have to be a good shot to use it," Jeb had pointed out. "And I don't think there's a man alive who won't quake in his boots if he's looking down the business end of a twelve-gauge shotgun barrel."

Tallie eased over to the wagon, remembering that Jeb had also told her never to point a gun at anyone unless she was willing to use it. *God in heaven,* she prayed, *don't let me have to* . . . Suddenly a big smile spread across her face as she saw that it was Jeb.

"Jeb! Am I relieved to see you!"

"Is something wrong?"

"I—uh—no, I just didn't know who it was, and I didn't expect you to come riding up before the herd got here."

"I told you this morning I was going to teach you to make biscuits, didn't I?"

Tallie laughed. "Yes, you did. I'd nearly forgotten."

"Well, let's get busy. We'll need them rolled out and baked so we can surprise the men tonight. What are you fixing to go with them?"

"I told Mr. Corliss, and he said stew would be better than beans, so he's out trying to get a jackalope for me. He said they're only found right here in Wyoming."

Jeb laughed. "Don't believe everything Mr. Corliss tells you. I think the meat he brings in will be a lot like plain old, everyday rabbit, but he's right. It will make a good stew to have with our biscuits."

Jeb showed Tallie the proportions she would need of flour, lard, salt, and water. When the dough was all mixed, he showed her how to roll it out. Then he handed her an empty can.

"What's this for?"

"It's a biscuit cutter. Use it to make as many rounds as you can."

Tallie cut out thirty-six rounds. "You think that's enough?"

"There are sixteen of us now, counting Corliss and you. Yes, I'm sure that's enough."

"Now what?"

"Put 'em in the Dutch oven, and nestle them down in the fire. They'll bake."

For supper that evening, Tallie served a savory rabbit stew along with the biscuits. These were the first biscuits the men had eaten since leaving on the trail drive, and they were obviously pleased.

"Don't get me none wrong, Miss Tallie," one of the men said. "I mean the truth is, the food you been acookin' is better 'n anythin' I've ever et out on the trail. But I was beginnin' to get me a hankerin' for some biscuits. And these you made tonight is as good as you'll find anywhere."

"I'd like to take credit for them, but I can't. Jeb made them."

"Whooee, Jeb. I never know'd you could make biscuits like that. If you was a purty woman, I'd marry you. Hell, you wouldn't even have to be purty, long as you can make biscuits like that."

A few of the others laughed and made jokes about Jeb making the biscuits, but they knew better than to push it too far. By the time supper was over, every ounce of the stew, and every biscuit, had been eaten. It was a well-fed and happy cowboy outfit that turned in that night.

SEVENTEEN

Tallie didn't know why she couldn't go to sleep. She certainly was tired enough, but no matter how many times she turned and repositioned herself, sleep continued to elude her. She sat up and looked out the back of the wagon at the sleeping men. She could hear snores from some of them, so she knew they were sleeping well.

Was it before midnight, or after? With sleep still unattainable, Tallie lit a lantern, took out her red notebook, and wrote more of her story.

The Lady and the Cowboy—Nora Ingram

John Tuttle's sister, Betsy, was a strong woman with a pleasant, though not beautiful, face, and quiet, observant eyes. The meal she served was simple fare delivered to the table not by serving girl or valet, but by the woman herself, and she offered no apology for the lack of servants.

Lady Anne found the simplicity to her liking,

for indeed she had had a surfeit of obsequious admiration, was tired of adulation, and was glad to see that John's sister very likely treated her as she would have treated any other visitor. She was sweet and kind; and what Lady Anne's Society friends might mistake as a dull lack of expression or vitality on Betsy's part, Lady Anne knew was naught but the refreshing quality of a woman who did not live a shallow life.

Could Lady Anne be happy living such a reserved life, far from London and the season, devoid of the company of titled lords and ladies? The answer was yes . . . with John Tuttle she could be very happy, for he had shown her what true love could be. Ah, but the sorrow of it all was that John was unaware of this secret love Lady Anne had for him. He did not know that he had but to ask for the lady's love and she would willingly give it.

Neither title nor social standing nor plays nor musicals nor ballets could compete with the love she felt in her heart for her magnificent cowboy. If only she could find the courage to tell him.

Putting down her pencil and closing her notebook with a sigh, Tallie felt herself still too much awake to be able to sleep, so she decided to take a walk. Within a moment she was completely away from the camp, swallowed up by the blue velvet of night in a soft, warm breeze that caressed her skin like fine silk. Overhead the moon was a brilliant white orb, and the stars glistened like diamonds.

Tallie walked down to the edge of the river, passing through the riparian vegetation that in places stood taller than she was. The surface of the water shone silver in the moonlight.

Dare she?

Why not? After all, the entire camp was asleep, except for the nighthawk, and he was out keeping an eye on the cattle. Tallie yielded to the appeal of the river. She walked down to the edge, then in her bare feet stepped into it.

Unknown to Tallie, Jeb was also awake and, having seen her walk away from the camp, had followed her.

He watched as she stepped into the water, her body partially hidden by the shrubs. She walked along the bank, stepping carefully among the rocks until she reached a deeper pool of water. When she stepped into the deeper water, she lost her balance and fell back.

Jeb started to go to her to see if she was hurt, but as he peered through the bushes, what he saw next held him back. She sat in the water and began to unbutton the shirt she had been wearing. Taking it off, she hung it on a branch. Then, cupping her hand, she began splashing the cool water onto her upper body as Jeb watched with fascination. She lay back in the water, which was barely a foot deep, keeping only her face protruding above the water. Arching her chin, she let the water flow through her hair.

As Jeb watched her in the spread of silver moonlight on the water's surface, he felt like Odysseus being lured by the sirens. He found an opening along the bank and walked quietly toward the water's edge, not wanting to frighten Tallie. When she became aware of his presence, she sat up.

"The water . . . " She stopped as she watched Jeb remove his trousers, leaving on his drawers.

"Do you mind if I join you?" He moved into the water, not waiting for an answer. He took her hand and helped her to her feet, then stepped out into the current of the river, being careful to stop before the water was above her waist.

There he turned to face her, and pulling her to him, he lowered his lips to hers and kissed her deeply as the cool water swirled around their bodies.

Tallie wound her arms around Jeb's neck and pressed herself closer to his body, letting her breasts, still covered with the thin cloth of her camisole, rest against the hard muscles of his chest. The swiftly moving water forced her lower body into contact with his burgeoning arousal, as her thighs pressed into his powerful legs. The only communication between them was of desire. He kissed her again and again, first in light, playful kisses, but she knew the instant the kiss filled with passion. His hardened lips sought hers with a hunger that caused Tallie to buckle from the current of the water, or from the current of her emotions—she couldn't tell. When he withdrew from the kiss, her lips were burning with desire, and Tallie initiated a reckless and demanding kiss. Neither Tallie nor Jeb spoke a word as they sought to satisfy each other's hunger for one another.

Jeb lifted Tallie off her feet and she wrapped her

legs around his body, his hardened arousal teasing her as he swayed back and forth in the water, at first gently and then with a rhythm that was as old as mankind. Abruptly, the movement stopped, and he lowered her to the riverbed as his head rested on her shoulder, his ragged breathing and his rapid heartbeat slowing.

She heard the agony in his muffled words: "I am so sorry, Tallie. I am so sorry."

She took his face in her hands, wishing there was more than moonlight to light his face. She kissed him with quivering lips, showing a tenderness that she had never before felt.

"Don't be sorry. This has been an incredible night. I only wish it didn't have to stop."

He kissed her lightly. "But it does have to stop. Come, let's go back to the camp." He held her hand as together they moved toward the bank of the river, where Jeb retrieved her shirt from the bushes. He put it around her and began to button it up, then boldly Tallie reached for Jeb's penis. He stilled her hand as he began to grow.

"I can't believe I'm saying this, because I want you more than I have ever wanted any woman in my life, but I will not make love to you. Not here, not ever."

"Why?" Tallie asked in a bare whisper.

Jeb kissed her on her nose. "Because"—he kissed her again—"you are another man's wife, and if I was your husband and a man did to you what I just did, I would kill him."

Tallie took a deep breath. This was the time. Now. "I don't have a husband."

Jeb pulled back from Tallie abruptly. "What did you say?"

"I'm not married."

"I don't understand. What happened to Arthur?"

"At my father-in-law's request, I divorced him. We are no longer married."

Jeb looked quizzical, then broke out in a wide smile. "Well, that changes everything." He kissed her deeply as he began to caress first her back and then her bottom, pulling her closer to him. Then he moved them to his own pile of clothing and lowered her to the ground. He moved over her, his engorged manhood once more erect as she entwined her legs around him, lifting her buttocks as he fumbled with the buttons of her wet drawers.

Then they heard in the distance the nickering of a horse as the nighthawks changed guard.

Jeb put his finger to Tallie's mouth as he raised himself to listen. All was well, but it brought Jeb back to his senses. This was not the place or the time to make love to Tallie. She deserved more than a rough tumble on the ground.

Jeb wrapped her in his arms. "We need to go back."

"I know," Tallie said with a long sigh. She felt sad that their time together was ending, but she accepted that Jeb was right.

"The next time we do this, I promise there will be no interruptions. It will be just you and me."

As Tallie and Jeb hurried back to the camp, they were unaware that Ken Corliss was sleeping under the hoodlum wagon. Their footsteps awakened him, and he rose to investigate who was approaching the camp. When he saw Jeb embrace Tallie before she entered the chuck wagon, a smile crossed Ken's face.

"Well, well, now that's interesting," he said so quietly that no one could hear.

Exhilarated by the cool water she had left, but equally so from the new turn in her relationship with Jeb, Tallie lay on her mattress tossing and turning. Sleep would still not come. She jumped up, tearing a page from her notebook, and began to write.

Dear Aunt Emma,

I can't begin to tell you the joy I am feeling. Tonight for the first time I had the courage to tell Jeb (the American whom I met at Badminton) that I am no longer married. I was worried as to how he would take it, but he said he was glad I was no longer married. You have been telling me that the truth would set me free. Why oh why have I not listened to you? Aunt Emma, I think that this man could be the one for me, the one who can make me as happy as Uncle Charles has made you. (Even though he does not play backgammon.)

In my excitement, I almost forgot to tell you what I am doing. I am a cook for Jeb's cattle drive. We are taking cows to a place called Montana. At first he was not happy that I insisted upon coming, but now I think he respects me for doing the job much better than he ever expected I could. And to be honest, I sort of surprised myself!

Tell Louisa she would be proud of me. One night I made a version of her plum heavies, but I had to use dried fruit. They weren't as good as hers, but nobody complained.

I hope you can tell that I am happy. I do miss you and Uncle Charles, but I do not miss, not for one scintilla of a second, the life that I wrote about in The Prince's Folly. *The other day while I was waiting for the men to come in, I reread the book. It's as if that life happened to another person.*

I don't know when I will be back in England. My friend Jennie is visiting her sister right now, and she tells me that the controversy surrounding the book has died down somewhat. She also tells me that the sales are going strong and she insists that I am a wealthy woman. It makes no difference.

I have learned so much about myself, something that you and Uncle Charles figured out long ago. Contentment is perhaps the greatest gift a person can receive. And right now, at this precise moment, I am content with what the future holds. (Of course happiness, and, dare I hope for it, love, are important, too.)

It is with much gratitude to you and Uncle Charles for the long-standing example of a loving relationship that I observed that I

*close this letter. Please give my best to every-
one.*
    With everlasting affection,
    Tallie

When she finished her letter, she folded it and
set it aside. Writing the letter seemed to release the
tension. She thumbed through her red notebook
and thought the Darwins would enjoy her story.
She added a happy ending just for Uncle Charles.
She would send this to them with her letter. This
time when she put her head on her pillow, she was
asleep instantly.

The next morning, for the first time, Tallie did not
awaken in time to fix breakfast, but Ken took up the
slack. He built the fire and had the coffee brewing
when Jeb entered the camp, his hair more tousled
than usual.

"Mornin', boss," Ken said.

"Where's the cook?"

"She's sleepin'. I saw her lantern lit way into the
night."

"You were awake?"

"I was."

Jeb gave Corliss a quick glance.

"Look, Jeb, you may be the boss of this here outfit, but I kinda like that little girl in there, and what
I'm about to say may be out o' line. But I'm gonna
say it anyways. I was hired to take care of Tallie,
and no matter what happens, I'm gonna do that."

Jeb lowered his head for a few moments, then
looked directly at Corliss. "Thanks, Ken."

"Now you go wake 'er up. She'll be mad as a wet hen if I take over her job."

Jeb walked toward the chuck wagon, stepping on the tongue and then parting the canvas flaps. What he saw made his chest swell. There she lay, her hair spread out around her, her lips pink and full inviting him to kiss them, but what took his breath away was her body. She lay naked before him, her breasts flattened, the pink nipples seeming to be hard even in sleep. His gaze traced her length, falling upon the reddish triangle of hair that formed at the V of her legs. He seared this picture in his mind, then closed the flap of the wagon and stepped off the tongue. With much noise and commotion he climbed the tongue again, yelling, "Sleepyhead, where's my cook?"

In just a moment, Tallie stuck her head out of the opening in the flaps. "Jeb, I'm sorry, I must have overslept."

He smiled broadly at her. "It's all right. Your partner took up the slack."

The herd reached Miles City ahead of schedule, and Jeb and the men put the cattle into the newly built corrals. The Northern Pacific Railroad had just been completed to this point, and the whole town was buzzing with activity. The cattle from the 76 outfit would be on the first train out, bound for the meatpacking markets of St. Paul.

Jeb had a lot of business to handle. Once he had completed the transfer of the cattle to the agent for the meatpacking company, he picked up the bank draft for the Great Western Cattle Company, the official name of the 76. He had cash in hand to pay the cowhands, so he rode back to the camp to meet the payroll.

"Men, we'll stay here two nights, so you all will get your chance in town, but decide among yourselves who stays in camp the first night. I know you all know Miles City and are familiar with its—let's say attractions and pitfalls. That's all I'm going to say, but if you find yourself in jail, unless you have a very good reason, consider yourself a resident of Montana. Do I make myself clear?"

"Yes, sir," they all said in unison, much as a troop of soldiers might address an officer.

"One more thing. I don't have to tell you this, but the soldiers from Fort Keogh hate cowboys. I would strongly advise you to stay away from them."

All the men lined up for their pay and headed to the river to clean up.

"And now there's pay for my cook," Jeb said, a big smile forming on his face as he handed Tallie $40. As she looked up at him, tears gathered in her eyes, and one escaped and rolled down her cheek. With his thumb, he wiped it away. "Ah, now it wasn't that bad, was it?"

"No, Jeb. It's wonderful. This money is the first I've ever had that has given me a real sense of satisfaction."

"You earned every penny, and you did a bang-up job of it. Why, old Tim Middleton may never get his job back—that is, if you decide to stay on."

"Well, that depends on whether I get to go to Miles City or not."

"Do you want to go?"

"I do—that is, if they have a post office and a store. I want to buy a dress and mail a package."

"Of course you do." Jeb laughed. "And here I thought you were a regular cowhand."

Tallie and Jeb rode into town with the other cowboys, who did much whooping and hollering along the way. She was wearing the outfit she had worn for the whole drive: work pants, a plaid shirt, and a Stetson. She had worn her hair in a topknot for much of the trip to keep it off her neck, and from the street she looked no different from any of the cowboys she was riding with.

Miles City had only two regular streets—Park Street, which ran alongside a little grove of cottonwoods, and Main Street. Main Street was just that. It looked as if it had been purposely divided into a "decent" side and a "bad" side. The bad side was filled with saloons and brothels. The decent side consisted of banks, a couple of lawyers' offices, a barbershop, some retail stores, and a hotel.

As they rode by one of the saloons, several soldiers were standing out front. One of the soldiers called out to them, "If you boys is comin' into town lookin' for whores, you're out of luck. We done got 'em all plumb wore out from bein' with real men, 'stead of a bunch of no-'count, small-peckered, bowlegged cowboy sons of bitches."

One of the cowboys looked over at the soldiers as if to respond to this challenge, but Will Tate cautioned him, "Let it be, Johnny. You heard what the boss said 'bout gettin' into a ruckus with the soldiers."

"Don't you fellas listen to them soldier boys," a woman's voice called. "Me an' the rest of the girls will show you a fine time."

The woman who called out was on a second-floor balcony, two buildings down from the saloon. She and another woman were leaning over the railing, looking down onto the street. Both women were wearing dresses cut so low that it looked as if their breasts were about to spill out. Tallie looked up at them in curiosity and shock at seeing women dressed in such fashion.

"You, honey," the woman called down to Tallie. "You're a cute one. I'll bet you ain't never even been with a woman before, have you?"

The other cowboys laughed, and blushing, Tallie looked down.

"Oh, my, Pearlie, what do you think? We've got us a shy young pup here. Tell you what, honey, you come on up here and me an' Pearlie will break you in proper, an' it won't cost you nothin'."

"Hey, boy, what's wrong with you?" one of the soldiers called out to Tallie. They're offerin' it to you free, and you ain't goin' to take 'em up on it?"

Will rode up alongside Tallie, putting his horse between her and the soldier who had called out. "Don't pay 'em no never mind, Miss Tallie," Will said quietly.

Jeb couldn't keep a straight face. It was amazing to watch how the cowboys had taken to Tallie and were now trying their best to protect her. They rode on a little farther, then Jeb asked, "Do you want to spend the night at the hotel, or do you want to go back to the camp?"

"Where will the men stay?" Tallie asked, and there was a polite titter of laughter.

"It's hard to say, Tallie. We'll not ask them," Jeb said.

"Well, I should ask, where will you stay?"

With that the men could not contain themselves, and the laughter rolled out of the cowboys easily.

"That's enough, boys," Jeb said, shaking his head good-naturedly. "Let's get you a dress, and then we'll talk about it."

In small groups the cowboys peeled off to one saloon or another until only Jeb and Tallie remained. They stopped in front of the mercantile store.

"I think this may be the best place to find you a dress. Why don't you take your hat off before we walk in." Jeb chuckled. "Otherwise they might not take you seriously."

Smiling, Tallie took off her hat, and they walked in. A tinkling bell on the door summoned a kindly looking grandmotherly woman. She smiled at them. "Welcome to Miles City. Are you railroad people?"

"In a way," Jeb said. "We brought a herd up from Wyoming and we're shipping them out on the first train to St. Paul."

"The 76 outfit?"

"That's right, but how did you know?" Tallie asked.

"Honey, in the West everybody is somebody's neighbor, and we all know everything about one another. With that accent, are you kin to the Frewens?"

"No, but they're my friends."

"Well, you can be thankful you're not related. How can I help you?"

"This is my cook"—Jeb draped his arm around Tallie—"and she wants to buy a dress. Can you fix her up?"

"That I can do. You just leave us women alone, and I'll make her the prettiest little thing in Miles City."

Jeb looked at Tallie. "I think she already is."

"Well now, isn't that a sweet thing for you to say to your girl?"

"Tallie, there's a restaurant in the hotel. When you finish up here, find your way there and I'll meet you."

Jeb stepped out onto the crowded street and made his way to the Cottage Saloon, directly across from the mercantile store. A big, burly man who said his name was Charlie Brown called to him when he entered, "Just help yourself."

"To what?"

"You must be new here. Everybody knows I give every cowpuncher that darkens my door their fill of stew. It's in the back."

"Well, that's mighty nice of you, but right now I think the only thing I need is a drink."

"I can fix that up, too," Charlie said. "What will it be?"

"Beer's fine."

When Jeb got the beer, he took it to a table, but before he had his first swallow, a big-busted woman came over and pulled out a chair.

"Do you mind, cowboy?"

"Have a seat. Charlie, send over a beer for the lady."

"It's Lily. Lily Davis. Where do you hang your spurs?"

"Down in Powder River country."

"Don't tell me you're part of that bastard outfit, the 76?"

"What's wrong with that outfit?"

"If you're on the Powder, you know. Those damn Englishmen think they own the world. They come over here with all their blue-blooded friends looking down their noses at anybody who's not a sir or a lord or a duke or some such title. They run around all over the Territory on their grand hunts killing any animal that walks and then take their trophy heads and leave the meat to rot. In the meantime, the little guys are starving and the Indians are being shipped off to reservations. You tell me about the Powder River."

"Well, Lily, I think you've told me, probably more than I want to know." Jeb drained his drink and stood. "Have a pleasant evening, ma'am."

That was enough. He would not allow Tallie to spend the night in Miles City. They would ride out to camp tonight.

When Jeb stepped into the dining room of the hotel, he looked around for Tallie, but he didn't see her immediately. Then he noticed a table in the corner with two men and a woman, the woman with her back to him, and another man standing over the table.

The woman was Tallie, and for an instant he felt a twinge of anger. What was she doing talking to men she didn't know? He had just left a woman who talked to strange men, and he knew what she was.

But this was Tallie.

He took a deep breath and approached the table.

One of the gentlemen stood and offered his hand. "Mr. Tuhill, I suspect."

Jeb was surprised to be addressed by name.

"Oh, Jeb, I've been entertained by these gentlemen until you arrived. This is Mr. Billings, who is a neighbor to Mr. Jerome, back in New York. And this is the Marquis de Mores, who is from France, and this gentleman"—she indicated the man who was standing—"is Mr. Huffman, who is a photographer. He's been trying to talk me into having my likeness taken with these gentlemen, but I told him I would only sit if you agreed to sit with me."

"Billings? Frederick Billings?" Jeb asked.

"He's with the railroad," Tallie said.

"With it? He's one of the original stockholders." Jeb shook his hand. "Mr. Billings, it's my pleasure to be among the first shippers of livestock out of Miles City, on your railroad."

"Wonderful. When the young lady mentioned she was visiting the 76, I connected that with the markup on the manifest."

"And the marquis is here looking for property somewhere. He wants to start a cattle ranch," Tallie said.

"Do you intend to buy it, or will you be putting your cows on the open range, too?" Jeb asked.

"With Mr. Billings's railroad, the opportunities

are limitless," de Mores said. "I think I am more suited to the Badlands, though, than I am to Montana or Wyoming." He twirled his mustache into a pencil-like roll, causing Jeb to feel an immediate disgust for the man.

"Gentlemen, will you be joining us for our dinner?" Jeb asked, knowing it was the expected thing to say, but hoping the answer would be no.

"Thank you for the invitation, but I have other obligations," Billings said. "My wife, Julia, will be delighted when I tell her that I've had the pleasure of sipping tea with the famous—or perhaps infamous—Nora Ingram." He took Tallie's hand in his and raised it to his lips. "Mr. Tuhill, my pleasure."

"It has been my pleasure likewise, mademoiselle," the marquis said as he departed with Billings.

"Perhaps, with the gentlemen gone, you would permit me to photograph you and your cowboy?" Huffman said.

"Jeb, would you mind?"

"Anything you say," Jeb replied.

"Good. If you will, my studio is in the back of the hotel. Is now a good time?"

"It's as good a time as any," Jeb said.

Tallie and Jeb followed Mr. Huffman into a small studio that was filled with photos. One wall was devoted to various pictures of animals, while another had nothing but pictures of soldiers. The other wall, with the greatest collection, was of Indians, some in ceremonial dress, but most were of Indians doing ordinary things.

Mr. Huffman posed Tallie and Jeb using various props: a buffalo skull, an Indian blanket, a saddle, a rope.

When he had them just the way he wanted, he placed his head under a small covering behind the camera, then reached around to remove the lens cap.

"One . . . two . . . three," he said, then the phosphorous powder ignited. "That's going to be a wonderful addition to my collection. Shall I make a copy for you?"

"Yes, and could you send an additional copy to Smith, Elder and Company, number fifteen Waterloo Place, London, England?" Tallie asked.

A broad smile came over Mr. Huffman's face. "Oh, my, is there a possibility that one of L. A. Huffman's photographs could wind up in one of your books, Miss Ingram?"

Tallie smiled. "Perhaps."

"I'll look forward to it. Good evening, Mr. Tuhill, Miss Ingram."

Jeb escorted Tallie back to the hotel restaurant, which was now beginning to fill with patrons. Not until they had sat at a table in the back did Jeb ask the question that had been hanging between them for the last hour.

"All right. What's all this about Miss Ingram?"

"You didn't say anything about my dress. Do you like it?"

"It's very becoming. You look good in gingham."

"How did you know that's what these little checks are called?"

"I just know. Quit stalling. What secret are you hiding from me now?"

Tallie took a deep breath. "Are we going to stay at this hotel tonight, or are we going back to camp?"

"What possible difference can that make?"

Tallie looked directly at Jeb, not moving a single muscle.

"I think it's best that we go back to camp, but not because of anything that just happened," Jeb said.

"Good. I will introduce you to Miss Ingram before you go to sleep tonight, but right now I'm anxious to eat a meal that I didn't have to cook."

EIGHTEEN

When Jeb and Tallie finished their meal, Tallie returned to the mercantile to pick up the bundle containing her trail clothes.

"Shall I change clothes before we start back?" Tallie asked.

"No, I sort of like the ranch-woman dress you're wearing."

"I'm going to take that as a compliment."

"And you should, but haven't I been complimenting you all evening? I've told you how proud I am for what you've accomplished on this trip. When I first met you at Badminton, I would never have expected you to fit in so well out here. And the thing I like most is how you treat everybody—the men, the shopkeepers, even Frederick Billings—you treat them all the same."

Listening to his praise, Tallie beamed. "Well, that's all well and good, Mr. Tuhill, but your kind words don't solve my problem."

"I don't understand, what's your problem?"

"That horse, this dress."

"Oh, no sidesaddle. I think we can take care of that." Jeb grabbed the reins of the horse Tallie had ridden and tied them to his own saddle. "Now you can ride with me."

He helped Tallie onto his horse, positioning her in front of him.

"I'm glad it's only a couple of miles back to camp," Tallie said, "because this could get uncomfortable."

"Not if I hang on to you." Jeb drew her back against him, his arm resting snugly against her waist as they set out.

Jeb was still confused by the Nora Ingram business. Why had she introduced herself as Nora Ingram? And what had Frederick Billings meant when he had called her the famous, or the infamous, Nora Ingram? Jeb's concern about that faded, though, replaced by the stimulation he was getting from the ride. She was leaning back against him—and he was very aware of the way she was sitting, with her body pushed against him, from his chest to his stomach to his groin.

When they got back to camp, several of the cowboys were sitting around playing cards.

"We didn't expect to see you two back this evening," one of the cowboys called out. "Wasn't Miles City exciting enough for you?"

"We came back because we missed you," Tallie said, and all the cowboys gave a cheer as she slid down off Jeb's horse.

"Don't you look purty in that fancy dress," Ken Corliss said. "We're glad you're back."

Jeb propped the wagon tongue up on a flour barrel and offered Tallie a seat. He went over to the fire where a pot of coffee was brewing, poured two cups, and brought one of them back to Tallie, then sat beside her.

"All right," Jeb said. "Who is Nora Ingram?"

"That would be me."

"I don't understand."

"Have you ever heard of Mark Twain?"

"Yes, of course."

"Do you know his real name?"

"It's Samuel Clemens."

"That's right. Mark Twain is his pseudonym. Nora Ingram is my pseudonym."

"Your pseudonym?"

"Yes, I'm a published novelist."

"Well, you're full of surprises. First, I find out you're not married, and now I find out you're an author, and not just any author, but one that someone as refined as—I believe he called her Julia—Billings would be happy to meet. I guess that pretty much puts a cowboy from Texas in his place."

"Jeb, that's not fair. Not two hours ago you were paying me compliments because you said I fit in so well out here, but now you're rebuking me for something you don't know anything about."

"That's right. I don't know anything about the *infamous* Nora Ingram because Lady Somerset never thought it significant enough to tell me. Did you think I wasn't sophisticated enough to handle the books you write?"

Tallie took a deep breath as she searched for a

plausible reason why she had not told Jeb about her writing. "My book—I have actually written two books, but only one has sparked a lot of interest, or perhaps I should say notoriety. When we stopped at Fort Fetterman, if you recall, the major's wife mentioned a book."

"Yes, I do remember there being talk of a book while we were having dinner."

"Mrs. Powell insisted that *The Prince's Folly* was not a book that she would allow her daughter to read. Well, that is my book. Unfortunately, it was not well received in England's high society either, and that's a big part of the reason why I'm here."

"Are you telling me you're in hiding?"

Tallie laughed uncomfortably because on one level that was exactly what she was doing. "I didn't do anything illegal, Jeb. I just stepped on some very influential toes. That's all."

"It must be some book to force you to come to this backwater country."

"Nobody forced me to do anything. I came and I am very glad that I came. Before you pass judgment on me, would you consider reading the book? I have it with me."

"Sure, I'll read it. I've got all night and all day tomorrow to hang around camp with nothing else to do, waiting for the men to get back."

That night Jeb sat by the hoodlum wagon, leaning back against the wheel, as, by lantern light, he started *The Prince's Folly*.

"Whooee, boss, I don't know what you've got there, but it must be some book if you'd rather lay around readin' than stay in town," Rudy Brock said.

"You don't know what's in this book," Jeb said.

"If it ain't one of Bill Cody's, I ain't likely to ever know."

"If it's good, I'll tell you about it." Jeb didn't say that Tallie was the author. He wanted to find out for himself why this book had caused such an uproar that she felt she had to leave England.

> The Duchess lay before the Prince, tame and unresisting, whilst there were raised no other emotions but those of pleasure. Though she be married, and not to the Prince, every part of her was open to the licentious courses of his hands, which traversed her whole body, slipping down lower into that soft, silky down that embellished the seat of the most exquisite sensation.

Jeb read the first paragraph and then closed the book and put it beside him. Did he really want to know what was in this book?

The Duchess lay before the Prince, tame and unresisting, whilst there were raised no other emotions but those of pleasure.

He picked up the lantern and, with the book, walked down to the edge of the river. Just two nights before, Tallie had told him she wasn't married and he had felt overwhelming joy. Now despondency came over him. Had the nighthawk not interrupted them, he would have made love to Tallie right then.

Made love. That was the right phrase. He knew being with Tallie would not be like poking any woman who had ever taken his money. He thought she was special, but here he was starting a book that she had written, and in the first paragraph she wrote about *the licentious courses* of the Prince's hands.

What had she told him in Chicago? *The Prince of Wales is not very happy with me right now.* And then there was her divorce. *At my father-in-law's request, I divorced him.* What right did he have to even dream that she could have any feelings for him? In the river had he *raised no other emotions but those of pleasure*?

What a fool he was. First Katarina and now Tallie.

Picking up the book, he returned to his place by the wagon wheel. He could not read about Tallie's being with another man after he had held her in his arms.

Tallie was unable to sleep that night. Several times she parted the canvas of her wagon to look out at Jeb, who sat unmoving for the entire night. What was he thinking? Did he find her book shocking or titillating or disgusting? Would he want nothing to do with her when he realized what she was capable of thinking, let alone what she would allow to be put in print for anyone to read?

Tallie saw Jeb finish the book and toss it aside. She couldn't tell from her vantage point if he had tossed it in disgust. So she dressed, putting on her trail outfit, and walked over to the hoodlum wagon and sat down in the grass where the book had landed. She picked it up, waiting for Jeb to comment.

"How accurate is that stuff?"

"It's a novel."

"So it's not true."

"No, I'm not saying that. The novel is true, but it's not necessarily factual."

"I don't get the difference."

"For writers there's a big difference between truth and fact. All fact is true, but truth doesn't have to be factual."

"So this"—he searched for the right word—"promiscuity you write about. That doesn't really happen?"

Tallie let out a long sigh. This discussion was going to be harder than she'd thought. "It does happen."

Jeb folded his arm and rested his chin in his hand. After a long moment he asked, "Are you the Duchess?"

Tallie cocked her head, not understanding what he meant.

"In the story. Are you supposed to be the Duchess?"

"No, that character is not based upon me. A writer doesn't have to experience everything she writes about."

"Well, maybe I'm too unsophisticated to figure out what's truth and what's fact, but Miss Ingram did a hell of a job convincing me that she knows what she's talking about." Jeb stood up and started walking away, kicking at clumps of grass as he passed them.

Tallie felt a hollow feeling in the pit of her stomach as she watched Jeb walk away. This damn book had caused her nothing but pain, and the next word in her thoughts was *heartbreak*. If she lost Jeb Tuhill, she would suffer heartbreak. Maybe he didn't know it yet, but she did. Jeb was worth fighting for, and she had no intention of letting him walk away from her thinking she was something that she was not. If she had to seduce him, she would prove that she was not the prototype for the Duchess.

When the first shift of cowboys returned from Miles City, and the second shift rode out, Jeb accompanied them, leaving Tallie in camp. She went down by the river and found a shady spot under a cottonwood. Taking off her shoes, she dangled her feet in the water, thinking of the feelings she had had just a few days ago when she had told Jeb she wasn't married. Right now, she could re-create in her mind his exuberance, his embrace, and his words: *That changes everything.* And then there was her euphoric letter to Aunt Emma. Happiness. True happiness. Was that a feeling she would never know?

"Miss Tallie, is everything all right with you?" Ken Corliss asked as he moved down the bank and sat beside her.

"Oh, Mr. Corliss." Her lip quivered as she spoke.

He patted her hand as it lay beside her. "How old are you?"

"I'm twenty-five."

"A long time ago I had a woman about your age. She ran off with some blowhard that, last I heard, took her to New Orleans. The biggest hurt in my life is that I never went after her. To this day I can see my Rachel. She was a pretty little thing." Corliss reached down and picked up a small rock from the river and turned it over and over. "I once heard a great man tell a bunch of people something that I never forgot. Old A. Lincoln hisself said, 'This, too, shall pass.' Whatever it is that's goin' on right now, take this rock, and put it in your pocket. When you get to feelin' down, take it out and say over and over, 'This, too, shall pass."

"Oh, Mr. Corliss." Tallie hugged him. "Thank you, thank you for your words and thank you for the pebble, but most of all thank you for being my friend."

"That I am, my girl. I got eyes. Ever'thing's gonna be just right."

Tallie grasped the rock in her hand as Corliss stood to leave.

Because she was exhausted, Tallie had no trouble falling asleep, and she was not aware when Jeb and the other men returned to the camp.

The next morning she was awakened early.

"Let's break camp and get out of here," Jeb yelled. "Grab a bedroll and some jerky and you can travel with me, or you can stay with the wagons and get there whenever. But I'm telling you now that we'll be pushing from sunup to sundown. I want to be back at the 76 in three or four days."

"Man, Jeb, are you trying to kill us?" Rudy Brock asked.

"No. You have the choice. Anybody that's riding with me, be ready in half an hour. The rest of you can stay with the wagons. Rudy, you take charge, since I gather you don't want to come with me."

"All right."

A couple of cowboys began scurrying around stowing their excess gear in the hoodlum wagon and putting together a pack that would go with them.

When Jeb had Liberty saddled and his gear packed, he got on his horse. He had not seen Tallie and was glad, because with Rudy in charge it would probably take the wagons a good week or more to get home.

He knew Bill Cody was coming in to guide one of Moreton's hunts the first week of the month, and Jeb decided he would insist that he go, too. He would relish taking a bunch of cullies up in the mountains where the air was clear and he could think. Hell, maybe Lady Somerset would go back with Count Kinsky and Lady Randolph if they hadn't already left. She needed to get back to her Marlborough Set, where he'd never have to see her again.

"Are we ready?" Jeb asked, looking around to see how many were going with him. He was shocked to see that Tallie was selecting a horse from the remuda. "You! What are you doing?"

"I'm riding back with you."

"Your job is to stay with the chuck wagon."

"I believe my job is over and I was paid forty dollars to prove it," Tallie said defiantly.

"You can't make this trip."

"I can."

"Well, I don't intend to wait around for you!" Jeb took off with Liberty at a gallop, and a couple of cowboys followed.

"Are you sure you want to do this, Tallie?" Ken Corliss asked.

"No horse can keep that up. We'll catch up. Besides, I've got my rock."

Corliss laughed uproariously. "Kid, you've got more spunk than anybody gives you credit for. I've got a couple of the boys who will bring the wagons in. Let's ride."

Tallie and Corliss rode at a brisk, ground-covering lope until the sun was a shining red ball just sinking below the western horizon, and they had not yet caught up with Jeb and the others.

"Miss Tallie, I think maybe we'd better call it a night."

"Jeb won't ride all night, will he?"

"No, their horses will be as tired as ours, maybe even more so, seein' as they been gallopin' some."

"They aren't likely to strike out on a different trail, are they?"

"This'll be the way they go."

"Then let's keep going until we catch them."

"Even if we don't need the rest, our horses do, else we might have one comin' up lame, and then it'll be a long wait for the wagons to pick us up.

Tallie's expression pleaded with Corliss.

"All right," he said, "we'll ride one more hour, and if we don't catch up with 'em, that's it. All I can say is, I hope he appreciates what I'm doing for 'im."

"You're a good man," Tallie said, and urged her horse to move.

Well after the shadows of the evening had set in, Corliss saw a tiny flicker. "That's a good sign. Looks like he lit a fire."

"Why do you say that's good? Wouldn't Jeb do that anyway?" Tallie asked.

"Not when you're livin' on jerky, and no coffee. He put out a light for us 'cause he 'spects we're comin' along behind him."

Tallie smiled. All day she had worried what Jeb's reaction would be if they caught up with him. She hoped Corliss was right.

The two riders approached the fire cautiously.

"Hello, the camp," Corliss called, stopping a hundred feet from the fire, the customary boundary for notifying someone before entering a campsite.

"Come on in," Jeb called. "I've been expecting you."

Corliss and Tallie rode in. She got off her horse, and when she tried to take a step, her legs buckled from having been in the saddle so long. Jeb was the first to catch her.

"You're a fool," Jeb said, but his voice was soft and not angry. He lifted her and carried her to his own bedroll, where she lay cushioning her head against her hands. She closed her eyes in weary exhaustion, but she had a smile on her face.

When Jeb rose, Corliss was standing there, his hands on his hips. "I should take you out in the weeds and whup you good for what you done to that little girl. She's rode harder'n ten cowboys today just to catch up with you. You could've slowed down. You knowed we was acomin'."

"I'm sorry, Ken. What can I say?"

"Don't say you're sorry to me, she's the one you done wrong, and now you'd better make it right, or you'll answer to me."

"You've taken this protective role to heart, haven't you?"

"Damn right, and proud of it. I'll take care of the horses."

Jeb went back to his bedroll and looked down at the sleeping Tallie. She looked so beautiful, so innocent. Yes, innocent. What if she had done the things he had read about in her book? If a man loved a woman, did her past even matter?

If a man loved a woman. Was he in love with Tallie Somerset? He didn't know. He certainly cared more for her than he had ever cared for Katarina, and he had been considering her to be his wife.

On this trail drive, Tallie had certainly earned her bona fides. She had worked without complaint, she had gained the respect of the men, and as evidenced by this day alone, she was tough. She would make a wonderful wife—a real partner—for a cattleman.

The next morning, Jeb held up until Tallie had awakened. It was well past sunup and he knew he had lost riding time, but now it didn't matter.

When she sat up, muscles ached that she didn't know she had.

"Good morning, sleepyhead," Jeb said when he saw her awake.

"I would never have thought the ground could be such a good bed." Tallie tried to stand.

"Are you sore?"

"I should ask that of you. Are you still sore at me?"

"No. I'm not sore at you, or even angry. I'm

sorry, Tallie." He pulled her to her feet and held her against his chest as he ran his hand through her tousled hair. "Would it make you feel better if you went down to the river and took a bath?"

"Will you get in the water with me?" Tallie said, not realizing that Corliss was now within earshot.

"I won't let him, and I'll stand guard for ya so nobody else comes near ya either," Corliss said.

"I'd love a bath. But do we have time?"

"We'll take the time," Jeb said. "Go with her, Ken."

The bath was therapeutic for body and soul. It took some of the soreness out, and she couldn't help but rejoice that Jeb wasn't angry with her. Apparently, he was accepting her even in his mistaken belief that she was the personification of the Duchess in *The Prince's Folly*. And she took great comfort in that because it made her dare to hope that he might actually love her.

When she returned from the river, Jeb had already saddled her horse for her, and he invited her to ride alongside him.

The ride today was as leisurely as the previous day's had been frantic. The horses were rested and the cowboys were relaxed. One man pulled out a harmonica and began playing. Everybody tried to teach Tallie the words to the songs as they rode along, and by the time they stopped for the night, she was quite proficient in cowboy ballads. Jeb had watched with admiration as more and more she assimilated into the group.

They made camp early that night. Corliss shot a couple of sage hens and set up a spit to roast them. After they had eaten, someone pulled out a deck of cards and they began to play poker. Tallie watched for a while, but resisted their invitations to join in.

"This was a fun day, Jeb," Tallie said as she drifted away from the cowboys. "These men are what a dear friend of mine would call the salt of the earth."

"Somehow, I don't think the dear friend you are talking about is Lady Churchill."

"Don't be so hard on her. She stood by my side when others ostracized me, first for the book, and then for the divorce. So no matter what she does, I will always be her friend."

"Is she the Duchess?"

Tallie laughed. "The Duchess is a composite of a lot of people, and I would have to say, Jennie is a big part of that person. If you ever got to know her well, you would love her."

"Like Kinsky does."

"No, that's different. She and Carl aren't in love, but they are lovers—and Randolph approves. He even refers to him as 'our Austrian connection.' But as I wrote in my book, English Society accepts that, as long as you don't go too far."

As long as you don't go too far.

Jeb wanted to find out who went too far in Tallie's marriage. What happened that was so egregious that it led to divorce? Jeb wanted to believe that it was something Arthur had done, but then he pictured the sallow-skinned, little, pharisaical bastard and his cutting comment about meeting her latest paramour. Whatever it was, he was sure it was Arthur's fault.

"Tallie, why were you and Arthur divorced? I can't understand how any man lucky enough to have a woman like you could ever let her go."

Tallie was quiet for a moment.

"I'm sorry. I had no right to ask."

"No, you have every right. It's just that—I've never told anyone the real reason, not even Aunt Emma, or Jennie."

Tears sprang to her eyes, and as one started to slide down her cheek, Jeb reached out to catch it with the tip of his finger. "You don't have to tell me anything." He placed his arm around her and drew her close to him.

"I need to tell you, Jeb. I married Arthur because"—she hesitated—"because he offered me security. He was kind to me after my father died, and I gratefully accepted that kindness, but the worst thing I did was to marry him because he promised to help me get my book published. What a horrible reason to commit your life to someone."

"Was it the book I read?"

"No. It was a book about a girl being an orphan. It was about my life with the Darwins."

"I don't understand. Was he jealous of you after the book was published?"

"He didn't care. He didn't care about me or anything that I did." She turned to Jeb and with a tormented voice added, "And when he took Eddy to a—the Queen accused him of corrupting her grandson, and then the duke came and . . . "

"That's why you divorced Arthur."

"I had to. The Queen was going to take the Beaufort title away if Arthur didn't leave, so they said I was the one who . . . " Tears were streaming down Tallie's cheeks as her voice cracked.

"Wronged Arthur," Jeb said, finishing for her as he held her tighter to his chest.

"Yes, but there's more I need to tell you. Arthur is a man who—how can I say this? He prefers the—intimacies—of other men."

"The self-centered little prick. Why did he ever marry you?" Jeb lifted her face to his and kissed her with a tenderness he was unaware he possessed.

When the kiss was over, he continued to hold her, as Tallie was now racked with sobs. He recognized how difficult it had been for her to tell him about this, and he felt honored that she had chosen to share her innermost turmoil with him. As he soothed her in her anguish, he thought that now she might be able to get on with her life. Could that life possibly be with him? He dared to hope.

The next couple of days were glorious in Tallie's estimation. She was experiencing a camaraderie that she had not known since her days spent in the company of the Darwin family, and she hated to see it come to an end.

Back at the 76 Ranch, Moreton was jubilant when Jeb presented him with a bank draft for $135,454.50.

"That much money for three thousand head of cattle? Is there any business in America—no, make that in the world—that has a greater return on your investment? How many did we lose on the way?"

"Eighty-seven, and we got forty-six dollars and fifty cents per head at the railhead on the day we delivered," Jeb said.

"What's your best estimate as to the size of our whole herd?" Moreton asked.

"I'd say better than thirty thousand head, give or take a couple of thousand."

A big smile spread across Moreton's face. "That means we've got close to one and a half million dollars running around out there someplace in this valley. Jeb, what does it look like up toward Miles City? Is the grass good enough that we can spread up the Tongue valley and across the Yellowstone into Montana?"

"The grass is there, but, Moreton, how big do you want this operation to be? There are a lot of people coming into this valley and—"

"I don't want to hear it. You sound just like some of the naysayers in the Cattlemen's Association. When our bank accounts rival the Vanderbilts' and the Astors', then I'll be satisfied."

Just then, Clara walked into the library where Moreton and Jeb were talking. "Do you recognize this lovely lady?" Clara made a sweeping hand movement toward the door. "May I present Lady Tallas Somerset, wearing the latest creation picked up by my darling mama at the Bon Marché in Paris."

Tallie stepped into the doorway, wearing a long, flowing, yellow gown that followed the curves of her body. Her shoulders were bare and the décolletage prominent.

"It's a good thing Tallie is not as fair skinned as I.

Otherwise there would be quite a contrast between her sun-bronzed face and her chest.

"My dear, I don't think Tallie's chest complexion is what draws either my or Jeb's attention. Would you concur?" Moreton turned to Jeb.

Jeb just shook his head. He would never get used to the English sense of humor.

"We've missed your company these last weeks, Jeb. Tonight, we will be saying farewell to Carl and Jennie. I intend to send them off with a barbeque, lest they think our fare is always caviar and capers. Can I count on you to attend?" Clara asked.

"After four days of jerky, barbeque sounds wonderful, but I will attend only if Lady Somerset promises she will come dressed as she is right now."

"That can be done," Tallie said with a little curtsy.

Like practically everything else that was done at the Frewens', the farewell party was extravagant. A table was moved down by the river under the cottonwoods, where the white linen tablecloths were laid with sterling-silver flatware and Imari-patterned china. Three silver candelabra were intertwined with fresh flowers brought in from Denver on the latest stage.

This was a barbeque, so beef cooked over an open fire was the main offering, but the side dishes were sliced fresh tomatoes, cucumbers in dilled sour cream, and husked corn. Jeb had assumed husked corn would be like the corn on the cob he had eaten his whole life. But that wasn't to be. Little bundles of corn husks were distributed with all the corn cut off the cob. Clara had declared it was vulgar to eat corn with your fingers.

Throughout the dinner, Kinsky and Jennie regaled everyone with tales of his prowess at the hunt that the two of them, along with a guide, had just concluded. Kinsky had taken two elk and one bighorn sheep, and he had sent their heads to a taxidermist in Cheyenne to have ready for shipment back to England. Jennie insisted she was going to hang the ram's head over her bed at St. James's Place, and everyone laughed uproariously thinking of Randolph's reaction.

Not until dinner was done, did Moreton clear his throat, then look over toward Clara. "It would seem that we can all speak with pride over recent performance, but I daresay that I have cause for the most pride." Moreton turned to Clara, who dropped her head demurely. "Do you want to make the announcement, or shall I?"

"I will defer to you, my love."

Moreton stood silently, smiling with adoration at his wife.

"Out with it, Frewen, what announcement?" Kinsky asked.

"Don't get impatient, this is too important. My dear friends, it is with great pleasure that I inform you—"

"I'm going to have a baby!" Clara interrupted.

Moreton laughed. "Darling, is that how you defer to me?"

"I'm sorry, I couldn't keep it a secret any longer, and it sounded like you were going to make a speech."

"Oh, Clara! This is wonderful news!" Jennie said. "I just wish I didn't have to go home."

"Don't worry, I won't be alone. Tallie will never leave me. Isn't that right?"

"Of course I'll stay, and I'll be the first person to hold your little one—that is, after you and Moreton."

"I'm putting my trust in you to take care of my sister, because if anything happens, you know who you'll have to answer to?"

When Tallie didn't answer the question, Moreton, Clara, and Jennie said in unison and with laughter, "Sitting Bull."

After congratulations were given and a toast was drunk to Clara and Moreton, Kinsky, once more, began to monopolize the conversation. "So, tell us, Jeb, how did our girl do on the . . . what do you call it? A trail drive?"

"I can't sing her praises enough," Jeb said. "She not only got every meal out on time, the meals were exceptionally good."

"They must have been," Moreton said. "The men are still raving over it, so much so that I think Hank is getting jealous."

Kinsky laughed. "I find this all very hilarious."

Jeb frowned. "Hilarious? How so?"

"Well, my dear boy, you have to understand this from my perspective. I have danced with this lovely young lady at the finest balls and parties in all of England. And just look at her now, so exquisitely dressed." Kinsky took in Tallie with a wave of his hand. "I'm sure you can imagine her at a party in the home of the Duchess of Marlborough or even at the Queen's court . . . " Kinksy put his hand to his mouth. "Oh, I guess that's not an option anymore after you so thoroughly exposed poor Bertie with your little book. But putting that little episode aside, I am having a most difficult time picturing Tallie in men's clothing. And then add to that, her cooking out of the back of a wagon for a bunch of ill-mannered, uneducated, coarse cowboys. It's just that I find it absolutely preposterous."

"You may consider them uneducated, and perhaps in the classical sense they are," Tallie said. "But as for being ill-mannered, or coarse, I found their behavior to be exemplary. So much so that the so-called gentlemen who are habitués of the London social set pale in comparison."

"My, my," Kinsky said. "My girl seems a little testy. Jeb, your cowboys must have made quite an impression on her."

"I am not your girl and I resent your saying that." Tallie pushed away from the table. "If you would excuse me." She got up and walked quickly up the rise to the ranch house.

"I say, I had no idea she would be so defensive of the common cowboy. What do you suppose got into her?" Kinsky asked after Tallie left.

"You did," Jennie said. "Who are you, of all people, to make such judgments?"

"Jennie, they're just cowboys. How could she possibly care anything about them?" Kinsky asked dismissively.

"If you would excuse me," Jeb said, rising from the table.

"Now look what you've done. This night should have been perfect, and you've ruined it for me," Clara said as she burst into tears.

"Please forgive me," Kinsky said. "This environment tends to make one lose all sense of propriety."

Jeb followed Tallie up to the house, where she was standing on the porch leaning against a post. When he arrived, he stepped up behind her and put his hands on her waist.

She leaned back against him, her head resting on his chest.

Her anger at Kinsky seemed to melt away as Jeb held her close to him.

"They don't understand," she said in a calm voice. "Ken Corliss, Will Tate, Rudy Brock, these are my true friends here."

"Oh? That's all well and good, but what about Jeb Tuhill?" Jeb teased.

Tallie didn't answer, but turned in his arms and, placing her hands upon his cheeks, kissed him. It wasn't a tentative kiss, it was firm and passionate, and Jeb returned it.

At that very moment a rider came galloping up, his abrupt arrival causing Tallie and Jeb to separate.

"Where's that bastard Frewen?" the man yelled.

"You'd better step inside, Tallie," Jeb said, pushing her toward the door.

"That's right, protect your own woman, but it don't make no difference about anybody else's wife and kids, does it? You can kill us or starve us out. It's all the same."

"Mr. Jones, I'm not sure I know what you're talking about."

"This. This is what I'm talking about." Jones threw a section of a fresh-skinned cowhide in front of Jeb. "Look at that brand."

"It's the 76. Did you kill one of our cows?"

"Damn right I did. About a hundred of 'em come stampedin' through my garden while my wife and kids was workin' the plot. They was lucky they didn't get trampled. The garden wasn't so lucky. Ever'thing in it was destroyed."

"You know this is free range, Mr. Jones. I'm sorry the cows ruined your crop, but I'm sure it couldn't be helped."

"Them cows wasn't runnin' free. My wife saw four men drivin' 'em, yellin' and hollerin' to get 'em to stampede. That's not an accident, and I intend to settle this with Frewen if I have to blow his damn head off." Jones dismounted and started up the steps.

When he got even with Jeb, Jeb reached down and grabbed the rifle with one hand, while pushing Jones back with the other. Jones lost his balance and let go of the rifle so he could catch himself. That left the rifle in Jeb's hands. Jeb jacked the lever several times until all the bullets were ejected.

Jones stood up, and seeing that Jeb was holding his rifle, he stared at him with defiance. "You know what this is all about. They want us all to give up what we've worked for. They want us to clear out, and if we don't do it, they'll starve us out or worse. But you tell that bastard Frewen and rest of the damn 'Association' that we're not leavin'. This is our country and we've got clear title to our land. We ain't leavin'."

"I'm sorry about all of this, but I can guarantee nobody from the 76 was involved," Jeb said.

"Is that there your brand?"

"That doesn't prove anything."

"When you come by to visit that day, I thought maybe you was someone I could trust. I see you ain't no different from the rest of them."

Jeb tossed the rifle back to Jones. "I'm sorry about your garden, Mr. Jones. And I assure you, I knew nothing about it."

"Tell Frewen we can form our own association, and he'll wish he never even heard of John R. Jones. You tell him that for me, mister."

Jeb watched Jones ride away until he disappeared.

Then Moreton stepped out from behind one of the outbuildings. "What was all that?"

"It was John R. Jones. He thinks someone from the 76 destroyed his garden."

"He doesn't know what he's talking about."

"That's what I told him, but look at this." Jeb threw the piece of cowhide to Moreton.

"He shot one of our cows?"

Jeb studied Moreton before he spoke. "How do you know the cow was shot?"

"Well, it was, wasn't it?"

"Yes, that's what John R. said. He also said our cows were stampeded through his garden. You don't know anything about that, do you?"

"If you're asking did I order his garden destroyed,

the answer is no. But I do know that the Cattlemen's Association has hired some people to find out if these squatters are rustling cattle."

"Jones isn't a rustler, Moreton. He's just trying to eke out a living and feed his family."

"Humph. Then he has nothing to fear from the Association."

NINETEEN

With the departure of Jennie and Kinsky, the day-to-day activity at the ranch was calm. Tallie spent much of her time with Clara, who was overseeing the making of a layette for what she referred to as *des espérances*, or expectation.

The idyllic mood was only disturbed by Moreton's frequent absences on what he said was Association business, and the gloomy despair that the whole country was feeling, as people were on death watch for President Garfield. It had been more than eight weeks since he had been shot, yet he clung to life.

"The paper says that the men who are treating the president may be doing him more harm than good," Tallie reported to Clara. "It says that the continued hypodermic injections of morphia have done as much as anything else to prevent any favorable issue of the wound. Had Mr. Garfield been at his own home in Mentor, Ohio, treated like an ordinary patient by his own family doctor, and not overdosed and overdoctored, as he has been, he might be a well man at this hour."

"That's what I think, too," Clara said. "Doctors don't always know what's best for their patients. Like with me. Mama says that I should come back to New York to have this baby, but I'll stay right here by Moreton's side. He does insist, though, that when the time comes, he'll send for a doctor from Cheyenne."

"I hope he does because I'm afraid I won't be much help as a midwife."

"Don't be silly. I won't need any help. Look at all the women around here who drop babies as easily as a cow drops a calf." Clara laughed and slapped her hand to her forehead. "Can you believe what I just said? Isn't that the crudest remark you've ever heard?"

"What is a crude remark?" Jeb asked as he joined the two women in the great room.

"I can't repeat it," Clara said. "It was just women talk."

"Well, I have some gossip that you ladies may want to hear, especially you, Tallie. Guess who is at Trabing right now and will be here within the hour?"

"Moreton!" Clara said excitedly.

"No, I'm afraid not. Buffalo Bill is coming."

"Oh, Jeb, you can't really mean that," Tallie said excitedly.

"Oh, but I do. And what's more, the reports are he's in the Deadwood Coach."

"That's the same coach that was robbed and Buffalo Bill had to go after the robbers after they shot the driver and passengers and left them for dead," Tallie said.

"That's how Bill wrote about it, but someone once told me there's a difference between truth and fact where writers are concerned. I think he got this stagecoach after it was abandoned someplace, and now he's fixed it up and it's sort of a novelty for him," Jeb said. "Today, he's bringing some of Moreton's guests in for a hunt."

"And Moreton's not here to entertain them," Clara said.

"Don't worry, Bill will take care of that," Jeb said.

"But Moreton should stop all this nonsense and stay at home."

The Deadwood Coach pulled up to Frewen's Castle amid a cloud of dust. Bill Cody, who was driving it, cracked his whip and fired his gun into the air and yelled, "Frewen! Frewen, Buffalo Bill is here!"

Jeb went out to welcome the stage, followed by Tallie and Clara.

"Welcome, Mr. Cody. I'm Moreton's wife, Clara, and this is my friend Tallas Somerset."

"And what a pretty friend she is," Cody said, looking at Tallie.

"I'm glad you made it."

"Jeb," Bill Cody said as he climbed off the stage, "I didn't expect to see you still hanging around these parts, but maybe this here lassie is adrawin' bees to the honey." Cody drew a flask of whiskey from his hip pocket and took a long swig. "I've brought some fine folks for Moreton, but where the hell is he?"

"Moreton has been absent quite often lately, at meetings and such. I really can't say when he will return," Clara said.

"He's not part of this new Cattlemen's Association, is he?"

"Why do you ask?"

"Because from what I hear, that's a powder keg waitin' to blow. Hey, I forgot. I've got some people that need to get out of this old rig."

Cody stepped back and fiddled with the door until he finally got it opened. "Sorry, folks, I got to work on that latch." Two men stepped out of the coach, followed by a woman and another man. "This here's Major Lewis Wise and his Aussie friend Frank— what's your name?"

"Frank Boughton."

"And this is Captain Sam Ashton, and his lovely wife, Rowena."

"How wonderful to have a woman visit us," Clara said. "We'll have a great time while the men are out hunting."

"Thank you very much, but I didn't come to visit. I came to hunt," Rowena Ashton said.

"Oh?" Clara said.

"I'm sure we can accommodate you," Jeb said. "Let's get everyone inside and settled, and then we can make plans for your hunt."

"That's wonderful. I don't believe I heard your name," Rowena said, taking Jeb's arm in hers as she went toward the door.

"Jeb Tuhill, ma'am."

It was funny seeing Rowena holding Jeb's arm and smiling up at him. She was openly flirting with him, and though Tallie was used to such overt flirtation among the people she knew in London, it seemed out of place here, and she had to check a little feeling of resentment.

That night, after a light supper, Clara thought of Cody's words about the Cattlemen's Association being a powder keg ready to blow. What was Moreton involved in, and where was he? She rose from her bed and went to sit at the window, and when she did, she saw Rowena Ashton walking along the path outside.

If Rowena Ashton could go on a hunt, she and Tallie could go as well. She went to her chests and began gathering clothes, both her own and some of Moreton's, which would be suitable for a trip to the mountains.

"Tallie, you know how you went on the trail drive?" Clara said the next morning as she barged into Tallie's room before she was out of bed.

"You're up early." Tallie yawned.

"Yes, and you need to be, too. Get your pants and shirts out and pack a warm coat. You said you wanted experiences? Well, get ready for another one, because we're going on this hunt."

"What? What are you talking about? You can't go; you're going to have a baby."

"Not until next spring I'm not, and I want to go. And this is the perfect time because Moreton isn't here to tell me I can't. I want to make him proud of me, just like Jeb was proud of you after the trail drive. Please, Tallie, say you'll do it."

"What if Jeb says no?"

"What if he does?"

"You know he won't let us go."

"Is he going to stop Rowena?"

"No, but that's different."

"How is it different?"

Tallie smiled. "You're right. It isn't different at all. All right, let's go."

Jeb was up early getting the horses and pack mules loaded. With Moreton gone, he hated to leave the ranch, but Fred and Will could manage everything.

It was past ten o'clock before Jeb and Cody had everything ready.

"These valises have to go, and two more sleeping rolls," Rudy Brock said as he approached Jeb with two saddled horses.

"If we take those, we'll need another mule."

"Will's bringing one."

"Who said we need more horses?"

"I don't know. Maybe it was Bill," Rudy said, avoiding Jeb as much as he could.

Rudy helped load the mule, and he put on an extra Sibley tent.

"What's that for?" Jeb asked. "Do they think this is our first hunt?"

"We don't have anything to say," Rudy said as he and Will hurried away from the staging area.

Then Jeb saw the hunters approaching.

Major Wise, Mr. Boughton, Captain Ashton, and his wife, he expected; Clara and Tallie he did not.

"Oh, no," Jeb said when they were within earshot. "Where do you two think you're going?"

"Hunting," Clara said.

"No, you're not going hunting, and that's final."

"Jeb," Tallie said, "did you want me to go on the trail drive? No, you didn't, but did I surprise you?"

"That was different. We're going up in the mountains, where it's going to be cold and uncomfortable."

"Rowena's going," Clara said.

"This isn't her first hunt."

"She had to have a first hunt sometime. We're going, and you can't stop us. If you won't let us ride with you, we'll ride behind you," Clara said.

"Tallie, talk her out of this. You know how uncomfortable camping can be. She's, she's . . . "

"Not helpless," Clara said.

Jeb took a deep breath, knowing that he couldn't stop them from going. "I plan for us to get to Beaver Creek Ranch tonight. That's thirty miles."

"I think I've already proven to you that I can ride long and hard."

Jeb took his hat off and ran his hand through his hair, then smiled and nodded. "Yeah, I reckon you have at that. All right, come along."

Tallie would never have suggested going on this hunt, but she was glad she had come. As they rode toward the mountains following the Red Fork, Tallie saw a buffalo. Jeb rode up beside her just to see her excitement and joy at the sight. At first there was just one, and then she saw two together, and a little farther along was a little string of animals, but then they rode over a little rise and there were hundreds of them, their shaggy heads lowered and their humped backs braced against the wind.

"They're beautiful, Jeb—no, that's not the word, they're absolutely regal. But why didn't we see any on the trip to Miles City? I thought they would be everywhere."

"At one time they were, but hunters took them out."

"You mean hunters like Buffalo Bill?"

"He killed his share, but he did it because our government hired him to do it."

"I'm glad I got to see such a magnificent sight before they're all gone," Tallie said.

"I'm glad, too. And I'm glad you insisted on coming along with us."

Tallie smiled as she and Jeb rode together in companionable silence. She knew in her heart that this was the kind of relationship Uncle Charles and Aunt Emma had. And she knew that they loved one another. Did she love Jeb Tuhill?

She remembered when she had gone to his cabin the night of the party. He had made her feel like no man had ever made her feel. And then in the water, when she had told him she wasn't married.

She knew why Arthur hadn't made love to her, but why hadn't Jeb? Was it something that she had done? She was so confused.

It was an excited group that pitched camp that night, high up on the mountain. A good number of blacktail deer and wapiti had been taken during the day's hunt, and bear tracks had been sighted. Cody explained that they would only stay in this camp for the night. Tomorrow, they would go higher up and scout the area for bighorn sheep as well as grizzly bears.

They sat around a blazing fire, telling stories about previous hunts until, one by one, the hunters went to their tents and crawled into their sleep sacks. Only Jeb and Tallie were left by the fire.

"It's going to get really cold tonight," Jeb said as he pulled his sleeping sack up beside the fire.

"Are you going to sleep out here?"

"More than likely. Somebody needs to keep the fire going all night. Why don't you come over here and sit beside me?" Jeb positioned his bedroll next to a fallen tree.

When Tallie sat down, Jeb lifted his sack so that the fur-lined top acted as a coverlet for her, and when he sat, he snuggled in beside her. "This will keep us warm," he said, his hip nestled next to hers. He could feel the heat of her body.

"What are you going to do, Tallie?"

Tallie wasn't exactly sure what Jeb was asking her, but she knew it wasn't about this hunt. "What do you mean?"

"About England."

"I wish I knew. I think you know that I really like it here, but once Clara's baby is born, I have no reason to stay. I have a house in England and my publisher is there."

"Can't you write in America?"

"Oh, yes."

"What if there was a reason to stay here? A good reason?"

Jeb turned to Tallie and gently hooked his finger

under her chin and lifted it until his lips came close to hers. The firelight caused his eyes to sparkle as he looked deep into her eyes. Then his lips closed over hers, the feeling one of a caress rather than a kiss. He didn't hurry the kiss, but let it linger on her lips. She felt her heart quicken when his tongue began to part her lips, then his tongue entered her mouth. In and out, in and out, in quick, little motions. After a long moment, they parted.

"Are you warm?" he asked. "If you are, you could take off your coat."

When their coats were removed, he rolled them into a pillow and slid down into the sack making room for Tallie to do the same.

Tallie hesitated for just a moment, then slithered into the warm cocoon that Jeb had made for them. He held her close to his body, his arms wrapped tightly around her.

"What if someone comes?" Tallie asked.

"Would you get out of a warm bag on a night like tonight?"

She answered by kissing him, and when she did, he shifted their bodies, lowering his hand to her shirt, where he began undoing the buttons. When the buttons were free, he started massaging her breast as his kisses grew deeper.

When she felt his arousal, with an instinct she didn't recognize she moved to the buttons of his pants, opening one and then another, until her hand sought the opening in his drawers. Tentatively she began to move her fingers ever so close, until she encountered a patch of coarse hair . . . and something more, something vibrant.

"Touch it," Jeb said in a hoarse voice.

"I can't." Tallie withdrew her hand.

Jeb took her hand in his and slowly moved it, this time unbuttoning his drawers as well. He placed her fingers on the tip of his penis, where a slight moistness was forming. "Wrap your hand around it, if you want to."

Tallie did as he invited, wrapping her hand firmly around his shaft. She ran her hand down to the base, then to the hard muscles of his abdomen as his penis stood erect and prodded into her own abdomen. Removing her hand, she pushed closer to him, allowing the hardness to thrust against her body.

Jeb found the buttons to her pants and fumbled with them.

Tallie smiled at him. "You're not very good at this, are you?" she teased.

Now the only thing between them was the light layer of her underwear, and she caught his hand and guided it to the slit in her drawers.

He grabbed his penis and moved it to touch her most private part, and with his hand he began moving his aroused member against her core, first slipping it between her legs, then bathing it in the juices that seemed to be oozing from her. He moved closer to her, and she clamped her legs, trapping him between them.

"I want to get out of my clothes," she whispered.

Jeb laid his face against her cheek. "Oh, Tallie, I shouldn't have done this."

"Why? Is there something wrong with me?"

"No, no, no," Jeb said almost in pain. "There's

nothing wrong with you, but this isn't the place. When I love you the first time, I want to make certain there's not a chance that someone would—"

Just then Clara called out, "Tallie, aren't you getting cold out there?"

"I'm fine, Clara. Jeb is keeping the fire going."

"All right."

Jake Slater and the four men with him crested a low hill and stared down at the dark cluster of buildings below.

"All right, fellas, you know what to do," Slater said. "Start with the barn."

All but Slater were carrying clubs, about half an inch in diameter and three feet long. Wrapped around the top end of the clubs were cotton sacks and strips of cloth that had been soaked in kerosene. The four men struck matches against their saddles, then lit the torches and started toward the buildings of the John R. Jones Ranch.

Inside the Jones house, eight-year-old Sammy Jones was awakened by a sound from outside. He wasn't sure what the sound was, he just knew that it was different from the ordinary night sounds. Curious, he got out of bed and walked over to the window—and saw five mounted men, backlit by flames, coming from the barn.

"Pa!" Sammy called. "Pa!"

"What is it, Son?" Sammy's mother's voice was muffled, and sleepy.

"The barn's on fire!"

"Oh, no! John! John! Wake up!"

John R. Jones woke up and knew immediately that something was wrong, seeing the walls of the bedroom painted orange by a flickering light. Moving quickly to the window, he saw five riders, four with blazing torches in their hands.

He started for his rifle, but his wife cut him off. "No, no, John. There're five men out there."

"Ethel, I can't just stand by and let them burn our barn."

"They've already done it. You can't do anything now except get yourself killed."

"Jones! John R. Jones, get yourself out here!" someone called from outside.

John reached for his rifle.

"No, John, please! Think of me and your children. They'll kill you if you go out there."

"I am thinking of my kids. They can't take what is ours."

"Jones, if you don't want your house burned down with you and your wife and younguns in it, get out here now!"

John, wearing a sleeping shirt, stepped out onto the front porch of his house. He could hear the animals in the barn screaming in terror.

"You're squattin' on open range, and you got no right to it."

"I have a deed of ownership to this land," John replied.

"That deed don't mean nothin'. The cattlemen was here first, and they don't want no trouble. Take your family and get out, or we'll burn your house down."

"Who's telling me to get out?"

"You know."

"I know it's not the law."

"The Cattlemen's Association is the law in this valley."

The braying of his mule and the cow became even more intense, and Jones stepped down from the porch.

"Where you think yer goin'?"

"My animals. Can't you hear 'em?"

"You don't need 'em. You're gonna be gone."

"You sick son of a bitch, I'm gonna get 'em out."

Slater pulled his rifle and fired two shots into the barn, and the animals grew quiet. He laughed a satanic cackle that made Jones cringe.

"Now don't say I ain't got the compassion. You can't win, Jones. Get your wife and kids and get out of here. And do it tonight. 'Cause the next thing we burn is gonna be your house."

Slater nodded to the others, and the men rode off. Not until they were gone did Ethel and the two children come out onto the porch. John put his arm around his wife and pulled her to him. She wept quietly as they stared at the burning barn.

They did not see a group of a dozen men watching from a distance. The men rode away in silence, the only sound the soft plod of their horses' hooves hitting the soil.

TWENTY

The next morning a beaver trapper wandered into the camp and, after having breakfast with them, reported some Crow Indians were hunting in the Bighorn Canyon, an area Bill Cody had scouted as the site for the next campsite.

"Is there a problem with the Indians?" Major Wise asked.

"No, but it's best to give them some room. We'll move south, there'll be plenty of game no matter where we go," Cody said.

It didn't take long to strike camp. When Tallie came out of her tent, she saw Jeb rolling up his sleeping sack, and she went to get a cup of coffee.

"Did the fire burn all night?" she asked.

Jeb turned toward her, and a slow smile crossed his face. "I don't know about your fire, but mine did."

She looked at him, a mischievous look coming into her eyes. "I was quite warm for the entire night, so, yes, I would say the fire was burning."

"It'll be cold again tonight so we'll have to keep it going."

Cody and the others joined Tallie and Jeb as they discussed the plans for the day.

"I want to break us up today," Cody said. "Jeb, you take the Ashtons, and I'll take the major and the Aussie."

"What about Tallie and me?" Clara asked.

"When we get to our next camp, you two can stay and tend the fire. Tallie can even start a stew for us," Cody said.

"No. I heard that trapper say he saw Indians."

"The Crow aren't going to bother us. They're out to get their winter supply of meat."

"We're not staying in camp by ourselves," Clara said.

"Fine. You two can go with Jeb."

Cody and the two men rode ahead and chose a good camping spot—close to a creek with good grass for the horses and at the edge of a piney wood. Even as they were setting up their camp, Frank Boughton saw two bears rooting for food among the fallen trees. Taking aim, he fired, but both bears disappeared into the woods.

"You missed," Ashton said.

"No, I'm pretty sure I hit one of them."

"If you shoot a bear, make sure you kill him," Cody said. "A wounded bear isn't something you want to mess with."

The day was most productive for hunting. Jeb's group came upon a band of at least four hundred wapiti with some fine bulls. Rowena took down three with fine heads, while her husband missed everything he tried to shoot. The women teased Captain Ashton and Jeb unmercifully about the superiority of their gender, and Captain Ashton and Jeb took it with good humor.

When they returned to camp, Cody's group had been equally successful. However, neither group had been able to bring down a bear. Boughton was excited because he had found a bison separated from its herd. The beast had three arrows embedded in its hump, and while Moreton's instructions were that buffalo were not to be killed on hunts originating from the 76 Ranch, they all agreed that Boughton was right to get it out of its misery.

That night there was much talk around the campfire. Everyone was excited about the animals they had seen and the heads they had brought into camp.

Jeb and Tallie exchanged glances during the whole evening, waiting until everyone retired so that they could once again enjoy the fire and share some stolen kisses. But tonight, Major Wise and Frank Boughton were telling stories about their trip to New Zealand, and Buffalo Bill Cody was entertaining them with stories of his stage performances. Even though the conversation was loud and raucous, Tallie kept nodding off.

"Tallie," Jeb said softly, "if you're going to be able to go out tomorrow, you'd better get some rest." He helped her to her feet and took her into her tent. As soon as they were inside, he grabbed her and kissed her. "I've been waiting for this all night, but they won't stop talking."

They exchanged a few more kisses, but the conversation and laughter just outside the tent made Tallie uneasy, so with one final good-night kiss, Jeb left her.

The next morning Frank Boughton told Cody that he wanted to get the head of the buffalo he had shot and take it back to Australia, so Boughton, Jeb, Tallie, and Clara set out in search of the animal. Cody took the others with him. A cinnamon bear had been seen nearby, and Rowena was bragging that she would be the first in the group to take a bear.

Boughton was unsure where he had left the buffalo, so his group spent some time looking for it. Then, searching the area through his field glasses, Jeb discovered it. All four dismounted and, tying up the horses, went across a small alpine valley, approaching the buffalo.

"I say, that is a magnificent beast, is it not?" Boughton said.

"Yes, it is," Jeb replied.

"I'll have the most coveted trophy in all of Australia." Boughton stroked the shaggy mane of the buffalo, almost as if he were petting a dog. "Could you give me a hand with the head?"

"Sure." Jeb laid his large-bore rifle, a Hawkins .50-caliber, alongside the animal. He liked to use the Hawkins because he knew it could stop any animal he might encounter, whereas the smaller-caliber rifles the others were carrying might not.

Taking a large hunting knife from a sheath on his belt, Jeb began severing the head. Boughton and Clara watched with fascination, but Tallie, thinking of the herd she had seen on the way to the mountains, and remembering Jeb's words, chose not to watch. She started back toward the horses.

"Tallie, wait until we all go back together," Jeb cautioned.

"I'm not going anywhere. I just don't care to watch. I'll be over here by the horses," Tallie said, her back turned to the scene.

As Jeb continued to work at detaching the head, all of a sudden Boughton raised his rifle to his shoulder. "Look! A bear!" he shouted excitedly.

The grizzly bear was just coming out of the tree line, drawn by the smell of the buffalo's blood.

"Don't shoot!" Jeb said. "A shot from your rifle won't stop him, and he could charge."

Despite Jeb's shouted caution, Boughton fired. Jeb saw a puff of dust fly up from the animal's shoulder where the bullet hit. The bear roared loudly, then started running toward them. Tallie saw the bear and, instinctively, started to run. Her running got the bear's attention, and he turned toward her.

Jeb had his big Hawkins in his hands by now, but Tallie was between him and the bear, and he had no open shot.

"Tallie! Get on the ground!" Jeb shouted. "Get on the ground!"

Boughton stood frozen, watching the bear advance toward Tallie, while Clara was screaming hysterically. Tallie continued to run, but the bear was closing on her.

"Fall down, Tallie! Do it right now!" Jeb yelled, his rifle on his shoulder, ready to shoot as soon as Tallie was clear.

Jeb knew that Tallie's natural instinct was to run, but he was counting on her to be courageous and, he hoped, to trust him enough to do something counterintuitive.

Tallie fell to the ground, but it was almost too late. The bear was upon her just as Jeb fired. Jeb's bullet was perfectly placed and penetrated the skull sending blood, brains, and bone spewing from the head. The bear fell, collapsing with Tallie partially under its dead body.

"Tallie!" Jeb shouted, running to her. She was lying facedown, her arms covering her tucked-in head. Jeb rolled the bear carcass off her, seeing her coat ripped and bloodied. His heart was pounding rapidly as he knelt beside her, saying over and over, "Don't die, Tallie, please don't die. I've just found you and I don't want to lose you. I love you."

When he gently turned her over, he was surprised to see a smiling Tallie looking up at him.

"Do you mean that? Do you really love me?"

He knelt to kiss her and held her to him. "I do, Tallie. I do love you."

Just then Clara and Boughton came running up to the pair.

"Is she all right?" Clara asked between sobs as tears streamed down her face.

"We haven't checked yet," Jeb said. "Do you hurt anywhere?"

"My arm. It hurts," Tallie said as she sat up.

Jeb checked and saw several marks across her

upper arm where the bear had clawed just as Jeb had shot it. Jeb's stomach began to churn and his face turned white as he thought about how close Tallie had come to death. He sat beside her and once more pulled her into his arms.

"You are one lucky lady," Boughton said.

Tallie, who seemed to be the one most in control, couldn't answer, but if she could have, she would have said that on this day she was lucky in more ways than one.

That night in camp, it was Tallie who had the story to tell. Her arm was sore, but her nurse was taking good care of her. Jeb had boiled some wapiti bones, and when they cooled, he scraped out the marrow and put that on her cuts, then rubbed a little of Cody's carbolic acid ointment over it, and the pain was subsiding.

"I think first thing tomorrow, we should get you back to the ranch," Jeb said as he sat in the tent beside Tallie. She was lying in her sleeping sack, made of opossum skin lined with beaver fur, and she was wearing a high-necked nightdress with long sleeves. Jeb cut the sleeve of her gown with his pocketknife and began rubbing more ointment on her wounds. Because of the location of the cuts and because of where Tallie had placed her arm, his hand was close to her breast. He continued to rub long after the ointment was worked into her skin.

"Is that the only place where I have scratches?" Tallie asked in a husky voice.

"I didn't look anyplace else. Do you think I should?"

Tallie reached to the neck of her nightdress and began to loosen the fasteners. In the light of the fire filtering through the walls of the tent, Jeb watched as the milky white of her chest became visible. Soon her gown was opened to her waist, and Tallie dropped her hands to her sides. Jeb moved the gown aside and stared at her breasts, then with his hand he began to rub her nipple, feeling rather than seeing the nipple harden beneath the pad of his thumb. Slowly, sensuously, he traced ever-widening circles, causing her skin to prickle. She arched her back, forcing her breast closer to his hand, and then he lowered his mouth to her, taking her nipple between his teeth, biting gently, all the while twirling his tongue around it. He moved to her other breast for a reprise.

Hearing laughter outside the tent, Jeb stopped his ministrations and closed up the sleep sack.

"Thank you, you've made it feel much better."

"Tallie, don't you think we should go back tomorrow? Just the two of us? We'd be in one sleep sack under the trees keeping one another warm."

"That sounds wonderful."

Jeb kissed her nose, then sat back on his heels, looking down at her. "You'd better rest well tonight because tomorrow night you may not get any sleep at all."

"Oh? And what is likely to keep me awake tomorrow night?"

"I am," Jeb said with a confident smile.

Clara, who shared the sleeping tent with Tallie and who had been outside with the others, came in then. "You should hear Boughton," she said, laughing. "According to him, if he hadn't slowed the bear down with his shot, it would have mauled all four of us."

"I hope you set him straight," Tallie said.

"My dear, Moreton wants money from him. I'll just let him brag."

Jeb and Tallie chuckled, then Jeb told the ladies good-night and exited their tent.

Tallie awakened during the night to hear Clara crying out.

"Clara, what is it?" Tallie asked as she crawled out of her bedroll.

"It's my stomach. I'm having terrible cramps." Clara was sitting and drew her legs up against her chest, burying her head on her knees.

"Let me get Jeb."

Jeb was sleeping by the fire and was awake the minute Tallie stepped out of her tent.

"Tallie? What's wrong?"

"Come quick. It's Clara."

Jeb entered the tent and lit a candle. When he did, he saw the dark red stain on Clara's nightdress.

"When did this happen?"

"What do you mean?"

"Look." Jeb pointed at the blood.

"Is it the baby?" Tallie asked.

When Clara heard her fear put into words, she began shrieking uncontrollably. "I want my mama, I want my mama," she said over and over.

Tallie tried to soothe her and comfort her, but she cried louder and louder.

"Get Bill to saddle two horses and gather up what

we need to get back. We're going to get her out of here."

"When?"

"Now. We're leaving right now."

"Two horses?"

"Yes, Clara will ride with me."

With Jeb holding Clara, and Tallie riding along behind, they left the camp well before sunup and traveled down the mountain with as much speed as Jeb dared. He hated to push Tallie so when he couldn't help her, but Clara was in and out of consciousness, and he knew they had to keep moving.

The next day they stopped only for calls of nature, when Tallie helped Clara as best she could. Jeb was glad they were off the mountain and onto the prairie by nightfall so that they could travel by moonlight.

After traveling all night, Jeb recognized that they were near the John R. Jones place, so he decided to go there and borrow a wagon to get Clara home. His arms were aching from holding her for more than twenty-four hours, and he knew Tallie was as tired as he was. Perhaps Mrs. Jones would also have a pallet that she could spare, and Tallie and Clara could rest as he brought them on home.

As they drew closer to the homestead, though, Jeb began to smell the acrid odor of smoke. When they came over the rise and looked down on the place, Jeb was shocked and came to a complete halt. Wisps of smoke were drifting up from a nearly burned-out fire, which had taken the house, the barn, and all the outbuildings of the John R. Jones Ranch.

This couldn't have been an accident. He wanted to go down and see if anything or anybody was around the rubble, but he couldn't—not with Clara barely hanging on to life in his arms.

"How could something like this happen?" Tallie asked. "Who lives here?"

"John R. Jones. The man who came to the 76 the night of the barbeque."

"Do you think it was some sort of accident?"

Jeb didn't answer, but clinched his jaw tightly. "We've got to get Clara home."

He kneed his tired horse and moved as quickly as was possible with an exhausted Tallie following along behind.

When Jeb and the two women arrived at the ranch just after sunup, Rudy was outside the barn and saw Clara on the horse with Jeb. "Jeb, what's up? What's wrong with Mrs. Frewen?"

"Hitch up Cody's stage, and get us ready to go as quickly as you can. Where's Moreton?"

"He's around."

"Help me get her down. Be careful with her, she's hemorrhaging and we need to get her to a doctor."

"Will!" Rudy shouted as he helped Jeb slide Clara down from the horse. "Get the coach hitched up!"

Jeb carried Clara over to the front porch and laid her down just as Moreton was coming out of the house.

"Oh, my God! What is it? What happened?"

"It's the baby, Moreton. We've got to get her to the fort doctor," Jeb said.

"Clara!"

Clara grabbed Moreton's hand and held it tightly. "I'm so sorry. I've lost our baby. It's all my fault," she said between sobs.

"Oh, Clara, it's not your fault. If we lose the baby, we'll make another one. We've got to take care of you."

Tallie came back outside in a clean gown and with as many Grundy cloths as she could find. "Get her inside, and let's change her gown."

With clean clothes on and the cloths positioned to slow the bleeding, Clara was placed inside the coach. Moreton and Tallie joined her, and soon both Clara and Tallie, exhausted from their long ride, were sleeping. Jeb had planned to drive the coach, but Rudy insisted on taking the reins. Within minutes, Jeb, too, was asleep on the top of the coach.

"I don't want to take my wife to Fort Fetterman," Moreton called to Rudy. "Let's take her to Cheyenne where she'll have a better doctor."

TWENTY-ONE

I'm sorry, Mr. Frewen. With the pain and the bleeding, there is no hope that the baby has survived," Dr. Kincaid said.

"And what about my wife? Is she going to be all right?" Moreton asked anxiously.

"She seems to be a healthy woman, and that's in her favor. I would say the prognosis is good that she'll recover. However, it will be a slow process. She's very weak. I want to keep her under observation here in the infirmary just to make sure the bleeding has stopped. Do you have anyone who can watch out for her?"

"I'll stay with her, Moreton," Tallie said.

"Young lady, it may take several weeks, even two or three months for her to fully recover."

"I understand."

"You look almost as exhausted as she does, my dear. If you're going to be the one looking out for her, why don't you take that bed next to her and get some rest yourself."

"Thank you, Dr. Kincaid, that will be most convenient," Tallie said. "Where will you be if I need you, Moreton?"

"At the Cheyenne Club. It's just down the street, and Jeb will be there, too."

"Very well. You two may as well get some rest as well. We're all exhausted."

Tallie was awakened late that night by Clara's crying. Getting out of bed, she crossed over to Clara, taking her hand in hers.

"Clara, what is it? I'm here."

"Where's Moreton?"

"He left a little while ago. He's been so worried about you."

"I need him to be with me. Please, Tallie, can you find him?"

"I know where he is. I'll go get him right now."

"Thank you, Tallie. You have been like a sister to me."

Pulling on her shoes and grabbing a wrap, Tallie stepped outside. As she started toward the Cheyenne Club, raindrops began to fall.

The lights of the club were glowing brightly as, inside, the members were engaged in various activities. She stepped in through the front door just as she heard the distinct clack of a billiard rack being broken.

"Madam, this is a gentlemen's club," a uniformed doorman told her in a stern voice.

"I know that, sir, but I must find Mr. Frewen, Mr. Moreton Frewen."

"He is a member."

"It's his wife. We brought her all the way from the Powder River, and she's very sick. She's asking for him and I must find him."

The doorman looked back over the room for a moment, then turned his attention back to her.

"I can't leave my post, but there's an outside entrance that women have used from time to time. When you reach the second floor, I believe you'll find Mr. Frewen in room number two."

The doorman turned away from Tallie, dismissing her.

Hurrying outside, she heard gales of laughter from inside punctuating loud conversation. It seemed so incongruous. Clara lay just a few doors away, weak from loss of blood and possibly dying, while here men were partying and laughing.

A flash of lightning illuminated the stairs as she climbed them to the second floor. When she reached the door, a peal of thunder caused her to shudder. Stepping inside, she walked down the quiet corridor until she found door number two.

"Moreton? Moreton?" she called as she knocked lightly. When he didn't come to the door, she knocked louder. "Moreton, it's me, Tallie."

The door opened, and to Tallie's surprise, Jeb stood in the doorway, his chest bare.

"Tallie? What's happened? Is Clara . . . ?"

"She needs Moreton. The doorman said he was in this room."

"He's in room three." Jeb stepped to the room next door and knocked loudly.

A moment later, a sleepy Moreton opened the door. "What is it?"

"Moreton, Clara is asking for you," Tallie said. "You need to go to her right now."

"I'll go with you as soon as I can get dressed."

"You, Moreton. She's asking for you," Tallie said. "She doesn't need me right now."

Moreton didn't answer but went back inside his room and closed the door.

Jeb and Tallie waited for him. When he emerged, he gave a little wave to them. "I'll stay the night with her." As he opened the outside door, he stepped into a cascade of water.

Tallie took a deep breath. "Clara needs him so much right now. I'm glad he's going to be with her."

"But where are you going to be?"

"I hadn't thought of that. There must be a hotel close by."

"No." Jeb opened the door to his room. "You stay here with me."

"I can't. The man downstairs said this is a gentlemen's club. No women allowed."

Jeb smiled, reaching for Tallie. "That's the man downstairs. The man upstairs has just asked you to stay with him."

Jeb lit a lamp as they entered his room, and it pushed out a golden bubble of light. The blankets on the oversize bed were thrown back where Jeb had just been sleeping, and Tallie realized that except for the few minutes in Jeb's tiny cabin at the ranch, this was the first time she had ever been in a man's bedroom.

As the storm continued to pound, she walked to

the window, pushing aside the heavy velvet drapes. "I'm glad we are not in our tents tonight," Tallie said, looking out onto the muddy street.

"If we were, how would we keep the fire burning?" Jeb asked as he came up behind Tallie, putting his arms around her and clasping his hands at her waist. She could feel his breath on her ear as he laid his cheek against her head.

She turned her face into his. "You kept my fire burning."

Jeb kissed her lightly, then pulled her up against him. "We didn't get a chance to lie together out under the trees."

"Is walnut a tree?"

"Of course it is, but why do you ask?"

"We could pretend the posts of the bed are trees."

Jeb laughed the deep rumble that Tallie knew so well. "Miss Somerset, are you asking me to bed you?"

"Well, I only see one bed and there are two people, so . . . "

Jeb spun her around and hugged her to him. He picked her up and carried her to the bed and placed her on it.

"I don't suppose you have your Mother Hubbard nightgown on under your clothes?"

"I don't have anything to sleep in."

"That won't be a problem."

Jeb began to loosen the buttons on the back of Tallie's dress as she sat on the edge of the bed. She leaned into him, resting her cheek against his bare chest, inhaling the scent of his body. When the dress was free, he lowered the top to her waist, being

careful as he removed her arm from her sleeve.
When he saw the healing scratches on her arm, he
ran his fingers over them, touching them ever so
lightly. "They don't look bad."

"I had a good nurse."

Jeb hugged her to him, holding her for a long
moment. "Do you realize what could have happened
to you?"

"I was never worried because I knew you would
take care of me. That's what heroes do."

"Oh, Tallie. What would I have done had I lost
you?" He stood her up, allowing her dress to fall to
the floor, then undid her camisole and dropped her
petticoat.

She stood before him in her drawers. Tallie felt
that she should be embarrassed, but she wasn't in
the slightest. After all, Jeb had seen her nude body
before, and it seemed so right to be open with him
in this way. She had never seen him fully naked,
though. Sitting on the bed, and with tentative hands,
she moved to the band of his pants, and finding the
button, she undid the top one. She looked up at Jeb,
who was standing in front of her, his eyes burning
with intensity. She went to the second button, then
hesitated.

If she let this go any further, would she know
what to do? Jeb mistakenly thought she was an
experienced woman. While he no longer mentioned it, she knew that with some of the liber-
ties she had allowed him to take, he must surely
believe she was knowledgeable about the things
that were in *The Prince's Folly*. What would he
do when he found out she was a virgin? He had

said he loved her, but she had never told him she loved him. She couldn't. Because what if when he found out, he didn't want her, just as Arthur hadn't wanted her? Tallie took a deep breath. Tonight was the night to find out.

Quickly she undid the rest of the buttons on his fly. When she did, she was shocked to see that he was not wearing any drawers. When she saw his arousal gaping from the opening of his pants, she was drawn to it. She examined it as if it were a thing of wonder.

Tallie touched his erection, running her fingers up its length. It was hard and hot, and she remembered when they had been at the hunting camp, the tip was moist, so while she held it in one hand, she touched the end, and moisture was there.

Then Jeb dropped his pants and, laying her gently back on the bed, removed her shoes and stockings and lifted her out of her drawers. He climbed into the bed beside her.

He began kissing her—first her throat, then behind her ear, then down her shoulders to the valley between her breasts. All the while he was kissing her, his hand was exploring her body, first her breasts, then her abdomen. Gradually his hand inched down to the mound of hair at the juncture of her legs. He let it lie there for just an instant, then his fingers began moving into that area where he had touched her before. This time no one would interrupt, so he didn't hurry. Slowly, he moved his fingers until they found her center. He dipped into that steaming cavern that was her core, now feeling the moisture. He found a little tip that rose against the stroking. At first he went slow, deliberately driving her, demanding that she cry out for more, but when she did not, he began to stroke faster and faster, all the while sending cascades of heretofore unknown pleasure spinning through her body.

What was happening to her? She had never been told, not by Jennie, not by anyone, and she had never ever read anything in a book that prepared her for the intense feelings she was experiencing. At first she tried to stop the feelings, tried to think of something else—her home, the ranch, anything—but then she thought about the bear.

She had trusted this man with her life. Now she was ready to trust him with the most fantastic feeling she had ever experienced. She lay back, spreading her legs wide to give his hand even greater access to the hub of her being. Grabbing his head, she urged him to take her breast into his mouth, and as she closed her eyes, she willed him to continue the movements that were building to something—something that she had never before experienced, but something that she knew would be wonderful, because Jeb, the man she loved, was bringing it to her.

A sensation began to build, first in the soles of her feet, and then a numbness hit her private parts. Then, as if she had been hit by a bolt of lightning, wave after wave of pleasure began coursing through her body. Her body bucked against him as she grabbed for his hand, not knowing if she was trying to stop him or urging him to continue. Finally, the spasms stopped and she lay back satiated, her body limp, her breathing ragged.

Jeb moved over her, kissing her again and again, as he held her limp body against him. "I love you. I love you. Do you know how much I love you?"

"Yes, and, Jeb, I love you, too."

When Jeb heard her say the words, he kissed her again, but this was not a kiss in the heat of passion. This was a kiss of love. For the first time in his life, he knew the difference.

Jeb was pleased with Tallie's reaction to what he had been doing to her, and now he was anxious to feel himself inside her warm body. He was sure she wanted him as much as he wanted her, and he began again, not with the patience he had used before, but with an unbridled intensity. He began brushing her core with his penis, arousing himself more and more, even as he felt her react to him. When he felt her moistness lathering his shaft, he lifted his hips and positioned himself to enter her body. He wanted his first stroke inside her to be one she would remember, but he knew that if he did it quickly, he would lose all control, and he wanted this lovemaking to go on and on. He wanted to watch her expression—to lock it in his memory— how she had looked the first time they had made love together. Lifting himself on outstretched arms, he held himself above her, watching her face as he entered her body slowly, barely touching the surface.

He pushed gently into her cavity, feeling the tightness of her, then moved a little more. The expression on her face, which had shone with exuberance, happiness, contentment, now changed to one he could not read.

"Tallie? Do you not want me to do this?" Jeb asked, not really wanting to hear her answer.

"I want you to go on more than I've ever wanted anything in my life." Tallie's eyes glistened.

Jeb held himself rigid. "Tell me, Tallie, was your husband . . . was he mean to you in any way?" Anger began to rise in Jeb as he thought of the little rat that had been her husband.

"No, Jeb. He was not, but . . . oh, Jeb, I'm a virgin."

Jeb withdrew immediately. "What did you say?"

"I'm a virgin. Arthur and I never consummated our marriage."

"But . . . how you reacted—your book—I thought . . . "

"You thought I knew what I was doing."

Jeb looked at Tallie, his eyes brimming with tenderness, but he did not speak.

"And now you don't want me," Tallie said, a dejected look crossing her face.

Jeb grabbed her and pulled her to him. "That's not true. It's just different when you're a virgin."

"What makes it different? You've said you love me. Isn't this a part of loving?"

"Of course it is, but the first time is a gift that a woman gives a man, and if that man and woman love one another, it's a moment to be cherished forever. I want your first time to be something you will always remember."

"Then love me, Jeb. Love me in every way."

"Oh, Tallie. I promise to love you."

Jeb pressed his body close to hers, bare skin against bare skin.

Tallie's heart was pounding so hard that she was sure he could feel it. Jeb began to kiss her, his kisses now familiar. But Tallie knew that these kisses were unlike the previous kisses they had shared. Before, they had been but teasing promises of what might be; these kisses were precursors of what was sure to come.

She knew there would be no interruption this time. She was inexorably committed to an experience that she had begged to receive, one that she had wondered about, dreamed about, and, without knowing the ecstasy, written about. Eagerly, she reached out for Jeb and pulled him to her. He moved over her and she felt his shaft slide in through her moist cleft. Slowly, he moved deeper into her cavity, until with one sharp thrust he burst through the membrane that had marked her as a virgin.

Once he was through, Jeb didn't stop, and his slow, sensory-laden thrusts fulfilled every fantasy she had ever imagined. She felt the penetration, long and deep, probing into that part of her never before touched. She lifted her legs and pushed up against his thrusts, savoring every erotic feeling of their coupling.

The storm outside made this moment even more intimate as they continued to make love, lost in their own world. There was only pleasure and the feel of her soft body, shaped so completely against his hard frame. Then, when she thought she had experienced every sensation there was to experience, his strokes grew even stronger, faster, and she reacted to it, not from skill or experience, but from primeval instinct. As the sensations grew stronger, she knew that something was ahead of her, that somewhere on this quest was a pleasure far beyond anything she had ever before experienced. The sensations grew, heightened, intensified.

Jeb had fought hard to control himself, not to let himself go, but to stay with her until she felt comfortable. He knew he could hold off no longer, and he found his own release, groaning in ecstasy as he emptied himself into her. Finally, totally satiated, he pulled himself free and lay beside her, cradling her head on his shoulder, his arm wrapped around her, feeling the gradually receding heat of her body. Tallie moved closer into his embrace, smiling contentedly.

They lay quietly in each other's arms for a long moment, listening to the rain outside, the thunderclaps no longer loud, but now a deep, far-off rolling, like timpani drums in an orchestral arrangement.

"Tallie, how is it possible?"

Tallie was silent for a moment longer, trying to find some way to formulate the answer.

"I mean, how is it possible that you, a married woman, could be . . . "

"A virgin?"

"Yes."

"Arthur was a husband in name only. He married me to keep down any speculation about—about himself."

"Then the book, the Society, your marriage—you are saying that in all this time you never . . . "

"I've never known a man before this moment. And never before have I ever wanted to make love. But I wanted to make love with you, Jeb. I love you as I have never loved another."

Jeb rolled over and kissed her. "It's a new moment. Do you want to make love again?"

"I'll make love with you anytime you ask."

Outside, a giant thunderclap crashed again. It was going to be a long night, and Tallie had never been happier in her entire life.

TWENTY-TWO

Jeb awakened as the sun was just rising. He got out of bed and padded over to the window to draw the curtains. When the light flooded into the room, he looked back at the sleeping Tallie. How had he ever thought she was like the people she had written about in her book? She had tried to tell him the difference between truth and fact, but he hadn't understood. They were from two different worlds, but somehow he was determined to figure out a way to make their two worlds one.

He walked over to the bed and sat down beside her. He loved to watch her. While he was sitting there watching her, his groin stirred, and soon he saw a smile form on Tallie's lips.

"You've been awake all along." Jeb bent down to kiss her. "Why didn't you say something?"

"Because it's the first time I've ever seen a man standing in all his glory," Tallie teased.

"I'll show you glory." Jeb climbed back in bed. He would never get enough of this woman.

About an hour later, Jeb and Tallie stepped out into the hallway, where Tallie headed for the outside door.

"Don't go that way," Jeb said.

"But the doorman will know I spent the night."

"It won't be the same one. Come on." Jeb took Tallie's arm and they went down the stairs into the foyer of the club.

"Oh, sir, I'm afraid you've violated the rules. This is a gentlemen's club, and if the membership finds out you have had a woman in your room, you may be asked to resign."

"I'll keep that in mind," Jeb said as they walked out onto the wide veranda and down the steps.

"I feel guilty," Tallie said.

"About last night? I don't."

"Not about us. I feel guilty because I left Clara."

"And who was with her? Her husband. By my reckoning, that's who should be staying with her anyway."

When they reached the infirmary, Jeb and Tallie let themselves in, the doctor apparently having stepped out. They expected to see Moreton, but when they looked into Clara's room, she was alone.

Clara barely raised her hand to wave when Jeb and Tallie entered. She looked pallid and weak.

"How was your night?" Tallie asked, clasping her hand.

"Fine."

"Where's Moreton?" Jeb asked. "Didn't he spend the night with you?"

"He did."

"Where'd he go? Do you know?"

"Cheyenne Club. A meeting." Clara looked away, staring at a bare wall. "Tallie, do you think he loves me, truly?"

"Oh, honey, of course he does. He was so worried about you. You should have seen him when we were getting you here," Tallie said.

"He must think I caused this because I made us go on the hunt."

"Clara, that's not true. If God wanted you to have this baby, nothing would have kept you from having it. I heard Moreton say you would make another little one, and when you are well, you know you will."

"Why did he leave me this morning? He's gone all the time."

"Do you want Jeb to find him and bring him back?"

"Will you, please?" she asked him, her eyes pleading.

"I'll find him and tell him you need him," Jeb said.

As Jeb walked back down the street to the Cheyenne Club, he wondered what meeting would be so important that it would keep Moreton away from Clara. No one had said anything to him about a meeting.

When he stepped through the front door of the club, he saw about fifty men gathered in a large room. Jeb didn't have to wonder if Moreton was at the meeting because he was conducting it. Jeb took a seat near the back. This wasn't just a coincidental meeting, not with this many people present, and if it was something that was planned, why hadn't he been told about it?

"I'm pleased to report the first phase of our operation has been completed," Moreton said. "A few days ago, the representatives of the Powder River Cattlemen's Association forcibly removed a squatter and his family off the open range."

"What do you mean 'forcibly'?" one of the men asked. "You vowed there would be no shooting. I for one won't hold truck with anyone getting shot."

Moreton shook his head. "Nobody was killed, nobody was even hurt. I've been told that Jones and his family are now staying in Buffalo."

"How'd you run him off?"

Moreton smiled. "Fires are a terrible thing. It seems a fire got—accidentally—started at the Jones place, and before you know it, why, his house, barn, and every outbuilding on the place was burned down."

"Accidentally started?" someone asked.

"Oh, quite accidentally, yes." Moreton laughed as he said the words, and the others laughed with him. "There are at least four other ranchers, chicken farmers, goatherds—whatever they prefer to be called—who have been selected to experience, shall we say, another accident. . . . "

"You son of a bitch!" Jeb shouted, jumping to his feet and pointing at Moreton. "You were behind it, weren't you?"

"Jeb, you're not a part of this, you don't understand," Moreton said. "You'd better just stay out of it."

"You're damn right I'm not a part of it! But I understand this. If you're burning out innocent families—families who have clear title to their land—you're nothing but a bunch of worthless out-laws!"

"Tuhill, there will be no profanity in this club. If you persist, we will have to ask you to leave," one fat, little man who was sitting in the front row said.

"I don't take kindly to being called an outlaw," another man said, and he stood, facing Jeb. His hand was near his pistol in obvious challenge.

"If you want to die right here and now, mister, you just make one move toward that gun," Jeb said coldly.

"Mr. Patterson, I don't think you want to do that," Moreton said. "Especially not in the club."

"What kind of men are you? John R. Jones, his wife, and two kids—what kind of a threat were they?"

"Look, Tuhill, I know you're Moreton's partner," Coble said. "And I know you're from Texas. But you don't understand how things are done up here, so why don't you just go on back to Texas before we force you to leave?"

"I've been thinking about this, Jeb," Moreton said, "and I believe our operation is going to be moving in a different direction. I'm not sure it's going to be a direction that you approve of, so I've taken the liberty to draw up a bank draft." He pulled an enve-lope from his pocket, then walked over and handed it to Jeb. "I want to buy you out, and I believe I've been more than generous. And, Jeb, I won't make the offer again."

Jeb took the envelope and removed the bank draft. It was for $250,000.

"Is that satisfactory?" Moreton asked.

"I'll leave today. And by the way—your wife needs you."

"Is Moreton coming?" Tallie asked when Jeb stepped back into the doctor's office. "Why didn't he come with you?"

"I don't know what he's going to do. Come. We need to talk."

"Is something wrong?"

Jeb didn't answer, but grabbing her wrap, he tossed it to Tallie and stepped out of the doctor's office. When she stepped out, he took her hand and led her down the street in the opposite direction from the Cheyenne Club.

"Where are we going?" Tallie asked, running beside him to keep up with his long strides.

"In here."

"A church? We're going to church?"

"It's as good a place as any."

They went into the small building, with six rows of wooden pews on either side of an aisle. A pulpit and a baptismal font were up front, and a pump organ sat to the side of the pulpit. Red hymnals were in racks on the back of the pews. Jeb held his hand out, inviting her to sit.

"Jeb, what's going on?"

"I'm going back to Texas."

"Jeb!" Tallie gasped. "You can't leave. Not now. What about us?"

"I have no choice. You remember the Jones Ranch that we saw on the way back from the mountain? The one that was burned out? Moreton did that."

"But he couldn't have."

"The meeting. The one he's at right now. There are at least fifty ranchers there, so no wonder Moreton wouldn't let us take Clara to Fort Fetterman. He insisted that we come all the way to Cheyenne because the bastard had a meeting to come to. He didn't care what was happening to Clara."

"Oh, no, poor Clara. But that still doesn't mean he burned the Jones Ranch."

"Oh, I don't think he did it himself, but he certainly knew about it, and right now, they're planning their next—accident. I can't be a part of that, Tallie. I won't be a part of it."

"But what about your money? You'll lose your investments."

"No, Moreton had thought about that, too. He bought me out. But the truth is, once I found that out, I was going back to Texas whether Moreton bought me out or not. And I want you to go with me."

"Jeb"—tears sprang to Tallie's eyes—"I want to go with you more than I have ever wanted anything in my life, but I can't go. I can't leave Clara, not now. She needs me."

"Let Moreton take care of her. She's his wife. You say that she needs you. Well, I need you, too. I love you, Tallie. I love you, and I want to marry you."

"Jeb, please, try to understand. I can't abandon Clara now. She considers me a sister."

"I understand, but it's time for you to make a choice. You're going to have to choose between Clara and me."

"Oh, Jeb, no. Don't make it so final. I have to stay with Clara. She's not only lost her baby, she thinks she's lost Moreton, too, and if he has become the man you say he is, she probably has. She wants to go back to New York, and she wants me to go with her. I have to see her through this. I'm honor bound to do so."

Jeb was silent for a long moment. Finally he stood and looked down at her, a pained look on his face. "Tallie, then this is good-bye."

"No, Jeb! No!" Tallie called after him, but he didn't look around as he walked out of the church.

Tallie sat there for how long she didn't know as tears streamed down her face. Eventually a door up front opened and a man, wearing a black suit, stepped out into the nave, then stopped when he saw Tallie sitting there.

"Miss, I didn't know anyone was here in the hour of our country's sorrow. May I help you?"

"No, I—thank you, no." Leaving the pew, she genuflected toward the sacristy, bowing her head, even though she didn't know if this was a church of the denomination where that was normally done.

As she walked back to the infirmary, she saw the flag at the post office. It was at half-mast.

TWENTY-THREE

One month later

Jeb had returned to Texas to find Two Hills Ranch had expanded, in both acreage and family members. Jonas had married Katarina, and they had a little, black-haired baby girl, named Elanabeth. They had met Jeb with some trepidation, but he embraced his brother warmly and offered Jonas his genuine congratulations. Jeb was happy to learn that Jonas had done a lot of "growing up" in the last few years and had taken over the management of half of the seventy-five-thousand-acre Two Hills Ranch.

"We'll be most happy to have you back. Pop needs help with his half of the ranch 'cause he just can't keep up with me," Jonas said. "I'm running more cows than he ever did."

Jeb smiled. "Jonas, it looks to me like you've got things well in hand here. I know Pop is happy to have somebody to compete against. But I think I'm going to start a ranch of my own."

"Good. We could call it Two Hills II."

"I don't think I'm going to stay in the Palo Duro."

"But why not? There's plenty of land here," Elizabeth Tuhill said.

"I know, Mom, but I'm going to find someplace else. But I'll say this—I'm going to stay in Texas."

"Oh, Jeb, you've been gone for over two years. Promise me you won't stay away so long this time," Jeb's mother said. "I've missed you."

Jeb smiled. "What if I promise to come back for Christmas? That is, if you make me some chicken and dumplin's."

"I'll do it, and I'll make fried apricot pies, too."

"You know what, Mom? I found something almost as good as your fried pies. They were called Mowbray pork pies. Do you think you could make some?"

"Pork pies? That sounds awful, Son," James Tuhill said.

"I guess it was where I ate them that made them so good."

A week later, Jeb was in Albany, Texas, sitting in the office of the North Texas Land Management Company.

Jason Greely, who was the land broker, had a map laid out on a large table, and he took his pencil and pointed. "I can get you a hundred thousand acres of land here in Shackelford County for a dollar an acre."

"A hundred thousand acres for a hundred thousand dollars? Are you sure that's the price?"

Greely stroked his jaw and shook his head. "I don't know, though. I mean, I figure in all fairness I need to warn you about this land."

"What about it?"

"Some of the water holes—not all of 'em, mind you, but I'd say the majority of 'em—are sometimes fouled. Some of 'em worse than others."

"What do you mean 'fouled'?"

"They call it something like pee-troll-eam, or something like that."

"Petroleum?"

"Yes."

"I can see how that could be a problem."

"But you got a couple of creeks runnin' through there, Battle Creek and Crystal Springs, where the water's always fresh. You could more'n likely close off the ponds that's polluted, keep your cows out of 'em, and you'd be all right."

"Yes," Jeb said. "All right, that is a way to handle it. I'll take it. How soon can I get a deed?"

"Oh, as soon as you can get your money together. They's a new bank in Breckenridge that's gettin' their loans out right quick if you need it. I know a fellow you can deal with. Name's Ketchem."

"Will you take cash?"

"Yes, sir, Mr. Tuhill!" Greely said with a huge smile. "We'll get the land filed, and by this time tomorrow, you'll be a rancher."

Jeb chuckled. "I'll be a landowner, Mr. Greely. I won't be a rancher until I'm running cattle on the place."

Once Will Tate learned that Jeb wasn't coming back to the 76, he left as well, coming all the way down by horseback, trading off between his horse and Liberty so as not to tire either of them excessively. Locating Jeb, Will and some of the cowboys from Two Hills Ranch came to help Jeb build Swangrove.

"Swangrove? What kind of name is Swangrove for a ranch?" Will teased.

"It's a fine name," Jeb said. "It's the name of a fancy hunting lodge over in England."

"Oh, yeah, I can see that. Would Miss Tallie have anything to do with it?"

"It's just a name."

"Ha. You can't fool me. It's a lot more'n a name. What I don't understand is what happened between you two. I thought you and her was hittin' it off real good."

"I guess it just wasn't to be," Jeb said. "I asked her to come with me, but she felt it was her responsibility to take care of Clara."

"I reckon so. Frewen sure didn't take care of her. They no more'n got back to the ranch before Frewen took 'em both and that French girl to Rock Creek and put 'em on a train for New York."

"Well, I hope they're all happy."

By the middle of December they had three buildings on Swangrove: the main house, which had a kitchen, a sitting room, and a bedroom; a bunkhouse, which was big enough to accommodate at least ten cowboys; and a barn, which was twice as big as the house, with a separate stall for Liberty that was paneled in tongue-and-groove lumber. Once the buildings were up, Jeb brought in his first fifteen hundred cows.

"What I want to know is, what kind of brand are we going to use for Swangrove?" Will asked Jeb.

"How about the letter *S*, which will look sort of like a swan's neck, then a curve through the middle of it, like a swan's wing."

"Yeah, all right, we can come up with somethin' like that."

New York

The city was getting ready for Christmas, with garlands of green tied with red bows on the lampposts. Some of the buildings were decorated as well, and here and there groups of carolers harmonized on street corners.

Tallie had her own room on the third floor of the Jerome Mansion, and in an attempt to cheer her up, Clara had put a Christmas wreath in her window.

"How long are you going to mope around?" Clara asked.

"I'm not moping."

"Oh? There've been half a dozen Christmas parties right here in New York and you haven't been to a single one of them. You didn't even go when Mrs. Astor invited you."

"I really haven't felt like going."

"That's a poor excuse."

"I got a letter from Aunt Emma. She told me Uncle Charles is very sick, and I'm thinking about going home."

"Well, why don't you book passage?"

"I just can't go."

"What's keeping you here?"

"I don't know, I just can't go. Not yet."

"I know what's wrong with you. You're in love. You're in love with Jeb Tuhill, aren't you?"

"I thought I was, but now I don't know. I told him I was coming to New York with you, but why didn't he come for me if he loved me? Why hasn't he written?"

"Did you write to him?"

"I don't know how to. I don't know where he went."

"That's not a problem. We'll just figure out a way to find him. The first time Moreton met Jeb he was in Texas, and surely Moreton will know where he lived. Someone will know where he is."

"But I thought you weren't even communicating with Moreton right now."

"For you, I would contact him."

"Oh, Clara, if you can find Jeb, you will make me the happiest person in the world. I love him more than I could have ever believed possible. My whole body aches for him."

"My name may be Frewen, but I'm still a Jerome. I'll find an address for the missing Mr. Tuhill."

"Perhaps we are star-crossed." Tallie forced a smile. "Star-crossed lovers. Isn't that material for a novel?"

"Don't let him get away from you, Tallie. He is a good man, and the two of you belong together."

There was a knock on Tallie's door then, and when Clara opened it, she saw Leonard Jerome standing there, holding a box.

"Papa, what is it?"

"This box just came for Tallie. It's from Downe, Kent."

"Oh, it must be a Christmas present from Aunt Emma."

Tallie put the box on her bed and opened it. Looking inside she saw a stack of books, bound in red, with the title in gold.

"What is this?" She picked up one of the books and read *The Lady and the Cowboy* by Nora Ingram. "How did this happen?"

An envelope was on top of the books, and she withdrew a letter.

> *My dearest Tallie,*
>
> *I hope the joy of this season finds you uplifted in spirit. Charles and I have detected a melancholy in your latest posts.*
>
> *I know that it was bold of me to submit* The Lady and the Cowboy *to Smith, Elder, but George was as enthralled with your story as we were. He felt it would be a perfect love story to reach his patrons in time for this Christmas season.*
>
> *Your story so bared your beautiful soul that Charles had to see it published while he still could. Tallie, our sweet Tallie, if you only knew what a tonic this has been for Charles in his twilight days. Thank you for sharing so much of your life with us.*
>
> *Love,*
> *Emma*

Tallie opened the cover, then gasped. "Oh, oh, Clara." Tallie's eyes welled with tears.

"What is it?"

"I had forgotten about this." She turned the book toward Clara. There, on the frontispiece, was a photograph of Jeb sitting sternly in a chair, staring into the camera, while standing just beside him, her hand resting on his shoulder, was Tallie.

"Oh, how beautiful!" Clara said. "It's just like a wedding picture!"

"For a wedding that will never be." Tears streamed down Tallie's cheeks.

Clara pulled Tallie into an embrace. "Don't give up yet. Just give me time to work on this."

Two Hills Ranch—Christmas Day 1881

"I have made chicken and dumplings, dressing, rolls, grapefruit, and fried apricot pies," Elizabeth said.

"Whoa, now I really am jealous," Jonas said. "You haven't done all that for me."

"Are you going to eat any of the dumplings?" Elizabeth asked.

"Only if I leave him a few," Jeb teased.

"Ha! Try and keep me from them."

"Will tells me your ranch is coming along fine," James said.

"I've got a long way to go before Swangrove starts turning a profit. But I think we've got a start."

"Are we going to gab all day? Or are we going to eat?" Jonas asked.

During the meal, Jeb learned that Katarina was pregnant with her and Jonas's second child. It was funny, two years ago that information would have disturbed him. Today, he was genuinely pleased for Jonas and Katarina. He also had to admit that he was a little envious, not jealous that Jonas had

Katarina, but envious of the happiness they obviously enjoyed.

Happiness that he had wanted with Tallie.

After their meal they went into the keeping room, where they opened presents.

Then Jeb's mother brought a package to him. "This came for you a couple of days ago. I don't know if it was supposed to be a Christmas gift, or if you were supposed to open it right away. But you didn't get here until this morning anyway, so here it is. Merry Christmas."

Jeb looked at the package and saw that it was from Clara Frewen. For a moment he considered throwing it away in disgust, but he decided to open it.

Inside were a letter and a book for Jeb.

Dear Jeb,

As Tallie's friend, I must tell you that I have watched her with some concern over these past months. I feel so terribly guilty that I persuaded her to come to New York with me. I thought I needed her, I thought I couldn't make it without her, but now I think my act was uncompromisingly selfish. Since arriving in New York, she has nearly become a recluse.

She is terribly in love with you, Jeb. And if there is any part of you that reciprocates those feelings, then I invite you to come to New York and make that love known to her. Tallie is much too dear to me for me to see her suffer so in mind and spirit.

Enclosed is her latest novel, The Lady and the Cowboy, *which will no doubt become another bestselling book. If after you read the book you can truthfully say that you have no feelings for her, then I will make no further entreaties.*

Yours affectionately,
Clara Frewen

Jeb excused himself from the others and went up to his room to begin reading. When he opened the book, a knot formed in his throat. There, staring out at him, was a picture of Tallie and him. He remembered its being taken by the photographer in Miles City.

My God, she was beautiful. What had he been thinking when he left her?

He didn't put the book down until he had read it through to the last page.

Lady Anne watched the rain move off the Thames, then slash down onto the roofs of London. Outside, a cat sought shelter beneath a garden table. Across the street a man hurried through the rain, holding an umbrella over him. The scene was reminiscent of an impressionist painting by Manet, but art meant little to her now because her heart was heavy.

Tears glistened in Lady Anne's eyes and she wished that her cowboy could be here to kiss them away. Surely more was meant to come from their relationship than this, John Tuttle in Texas and she half a world away, her heart aching for him. Did he love her? Or had she been but a game for him, a test to see if he, an ordinary cowboy, could conquer a lady of title?

Lady Anne closed her eyes and whispered a prayer. "Please, Lord, fill John's heart with love for me as I so love him."

That simple prayer seemed to relieve some of the heartache because she began to hope, no, to believe, that she would see him again. She dried the tears from her eyes even as the sun appeared over a city that glistened with promise.

"He will come," she said aloud. "I know that he will come."

It was nearly midnight by the time Jeb finished reading Tallie's novel, but he still couldn't go to sleep. Instead he lay in his bed with his hands folded behind his head, staring up into the darkness.

Could it be true that she loved him as much as he loved her? Or were these merely carefully constructed words, the tool of an accomplished novelist?

When Jeb came downstairs the next morning, Jonas was the only one at the kitchen table. He was drinking coffee and got up and poured a cup for Jeb.

"Will tells me that you fell for some English girl who was up at Frewen's place. He says you've been pining over her ever since you came back."

"Will talks too much."

"It's true, isn't it?"

Jeb didn't answer.

"Where is she now? Is she still in Wyoming?"

"She's in New York."

"How do you know?"

"The letter I got last night. It was from Moreton's wife."

"God in heaven, man, if you love this woman, and you know where she is, don't throw your chance away. Go get her."

"It's not that easy, Jonas. Even if I did go after her, there's no guarantee that she will come back with me."

"There's no guarantee? Jeb, I'm goin' to tell you something that I know you have heard before, because it's something that Pop says. There is only one guarantee in life, and that is that someday we're all going to die. You're never going to know whether or not she'll come back with you unless you go to New York and ask."

Jeb smiled, then reached out to take Jonas's hand in his. "You're right, little brother, I'm never going to know unless I try."

New York—January 1882

Twelve days from the day Jeb had received the book and the letter from Clara Frewen, he was standing in front of Grand Central Depot in New York. He had not bothered to gather a wardrobe for the trip, coming instead in the same clothes that he wore around the ranch. His Western garb and his Stetson hat made him stand out among the bowler-topped gentlemen of the city, and he was well aware that he was gathering stares.

He had thought about sending a telegram, but hesitated because he was afraid he might get an answer telling him not to come.

All right, he was here, so what should he do now?

Whatever that was, he was on his own. On his last visit to New York, though he had been wearing the dandified clothes of a "gentleman," he had seen examples of most ungentlemanly behavior among such men. Then, he had told Mack that he felt like a mule in horse harness.

Today he was dressed like a cattleman, a real cattleman, not some fancy-dressed dude who only played at it. He was comfortable with his clothes, he was comfortable with his place, and he answered to no man but himself.

But how would Tallie react? Would she receive him or would she send him away?

It was too late to worry about that now. He had come this far, and he would not be denied. Summoning a cab, he took it to the Jerome Mansion at Madison Square and Twenty-sixth Street.

Clara and Tallie were sitting in the library when the butler came into the room with a discreet clearing of his throat.

"Yes, Mr. Walker, what is it?" Clara asked.

"There is a rather, ahem, peculiarly dressed gentleman inquiring about Lady Somerset."

"How do you mean 'peculiarly dressed'?"

"He is wearing a sheepskin coat and a big hat. I would suggest that he is a common workingman, but he asked to see you."

Clara and Tallie looked at each other.

"Clara, you don't think . . . ".

"I do think, Tallie," Clara said with a broad smile.

"But if that's true, what's he doing here?"

"Well, if my letter had anything to do with it, my guess would be that he has come to take you back with him."

"Your letter? You sent him a letter?"

"Did I not tell you I would find him? So, what do we do, Tallie? Do I receive him, or not?"

"I—I don't know. It's all so frightening to me."

"Frightening? This coming from a woman who made a cattle drive and was mauled by a bear?"

"Shall I tell him you aren't receiving?" Mr. Walker asked.

"It's up to you, Tallie, though you might want to consider that he's come two thousand miles to see you. I wouldn't be so quick to send him away."

"Mr. Walker?" Tallie said.

"Yes, ma'am, shall I show him in?"

"No."

Clara looked at Tallie in confused disappointment.

"I will show him in myself," Tallie said as a broad smile spread across her face.

Jeb was convinced he had made a big mistake. He had no business being here . . . who was he to think that Tallie could feel for him the same way he felt for her? He turned toward the door, hoping he could be gone before the butler came back to tell him he was wasting his time. Then he heard his name called. He recognized the voice at once and whirled around to see Tallie coming toward him.

"Tallie?"

Tallie rushed into his arms, and the two of them

stood in the foyer for a long moment, lost in each other's kiss.

When they separated, Jeb smiled down at her. "Tell me, Tallie, did John Tuttle get his Lady Anne?"

"What do you think?"

"If you are Lady Anne and I'm John Tuttle, then I say yes. You're going back to Texas with me if I have to carry you."

"Oh, my sweet Jeb, I would go back to Texas with you if we had to ride double all the way."

EPILOGUE

As the Ford Tri-Motor airplane touched down lightly at Floyd Bennett Field in New York City, Tallie gazed through the window at the whirling propeller on the engine nacelle that hung from the right wing. She and Jeb had left Dallas the day before, had laid over in St. Louis last night, and were in New York in time for dinner. She couldn't help but compare that speed with that of the first cross-country trip she had made with Jeb, when it took them eleven days to reach the 76 Ranch in Wyoming from New York.

The 76 had gone bankrupt many years ago, but Swangrove had transitioned from cattle to oil, and the Tuhill family was among the wealthiest in Texas. They had come to New York for Tallas Cameron Tuhill's acceptance of the Pulitzer prize for *The Man from Downe*: *A Personal Biography of Charles Darwin*.

The plane, which bore the logo SWANGROVE OIL, followed the ground guide to its parking place.

When the propellers spun to a stop, the pilot and the copilot stepped back into the plush cabin.

"Mrs. Tuhill, I've just received word on the radio that Mayor La Guardia will send his car out to the plane to meet you."

"Thank you, Michael," Tallie said.

Ten minutes later, they were riding in the backseat of the mayor's Packard, and Tallie looked over at Jeb. To some, Jeb might look like an old man. His thinning hair was stark white, he wore glasses to read, and the hand that reached over, familiarly, comfortably, to take hers was lined with age.

But Tallie saw none of that. Tallie saw the young man she had examined in her hand mirror as he rode alongside the stagecoach on that day, so long ago, when first they were going to Moreton Frewen's ranch. She saw a shock of wheat-blond hair that tumbled onto his sun-bronzed forehead, deep blue eyes, broad shoulders, a trim waist, and muscular legs.

The Packard glided through the streets of New York, the passengers in its backseat hand in hand. For fifty years, their hearts had beat as one, and he lifted her hand to his lips to kiss it.

"Tallie?"

"Yes?"

"May I tell you that I love you? Or have I already said that?"

"You can never say it enough," Tallie replied.

"I am the luckiest cattleman in the world."

"And I am the happiest woman."

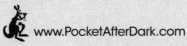

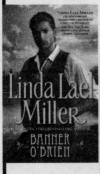

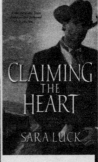